Beauty, Beast, and Belladonna

Maia Chance

BERKLEY PRIME CRIME, NEW YORK

**BERKLEY
PRIME
CRIME**

An imprint of Penguin Random House LLC
375 Hudson Street, New York, New York 10014

BEAUTY, BEAST, AND BELLADONNA

A Berkley Prime Crime Book / published by arrangement with the author

ISBN: 978-0-425-27164-3

PUBLISHING HISTORY
Berkley Prime Crime mass-market edition / February 2016

PRINTED IN THE UNITED STATES OF AMERICA

10   9   8   7   6   5   4   3   2   1

Cover art by Brandon Dorman / Peter Lott Reps.
Interior text design by Kelly Lipovich.

**Penguin
Random
House**

Beware of allowing yourself to be prejudiced by appearances.

—Gabrielle-Suzanne Barbot de Villeneuve,
Beauty and the Beast (1756)

Author's Note: Readers familiar with the countryside around Sarlat and the Vézère valley in France will, I hope, forgive me for shrinking the landscape in order to avoid too much time spent on horses and in carriages.

1

⚬✕⚬

The day had arrived. Miss Ophelia Flax's last day in Paris, her last day in Artemis Stunt's gilt-edged apartment choked with woody perfumes and cigarette haze. Ophelia had chosen December 12, 1867, at eleven o'clock in the morning as the precise time she would make a clean breast of it. And now it was half past ten.

Ophelia swept aside brocade curtains and shoved a window open. Rain spattered her face. She leaned out and squinted up the street. Boulevard Saint-Michel was a valley of stone buildings with iron balconies and steep slate roofs. Beyond carriages and bobbing umbrellas, a horse-drawn omnibus splashed closer.

"Time to go," she said, and latched the window shut. She turned. "Good-bye, Henrietta. You will write to me—telegraph me, even—if Prue changes her mind about the convent?"

"Of course, darling." Henrietta Bright sat at the vanity table, still in her frothy dressing gown. "But where shall I send a letter?" She shrugged a half-bare shoulder in the looking glass. Reassuring herself, no doubt, that at forty-odd years of age she was still just as dazzling as the New York theater critics used to say.

"I'll let the clerk at Howard DeLuxe's Varieties know my forwarding address," Ophelia said. "Once I have one." She pulled on cheap gloves with twice-darned fingertips.

"What will you *do* in New England?" Henrietta asked. "Besides get buried under snowdrifts and puritans? I've been to Boston. The entire city is like a mortuary. No drinking on Sundays, either." She sipped her glass of poison-green cordial. "Although, all that knuckle-rapping *does* make the gentlemen more generous with actresses like us when they get the chance."

"Actresses like us?" Ophelia went to her carpetbag, packed and ready on the opulent bed that might've suited that princess sleeping on a pea. Ladies born and raised on New Hampshire farmsteads did not sleep in such beds. Not without prickles of guilt, at least. "I'm no longer an actress, Henrietta. Neither are you." And they were *never* the same kind of actress. Or so Ophelia fervently wished to believe.

"No? Then what precisely do you call tricking the Count de Griffe into believing you are a wealthy soap heiress from Cleveland, Ohio? Sunday school lessons?"

"I had to do it." Ophelia dug in her carpetbag and pulled out a bonnet with crusty patches of glue where ribbon flowers once had been. She clamped it on her head. "I'm calling upon the Count de Griffe at eleven o'clock, on my way to the steamship ticket office. I told you. He scarpered to England so soon after his proposal, I never had a chance to confess. He's in Paris only today before he goes to his country château, so today is my last chance to tell him everything."

"It's horribly selfish of you not to wait two more weeks, Ophelia—two measly weeks."

Not this old song and dance again. "Wait two more weeks so that you might accompany me to the hunting party at Griffe's château? Stand around and twiddle my thumbs for two whole weeks while you hornswoggle some poor old gent into marrying you? Money and love don't mix, you know."

"What? They mix beautifully. And not hornswoggle, darling. Seduce. And Mr. Larsen isn't a *poor* gentleman. He's as rich as Midas. Artemis confirmed as much."

"You know what I meant. Helpless."

"Mr. Larsen is a widower, yes." Henrietta smiled. "Deliciously helpless."

"I must go now, Henrietta. Best of luck to you."

"I'm certain Artemis would loan you her carriage—oh, wait. Principled Miss Ophelia Flax must forge her own path. Miss Ophelia Flax *never* accepts handouts or—"

"Artemis has been ever so kind, allowing me to stay here the last three weeks, and I couldn't impose any more." Artemis Stunt was Henrietta's friend, a wealthy lady authoress. "I'll miss my omnibus." Ophelia pawed through the carpetbag, past her battered theatrical case and a patched petticoat, and drew out a small box. The box, shiny black with painted roses, had been a twenty-sixth birthday gift from Henrietta last week. It was richer than the rest of Ophelia's possessions by miles, but it served a purpose: a place to hide her little nest egg.

The omnibus fare, she well knew from her month in Paris, was thirty centimes. She opened the box. Her lungs emptied like a bellows. A slip of paper curled around the ruby ring Griffe had given her. But her money—all of her hard-won money she'd scraped together working as a lady's maid in Germany a few months back—was gone. *Gone.*

She swung towards Henrietta. "Where did you hide it?"

"Hide what?"

"My money!"

"Scowling like that will only give you wrinkles."

"I don't even have enough for the omnibus fare now." Ophelia's plans suddenly seemed vaporously fragile. "Now isn't the time for jests, Henrietta. I must get to Griffe's house so I might go to the steamship ticket office before it closes, and then on to the train station. The Cherbourg–New York ship leaves only once a fortnight."

"Why don't you simply keep that ring? You'll be in the middle of the Atlantic before he even knows you've gone. If it's a farm you desire, why, that ring will pay for five farms and two hundred cows."

Ophelia wasn't the smelling salts kind of lady, but her fingers shook as she replaced the box's lid. "Never. I would *never* steal this ring—"

"He gave it to you. It wouldn't be stealing."

"—and I will never, ever become . . ." Ophelia pressed her lips together.

"Become like *me*, darling?"

If Ophelia fleeced rich fellows to pay her way instead of working like honest folks, then she couldn't live with herself. What would become of her? Would she find herself at forty in dressing gowns at midday and with absinthe on her breath?

"You must realize I didn't take your money, Ophelia. I've got my sights set rather higher than your pitiful little field-mouse hoard. But I see how unhappy you are, so I'll make you an offer."

Ophelia knew the animal glint in Henrietta's whiskey-colored eyes. "You wish to pay to accompany me to Griffe's hunting party so that you might pursue Mr. Larsen. Is that it?

"Clever girl. You ought to set yourself up in a tent with a crystal ball. Yes. I'll pay you whatever it was the servants stole—and I've no doubt it was one of those horrid Spanish maids that Artemis hired who pinched your money. Only keep up the Cleveland soap heiress ruse for two weeks longer, Ophelia, until I hook that Norwegian fish."

Ophelia pictured the green fields and white-painted buildings of rural New England, and her throat ached with frustration. The trouble was, it was awfully difficult to forge your own path when you were always flat broke. "Pay me double or nothing," she said.

"Deal. Forthwith will be *so* pleased."

"Forthwith?" Ophelia frowned. "Forthwith Golden, con-jurer of the stage? Do you mean to say *he'll* be tagging along with us?"

"Mm." Henrietta leaned close to the mirror and picked something from her teeth with her pinkie nail. "He's ever so keen for a jaunt in the country, and he adores blasting at beasts with guns."

Saints preserve us.

Ophelia meant to cling to her purpose like a barnacle to a rock. It wasn't easy. Simply gritting her teeth and *enduring* the next two weeks was not really her way. But Henrietta had her up a stump.

First, there had been the two-day flurry of activity in Artemis Stunt's apartment, getting a wardrobe ready for Ophelia to play the part of a fashionable heiress at a hunting party. Artemis was more than fifty years of age but, luckily, a bohemian and so with youthful tastes in clothing. She was also tall, beanstalkish, and large-footed, just like Ophelia, and very enthusiastic about the entire deception. "It would make a marvelous novelette, I think," she said to Ophelia. But this was exactly what Ophelia wished to avoid: behaving like a ninny in a novelette.

And now, this interminable journey.

"Where are we now?" Henrietta, bundled in furs, stared dully out the coach window. "The sixth tier of hell?"

Ophelia consulted the *Baedeker* on her knees, opened to a map of the Périgord region. "Almost there."

"There being the French version of the Middle of No-where," Forthwith Golden said, propping his boots on the seat next to Henrietta. "Why do these Europeans insist upon living in these godforsaken pockets? What's wrong with Paris, anyway?"

"You said you missed the country air." Henrietta shoved his boots off the seat.

"Did I?" Forthwith had now and then performed conjuring tricks in Howard DeLuxe's Varieties back in New York, so Ophelia knew more of him than she cared to. He was dark-haired, too handsome, and skilled at making things disappear. Especially money.

"You insisted upon coming along," Henrietta said to Forthwith, "and don't try to deny it."

"Ah, yes, but Henny, you neglected to tell me that your purpose for this hunting excursion was to ensnare some doddering old corpse into matrimony. I've seen that performance of yours a dozen times, precious, and it's gotten a bit boring."

"Oh, do shut up. You're only envious because you spent your last penny on hair pomade."

"I hoped you'd notice. Does Mr. Larsen have any hair at all? Or does he attempt to fool the world by combing two long hairs over a liver-spotted dome?"

"He's an avid sportsman, Artemis says, and a crack shot. So I'd watch my tongue if I were you."

"Oh, dear God. A codger with a shotgun."

"He wishes to go hunting in the American West. Shoot buffalos from the train and all that."

"One of those Continentals who have glamorized the whole Westward Ho business, not realizing that it's all freezing to death and eating Aunt Emily's thighbone in the mountains?"

Ophelia sighed. Oh, for a couple of wads of cotton wool to stop up her ears. Henrietta and Forthwith had been bickering for the entire journey, first in the train compartment between Paris and Limoges and then, since there wasn't a train station within fifty miles of Château Vézère, in this bone-rattling coach. Outside, hills, hills, and more hills. Bare, scrubby trees and meandering vineyards. Farmhouses of sulphurous yellow stone.

A tiny orange sun sank over a murky river. Each time a draft swept through the coach, Ophelia tasted the minerals that foretold snow.

"Ophelia," Forthwith said, nudging her.

"What is it?"

Forthwith made a series of fluid motions with his hands, and a green and yellow parakeet fluttered out of his cuff and landed on his finger.

"That's horrible. How long has that critter been stuffed up your sleeve?" Ophelia poked out a finger, and the parakeet hopped on. Feathers tufted on the side of its head and its eyes were possibly glazed. It was hard to say with a parakeet. "Poor thing."

"It hasn't got feelings, silly." Forthwith yawned.

"Finally," Henrietta said, sitting up straighter. "We've arrived."

The coach passed through ornate gates. Naked trees cast shadows across a long avenue. They clattered to a stop before the huge front door. Château Vézère was three stories, rectangular, and built of yellow stone, with six chimneys, white-painted shutters, and dozens of tall, glimmering windows. Bare black vegetation encroached on either side, and Ophelia saw some smaller stone buildings to the side.

"Looks like a costly dollhouse," Henrietta said.

"I rather thought it looked like a mental asylum," Forthwith said.

Ophelia slid Griffe's ruby ring on her hand, the hand that wasn't holding a parakeet. Someone swung the coach door open.

"Let the show begin, darlings," Henrietta murmured.

A footman in green livery helped Ophelia down first. Garon Gavage, the Count de Griffe, bounded forward to greet her. "Mademoiselle Stonewall, I have been restless, sleepless, in anticipation of your arrival—ah, how *belle* you look." His dark gold mane of hair wafted in the breeze. "How I have longed for your presence—what is this? A *petit* bird?"

"What? Oh. Yes." Ophelia couldn't even begin to explain the parakeet. "It's very nice to see you, Count. How long has it been? Three weeks?"

Griffe's burly chest rose and fell. "Nineteen days, twenty hours, and thirty-two minutes."

Right.

Forthwith was out of the coach and pumping Griffe's hand. "Count de Griffe," he said with a toothy white smile, "pleased to meet you. My sister has told me all about you."

Ophelia's belly lurched.

"Sister?" Griffe knit his brow.

"I beg your pardon," Forthwith said. "I'm Forthwith Stonewall, Ophelia's brother. Didn't my sister tell you I was coming along?"

The *rat*.

"Ah!" Griffe clapped Forthwith on the shoulder. "Monsieur Stonewall. Perhaps your sister did mention it—I have been most distracted by business matters in England, *très* forgetful . . . And who is this?" Griffe nodded to Henrietta as she stepped down from the coach. "Another delightful American relation, eh?"

It had *better* not be. Ophelia said, "This is—"

"Mrs. Henrietta Brighton," Henrietta said quickly, and then gave a sad smile.

Precisely when had Miss Henrietta Bright become *Mrs.* Henrietta Bright*on*? And . . . oh, merciful heavens. How could Ophelia have been so blind? Henrietta was in black. *All* in black.

"Did Miss Stonewall neglect to mention that I would chaperone her on this visit?" Henrietta asked Griffe. "I am a dear friend of the Stonewall family, and I have been on a Grand Tour in order to take my mind away from my poor darling—darling . . . *oh*." She dabbed her eyes with a hankie.

Griffe took Henrietta's arm and patted it as he led her through the front door. "A widow, *oui*? My most profound condolences, Madame Brighton. You are very welcome here."

Ophelia and Forthwith followed. The parakeet's feet clung to Ophelia's finger, and tiny snowflakes fell from the darkening sky.

"You're *shameless*," Ophelia said to Forthwith in a hot whisper.

Forthwith grinned. "Aren't I, though?"

2

⌒⌒

Ophelia's conscience demanded that she call off the
entire visit *now*. Because, well, the gall of Henrietta
and Forthwith, springing those fake identities on her at the
last minute. On the other hand, she didn't have a centime to
her name. Griffe would surely kick her out on her ear when
he learned she was a fraud. She needed a little more time to
cook up a plan.

She was led upstairs to a chamber with a canopied bed,
walls painted with dark forest scenes—trees, rivers, castles,
and wild animals—and a carved marble fireplace. Footmen
brought up the two trunks of finery borrowed from Artemis
Stunt, and then a maid arrived.

The maid, a beautiful blond woman of about thirty years
with the full, sculptured figure of a Roman statue, tapped
her chest and called herself Clémence. As Clémence hung
the finery in the wardrobe, she furtively inspected Ophelia
from top to bottom. Then she led Ophelia down a creaking

corridor to a small bathing chamber. Marble from floor to ceiling, with a tinned copper tub and gold water spigots shaped like duck heads. Clémence ran the bath, gave Ophelia a cake of soap and parting glance of disdain, and left Ophelia to bathe.

How discomfiting, having people tend to you. Especially when they made you feel that *you* ought to be waiting on *them*.

After her bath, Ophelia returned to her bedchamber, dried her hair before the fire, and arranged it in a frivolous braided knot. Then she squirmed and laced herself—she would *not* ring for Clémence—into corset, crinoline, evening slippers, and Artemis's green velvet dinner gown.

After that, she checked on the parakeet. Griffe had sent up an unused brass birdcage from somewhere, its bottom lined with newspaper. Ophelia hung the cage near the fireplace with a saucer of water and a little bowl of bread crumbs. The parakeet was fluffed up, its eyes mostly shut. "Are you all right?" Ophelia whispered.

The parakeet ignored her.

Outside the windows, snow blew sideways through blackness. The *Baedeker* claimed that it never snowed in the Périgord.

A rap on the door.

"Entrez," Ophelia called. She was picking up licks of French.

Clémence had returned, carrying an envelope. She gave it to Ophelia in sullen silence and left.

Ophelia looked at the envelope—it read *Mademoiselle Stonewall*—and sighed. She knew that sloped, smeary handwriting. Although she hadn't seen the Count de Griffe since the day after she'd accepted his marriage proposal, he'd written her daily rhapsodic letters from England. Luckily, she'd been spared the need to reply because he had been traveling.

She tore open the envelope and read,

Dearest Mademoiselle Stonewall,

It is with a swollen heart and fevered brow that I welcome you at last to this, my ancestral home. How ardently I dream of showing you every inch of this sacred place, the formal gardens by moonlight, the riches housed in the library, the Roman statues alongside the ornamental canal, the fruits and blooms in the orangerie. How I long, too, to show you the more intimate features of your future home.

Ophelia's palms started sweating.

For instance, my late mother's own wedding gown, preserved in delicate tissue in a box, and the nursery and schoolroom where I once romped and studied and where, God willing, our own children will romp and study, too.

Ophelia went to a side table, where she'd seen a decanter of red liqueur. She poured herself a small glass and drank it down. Cherry. She coughed. She wasn't really a tippling lady, but the image of a half dozen hairy baby Griffes crawling around in diapers required blurring.

She turned back to the note.

We did not enjoy even one moment alone upon your arrival today. Might I beg you to join me at half past eight this evening—dinner will be served at nine o'clock—in the ballroom? There is so much in my heart I must convey, ma chérie—may I call you that?—and a pressing question I must ask.

> *Your most humble and obedient admirer, Griffe*

Oh, lorks.

Ophelia checked the mantel clock. Almost half past eight

already. She stuffed the note in a drawer and sat down to wallow in guilt until nine o'clock. She'd rather stick her hand in a beehive than be alone with Griffe. She could tell him she'd fallen asleep.

At two minutes till nine o'clock, Ophelia slid on Griffe's ruby ring, over her satin elbow glove. The ring was heavy, and too tight. Probably served her right. She trudged downstairs.

At the bottom of the stairs, she turned left and found herself in a long, dim gallery with a checkerboard floor and tall windows. Snow piled up in the corners of rattling windowpanes. Gleaming suits of armor lined the gallery, along with a couple of cannons and cases displaying swords, bows and arrows, and guns.

Griffe's voice boomed from beyond the far doorway. Drat. Ophelia didn't relish the notion of meeting him here. Too dark.

His voice again. Closer.

Ophelia dodged behind a suit of armor, one of four standing close together. She was hidden.

Griffe speaking. She caught the words *perhaps* and *dinner* . . . Wait. Ophelia held her breath. Her eyes slid sideways.

Someone *else* was hiding behind the suits of armor, not three feet away. A tall, shadowy male form—

The man cleared his throat.

She'd know that *ahem* anywhere. Yet how could it—why—what was *he* doing here?

"Professor?" Ophelia whispered. "Professor Penrose?"

"Ah, it *is* you, Miss Flax," Penrose murmured. "How good to see you."

"What are you doing, hiding back here?" Ophelia's eyes adjusted to the faint light. Penrose held a wineglass and wore evening clothes. She saw the glow of his spectacles, his square shoulders, the line of his clean-shaven jaw. Her heart skittered. "I thought I'd never—"

"I merely wished to inspect the mechanism at the back of this helmet." Penrose tapped one of the knight's helmets. It clanged softly. "Fascinating type of hinge."

"In the dark? Stop fibbing. Who are you hiding from?"

"Who are *you* hiding from?"

"Griffe said nothing of you being here." If Griffe *had* said something, Ophelia would've never come. Penrose had told her *I love you* three weeks ago, right after she'd impulsively promised her hand to Griffe. She fancied she'd broken the professor's heart. She'd broken her own heart, too, and since broken hearts must be let alone to mend, she'd banished him from her thoughts.

Another disaster.

"It was a last-minute invitation," Penrose whispered.

"Professor, if you happen to notice . . . anything odd. I mean to say, well, I still haven't gotten the chance to tell Griffe that I—"

"That you aren't Miss Stonewall, the Cleveland soap heiress?"

Ophelia swallowed. "Well, yes. And Henrietta is here, too—"

"Henrietta Bright? On the husband hunt, I suppose? Not to worry. Your secrets are safe with me."

Griffe said loudly, "He cannot be far, my dear." He was inside the gallery now. "Shall we seek for him in the gaming room? It is through the artillery gallery here."

"I suppose so," a woman said in a crisp British accent. "I can't think why he would simply disappear like this before dinner."

"Penrose is a scholar, Mademoiselle Banks," Griffe said. "Scholars become engrossed in their studies, I understand, to the point of sheer distraction and forgetfulness. Perhaps he has gone not to the gaming room but to the library? Come along. We will find your mislaid fiancé yet."

Fiancé?

Oh.

Griffe and Miss Banks passed by in a breeze of lilac perfume and silken rustles. Penrose didn't move a muscle.

"Dreadfully rude of him." The woman's voice was sulky. "Once we are married, I'll insist that he remedy his ways."

"You may insist," Griffe said, "but gentlemen rarely undergo change. Particularly after matrimony."

Their footsteps receded.

Ophelia whispered to Penrose, "I recall you speaking of Miss Banks with great enthusiasm last month in Paris. Congratulations on your engagement. Your *swift* engagement."

"Miss Flax. What I told you three weeks ago . . . I beg your pardon about all that." Penrose adjusted his spectacles. "I was rash and, indeed, mistaken. Paris had gone to my head, I suppose."

"I see." He'd taken that *I love you* back. Well. What an absolute *relief*.

"I do hope I did not cause you a moment of unease," Penrose said.

"Unease? No. Certainly not. I will see you at dinner, I reckon." Ophelia stepped out from behind the suits of armor and hurried in the opposite direction from that in which Griffe and Miss Banks had gone.

And this lump in her throat? Well, it must be that she was thirsty from traveling all day.

Gabriel Augustus Penrose, Fifth Earl of Harrington and lecturer of philology at St. Remigius's College, Oxford, was accustomed to sitting firmly in the saddle at all times. Events rarely unhinged him. And by Jove, he'd known all along that Miss Flax would be here and that she was still engaged to marry Griffe.

Her serene oval face, just shy of beautiful. Those darting, dark eyes of hers like the centers of poppies. The glossy upswept hair, her queenly posture—none of it moved him anymore.

So why was it so dashed difficult to chew this roast venison?

"Do tell everyone why you are here, Lord Harrington," Bernadette called from the foot of the dinner table. Mademoiselle Bernadette Gavage, Griffe's sister, was a sturdy, genteel lady of middle years with the misfortune of having, like her brother, one long eyebrow instead of two shorter ones. "Besides for the shooting, that is. Your work is terribly fascinating."

Gabriel washed venison down with wine. "There is an old woman in the village here who knows an unusual version—a local version—of the tale *La belle et la bête—Beauty and the Beast*. It seems that her memory is, alas, rapidly fading. I happened to dine with Griffe in England last week and he invited me here, knowing my scholarship concerns, in part, fairy tales. I will commit the old woman's tale to paper before it is lost forever." Gabriel raised his wineglass. "To my host and hostess."

"No, no," Griffe said at the head of the table. "To beauty." He tilted his brimming glass towards Miss Flax. She sank lower in her chair.

Ivy Banks, Gabriel's betrothed, blushed. She had mistaken Griffe's toast to be in her honor. An honest mistake; Ivy was a dainty beauty of twenty-four with a peaches-and-cream complexion, a heart-shaped face, and masses of light brown curls. "To the hunt," she said gaily.

Everyone toasted. Footmen poured more wine. Gabriel refused a third glass. Another course was served, strange, fibrous root vegetables in truffle and juniper sauce. Griffe ate with gusto, grunting softly as he sawed his meat. Flecks of sauce stuck to his stubbled jaw.

On Gabriel's right, Albert Banks checked his pocket watch for the fifth time since dinner had begun. Gabriel's future father-in-law was severe, gray-muttonchopped, and rotund. He owned many wool and silk mills in the northwest of England, and he doubtless had work he wished to complete before bed. Banks had come along on this trip because

Ivy had insisted upon coming, and Ivy and Gabriel could not travel without a chaperone. Banks couldn't say no to his darling, motherless child.

Thorstein Larsen forked up truffles with relish on Gabriel's left. Larsen was an elderly, smallish Norwegian gent with side-whiskers stained yellow from tobacco. Larsen seemed oblivious to the general conversation. He kept saying things such as "We will track those boars easily in the snow tomorrow," and "Those beasts do not stand a chance with Griffe's pack of hounds—fine creatures."

"I always pity the boars," Bernadette said in response to one such comment. "Snuffling about the wood in peace and then—bang!—out of nowhere, a hunter kills them."

"They are monsters, dear lady," Larsen said. "Their tusks will gore you straight through."

Bernadette touched the brooch pinned to her bodice.

"I am so eager to hunt tomorrow," Henrietta said to Larsen with a crafty shift of her décolletage. She slid Gabriel a nervous look. Gabriel supposed that Henrietta feared he'd betray her wealthy-widow scam.

Banks whispered in Gabriel's ear, "Strange coincidence that *he* turns up here, what?"

"Who?"

"That Norseman. Larsen." Banks hacked a dry cough into his napkin.

"What ever do you mean? Have you made his acquaintance previously?"

"Know him by reputation," Banks said darkly, and beckoned a footman to refill his wineglass.

Larsen was in timber, herring, copper mining, shipping, and the ice trade. Gabriel supposed he and Banks must have crossed paths in business at some juncture.

Across the table lounged the slick, vapid young chap claiming to be Cleveland soap heir Forthwith Stonewall. Gabriel assumed Forthwith was another actor. Poor Griffe. A château full of American actors, and not a clue.

Moldy, runny cheeses and hothouse pomegranates were served for dessert. As the last plate was cleared, Griffe's wineglass was topped yet again, and he stood on swaying legs. "A toast."

"Another?" Ivy pursed her lips.

"In this, the valley Vézère," Griffe said, "a long tradition exists of weddings, important weddings, fateful weddings, on the winter solstice, the longest, the most enchanted night of the year."

Bernadette nodded, and Miss Flax's face turned pink.

Gabriel's heart, unaccountably, wrung itself.

Miss Flax said, "Perhaps we should—"

"So it is with deep pleasure, gratitude, and *grande joie*," Griffe said, "that I announce my marriage to Mademoiselle Stonewall in five days' time, on the twenty-first of December. Here, in the château chapel."

Silverware clanked on china, and Henrietta squealed.

Miss Flax was pale as everyone turned to congratulate her. She mumbled her thanks, looking every inch the bashful bride-to-be.

Gabriel decided another glass of wine would be rather nice, after all.

3

Everyone got up and filed into the grand salon, with its splendid mural-covered walls, carved furniture, huge gilt mirrors, and faded carpets.

Ophelia wouldn't panic. She would *not*. She itched to corner Griffe and give him a piece of her mind about pulling that wedding date—in five days!—out of his hat. What about her fake parents in Cleveland? Weren't *they* invited?

But Griffe was as drunk as a skunk. No, she would call it off in the morning, give his ruby ring back, tell him the truth, and be on her way. Even if it meant wading through snowdrifts to golly-knew-where. Would Artemis mind if she pawned this fancy dinner gown for a ticket back to Paris?

Forthwith grandly announced that he would perform a conjuring trick.

Ophelia cornered him. "Truly?" she whispered through tight teeth. Forthwith was placing two flowerpots on tall, narrow, cloth-covered stands. "Magic, dear brother?"

"My sister is weary of my tricks," Forthwith said loudly

over his shoulder to the others. "I am a bit of an amateur conjurer, as all of our circle in Cleveland will attest. Poor Ophelia has endured countless parlor shows, and, as a girl, she even acted as my assistant."

"Did you saw her in half?" Henrietta asked.

Forthwith smiled. "No, I simply made her disappear. Most enjoyable for everyone."

Professor Penrose caught Ophelia's eye. She'd been making an effort not to look at him, for his keen hazel eyes behind his spectacles, his straight dark eyebrows, his square chin, and his brown, wavy hair worn longer than she remembered, well, they made her throat squeeze. She looked away.

"Now, if you will seat yourselves on these sofas here," Forthwith said, "—yes, that's excellent—I shall perform our dear mother's favorite trick, 'The Magic Rosebush.'" He tilted the flowerpots on the stands. "Observe: There is nothing in these pots but sand."

Everyone murmured in agreement.

"Good," Forthwith said. "Now I shall plant a few seeds." He drew something from his waistcoat pocket and sprinkled it in the sand. Then he produced a large white paper cone, showed it was empty inside, and placed it over the pot. "The seeds, you see, require darkness in order to germinate." He snapped his fingers and removed the cone. A little green sprout had appeared in the sand. "And so life begins anew, with a single hopeful sprig." He fiddled with the cone and the second pot, and another green sprout appeared.

Everyone clapped and murmured. Everyone, that is, except Ophelia. Forthwith was up to no good.

"Next," Forthwith said, "I will . . ." His voice trailed off, because Griffe was whispering loudly with a footman.

Forthwith crossed his arms.

"Then bring them in!" Griffe bellowed to the footman. The footman scurried off. Griffe addressed everyone, his face red with drink. "Most strange. A stagecoach has broken down outside the château gates, and the travelers have taken refuge here—the snow and wind—ah. Here they are."

The footman led three people into the salon, all bundled in furs that dripped melting snow: a wizened little lady with windblown bouffant hair; a bald, stoop-shouldered man; and a bland, youngish man.

"This *is* very awkward," the bland one said in a gentleman-like British accent. "I do beg your pardon—is it the Count de Griffe?—ah, yes, good, so pleased to meet you. Thank you for your kindness. It seems our stagecoach—coming from Sarlat, you understand, heading for Bordeaux—has broken down. Something to do with the mechanism of the thing—the whipple something or other, the driver said—simply gave way, and as we were just by your gates when it occurred, we all trooped up the drive. The driver took the horses to your stables. Wretched weather."

"You are welcome to stay here," Griffe said. "This is not a night for anyone to be abroad. It is a wonder that your coach set out at all in this storm."

"Yes, well, I fancy that the coachman thought it would blow over quickly. Everyone says these sorts of storms never happen in this region. But I forget myself. I am the Reverend Mr. Cecil Knight of Cricklade, Gloucestershire." He gestured to the old lady. "And this is—is it Madame Dieudonné?"

Madame Dieudonné nodded and made an antique curtsy. As she did so, her fur cloak fell open to reveal a small, frizzy white poodle tucked inside. "This is little Meringue," she said with a laborious French accent. She patted the poodle's head. Meringue lifted his lip and growled.

"This is Monsieur Tolbert," Knight said, gesturing to the stoop-shouldered man, "who, I learned upon meeting him two hours ago in Sarlat, is an esteemed scholar from Paris."

"A zoologist." Tolbert twiddled gloved fingers. "It is nothing to interest the layman."

Knight said, "There is one more traveler, my young charge

Master Abel Christy. He has been taken to the kitchens to be fed."

Complete introductions were made all around. Meanwhile, Forthwith fidgeted with impatience.

"Please, sit," Griffe said to the new arrivals, "and my servants will take away your coats and bring you food and wine."

"No wine for me, thank you," Knight said, wearing a pious expression. "Wine is the work of dark forces, I'm afraid."

"Priests in *this* country drink wine," Griffe muttered.

"Mr. Knight, what has happened to your neck?" Ivy exclaimed.

"Daughter," Banks whispered, coughing a little, *"where are your manners?"*

Ivy cast her eyes to her lap, but now everyone was goggling at Knight's throat. An angry red scar, four inches long, stretched beneath his jaw.

Knight touched the scar. "The natives in Africa do not always respond well to missionary efforts, poor benighted souls. . . ."

Everyone nodded and murmured. But Ophelia noticed that Knight licked his lips in a nervous fashion.

"Please, Monsieur Stonewall," Griffe said. "The magical rosebush trick."

Forthwith resumed his trick. He placed a paper cone over the first pot, removed it and—ta-da—a rosebush appeared. He did a few more maneuvers with the cones, and a rosebush appeared in the second pot. They weren't paper roses, either. They were real.

Everyone applauded. Ophelia's keen eye noted that the stands upon which the flowerpots rested were tall for a reason: to hide the *third* paper cone that no one else had seemed to notice, the cone used to conceal and transport the rosebushes. And the first two cones, well, Ophelia would bet her boots that they had holes in the top through which Forthwith dropped his little green sprouts.

"Those are roses from my own orangerie," Griffe said. "As Monsieur Stonewall must know. Note their peculiar crimson and white stripes."

The roses made Ophelia think of candy canes.

"They bloom the winter through," Griffe said, "and they are the only bushes of la Belle de la Périgord roses in the world."

"Ah, I have heard of the variety," Mr. Banks said. "I am something of a botanical enthusiast at home, am I not, Ivy?"

Ivy smiled and patted his arm. "Papa's most recent hobby."

Banks said to Griffe, "A single rose hip filled with this flower's precious seed would fetch an immense sum from horticulturists in England. They are eager to possess rare varieties."

Madame Dieudonné murmured, "*Incroyable*," as she petted her poodle, and Knight said, "Oh, indeed?"

"I have prosperity enough without plundering the plants in my orangerie," Griffe said. "What is more, I would rather possess something rare and precious than share it." His bleary eyes fell upon Ophelia.

Ophelia tried to disappear into the sofa cushions. How long till she could flee to her bedchamber? She would have claimed a sick headache if she weren't worried that Griffe would insist upon tending her himself with a cold compress and love poems.

When the after-dinner conversation turned to the topic of comic operas, Gabriel wandered away from the others, hands in pockets, in search of diversion.

He would've liked to retire, but he felt the expectant eyes of both Ivy and her father boring into him. Miss Flax, of course, looked at everything *but* Gabriel. Why did she seem so miserable? She had gotten everything she'd gambled for in becoming engaged to Griffe: title, financial security, and, indeed, she'd gotten the better of Gabriel, too. It had taken a good deal of effort not to think of her these three weeks past, but he'd managed rippingly. For the most part.

Tolbert, the Parisian zoologist, bent over a book at the far end of the salon. His forehead puckered, his thin lips worked, and he did not notice Gabriel until Gabriel stood just beside him.

Tolbert started and slapped the book shut, but not before Gabriel had seen a pencil sketch of a jawbone with square teeth and two short tusks.

"I beg your pardon, but you are Étienne-Frédéric Tolbert, correct?"

"Oui."

Ah. He was indeed *that* Tolbert. The Tolbert who had a few years ago made off with a bone of the great fossil lizard *megalosaurus* belonging to his place of work, the Muséum national d'histoire naturelle in Paris. The theft had been gossiped about among academics, although the museum had kept the business hushed up to avoid scandal. Surprising that Tolbert had kept his post. But surely he'd missed out on promotions as a result of the theft.

"Are you on your way to Paris?" Gabriel asked.

"Only to Bordeaux. An important parcel awaits me at the port, shipped from London. I cannot trust anyone to transport it safely to me."

Intriguing. Perhaps the parcel contained a fossil. "Then you are staying in the Périgord?"

"How inquisitive you are. Yes, I have been in this region for nearly one year, staying in let rooms in Sarlat, conducting research on fossilized ferns."

"Ferns? But I could not help but notice your drawing," Gabriel said. "Is it your own?" The book was cheaply bound, like an artist's sketchbook.

"Ah, *oui*, but I am most certain—Lord Harrington, was it?—that it is of no interest to a sporting gentleman."

"I am not a sporting gentleman, actually. I am a philology lecturer at Oxford."

"Ah. Still, fossils are nothing to concern gentlemen in the less *rigorous* fields of science." Tolbert stuffed the notebook inside his rumpled brown jacket. His hairy small hands shook.

"Your sketch appears to be that of a primitive human jawbone, is that correct?"

"*Oui, oui*—that is all. An ancient, perhaps prehistoric human bone—"

"Yet it had boar's tusks."

A long pause. Tolbert scratched the tip of his hooked nose. "It is possible."

"The remains of some heretofore unidentified hybrid species, perchance, part human and part boar? I read of the recent discovery of the creature *archaeopteryx* unearthed in Bavaria—you've heard of it?—that bridges the gap between reptilian and avian species."

"I know quite well of *archaeopteryx*. But my own sketch—pah!—entirely unimportant and dull." Tolbert made an awkward nod as he stood. He left the salon, head down, without bidding the others good night.

Curious. Gabriel watched Tolbert retreat. He had never before heard an academic describe his own work as unimportant or dull. Unless they were lying.

When Ophelia at last arrived in her bedchamber, the fire had gone out and the parakeet's head was tucked under its wing. By wavering candlelight, she washed and changed into her nightgown. Outside, wind whooshed and snow kept mounding up. From next door came the sound of Larsen's vibrating snore. She'd seen him go into his chamber when she'd gone into her own.

She curled up in bed and put a pillow over her head, unable to shake a sense of doom. Maybe it was only that she'd eaten too much of that runny cheese at dinner.

A sleepless hour passed. Continuous snoring, continuous

snow. Ophelia's nightgown was tangled around her legs when she heard stealthy footfalls in the corridor. Heart in her throat, she threw off the bedclothes, tiptoed to the door, and peeked out.

She caught the briefest glimpse of Griffe's burly form as it disappeared around a corner at the end of the corridor.

What was *he* doing, prowling around here at this hour? Bernadette had said that the family had its own wing on the other side of the château. Ophelia pushed a hefty chair against the door and tipped it under the doorknob. Just in case.

Later, she surfaced from a thick black sleep, aware that something had changed. She lay motionless. Larsen was still snoring. But—yes, that was it. *Moonlight.*

She got out of bed and went to the window. It had stopped snowing. The sky radiated with the light of the almost-full moon, and only a few silky clouds remained. Ophelia's chamber overlooked the side of the château. Snow-covered ground spread pristine all the way to the edge of a long, low building. She couldn't be sure, but there seemed to be a faint light inside the building.

She checked the mantelpiece clock—fifteen minutes until two o'clock—and went back to bed.

Ophelia woke for the second time to sunlight.

She swung her legs out of the bed. She must make haste. She would dress, break things off with Griffe, and somehow get to the nearest town. She'd figure out her next move there.

The parakeet didn't cross her mind until she'd tied herself into corset and crinoline.

She went to its cage. "Don't you like bread crumbs?" she said. The bowl of crumbs was untouched, and the parakeet looked melancholy. Ophelia couldn't in good conscience leave without first making certain the parakeet wasn't going to kick the bucket. Seeds. Birds required seeds. The kitchen, maybe, or—yes, the orangerie, which was only a fancy sort of greenhouse. She was fairly certain that the long, low building visible from her window was the orangerie. She'd find seeds in there.

She finished dressing in a blue woolen day dress and boots. She wouldn't need a cloak for only a few minutes out of doors. After a goodly number of wrong turns and one back stairway, she found a side door leading out.

She stumbled into a foot of wet snow. The orangerie was three dozen yards away, with a flat roof, carved embellishments, and a row of big arched windows.

Halfway there, Ophelia heard screaming. A woman's screams, bleating and high-pitched.

Ophelia plowed forward. By the time she reached the orangerie door, her skirts were caked with snow and her boots were leaking. She opened the door and balmy air puffed out.

"Mademoiselle Stonewall," a woman called behind her.

Ophelia turned. Bernadette was staggering through the snow, fear contorting her face. "The screaming," Ophelia croaked. A waste of breath; those piping screams didn't need pointing out.

Ophelia stepped into the orangerie, Bernadette right behind.

The screaming stopped.

Gurgling water—a stone face on the wall spouted into a basin filled with lily pads. Rows of potted orange trees stretched the length of the building. Between the orange trees, iron benches billowed with other kinds of plants. The air smelled of decay and green growth.

A whimper.

Ophelia and Bernadette followed the sound.

At the end of a row of rosebushes, a plump woman in a brown gown and apron clutched her skull and rocked herself.

"Marielle?" Bernadette said. "What is the matter, Marielle?"

Marielle pointed to something that Ophelia could not see, obscured behind potted rosebushes.

Ophelia and Bernadette looked around the bushes.

"Mon Dieu." Bernadette clapped her hands over her mouth.

"Oh my Mabel," Ophelia whispered.

Ophelia had seen a few dead bodies, but she still wasn't prepared for the sight of the vicar, sprawled on the floor and clutching a red-and-white-striped rose. He wore the same suit of clothes she'd seen him in last night. His mouth was wide, his skin rashy, and bloody scratches striped his cheeks. The worst part of it was the deep, shiny gouge at one side of his belly. Nausea slopped over Ophelia, and she looked away.

"La bête," Marielle whispered.

"La bête?" Ophelia said. "The . . . beast?"

"She is in shock." Bernadette took Marielle's arm and drew her away.

Marielle babbled breathlessly in French.

"What did she say?" Ophelia asked Bernadette.

"She is—the village folk here, they are . . . superstitious," Bernadette said. "She says that the vicar was gored to death." Marielle spoke rapidly, eyes wild, gesturing with her hands. Bernadette translated. "The mark on his belly—that terrible gouge—it is the mark of the Beast."

"What beast?" Ophelia asked.

"The Beast of Vézère—it is a legend only, you must understand, and Marielle—my cook—she is upset—"

"What is the legend?"

Bernadette stroked Marielle's back. "It is silly, but, well, it is said that if a person drinks water from a certain enchanted spring, he might become a—a creature, half man and half, well, it is silly to say, but half boar—but I really must take her—"

Marielle was babbling again.

"She says that the winter solstice draws near," Bernadette said, "and the moon is waxing."

"This beast thing—it enjoys the moonlight?"

"Yes. All nonsense, of course, and I see the doubt in your eyes, Mademoiselle Stonewall, and I entirely agree. It is clear that Monsieur Knight met with a terrible accident of some kind, and—well, I must take Marielle away and summon help—my brother will know what to do, and I—oh—please stay here and make certain nothing happens to—oh dear. You are so very self-possessed. . . ."

Ophelia nodded. Bernadette was already leading the sobbing Marielle away.

Ophelia was left alone with the body.

4

Holy Moses, the *body*. Despite the orangerie's tropical air, Ophelia felt clammy. Soon, the orangerie would be swarming with folks. The gentlemen would take charge, send the ladies away to sniff vinaigrettes and drink sherry, and that would be that.

Last chance to satisfy her curiosity; she took another look at the vicar.

A wooden bowl lay upside down beside him, and greens were scattered. Marielle had probably been cutting greens for the kitchen when she found the body.

The striped rose in the vicar's hand matched the roses in the pots around him. La Belle de la Périgord, the rare variety everyone had made a fuss about last night. Now *this* was mighty peculiar: The vicar's fingers were clenched like talons, so he wasn't actually holding that rose. The rose was *propped* between his fist and chest.

The rose had been placed there after his death. Why? And could Marielle have done it?

Or . . . had the vicar been *murdered*?

Ophelia looked around with sharper eyes.

Red blotches—wine—down the vicar's shirt front. Hadn't he refused wine last night, claiming he never drank the stuff?

A tiny glass bottle lay beside the vicar's head. Ophelia bent to inspect it. The bottle hadn't a label or a cork, and it was empty. Odd.

Many pots had been knocked down, spraying black dirt, wrecked plants, and clay shards across the floor. Had there been a struggle here?

Ophelia lifted her skirts to step around the body, and went up the aisle between the rows of plant racks.

Something popped beneath her heel. She checked the bottom of her boot. She had trodden upon a blackish purple berry. A broken bush lay at her feet, surrounded by spilled dirt and a shattered pot.

She knew those berries. Belladonna. Deadly nightshade. Whatever you called it, a handful of berries could kill a man. Kill him awfully, with convulsions that would cause him to, say, thrash around and knock down potted plants.

She scanned the racks. More belladonna bushes—who would need all that?—and wolfsbane, wormwood, chamomile, and hogwort. Medicinal plants, but strong ones. Ophelia's mother had taught her about these. Halfway down the aisle, the medicinal plants gave way to culinary herbs—rosemary, thyme, lavender, and chives—and these, too, had not escaped damage.

Hanging on the stone wall was an iron rack, from which were suspended gardening tools—shovels, trowels, a broom. And a pitchfork with sharp curved prongs. Prongs caked with blood.

That was how the vicar had gotten his "beast" goring, then. It was a wonder that the pitchfork was still hanging up, but then, it was suspended by a leather strap.

Ophelia froze. Men's voices outside.

She returned to the vicar's body. Yes, his pupils were dilated, a sure sign of having eaten belladonna. And what was this? His waistcoat pocket bulged with some small object. Ophelia crouched and pulled it out. A brown glass bottle labeled "For Heart Complaints."

The men's voices echoed, inside the orangerie now, and footsteps sounded on stone. Ophelia slipped the bottle back into the vicar's waistcoat pocket and stood.

Griffe and Banks rushed down the aisle of plants, with Professor Penrose and Ivy close behind.

"*Ma chérie*, how terrible for you," Griffe said, brushing Ophelia's cheek with the back of his fingers.

She tried not to cringe.

"I have sent the stable boy into Sarlat to fetch a doctor." Griffe's bloodshot eyes fell on the body, and a muscle in his cheek twitched. "The police, too—I see that no doctor will be needed. In this snow, the boy will have a difficult ride, although it is but three miles to town."

"Are you well, Miss Stonewall?" Penrose asked Ophelia.

She nodded.

"Good God," Banks muttered when he saw the body. He wrapped his arm around Ivy and whispered into her hair, "Pray do not look, child."

Ivy twisted to see. "But what is that? The small bottle, beside his head? Why, that is my own bottle of traveling sickness tablets, except all the tablets are gone. Whatever could it be doing here? Did he—could the vicar have stolen it from my chamber?"

"Ivy, go back to the château," Banks said. "This is no place for a lady."

"Traveling sickness tablets?" Ophelia asked Ivy.

"Ships and trains and coaches make me frightfully ill. Mr. Knight must have done himself in with my tablets. He took them all—see?—and they are made from *atropa belladonna*—deadly nightshade. The chemist told me as much."

Belladonna? *More* belladonna? "Surely your traveling

sickness tablets were not potent enough to do in a grown man," Ophelia said.

"If he had a weak heart, perhaps," Banks said.

"Look at the way the rose is clasped to his chest," Ophelia said. "It seems he was not really *holding* it, but—"

"We will leave these matters to the Gendarmerie de Sarlat," Griffe said. "You must be greatly shocked, Mademoiselle Stonewall. Please, go to the house."

"You as well, Ivy," Banks said.

Ophelia turned down the aisle of plants, although she didn't fancy being sent away like a bad puppy. Ivy minced ahead of her, lifting her skirts above the dirt and smashed plants. In a few moments she disappeared through the door.

Ophelia went more slowly, holding her elbows, her nerves like flyaway threads. Near the end of the aisle, where orange trees stood laden with fruit, a motion caught her eye. She stopped and peered through the stiff leaves.

A small form—yes, a plump child in a grown-up suit of clothes, with a brown complexion and black curls—scrambled to his feet. He stuffed something in his jacket pocket.

"What are you doing?" Ophelia whispered. "There's a dead man in here." She looked down the aisle to the men standing over the body. Oblivious. She looked back through the leaves; the boy had vanished.

He must've been the young charge the vicar had been escorting to England. But why in tarnation had he been in this gruesome place?

Outside, Ophelia circled the orangerie. No footprints in the snow at the back, but too many to count at the front, now that half the household had been stomping around. If footprints could've been a clue to the mystery, well, they were all spoiled now.

She went back into the château, all the while thinking that she should fetch her cloak and bonnet and go for a walk.

It was snowy, yes, but until the police came and went, she wouldn't have a chance to break things off with Griffe. How could she simply sit still? Then she remembered the parakeet and its untouched bread crumbs.

She poked around until she found stairs coiling down into the smoky kitchen. Copper pots gleamed on stone walls, and something meaty bubbled on the hulking black cookstove. A maid chopped mushrooms at a big wooden table, talking with another maid. They both froze and lifted wide, fearful eyes when they saw Ophelia.

They'd heard about Knight's death, then.

"Birdseed?" Ophelia said to the maids. "Um, *cuisine de oiseau?*" No, that couldn't be right.

One maid pointed at a pheasant dangling from the ceiling next to a bundle of garlic.

Ophelia shook her head. What was the word for pantry? Oh, yes. *"Garde-manger?"* she said.

The maid tilted her head towards a stone passage and went back to chopping.

Ophelia found the pantry, a musty chamber filled with clay pots, jars, burlap sacks, and baskets of onions and apples. After a few minutes of looking, she found a jar of sunflower seeds. She took the jar and went upstairs.

Before she reached the staircase leading to the upper chambers, Bernadette waylaid her in a corridor. "Do you require a glass of cordial, Mademoiselle Stonewall? You have had such a shock. Or coffee, perhaps? I have sent for some. Waiting for the doctor and police to arrive, well, one must do something to distract oneself."

"Oh. Hello. Nothing for me, thank you."

Bernadette's face fell. She wanted company.

"Well, perhaps coffee," Ophelia said. She had developed a taste for coffee while working in P. Q. Putnam's Traveling Circus. The Astonishing Aerial Twins, Alphonso and Allegra

Vito, used to prepare it for her in a funny silver pot in their wagon.

"Ah, *bon*. Come in, please." Bernadette led Ophelia into a salon with paneled walls and blue damask upholstery. "What is that little jar you are holding?"

"Seeds for my parakeet." Ophelia nodded in greeting to Ivy, who lolled against a cushion with a book facedown on her lap.

"How eccentric of you to have brought a bird all this way," Ivy said, twirling a ringlet around her finger.

"Poor thing," Bernadette said. "I always think such little creatures should be set free into the wild."

"A parakeet wouldn't last in this climate," Ophelia said.

Did Bernadette's eyes look *teary*? "Please do stand just there," she said to Ophelia, pointing to a spot next to a harpsichord.

Stand?

"You are not wearing the ruby ring?" Bernadette asked, now gathering up something white and gauzy from a basket on the floor.

"I seem to have forgotten to put it on."

Bernadette came at Ophelia with the white gauzy thing. "I am so glad I found you, for I have been mending my mother's wedding veil."

Ophelia's tongue stuck to the roof of her mouth.

"Is it to your taste? I mean to say, if you had other plans for your bridal garments, then. . . . But when my brother announced that the wedding would be in but five day's time, my thoughts flew to Maman's gown and veil."

"The news seemed *very* sudden," Ivy said. Her wide blue eyes drifted to Ophelia's belly.

Merciful heavens. Is *that* what people thought the hurry was about? Her belly? Ophelia's ears burned.

"There is so much to see to before the wedding," Bernadette said. "The cakes and meats, the flowers—"

"The invitations, of course," Ivy said. "*Such* a pity that your parents won't be able to attend due to the short notice, Miss Stonewall."

Ophelia opened her mouth.

Bernadette went on, "I had always hoped to wear Maman's gown and veil at my *own* wedding." A heavy pause. Bernadette's shoulders sagged. Then she said brightly, "This veil—is it not splendid? It is nearly seven feet long—"

"Should just hit the floor, then," Ivy said.

"—and made of the finest Brussels lace. There are only a few bits to be mended, some of the embroidered flowers at the bottom, and a moth hole here and there. Now. Allow me to see it on you." She draped it over Ophelia's head.

Ophelia stood stock-still, clutching the jar of seeds to her chest. The veil smelled like dust and camphor. Only a few more hours of this ruse, and then she'd break it off with Griffe. A few more hours. "Who tends to the plants in the orangerie?" she asked Bernadette. "Is it Marielle? I noticed there were some . . . potent medicinal plants there."

"How do you know of such things, Miss Stonewall?" Ivy asked.

"Books."

"Ah."

Bernadette fiddled with the veil around Ophelia's face. "Marielle does not tend the plants, no, although she does go into the orangerie every morning to cut herbs and greens for her cooking. The plants are cared for by our old gardener, Luc. Luc also keeps the orangerie's coal furnace going, the furnace that heats the water for the pipes beneath the floors to keep it so warm in wintertime. But we should speak only of joyful things." She swept the veil off. "Please, sit while I work. Ah, here is Clémence with the coffee."

Clémence, the beautiful, statuesque maid, carried in a tray with a coffee service. When she saw Ophelia in the veil, she stumbled and nearly dropped the tray.

"Clémence!" Bernadette said. "Not with Maman's Limoges cups."

Clémence, eyes cast down, arranged the coffee service on a table and left.

"The servants are upset about poor Monsieur Knight," Bernadette said, pouring coffee. "I am surprised at Clémence, however. She is the most sensible of them all. So very devoted to the family. Sugar and cream, Mademoiselle Banks?"

Ivy nodded.

Bernadette went on, "I do apologize if the coffee is bitter. Only Marielle makes coffee correctly, and I gave her the rest of the day off. She was so shaken by seeing the vicar."

"Did you hear what the servants have been saying about this beast thing?" Ivy asked. "That it walks upright, like a man, but with the hideous head of a boar—"

"Oh, do not speak of it," Bernadette whispered.

Ivy shrugged.

Ophelia tried to pry more about the gardener and the orangerie out of Bernadette, but Bernadette kept steering the conversation to the weather, weddings, and Ophelia's supposed life amid Cleveland's high society. Ivy listened in silence, sipping coffee and looking amused. Ophelia was relieved when Tolbert, the Parisian zoologist, appeared in the doorway.

"Monsieur Tolbert," Bernadette said. "Do come and take some coffee with—"

"No time, no time." Tolbert shifted his weight from foot to foot. "Something has been taken from my chamber. Are your servants in the habit of stealing?"

"Most certainly not," Bernadette cried. "Monsieur Tolbert, what has been taken? If it is an article of clothing, surely the servants meant to launder it, or—"

"A scientific specimen of great, no, of *astounding* and irreplaceable value." Tolbert's voice shook. "I demand that you summon your servants, all of them, so that I might interrogate them."

"I will do no such thing. My servants do not steal."

"Very well, then. I am forced to take matters into my own hands." Tolbert swung around and left.

"Prickly little gentleman, isn't he?" Ivy said. "Reminds me of the evil gnome in a storybook I once had."

Bernadette's fingers trembled as she took up the veil, needle, and thread. "I cannot think why he is still here. I understand he has rooms in Sarlat."

Hours passed. Bernadette worked on mending the veil, Ivy read, and Ophelia by turns tried on the veil for Bernadette and fretted.

She saw men through the windows, slogging through snow at the front of the château. She went to the windows. "The count and Professor Penrose," she said. "And two gendarmes." She recognized their blue peaked caps from her run-ins with the police in Paris. Another man wore a bowler hat and a greatcoat, and a wagon with a black horse stood in the drive. "And a doctor, I suppose." The four men disappeared around the corner.

"Come, Mademoiselle Stonewall, and try the veil again," Bernadette said. "I have mended the last moth hole."

5

"His heart?" Gabriel said in disbelief to the doctor from Sarlat. They, along with two gendarmes, stood beside the doctor's wagon in the slushy front drive. They had not spent more than ten minutes examining the scene in the orangerie. "Really? Does a thrombosis—"

"Thrombosis *or* angina," the doctor said. "I cannot be certain which."

"All right, then, does either affliction cause a man to convulse for such a prolonged period that he would be able to create such disarray—all those broken plants and pots? That he could wound himself so grievously on a hanging pitchfork? There are belladonna plants growing in that orangerie." While waiting for the doctor and the police, Gabriel had read in the château library about the effects of ingesting *atropa belladonna*. These included convulsions, staggering, loss of balance, dilated pupils—all of which Gabriel had noted the vicar had had.

"The death throes of a heart complaint sufferer have many variations, monsieur." Dr. Duclos, young, boneless, and bored, adjusted his hat.

"We found a bottle of heart complaint tablets in his waistcoat pocket," one of the gendarmes said. "He did not get to them in time."

And that sewed the whole thing up. They would take the body to the morgue in Sarlat, where it would wait until the vicar's parish in England was reached by telegram. The vicar's belongings were still in his bedchamber and to be left there until the parish was heard from.

"There is also the matter of the young boy who was traveling with Mr. Knight," Gabriel said. "Master Christy. What is to become of him?"

"That is a domestic affair, monsieur. You are welcome to sort it out yourself. Good day."

Gabriel felt uneasy as he watched the wagon rattle away down the drive. He turned and went inside to tell the others the doctor's judgment.

Ophelia was trapped under the wedding veil when she saw, through the window, the vicar's shroud-draped body being loaded into the wagon. She watched as the doctor and gendarmes spoke with Penrose and left.

Now might be a good time to break things off with Griffe.

"Where is your brother?" Ophelia asked Bernadette, who was fiddling with the veil.

"I do not know. Riding, perhaps. He rides a great deal, looking over the estate. He is restless. Do not worry— he will be back in time for luncheon. He never misses a meal, my dear. And I am certain, once there are children"— a peek at Ophelia's midriff—"well, he will become more settled."

Right. Time to change the subject. "What do you suppose happened to Mr. Knight?"

"Why, suicide," Ivy said, glancing up from her book. "Don't you remember my stolen medicine bottle?"

Bernadette stopped fussing with the veil. "My own father died of a heart attack, and there was something about poor Monsieur Knight's face that reminded me—oh dear, but we really should speak of something else. Weddings, perhaps?" She sniffled.

"What is the matter?" Ophelia asked, touching Bernadette's shoulder.

"Oh, nothing."

"You're weeping."

Ivy said, "Talk of weddings is not always pleasant for maiden relations."

Ophelia frowned at Ivy, who narrowed her eyes and smushed her lips.

Ophelia had seen that look before, on a five year-old who'd been denied an ice cream.

"Well, it is a trifle," Bernadette said, blinking away tears, "and I did not mean to mention it with all that is happening, but a small item has gone missing from my bedchamber. Nothing of great value, but it was something very dear to me. Now that Monsieur Tolbert says that he, too . . . oh, *là*."

"Stolen?" Ophelia asked. "What was it?"

"It is *so* difficult to find trustworthy servants," Ivy said.

"My servants would never steal!"

A rap sounded on the salon door, and Professor Penrose stepped inside. His eyebrows lifted when he saw Ophelia in the veil.

"*There* you are," Ivy said impatiently.

"The doctor and the police have come and gone," Penrose said. "They've taken Mr. Knight's body away. The police will telegraph his parish in England. They asked that his things be left here in the château until further notice."

"What did they say he died of?" Ophelia asked.

"His heart failed—either by a thrombosis or an angina. Clotting or constricting. Either way, natural causes."

Natural causes? How did that account for the empty bottle of Ivy's traveling sickness tablets? And the convulsing, the dilated pupils, the belladonna berries . . .

"What a relief to have that done with," Ivy said. "Will you take coffee with us, Lord Harrington?"

Penrose cut a glance to Ophelia and away.

Did *he* suppose the hurried-up wedding was on account of her belly, too? Ugh.

"I wish to visit the old storytelling woman in the village, Madame Genepy," Penrose said.

"I will come with you." Ivy set her cup down and stood. She turned to Bernadette. "It is curious that something was stolen from you and from Mr. Tolbert, for you see, last night an amethyst bracelet was stolen from my own chamber, and Father said he is missing a pair of diamond cuff links."

The ruby ring. Oh, golly. What if—? "Your traveling sickness tablets were taken, too," Ophelia said to Ivy.

"Indeed. There is a thief afoot."

Ophelia removed the veil and placed it in Bernadette's hands. Then she grabbed her jar of sunflower seeds. "I've just remembered something that I—please excuse me." She strolled calmly to the salon doors, nodding as she passed Penrose. Once she was in the corridor, she hitched up her skirts in one hand, clutched the jar with the other, and ran.

"Miss Stonewall," Penrose called.

She ignored him.

Upstairs, she burst into her bedchamber, panting, and ran to her vanity table. She set down the jar of sunflower seeds and opened the little box.

The slip of paper was there.

The ring was gone.

Ophelia stared blankly into the box until the parakeet chirped.

She looked at the slip of paper with disgust. On it was written a favorite saying of hers:

I make my circumstance.

Apparently, she didn't.

She replaced the box's lid. Numb, she exchanged the parakeet's bread crumbs for sunflower seeds, and by the time she'd refilled its water dish, the parakeet was crunching away.

Someone had stolen the ring. How could she break off her engagement to Griffe now? If she told him she was really an out-of-work actress and a seasoned confidence trickster, he would assume *she'd* stolen the ring. Her dignity was on the line. Griffe might even have her arrested.

She had a hunch that Knight had been killed by the thief who had stolen her ring, Banks's cuff links, Ivy's bracelet, and whatever Bernadette and Tolbert were missing. If she could figure who killed the vicar, then she'd have her thief, and if she had her thief, then she could get the ring back.

The clincher was Ivy's bottle of traveling sickness tablets; that bottle was out of place. Ophelia wondered if the thief had stolen all those things from people's chambers as they slept last night, and then gone on to kill Knight—maybe because Knight knew of their stealing. Then, for some reason they had dropped or placed the empty traveling sickness bottle by the body.

Ophelia tallied up the possible suspects. The storm last night had been severe enough to rule out interlopers; the murderer, if Knight had truly been murdered, was among the occupants of Château Vézère. One of the servants, one of the guests, or . . . or Griffe or Bernadette? Ophelia couldn't picture her host and hostess killing anyone. Nor could she, for that matter, suspect Henrietta, who was as self-absorbed as a baby but not the violent sort. Forthwith? Possible. Larsen? No—she'd heard his snoring all night. Tolbert and that funny old woman with the poodle, Madame something or other, could not be discounted. Neither could Ivy or Banks.

That was a bundle of suspects.

Professor Penrose had said that the vicar's things were to be left in his bedchamber. So that was the place to start.

The first matter of business was to locate Knight's chamber. Bernadette, Griffe, or a servant would know where it was, but Ophelia couldn't have anyone know she was snooping. Château Vézère was large but not palatial; she could poke around and see if could find it.

Beetle-browed Griffe ancestors decorated the corridor. Just next door was Larsen's chamber. Ophelia tried the door after that. Unlocked.

Inside, Henrietta slept in a canopied bed, mouth ajar, a satin mask over her eyes.

The last door led to the newfangled water closet—Griffe was keen on such scientific improvements—and after that, the marble bath chamber.

Ophelia turned and went the other way, past the grand staircase and through to the other wing.

Halfway down the corridor, a furtive motion made her stop. There, behind that bulky chair . . . somebody on hands and knees . . . why, it was the chubby, dark-skinned boy she'd seen in the orangerie earlier. She moved stealthily closer, stopping only inches from him. He was inspecting a chair leg, and he did not seem to notice her presence. Was he deaf?

Ophelia cleared her throat.

The boy started with a gasp, and then glared up at her. "I say! What are you playing at, sneaking up on me in that fashion? You'll give me a fit of apoplexy, and seeing as I am only thirteen years old, that would be a feat indeed. And speaking of *feet*—" He smirked down at Ophelia's somewhat large boots.

"Don't you *dare* comment," Ophelia snapped. Instantly,

she felt ashamed. He was only a child. A child who spoke like the British members of parliament in Howard DeLuxe's *A Penny for Your Thoughts*.

The boy stood, brushed off the knees and sleeves of his little man suit, and held out a hand. "Master Abel Christy."

Ophelia shook his hand, bare and pudgy. "Miss Ophelia Stonewall. You are Mr. Knight's charge."

"A transitory arrangement, but yes. I'd only just met him when he collected me from my ship in Marseille. As my escort, you see. I'm considered too young and too small to travel alone, although as anyone might discern, I am quite capable of managing."

Maybe, but Ophelia noticed that Abel *wasn't* able to manage the two small hairs on his spotty chin.

He went on, "As it turns out, I would have been better off without him—I'd be in London by now if I'd been left to my own devices."

"Then Mr. Knight was a stranger to you?"

"Yes. An acquaintance of my protector, Sir Percival Christy. They met in Kenya at one time or another, where Mr. Knight was preaching to the heathens and all that."

Knight had had a pasty complexion. How had he managed to preserve that under the African sun? Then again, he'd had that ghastly scar on his throat.

"And to where are you traveling, Master Christy?"

"Back to school. The Warbridge School?"

"Haven't heard of it."

"Really, you Americans are so marvelously provincial. It's almost as though you lived on the surface of a distant star."

"Where is the Warbridge School, then?"

"England." Abel looked glum. A fleck of some sort of custard was stuck to his cheek. "Of course, it's the Christmas holidays just now, but Sir Christy was all in a lather to return to his expedition. He is currently engaged in an expedition to discover the source of the Upper Nile."

"Oh?"

"No one can find it, you see. The rivers become like mazes in the highlands."

"Surely Africa is too far from England to simply gallivant down there on one's school holidays."

"Death in the family."

"I am sorry."

"No need. Grandfather was ninety-seven years old, and his funeral was attended with all the pomp owing a . . . king." Abel flicked something from his cuff and puffed out his cheeks.

"King?"

"Of Nubia."

"How grand." Abel seemed to expect kowtowing from Ophelia. Not in the cards, even if his grandfather really *was* a king. Which was questionable. Thirteen-year-old boys weren't known for their honesty. "Tell me, how did you recognize Mr. Knight in Marseille if you'd never met him before?"

"I didn't. He recognized me. I mean, as soon as I'd reached the bottom of the gangway, there he was, saying he was the Reverend Mr. Knight, and that was that. Nasty man. Kept making little remarks to me about ankle biters and such, although I calmly told him that I have already exceeded his cerebral abilities. Why are you asking so many impertinent questions?"

"Because I'm curious about how Mr. Knight died."

"But I was told by the cook that the doctor chalked it up to a heart ailment. Not, mind you, that *she* believed it for a second. She postulates that Mr. Knight was gored to death by a mythical beast. Very quaint."

Ophelia hesitated, reminding herself that she was speaking with a child. But Abel was no ordinary child. "I don't believe he died a natural death."

"Murder, then?"

"You aren't going to have nightmares about this and blame me, are you?"

"I sleep the sleep of the innocent."

"That reminds me—what were you doing skulking in the orangerie, and what are you doing in this corridor?"

"Skulking?" Abel looked insulted. "You misunderstand. I am adding to my collection." He reached in his jacket pocket and withdrew a small corked vial. A fat white grub lay inside. "This is an *anobium punctatum* larva. Furniture beetle. The larvae bore through wood—see the holes?"

Ophelia looked. The chair was indeed stippled with holes. "You're a bug collector."

"I prefer entomologist, but yes. In the orangerie earlier, I was merely pursuing a glorious specimen of *cetonia aurata*—rose beetle. Normally the adults perish in the autumn, but in that artificial climate, they have survived."

"But the body . . ."

"Well, I didn't *look* at it."

"Do you know which bedchamber was Mr. Knight's?"

"Going to have a little sleuth?"

"I beg your pardon?"

"I've read Poe's detective tales. I'll come with you. I don't think much of Americans, but you seem all right."

"No. This isn't a game. A man may have been"—Ophelia lowered her voice— "may have been *murdered*."

"I could help you. I enjoy deductive reasoning as much as the next chap."

"I don't require help."

"Do you know where Mr. Knight's chamber is?"

"Well—"

"Come on. I'll show you."

6

K night's chamber was third on the right. Ophelia and Abel crept in and shut the door.

"The bed doesn't appear to have been used at all," Ophelia said, mostly to herself. Abel rubbed her the wrong way, and on top of that, she felt silly and ashamed that a thirteen-year-old nipper *could* rub her the wrong way. "Knight had stayed up before his death, then—he hadn't been roused from his slumber to go to the orangerie."

"There is his trunk," Abel said, pointing to a large, domed affair with brass ribs and tacks.

They went over, and Ophelia swung it open. The scents of bay rum aftershave lotion and exotic dust wafted up.

"What a mess." Ophelia prodded the tangle of garments and hats inside the trunk. "Was the vicar a sloppy fellow?"

"No, actually. Mr. Knight struck me as the sort who had a fire poker up—"

"I see," Ophelia said quickly. "A stickler."

"He *was* a vicar."

"Then someone has been rummaging through his trunk already." Ophelia removed the items from the trunk, one by one, and stacked them on the floor. Some clothes were made for a warm climate—white flannels and linen shirts and a straw hat—while others, like the greatcoat, beaver hat, and woolen suits, were made for a European winter.

"Everything looks to be the first-rate quality," Abel said.

"Well-worn, though."

"Well, the kingdom of heaven and all that."

"Here's his Bible." Ophelia flipped through. It was tissue-paged and floppy. Some pages were translucent with finger oil. An envelope fell out.

"Aha!" Ophelia and Abel exclaimed in unison. Abel made a grab for the envelope, but Ophelia nabbed it first. Return address one D. J. Montgomery, Esq., in London.

"That's Sir Christy's solicitor," Abel said.

The seal was broken. The letter read,

Dear Mr. Knight,

Thank you for agreeing to escort young Master Christy from Marseille to London. Upon his safe arrival at my offices, you will receive recompense of two hundred pounds sterling for your trouble. I am afraid, however, that if he is not delivered by the twentieth of December, you will be required to wait one month to collect this recompense, as I will be going abroad.

I wish you safe travels.

Sincerely,
D. J. Montgomery

Abel pouted. "I had no notion the solicitor was *paying* people to herd me about. Makes me feel a bit like a sheep."

"I wouldn't feel too badly." Ophelia replaced the envelope in the Bible and dug through to the bottom of the trunk. A pair of riding boots, neatly folded nightshirts— "What's this?" She pulled out a bundle wrapped in twine.

"Any detective would open it."

Ophelia didn't need convincing. She undid the twine, and several bobbins clattered to the floor and rolled. She picked one up. "Embroidery thread?"

"Looks like silk—what colors. Could Mr. Knight have been stitching a sampler?" Abel snickered.

"Perhaps these were a gift for a lady back in England."

"Silk doesn't come from Africa, you know. It comes from India and China."

"Well, goodness knows where he got these. Come on, help me pick them up."

After rewrapping the bobbins, Ophelia patted the trunk lining for good measure. It was baggy from use. "There *is* something . . . something under the lining. Feels like it might be a cuff link. Mr. Banks is missing a pair of diamond cuff links, by the by. Here's a hole . . . what's this?" She held up a tiny gray thing. "A tooth?"

"Allow me." Abel snatched it.

"Hold it, whippersnapper."

Abel rolled his eyes. "I've been called *whippersnapper* more times than I can count. Tiresome. Now, look. It's a fossilized tooth. See how, instead of being formed of tooth enamel, it appears to be made of stone? It's very, very old."

"It's a pig's tooth," Ophelia said. As a girl she'd tended a sow named Hecuba. "A molar."

"Mr. Knight must have been some sort of amateur naturalist." Abel tucked the tooth in his pocket.

"Give that to me."

"But I've begun a small fossil collection in the dormitory at school."

"*I'm* investigating. You're simply—simply assisting. Temporarily." Ophelia held out her hand.

Abel heaved a sigh and handed over the tooth. "What are we going to do next?"

Ophelia stood. She meant to begin her search of every suspect's bedchamber, but she had no intention of allowing Abel to tag along. "Perhaps, after doing a quick search of the rest of this chamber, we ought to check and see if there are any fresh pastries to be had in the kitchen."

Abel's face brightened. "I suppose enormously rangy ladies like you require loads of pastries and so forth to keep you going?"

"Yes indeed," Ophelia said with a tight smile. "Almost as much pastry as cheeky youngsters with custard on their faces."

Abel whipped out a hankie and dabbed his lips.

"More to the left," Ophelia said, tapping her cheek, and went to look under the vicar's bed.

Gabriel searched for young Master Christy but could not find him. He meant to learn from the lad who would be the best person to contact regarding his current predicament.

After that, Gabriel, Ivy, and Banks rode the mile to Madame Genepy's house. The yellow stone farmhouse squatted at the edge of a snow-covered field. Behind the house, a line of bare trees marked the banks of the Vézère River. The village lay just across the field, a hodgepodge of snowy roofs and stone chimneys.

"How sweet her house looks," Ivy said as Gabriel helped her down from her horse. Her gloved hand lingered in his, and she smiled up at him.

A besotted man would've said, *How sweet YOU look, my dear.* "Quite," Gabriel said, gently removing his hand from Ivy's.

Banks thudded down from his own horse. "Griffe complains about how backward his peasants are—resistant to his efforts at improving their lots and so forth—but I find this all rather charming. Quite like stepping into the pages of a picture book, what?"

"I do agree," Gabriel said, going to the door. Not a single footprint marked the snow around the house. He knocked.

A woman opened the door. She was short and blowsy, thirty-odd years, with mussed brown hair. *"Oui?"* she said in a coarse voice.

Gabriel continued in French, since Banks and Ivy were fluent. "Good afternoon. I am Professor Penrose, a guest of the Count de Griffe. With me are Mr. Banks and his daughter, Miss Banks. Would you be so kind as tell me if Madame Genepy is within?"

"Grandmother, you mean. Yes. Snoozing by the fire as always. What do you want with her? Are you some sort of doctor?" The woman looked Gabriel up and down. "Where is your bag? Are not doctors supposed to carry bags?"

Gabriel explained to her that he was a scholar of folktales and that he wished to hear Madame Genepy's story of *La belle et la bête*.

"That sorry old tale?" The woman's expression closed. "Changes it every day, she does. No one knows which version is the correct one anymore. But seeing as you have come all this way through the snow, you may as well come in and hear for yourself the nonsense she spins. My name is Lucile, by the way. I do not live here—have a husband and house in the village—but when the snow started coming down so thick yesterday evening, I came here to look after Grandmother." She led them into a low-beamed room stinking of cat urine and wood smoke. A small fire crackled. A film of dust coated everything, and balls of cat fur lurked in the corners. A frail, shawl-wrapped old woman curled against the chimney corner. She was snoring. A cat sat alert on her lap, yellow eyes unblinking.

Lucile roused Madame Genepy. "Grandmother, wake up. Visitors."

Madame Genepy's eyes slowly opened. "Visitors?" she said in a creaky voice.

"They wish to hear one of your stories, Grandmother."

Lucile turned to the visitors. "I have cleaning to do. I will be in the next room." She slouched away.

Madame Genepy watched blearily as Gabriel, Ivy, and Banks removed their cloaks and sat.

"What is that you are wearing, child?" Banks whispered harshly to Ivy.

Ivy tensed. "It's only a *dress*, Father," she said softly.

"A *cotton* dress, Ivy. You know what I told you about—" Banks stopped, realizing that Gabriel was listening. He flushed.

Ivy stared at the floor.

Well, well. Was this a crack in the idyllic father-daughter rapport? And about a cotton dress?

"I am so pleased to meet you, Madame Genepy," Gabriel said, taking a notebook and pencil from his inner jacket pocket as he sat. "I would be most obliged if you would relay to me—to us—the tale of *Beauty and the Beast*. *Your* tale."

"The favorite tale," Madame Genepy said. "The tale everyone asks for."

"And you know a version rather different than those found in storybooks," Gabriel said.

"Yes. My grandmother taught it to me, asked me to remember it by heart, as I sat in the kitchen with her preparing food. She said I was a born storyteller, like she was, my memory so sharp and my tongue so keen." She stroked the cat.

"And how does this story go?"

"My tongue is no longer so keen. Yet my memory is good. They say it is fading, they try to tell me I do not remember the stories correctly anymore, but I do." Madame Genepy lay her head against the side of the chimney and shut her eyes.

"Perhaps we ought not trouble her," Banks said, picking cat hairs off his sleeve.

Lucile looked around the doorway, holding a broom. "Grandmother!" she said sharply. "Wake up." Lucile turned to the visitors. "You will have a trying time getting even a piece of a story out of her. She fades in and out, and her memory is fading, too. Each time she tells her tales now, they come out differently. We no longer know what the original story was."

Madame Genepy snuffled awake. "You girl—who are you?"

"I am your granddaughter, Lucile."

"But I have never seen you before."

"You see?" Lucile said. She stomped away with her broom.

Gabriel was certain that Lucile was going to listen to everything from out in the corridor.

With a few more promptings, Madame Genepy at last began her story. "In this land before time began, the Mother of the Seasons made this land lush with animals. She presided over a kingdom of great palaces. Palaces of stone they were that reached deep into the earth, into the very womb of the earth."

Banks coughed and Ivy blushed.

"In the most splendid palace of all lived a beast. Fearsome he was, and gorgeous, with the body of a young man and the furred face, the tusks, the all-knowing dark eyes of an animal."

The cat growled, and Gabriel noticed that it didn't look quite domesticated with its bob tail and tufted ears.

"Oh dear, where was I?" Madame Genepy said.

"The beast," Gabriel said. "Great palaces of stone. Castles, I suppose you mean by that?" Ruined castles studded the Dordogne and Vézère River valleys. From a distance one could not always distinguish between a ruin and a natural stone outcropping. And some castles were built over the natural limestone caverns with which the region was honeycombed. These caverns, Gabriel had heard, boasted stalactites and stalagmites.

"You spoke of a beast, madame," Ivy said.

"A beast?" Madame Genepy clawed at her shawl. "Once, there was no divide between human beings and beasts, but now, the Mother of the Seasons has allowed only one reminder of what once was. He stalks the hills."

"What does he look like?" Gabriel asked.

"He?" Madame Genepy's eyelids quivered. "Beasts everywhere in these woods. Teeming with beasts. With fangs and claws and tusks. Hideous white stags with sharp golden antlers, too. Beware!"

The cat hunched and hissed. Lucile rushed in and wrapped an arm around her grandmother's shoulders. "Calm down," she murmured. Lucile looked at the guests. "You see? Only nonsense. They do not even sound like real stories anymore. You must go. She gets herself worked up, and then her heart—"

"Of course," Gabriel said, attempting to squelch his frustration. He stood. "I am very sorry to have upset her. Perhaps we might call again on another day?"

"Perhaps," Lucile said, not meeting his eye.

Gabriel, Ivy, and Banks bundled up and went back outside into the clear, sharp air.

7

~~~

Abel seemed to think that he was going to assist Ophelia in all further inquiries into the vicar's death. However, Ophelia planned to escort him to the kitchen, set him before a plate of pastries, and make an escape. After a fruitless search of the rest of the vicar's bedchamber, they set off for the kitchen.

Along the way, Abel complained of his bedchamber in the servants' quarters of the château—"like the garret of a consumptive playwright" was how he described it—about the rations at the Warbridge School—"you could use the morning porridge for spackling walls"—and how Château Vézère's food, though "rather good," was not sufficiently bountiful.

"But you are an unexpected guest," Ophelia said. "Surely they would've made more food if they had expected more guests."

"This is a château, not a monastery, for heaven's sake. And besides, there ought to be an outright *feast* going on, for I'm told there is to be a wedding in four days." Ophelia was half convinced that Abel had looked at her belly.

Oh, the shame. She quickened her pace. "Why has Mademoiselle Gavage relegated you to the servants' quarters, Master Christy?"

"She is unaware of my royal blood. Oh, and she said something about having run out of the usual sort of guest chambers."

They passed the dining room. Men's voices within. Had Griffe returned from his ride?

"Wait," Ophelia whispered, stopping Abel with a hand. She poked her head through the dining room door.

No Griffe. Forthwith and Larsen were eating a late breakfast. They sat cater-cornered, speaking in low, earnest tones, and they didn't notice Ophelia at once. She caught Forthwith's words *buffalo* and *invest*. Then she heard him say, "Father is hell-bent on me taking over his soap manufactories. Can't stand the thought of me going into things for myself. It's Oedipal is what it is."

Larsen grunted and nodded.

Forthwith glanced up, and his face hardened. "Oh, sister dear, loitering about like a ghoul again?" he called.

"Oh. Hello. No, I haven't—well, I haven't had any breakfast yet." Suddenly, Ophelia felt half starved. More importantly, she felt the need to monitor Forthwith and whatever he was plotting. She was, in a way, responsible for his presence in the château. It felt like she'd released a python into the house. "I'll meet you in the kitchen," she whispered over her shoulder to Abel.

Abel craned his neck to see what was on offer on the dining table.

"No. Don't go in there," Ophelia said.

"I certainly will—and you resemble a choleric nursery maid when you pull that face." Abel toddled into the dining room. "I see those custardy tart things that have run out below stairs." He plopped onto a chair and introduced himself formally to Forthwith and Larsen.

Ophelia sighed, and went to the table, too.

"Good morning, Miss Stonewall," Larsen said.

"My dear sister's got the most awful habit of eavesdropping," Forthwith said. "Made Mother despair of her ever finding a husband who wasn't a criminal or a deaf-mute. But then, Griffe doesn't seem to mind, does he?"

"Would you pass the coffee?" Abel said.

"Young lad like you ought to be drinking good goat's milk, not coffee," Larsen said. "Coffee will stunt your growth."

"I really don't care. It is my mind I am concerned with. I'll leave the brute force to other men."

"That's the spirit, little fellow," Forthwith said, but his smile slipped away under Larsen's sharp glance. He meekly passed Abel a pitcher of milk.

"What are you speaking of with Mr. Larsen, dear brother?" Ophelia asked. "Something about investments?"

"Gentlemen's business," Forthwith said.

"Oh? Father will be so pleased to learn you are at last turning to business after your dissolute style of living these many years past."

"What is that?" Larsen asked. He looked at Forthwith. "I thought you said you have done this sort of thing before. Dissolute, your sister says?"

"An exaggeration. I have been somewhat taken up in sporting life—"

"Gambling?" Larsen asked.

"No, no. Hunting. Fishing."

Larsen relaxed. "Nothing wrong with that. You call hunting and fishing dissolute, Miss Stonewall? Why, they are healthful pastimes, in keeping with the laws of nature."

"Dear Ophelia was raised as a lady," Forthwith said, "and I for one will not corrupt her delicate sensibilities by speaking of commerce in her presence. Mother would be furious with me." He stood. "Mr. Larsen, shall we resume our little chat out in the field? My fingers positively itch for a shotgun."

"*Ja, ja,*" Larsen said. "Too late to take the dogs out today—that vicar dying put a damper on things—but we might go and rustle up some game birds."

"Marvelous." Forthwith flashed a white smile and sauntered out.

Larsen picked up a newspaper and began to read. Abel was chewing pastries, full chisel. Perfect. Ophelia got up.

"Wait. Where are you going?" Abel called through a mouthful.

"To practice the harp," Ophelia said over her shoulder.

The sorry truth was, Ophelia still had no clear idea who might've stolen her ring and murdered Knight. Checking everyone's chamber, one by one, was the only thing she could think of to do.

She *would've* liked to start with Forthwith's. He was up to something, speaking to Larsen of investments when he had as much business experience as a kipper. But Forthwith could be in his chamber now.

So she'd try other bedchambers. *Any* other bedchambers.

She rapped on the door next to the vicar's. No answer. She looked in. Unoccupied. Filmy garments oozed from a traveling trunk, and the bedclothes were knotty. Jars, bottles, and brushes littered the dressing table. This couldn't be Bernadette's chamber—too messy, too vain. Could it be Ivy's? No. Ivy did not use face paint, and there was a box of complexion powder and a pouf over there.

This must be Madame Dieudonné's chamber.

Ophelia stole inside.

She began with the dressing table. The powders and complexion creams were of the first quality, beautiful boxes and jars with gilt French lettering. A set of ivory false teeth in a box. Perfume bottles nestled in a velvet-lined case, wafting intricate aromas. Ophelia sneezed, which was why she didn't hear the door open.

"*Pardonnez-moi,*" someone said behind her.

Ophelia turned.

Madame Dieudonné stood in the doorway, clutching a wrapper about her. She was utterly bald, her withered face pink from the bath.

The little white poodle charged at Ophelia, yipping, teeth bared, the blue bow on his topknot bouncing.

"Meringue!" Madame Dieudonné shrieked.

Ophelia bent and held out her hand. Meringue skidded to a stop, sniffed her hand, and seemed placated. Back in her circus days, Ophelia had been a trick pony rider as well as the partner of a poodle who jumped through flaming hoops. She reckoned she had a way with animals.

"Why are you in my chamber, mademoiselle?" Madame Dieudonné said, her accent garbled by her lack of teeth. She shut the door behind her and came towards Ophelia.

"Oh. I was—I believed this was my friend Mrs. Brighton's chamber, and I wished to borrow a little perfume. I forgot to pack any, you see, and I feel quite lost without it."

"Perfume?" Madame Dieudonné lowered herself creakily onto the dressing table stool. She pushed the false teeth into her mouth. "*Mais oui.* I have many. Choose one."

"Thank you so much." Ophelia studied the perfumes, wondering which would be the least likely to attract fops or muskrats.

Meringue sniffed avidly at Ophelia's ankles. He lifted a hind leg.

"*Non!*" Madame Dieudonné swooped Meringue into her lap. She uncapped a jar of complexion cream. "One must tend to one's complexion even in the midst of terror." She dabbed cream on her bald scalp. "That is what I was taught. Troubles will come and go, yet at the end of the day a lady is still expected to be beautiful."

"You refer to the death last night?" Ophelia said, selecting a crystal perfume bottle.

"Death, my dear? Don't be coy. We all know it was a murder."

"We do?"

"Empty bottles of poison? Stolen jewelry? Noxious berries? *Mais, oui.* Playing naïve is all very well when the gentlemen are present, but we ladies must not try to deceive each other when we are alone." Madame Dieudonné tapped her temple. "I am working the puzzle out. Only a few pieces remain unaccounted for."

"Such as?"

"I must not say. It could be *dangereux.* Monsieur Knight's death did not surprise me, you understand. I knew that he was not a good man the moment I saw him boarding the stagecoach in Marseille. He was a man with the enemies."

"How did you know?"

"There was something, oh, I do not know, something cheap and *shifty* about him. He did not speak kindly to the boy from *Afrique.* He seemed to be fleeing something. *Mais,* I would never trust a man of the cloth."

"Was anything stolen from you last night?"

"A pearl necklace, *oui.*"

"But you noticed nothing?"

"Nothing. I sleep deeply, always. I take a sleeping draught."

"How do you know about the belladonna berries? Did you enter the orangerie this morning?"

"I was told of the berries by—who was it? I cannot recall. My memory has never been terribly good. As a girl, I was always too busy with my many beaus to cultivate my mind."

"If you reckon it was murder, who do you suppose did it?"

"How would I know? All of you—*all*—are strangers to me." Madame Dieudonné flicked her eyes down and up Ophelia, appraising. "Tell me, Mademoiselle Stonewall, how does it feel to be a humble American girl betrothed to a European nobleman of such an illustrious lineage?"

"Oh. Well, I—I suppose it feels very nice."

"Simply remember, my dear, that beauty does not last."

"If you refer to the Count de Griffe, I assure you that my regard from him does not rest upon his outward appearance."

Madame Dieudonné cackled. "A wit, as well. But I refer to *your* beauty, not Griffe's."

"Mine?" Ophelia was no beauty. She was too beanstalky and her face too, well, *simple*. Stripped down. Basic.

"You have a certain quality that some gentlemen admire. And I assure you, it will not last. Look at me! Men are fickle. Disgusting. They will feign adoration only to toss you aside like yesterday's underclothes. They will clamor for a spot on your dance card one season, and pretend not to know you at all—at all!—the next time you meet."

"I beg your pardon, but did you . . . had you made the acquaintance of Mr. Knight before you met him in Marseille?"

"*Sacré bleu*, not *him*." Madame Dieudonné watched with maternal pride as Meringue contorted in order to slurp his nether fuzz. "Do you suggest that *I*—"

"Of course not. You are journeying to Paris?"

"Yes, to stay with an old friend. I resided in the Côte d'Azur for too long, I am afraid, and things between me and the creditors at Monte Carlo became *terribly* dull." Madame Dieudonné opened a hatbox on the floor beside her and lifted out a large, blond, bouffant wig. She placed it on her head. Then she selected a pot of rouge and dabbed spots onto her cheeks. "Would you like some rouge, Mademoiselle Stonewall? You appear pale."

"Oh. No, thank you. I must be going. I'll see you at luncheon, surely." Ophelia hurried towards the door.

"But you did not select a perfume," Madame Dieudonné called.

"Later, perhaps."

* * *

Back in the corridor, Ophelia's lungs were tight with excitement. Madame Dieudonné seemed to have known a gentleman in the château before, and not only that, she was furious with him. Had that gentleman been the vicar?

She tried the next door. Another bedchamber, but an unoccupied one; there wasn't even a coverlet on the mattress. The door after that led into a lady's room, and Ophelia knew it was Ivy's because it smelled of her lilac perfume.

Ophelia tiptoed in.

Jars and ornaments on the dressing table lay in regimental rows and at right angles. The many rich gowns in the wardrobe were arranged according to color. The book at the bedside was in German, but it had enough diagrams for Ophelia to figure it was a technical book about architecture.

Ivy was a military captain trapped in a damsel's body.

Ophelia didn't find the ruby ring or anything else of interest. She crept out.

She rattled a few more locked doorknobs. Then, pounding footsteps. She pressed herself against the wall. A maid rushed past, tears coursing down her face and a bucket of coal swinging in her hand. She didn't even see Ophelia.

Upset about the beast, maybe?

No.

"Hello, Mr. Tolbert," Ophelia said.

Tolbert slunk along the corridor, hands in pockets. He didn't answer, but his nostrils shuddered.

"Quizzing that maidservant about whatever it is you're missing?" Ophelia asked.

"What business is this of yours?"

"What was stolen from your bedchamber? Perhaps I could help you find it."

Tolbert curled his upper lip and sniffed.

Ophelia took another stab. "By the by, Mr. Tolbert, where were you headed on that stagecoach?"

"A very important parcel is waiting for me at the port in Bordeaux."

Oh, really. "Then you must be in a dreadful hurry to be on your way."

"Pah! I will not be on my way until I find what was stolen from me."

"Where do you live?"

"In Paris."

"What are you doing in this region?"

"Working. Pray, cease prying into my affairs." Tolbert shoved past.

Ophelia sighed. She continued trying doors until she ran out. Many were locked. Others led to chambers that appeared to be unused.

At the end of the line she turned, and stopped short. Abel blocked her path, plump arms folded. "The *harp*, Miss Stonewall? There is no harp in Château Vézère."

"Yes, I noticed that."

"I believe you're avoiding me."

"No, I'm not."

"You are. Is it because I told you my grandfather was a king?"

"No."

"Is it because of my complexion?"

"Certainly not."

"Because you would not be the first person to be alarmed by my complexion, which is sad, really. It points to an impoverishment of imagination, since not everyone is as pinched and white as Robby St. John's pet mouse."

"Who is Robby St. John?"

"He's at school. Thinks he's better at geometry than I am, but that's only because he cheats on his exams. Sticks a bit of paper with the formulas written on it up his cuff."

"I'm not avoiding you, Master Christy. It is simply that, well, I prefer to work alone."

"How stoic of you. I could contribute to your investigation, you realize. I have clues."

"You do?"

Abel made a know-it-all nod. "Would it interest you to learn that the stagecoach driver—he's called Gerard—deliberately broke the coach's whippletree?"

8

"What?" Ophelia said.

"The whippletree," Abel said. "You know, the wooden beam sort of thing with the iron rings that the horses' harnesses are hooked to on the—"

"I *know* what a whippletree is."

"The village blacksmith is supposedly mending it."

"And the driver broke it deliberately?"

"Well, I did not see it happen, precisely, but I did see him doing something with a rather hefty pair of metal cutters. It was snowing hard last night, you understand, and dark—although Gerard had a lantern. We'd stopped just outside Château Vézère's gates, although at that juncture I didn't know that's what they were. I assumed Gerard merely wished to relieve himself, particularly since I'd seen him swilling wine at the Sarlat Inn earlier. But I heard—or rather, *felt*—a kind of clanking, so I poked my head out and saw him going at the rings with the metal cutters. But then Mr. Knight and that crusty zoologist—Tolbert, is it?—and the frightening old woman with the poodle and the fallen-soufflé face all shouted that I was letting the snow in, so I shut the door."

"Then the driver *meant* for the stagecoach to break down."

"I thought that was rather obvious." Abel pulled something from his pocket, wrapped in a handkerchief. A sticky-looking cake. He took a bite.

"You keep cake next to the insects in your pocket?" Ugh.

"The larva is in a vial. Perfectly sanitary."

Ophelia had her doubts. "What if the driver damaged the whippletree in order to give himself the opportunity to, well, to *do in* the vicar?" She started down the stairs.

Abel trotted behind her. "I'm certain he did not kill the vicar. My room is next to his, you see, and the walls in the servants' quarters are thin, so thin that I was forced to endure listening to Gerard and a lady giggling and carrying on through the night."

"You needn't—"

"They were playing hide-and-seek, from the sound of it."

Oh, goodness. "That must have been it." Ophelia lowered her voice. "Who was the lady?"

"How would I know? They all sound the same when they're giggling like that. Bit like guinea pigs. At any rate, Gerard strikes me more as the sort who would damage his own carriage in exchange for a bribe. Not an enterprising chap, you see."

"If someone bribed him to damage his coach, then that means someone may have planned Mr. Knight's death. Planned it out in advance."

"You mean to *lure* Mr. Knight to the château?"

"Yes."

"It couldn't have been planned *too* far in advance, because our route through this region was not Mr. Knight's original plan. We only came through the Périgord because of some problem with the train. Would you slow *down*? I've got a stitch in my side now. In Nubia, men carry me about on a litter, you realize."

"What about at your school in England?"

"Well, no."

"What was the problem with the train?"

"I haven't the slightest notion. Broken, I suppose. So in lieu of waiting about for the train, Mr. Knight decided we ought to take the stagecoach to Bordeaux and then board a ship to London from there. He was exceedingly impatient for a vicar. His sermons were doubtless blessedly short."

"How long ago did you leave Marseille on the stage-coach?" They reached the bottom of the stairs and paused.

"It took us five days of travel to reach Sarlat."

Ophelia would wager that Knight didn't wish to wait around for fear of losing out on the reward waiting for him at the London solicitor's office. And the Monte Carlo creditors were surely Madame Dieudonné's reason for not waiting around for the train to be fixed, either. "Where do you think Gerard is now?"

"In the kitchen soaking up wine, or stuffing his face with food and harassing the maidservants." They turned towards the kitchen stairwell. Abel trotted beside Ophelia, panting. "Repulsive, his behavior with the girls, although it is not *entirely* uninteresting. One is able to appreciate it in the same way one appreciates the breeding habits of mayflies. You know, your rather diabolical theory narrows down the suspects, by eliminating those traveling *in* the coach."

"You mean Madame Dieudonné and Tolbert."

"And myself," Abel said, squaring his shoulders. "Or did you assume that I am incapable of murder simply by virtue of having not yet reached my full adult height?"

"Of course not. I assumed you were not capable of it because murdering a person is horribly unreasonable."

Abel liked that.

The kitchen bustled with servants preparing luncheon. Ophelia and Abel hesitated on the bottom step. "Do you see Gerard?" Ophelia whispered.

"No. Let's check his chamber."

"Where is that?"

"Up in the Antarctic garret, next to mine. But allow me to catch my breath, first."

They hiked all the way to the top floor, this time by way of a dank-smelling servants' stair. Abel led the way into a chamber.

A man sprawled asleep on a dumpy bed crammed under the eaves. His mouth gaped, revealing crooked brown teeth. He was perhaps fifty years of age, with pebbly skin, greasy graying hair, and a shearling vest. He held a licked-clean chicken bone like a baby rattle. The room stank of wine and underarm.

Ophelia cleared her throat. "Monsieur Gerard? Wake up, monsieur."

Snores.

Abel, wearing a look of distaste, stepped forward and prodded Gerard's leg.

Gerard mumbled something and rolled over.

"He's been at the wine like a calf at a teat," Abel said. "I fancy there won't be any waking him for hours yet."

Ophelia felt like yelping with impatience. "Very well." She turned to go.

Abel caught up with her. "Don't attempt to tell me that you mean to practice the harp."

"I'm going to speak with the village blacksmith, who's repairing the whippletree. He'll be able to confirm if it was cut deliberately or not."

Abel balked. "I don't know. . . ."

"You don't wish to miss luncheon, do you? It smelled so savory and—"

"I am coming along."

"No."

"You require my assistance. I've been rigorously trained in classical logic. I work out Aristotelian syllogisms while I nap."

"Doesn't sound very restful. Tykes like you need their shut-eye."

"Do you speak French, Miss Stonewall? Because I'd guess that the blacksmith does *not* speak English."

Drat. "Very well. Meet me downstairs in ten minutes."

Ten minutes later, Ophelia was bundled in her borrowed cloak and bonnet. She found Abel in the foyer, up to his ears in a puffy fur coat with a fur hat pulled low over his forehead. He resembled a well-fed beaver.

Outside, the sky was a damp, bruised gray. They walked down the snowy drive. The château gates stood open to the main road, and from there it was a several minutes' walk into the village of Vézère.

Stone houses with slate roofs and wooden shutters hunkered. Smoke puffed from chimneys. In the pasture at the edge of the woods, a cluster of sheep, roly-poly in their winter fleece, nibbled at grass poking up through the snow.

"Did you bother to ask anyone where the blacksmith's shop is?" Abel asked, mincing around a puddle.

"I didn't need to. I grew up in a village. Do you hear that clanging?"

"Yes."

"That's the blacksmith, hammering."

Abel stopped. "Perhaps we should come back tomorrow. It's growing late—"

"Late? We haven't even had luncheon yet." Ophelia looked at Abel sharply. His eyes were huge. "Are you . . . afraid of something?"

"Certainly not. The very thought. Fear is the bilge of poorly educated minds."

"Well, come along, then."

"No."

"Why?"

"If you must know, it is because I—well, I've got the most awful pain in my side, and I feel I must return to the château and rest."

"Fiddlesticks. You're frightened of the blacksmith. Why?"

"I've never met the chap."

"Then what is going on?"

Abel scratched his round little nose. "In my country, blacksmiths are . . . well, people say—there are legends, I mean—that blacksmiths turn into hyenas at night."

"Hyenas?"

"You said you wouldn't laugh."

"No, I didn't. Anyway, I'm not laughing. But Abel, we aren't in your country; we're in France, and even though everyone is talking about beasts, the only animals I've seen are a poodle, a parakeet, horses, and a herd of sheep. Come on."

The blacksmith's shop was entirely open on one side, and the heat from the fire had melted the snow in an arc. A huge man hunched over an anvil, beating rhythmically with a hammer on a glowing bit of metal that he held between pincers.

"Well, if it isn't Hephaestus," Abel muttered, trying to sound cocky.

When the blacksmith caught sight of Ophelia and Abel, he froze, hammer in midair. He said something gruffly in French, and Abel responded in a reedy voice, cowering against Ophelia.

"What did he say?" Ophelia whispered.

"He asked who we are—I told him that—and our business. He's rude, I'll have you know. A brute. His name is Marcel."

Marcel stalked towards them, hammer at his side. Muscles bulged in his arms, chest, and neck. His unusually wide-set eyes were reminiscent of a bull's. The red glow from his fire threw the pocked skin of his cheeks into sharp relief.

Ophelia took an involuntary step back. "We wish to know about the stagecoach whippletree that you have been tasked to fix," she said in her boldest tone.

Abel translated. Marcel snorted and said something that Abel translated as, "What do you wish to know—and what business is it of yours?"

Ophelia said, "Because we wish to know if it was damaged on purpose."

Marcel spoke, and Abel translated, "I could tell you, but it will cost you."

"A bribe?" Ophelia whispered to Abel.

"I *told* you blacksmiths are a dubious sort," Abel whispered back.

"But I haven't any money. Wait." Ophelia reached under her bonnet and removed a hairpin. It was mother of pearl, belonging to Artemis Stunt. Ophelia would figure out a way to replace it later. "Offer him this."

"I won't go an inch nearer to that brute."

"Fine." Ophelia went to Marcel and held out the hairpin. He looked at it appraisingly and pocketed it.

Ophelia darted back to Abel's side, feeling ridiculous. This fur-wrapped cream puff of a child couldn't protect her from a flea.

Marcel said something. Abel translated, "The whippletree was broken deliberately. Three iron rings had been clipped with metal cutters, and then on the way here from the château gates, the wooden part snapped. He says he can't do anything in the way of fixing the thing until a beam of ironwood arrives from Bergerac—evidently whippletrees require perishingly strong wood because of all the weight they bear. Oh, and he says he will slit our throats in our beds if we or any other outsiders come snooping about his hut again."

Ophelia and Abel practically tripped on each other in their haste to get away.

In truth, *La belle et la bête* had always bored Gabriel. Fairy tales obsessed him, to be sure, but this particular tale was an exception. For while most literary fairy tales had their roots in old traditions, passed down by word of mouth for generations, *La belle et la bête* had never been anything but a product of Parisian authoress Gabrielle-Suzanne Barbot de Villeneuve's eighteenth-century fancy. In some sense, it wasn't even a proper fairy tale.

Except.

Except that the beginning of Madame Genepy's tale had made mention of a stone castle that stretched deep into the womb of the earth. If the tale she had learned from the lips of her grandmother was even a *relatively* unadulterated version of a medieval tale . . . how special, and how incredibly rare. That would turn everything scholars believed about *La belle et la bête* on its ear. *If* Gabriel could date it.

After leaving Madame Genepy's house, Ivy insisted upon a ride along the valley road, claiming boredom and a desire for exercise in the fresh air. Although Gabriel was burning to go to Château Vézère's library—alone—a sense of duty compelled him to agree. So they, along with Banks, set out along a winding, snowy road that traced the black river.

When Ivy rode ahead of them, Gabriel said to Banks, "Miss Banks's cotton dress . . ."

"Pshaw," Banks said with a dismissive wave.

"Is it because you mill silk and wool?"

"Yes. No need for that nasty stuff."

"But surely there is a great demand for cotton. I understand that during the war in America a few years back, the British embargo on Southern cotton resulted in a few fortunes being made in cotton, what with the trade in cotton from Egypt and India opening up—"

"Of course, of course." Banks's face looked purplish and congested, although maybe it was only from the cold air. "But Egyptian cotton's poor quality, too—so's Indian—no doubt about it. I only deal in quality goods, Lord Harrington. That's something you must know about me. I don't stand for any nonsense."

No, he did not. Gabriel had learned that Ivy and her father

shared a complex bond. After Ivy's mother had died in child-birth, it had been Ivy and Papa, allied against the world. Yet at the same time, Banks had overseen his daughter's education with a hawk's eye and, Gabriel suspected, at times an iron fist. Banks was a self-made man, and he was determined to make a true lady of his daughter. At times Gabriel feared that Ivy had suffered somewhat for lack of tenderness. She was sweet, but she was also a bit, well, *cold*.

By the time they arrived back at the château, Gabriel was jumpy with impatience.

"I must go to the library and write down what Madame Genepy told us," he said to Ivy and Banks in the stables.

Ivy's lower lip protruded. "What about luncheon, Lord Harrington?"

"Soon," he said over his shoulder.

The library was unoccupied, and he shut himself in. Hazy light illuminated carved shelves packed with books. Oak tables and high-backed chairs stretched the marble-tiled length. A huge globe squatted on a brass stand.

Gabriel methodically searched the shelves. He saw a remarkable collection of French literature, and books in countless other languages as well. Portfolios of prints. Sets of encyclopedias. Even a book of French railway timetables. Gabriel smiled. A comprehensive collection, indeed.

He soon found what he was searching for: a cabinet of drawers. His fingertips tingled. He opened the top drawer. Crumbling old maps of the world, some so antiquated, the New World was a mere blank. The drawers hadn't prevented the vellum and parchment from acquiring a thick film of dust.

The next drawer held maps of Europe and France, and the drawer after that, at the top, a map marked *Vallée Vézère*. His breath quickened. He pulled it out and placed it on a table.

He longed to hear the rest of Madame Genepy's tale, but in the meantime he could locate the medieval castles in the valley. One of them could be the original location of Madame Genepy's tale.

Dust blurred the hand-drawn map. Except . . . what was this? Oval fingerprints, *fresh* fingerprints, spotted the edges, and two round sections had been rubbed clean, as with a handkerchief. The rubbed-clean portions lay along a tributary of the Vézère River, back into what appeared to be the hills, and both stopped at the word *grotte*. Cave.

Someone else had already examined this map, very recently. Gabriel fancied he knew who: Tolbert.

Ophelia saw Griffe riding his horse into the château stables just as she and Abel were returning from their visit to the blacksmith. Her stomach flipped.

"Thank you for translating for me, Master Christy," she said. "I must go speak to the count." If she could convince Griffe to stall the wedding, she'd have more time to find the ring.

"Not too keen on your better-half-to-be?" Abel asked.

"Nonsense."

"You look like a cat who's about to expel a hair ball."

"I will see you later, I am certain." Ophelia went towards the stables.

"Why are you certain?" Abel shouted after her. "You forget they're holding me prisoner in the attic!"

When Griffe saw Ophelia enter the stables, something unreadable washed over his heavy features. "Mademoiselle Stonewall. But why do you venture into this so lowly place, eh? This is no place for a tender rosebud." He proferred his arm.

Ophelia reluctantly took it.

They strolled out, past the orangerie and into the terraced formal gardens behind the château. Snow piled on balustrades, hedges, and fountains. Water dripped from statues. Puddles glistened on geometric paths.

"You have been absent for hours, *monsieur le comte*," Ophelia said as a way to begin the conversation.

"Ah, if you mean to monitor my movements, Mademoiselle

Stonewall, that will prove a fruitless endeavor. I will not be beholden to any woman, no matter how *belle*."

Ophelia stiffened. Griffe had never before spoken to her like that. "It is only that we have not been alone for a moment since, well, since my arrival—"

"Is that not what you desired? You did not meet me in the ballroom as I requested in my note yesterday evening."

"Oh. Yes. Well, I fell asleep—"

"That is not what Clémence told me."

Clémence was *spying* on her? "I don't know what your servants presume to—"

"Clémence is devoted to the family. She has been with us since she was a young girl. Come now, Mademoiselle Stonewall. Do not attempt to fool me. You did not wish to meet. *Qu'est-ce que c'est?* Do I disgust you?"

"What? No, of—of course not." She took a breath. "I wish to speak of the wedding. You might have consulted with me. What of my parents in Cleveland? What of my friends?" Ophelia pulled her arm from Griffe's and turned to look up at him. "You can't go springing things like that on a lady. I ought to have a say in the matter."

"Ah, *oui*?" Griffe suddenly seemed too large, his eyes penetrating. "Is there some reason you wish to delay the wedding? Two people deeply in love do not require pomp and display to marry—or do you have something you wish to say to me?"

"For starters, I'll have you know that everyone suspects that the hasty wedding is on account of . . ." Ophelia's cheeks burned. "On account of, um, a third party."

"Eh?"

"A very *small* third party?"

"A babe?" Griffe burst out laughing.

"My dignity is at stake," Ophelia said. "Does that not trouble you?"

He kept laughing.

Oh, how she would've relished throwing that confounded

ruby ring at his feet. But the ring was gone, and so she was stuck. "I saw you prowling through the corridor outside my chamber last night," she blurted.

"Ah, *oui*? You will soon grow accustomed to that, *chérie*."

Ugh. "I beg you to change your mind about this rushed wedding. Let us marry in the springtime, with the flowers blooming and the birds chirping, and my parents—"

"*Non*." Griffe's face was cold, his voice flat. "We marry in four days."

Ophelia hated being told no more than anything in the world. She ached to scream *WHY?* and kick something. Instead, she summoned all her acting abilities to say "Very well," to meekly bow her head, to walk quietly away.

The rest of the afternoon and early evening was wasted checking for Gerard in his chamber and in the kitchen. The stagecoach driver seemed to have disappeared. Ophelia's only consolation was that his satchel was still in his chamber (filled with unclean garments and nothing else) and that he had a lady friend in the château with whom to play hide-and-seek.

9

⁕

Dinner was subdued, although everyone consumed quite a lot of wine in a dogged sort of way. Gabriel noticed that Miss Flax did not once look at Griffe, who was for his part drinking heavily again. Bernadette did not touch her fish or meat and ate only vegetables. Odd.

Tolbert, spine curved like a spigot, kept his eyes on his plate. Gabriel had ridden up the tributary valley that afternoon in search of the caves marked on the map in the library. Why, he wasn't certain. There was simply something *to* all this. A legendary beast, which some of the locals still feared. A local tale about a beast. And now, a furtive zoologist on the hunt for, quite possibly, the fossilized remains of said beast.

How this connected to fairy tales, Gabriel couldn't picture. But he *tasted* it: the magic.

He hadn't found the first cave. The sun was behind the hills by then, so he'd turned back. Next, he'd figured out which chamber was Tolbert's, in the hopes of discerning what he was about. But it had been locked up tight.

After dinner, everyone was compelled to view Forthwith's conjuring tricks in the salon, and then to listen to Ivy and Henrietta sing songs to Bernadette's pianoforte accompaniment.

Ivy's performance of Brahms was pitch-perfect, if mechanical. Henrietta's selection was a saucy Spanish song, to which she flicked a fan and batted her eyelashes at Larsen.

When Henrietta was through, Ivy said in a sweet voice, "How nice, Mrs. Brighton, that you are feeling well enough— as a recent widow, I mean—to perform such an *enthusiastic* song."

Gabriel had always fancied that Ivy said such things out of childlike honesty. Now, he wondered. Ivy was intelligent. She could read Latin, Greek, and even bits of Old Norse. So how could she be so obtuse when it came to the feelings of others?

"And do you know, it is so strange," Ivy said to Henrietta. "I feel as though I have seen you before."

Panic flashed in Henrietta's eyes, but she smiled. "Why, I did not know you had traveled to Cleveland, Miss Banks. Did you attend the symphony while there? The fine art museum, perhaps?"

"No, it's not that," Ivy said.

"My precious Ivy never forgets a face," Banks said. He coughed.

"Are you well, Monsieur Banks?" Bernadette asked.

"He is as healthy as a horse," Ivy said quickly.

Truth be told, Banks *was* a bit qualmy-looking.

Gabriel wandered away from the group. Forthwith took to the piano, accompanying Ivy.

"Professor, take a gander at this." Miss Flax plopped down next to Gabriel on a secluded sofa and wiggled out something from beneath her elbow glove. She dropped it in his hand.

Gabriel's spirits rose. Was it wrong for his spirits to rise, when they were both engaged to others? Probably.

He poked at the thing in his hand. "I daresay this is a fossilized tooth. I am no dentist, but I believe it is—or, *was*—a human tooth."

"I fancied it was a pig's tooth. See how it has so many little bumps? Human molars don't have half as many."

"Ah, yes. Tubercles, I believe those bumps are called."

"You'd make your dentist proud."

"Where did you get this?"

"That's the funny thing. I found it in the dead vicar's trunk."

"I suppose I'd better not ask why you were looking in his trunk."

"Don't bother."

"All right. And were there other fossils?"

"No. Only his clothes and shoes and things, a Bible, a letter from Sir Christy's lawyer in London, bobbins of silk thread, and this tooth, stuck underneath the trunk's lining."

"Yesterday evening I happened to see a sketch in the notebook of Tolbert—where has he gone, I wonder?" Gabriel glanced about the salon. No Tolbert.

"Back to study in his chamber, I'd wager."

"I saw a most puzzling sketch, of a jawbone that appeared to possess both human and, well, *boarlike* traits."

"Go along! A boar man?"

"As outlandish as it seems, yes. I wonder if this tooth came from that jawbone."

"It must be a hoax. Or a mistake. Either way, Tolbert said he was searching for something that had been stolen from his chamber. Do you suppose this tooth—or even an entire jawbone—was what he was missing?"

"That does not seem unlikely."

"But that means that the jawbone may have been in the vicar's trunk."

"Yes. But then removed—less one tooth."

Miss Flax was frowning again, that look of fierce concentration Gabriel had not too long ago been smitten with. He ran a finger beneath his collar. Deuced hot in here.

She said, "All this time, I've supposed that the murderer—"

"Murderer?" Gabriel glanced over at the group. Ivy was trilling out an aria; no one would hear. Still, he lowered his voice. "Miss Flax, tell me precisely why you believe the vicar was murdered."

She told him how she had reasoned that Ivy's stolen bottle of traveling sickness tablets was out of place next to the vicar's body. How several people in the château had had items stolen from their chambers last night. How she figured that the vicar might've suspected, or even cornered, the thief and paid a deadly price. How the stagecoach driver broke the whippletree on purpose.

"Indeed?"

"The village blacksmith confirmed it."

"How industrious you are, Miss Flax. I briefly met the driver, Gerard, in the château stables. A most unseemly fellow."

Miss Flax was barely listening to him. "I've been supposing that the murderer and the thief were one and the same," she said, "but what if the *vicar* was the thief?"

"Then where are all of those stolen items now?"

"Well, someone else must've stolen them *again*. From his trunk, I'd guess, if this tooth is really from Tolbert's stolen jawbone."

"That is excessively complicated, is it not?"

"Nothing wrong with a little complication here and there. Do you have any better notions?"

"No. And this time, I am blessedly free of being entangled in this death—as are you, I should point out."

"Not quite." Her shoulders drooped.

"What is it?

"What?"

"How are you entangled?"

"I'm not."

"I don't believe you."

"Nothing I can do about that."

Gabriel gave the tooth back to her. As intriguing as a boar-man fossil might be, it wasn't in his realm of expertise—or fascination. Miss Flax hid it under the edge of her elbow glove in a deft way that made him wonder, not for the first time, if she'd ever been a pickpocket.

"Did you manage to hear the tale of the old village woman?" Miss Flax asked.

"Only a snippet, but it was rather intriguing." Gabriel told her about Madame Genepy's mention of castles, and how he thought that might enable him to date the tale, not to one hundred years ago, but to the middle ages. "It would be a scholarly coup."

"Not only scholarly." Miss Flax's dark eyes seemed to delve straight into Gabriel's heart. "I'd say it's rather grati-fying to your fairy tale obsession, isn't it, professor?"

"Need I answer?"

"I've never read the tale, you know."

"What? Never? I'll give you a copy at once. There's an English translation floating about the château. I would be most interested to hear what you think of it."

A piercing cry made them both spin around on the sofa. Ivy's aria came to a warbling stop. Bernadette was yanking a long, gauzy white thing from Meringue's jaws.

"Let go, you vile animal!" Bernadette screamed in French. "Maman's wedding veil! Oh, he will ruin it!"

"He is not vile," Madame Dieudonné snapped.

"Allow me," Forthwith said. He grabbed Meringue's sausage-like body and pulled. Meringue shook the veil back and forth as though breaking a hare's neck.

"You do not know how to manage beasts," Larsen said. He bent over and squeezed Meringue's snout on either side. Meringue's mouth popped open.

Bernadette seesawed the veil from his teeth and bundled it into her arms. "What is this?" she said in English, sniffing the veil. "Who has smeared the veil with pâté de foie gras?"

Her voice cracked. *"Who has done this?"* Her eyes fell on Miss Flax. Everyone else swiveled to look at Miss Flax, too.

Miss Flax seemed to be frozen, lips parted, eyes round.

"Someone who wishes to delay the wedding, quite obviously," Larsen said. "Come now, what became of the music?"

At bedtime, Ophelia thought the parakeet might enjoy an airing. But when she swung open its little door, the parakeet looked offended.

"Oh, fine. But I see you've eaten piles of sunflower seeds."

Ophelia readied herself for bed. She couldn't sleep. She tried to take her mind off things by reading the English copy of de Villeneuve's *Beauty and the Beast* that Professor Penrose had given her. It was artificial and even dismaying, especially the insistence on womanly self-sacrifice and submission. Ugh. Although, Ophelia's Yankee spirit liked the line "patience, perseverance, or all is lost."

She tossed the book aside. She thought about the stolen ring, the looming wedding, her suddenly sinister fiancé, and the way everyone had looked at her as though *she* had smeared pâté on that veil. Meanwhile, the ruby ring could be *anywhere*. Luckily, she had a lifeline: The stagecoach driver, Gerard, had cut the whippletree rings. He must know something. Wherever he was.

Patience, perseverance, or all is lost? No truer words had ever been written. Ophelia turned down her gas lamp and went miserably to sleep.

In the morning, Ophelia dressed herself. She refused to summon that spying Clémence. Lucky for Ophelia, she didn't require tight corset laces. If the fashion was an hourglass shape, well, her shape was more like a *water* glass.

All Ophelia could think of was finding the stagecoach

driver, Gerard. Unfortunately, before bed last night she had promised to meet Bernadette in her boudoir before breakfast. Ophelia suspected that Bernadette wished to privately confront her about smearing pâté on the wedding veil. Ophelia changed the parakeet's seeds and water and arranged its cage closer to the sunny window. The newspaper at the bottom of the cage would need changing soon.

"Come in," Bernadette called in response to Ophelia's knock.

Ophelia stepped into an airy, feminine boudoir, which lay in the family wing of the château.

Bernadette sat at a desk, writing. "I am just finishing some invitations, Mademoiselle Stonewall. Garon asked that the ceremony be kept small, but I must invite the neighbors. There is General de Beauchamp in Beynac, and Princess Marguerite of Poland lives not far away in Turenne."

"Oh, good," Ophelia said, feeling queasy. She went to a wardrobe, upon which hung a cream silk dress. "This is your mother's gown?"

"*Oui.*" Bernadette stuck her pen in its holder. "Is it not beautiful? I do hope it fits."

Then Bernadette didn't mean to demand an explanation for the pâté? What a relief.

Ophelia touched the gown. A high-waisted bodice gave way to a cascade of skirts. "It's lovely, but isn't it, well, I am not certain it will be a good fit." The hem would fall to Ophelia's shins, while the bodice was wide enough for Ophelia and a cat.

"Well, of course. That is why I wished for you to come this morning and try it on." Bernadette bustled over. "Would you undress behind the screen in the corner, there? We will just take in the bodice and sleeves and let out the hem, and it will fit you like a glove. Go on, then. What are you waiting for? We must breakfast, and then set out on the hunt. I hoped to pin it for the maid to sew today. The clock is ticking."

Ophelia didn't need reminding.

10

After Bernadette finished pinning the wedding gown, Ophelia dressed again and went downstairs. She was ravenous, but before breakfast she wished to have another look for Gerard.

She took the back stairs to the third-story servants' quarters, where Abel had led her yesterday.

Gerard's door was ajar, but when Ophelia put her eye to the crack, she saw nothing but a messy bed, the valise, an empty wine jug on the table, and—ugh—an *un*emptied chamber pot.

Well, he had come back.

She hurried downstairs, *all* the way down, to the kitchen.

The cook who had discovered the vicar's body, Marielle, stirred a pot. A maid pushed past with a tray loaded with bread rolls. Both servants had wide, darting eyes. Almost as though they were *afraid* of something.

"Oh, hullo, Miss Stonewall," Abel called from the plank table. "I suppose you're looking for me?"

"Not exactly."

"Oh, no?" Abel scowled as he stuffed a chunk of butter-dripping roll in his mouth. "Done with me, are you? I think you'll find that, this being *France* and all, most people only speak French. You're shipwrecked without me."

Ophelia went to the table. "I'm looking for Gerard. Have you seen him?"

"I saw him relieving himself out the window this morning."

"Oh."

"And then I saw him riding away down the château drive. Lopsided, mind you, and smoking a cigarette, but somehow managing nonetheless."

"Did you ask him about"—Ophelia leaned forward and lowered her voice—"about cutting the whippletree rings?"

"Certainly not. I don't have a death wish. I only *saw* him— I didn't speak with him. Who put the coffeepot all the way at the other end of the table? The servants are unaccountably lax this morning. Pour me another cup of coffee, would you?"

"I'm not your butler."

"You're already standing."

"Get it yourself."

"I'm going to be a king one day, you realize."

"I don't even pour coffee for kings."

"Well, *I* don't fancy helping you with your sleuthing anymore."

"Fine."

"I think I'll go hunt rose beetles in the orangerie, instead. Why should I work for you? You're only an American. I'd much rather speak to, oh, to Lord Harrington. Now *there* is a nobleman. We're different than the rest of you, somehow. We had a nice chat yesterday, actually. He said he'd telegraph Sir Christy's solicitor on my behalf." Abel puffed himself up.

He was a child. Only a child. Ophelia took a deep breath. "I would be most obliged if you'd come find me when Gerard returns."

"Gerard is a low character, Miss Stonewall, or hadn't you

noticed? He keeps a revolver tucked in his trousers. He's dangerous as well as loathsome."

"A revolver?"

"*If* he returns, you should give him a wide berth."

"Do you suppose he won't return?"

"He will. Abundant wine here at the château—he found the cellar, it's unlocked, and it's got hundreds of barrels. His notion of paradise. No, we're all stuck here until that brute of a blacksmith mends the whippletree. I can't think why it's taking so long."

Nor could Ophelia. Unless the blacksmith was deliberately dilly-dallying.

In the breakfast room, Griffe, Banks, and Larsen conversed in serious tones. They fell silent when Ophelia entered.

"Mademoiselle Stonewall, good morning," Griffe said. "How well you look in that dress. *Charmant.*"

How dare he compliment her after refusing to discuss their wedding date yesterday? Did he take her for a spineless dupe? On the other hand, Ophelia wasn't able to tell him exactly what she thought of him, on account of the missing ring, so she probably *did* seem like a spineless dupe. How maddening.

"What is the matter?" Ophelia asked the men. "Is someone ill?"

"No." Griffe and Larsen exchanged a glance.

"Ladies ought not hear of such things," Banks said.

"We are stronger than you might suppose." Ophelia sat. "Has someone died?"

"Only a sheep, in a pasture just outside the village," Griffe said.

"Attacked by a beast," Larsen said, tapping his fingers on the table.

"Was it a wolf?" Ophelia asked.

Silence. Banks coughed.

"Tell me," Ophelia said.

"It is rather gruesome, my dear, and not fit for delicate ears," Banks said.

"I haven't got those."

Griffe sighed. "The sheep appeared to have been gored."

"Gored!" This must be why the servants in the kitchen had seemed frightened. "By a wild boar?"

"It appears so."

"I didn't know that wild boars ate the flesh of large animals," Ophelia said.

"They do not. At least, not ordinarily. Perhaps there is an overgrown boar gone mad. . . ."

"The peculiar thing is," Larsen said, still drumming his fingertips, "the ewe's throat was *torn out*." His normally vague eyes gleamed.

"Surely wild boars do not do *that*," Ophelia said. True, boars had tusks. But other than those, all of their teeth were the squarish, vegetable-chewing sort.

"My theory is that there were two beasts at work," Banks said. "A wild boar—hence the goring—*and* a wolf."

Larsen nodded. "The wolves are known to go mad in these parts. Have you heard, Miss Stonewall, of the Wolves of Périgord?"

"Um. No."

"One hundred years ago, a pack of man-eating wolves roamed this region in the dead of winter. They killed nearly twenty people and maimed many more, until they were finally slain by a hunter. The hunter, I must add, was over sixty years of age, and when he killed the marauding wolves, he was rewarded by the king of France." Larsen narrowed his eyes, as though envisioning a king placing a garland on his yellow-whiskered, balding little head.

"That explains it, then," Ophelia said. "More marauding wolves killed the ewe." She tried to sound crisp and rational, but her guts were twisting. If there *were* man-eating wolves roaming the countryside, she for one wasn't eager to set foot outside.

"Alas, the villagers—and all of my servants among them—murmur their stories and tremble with fear," Griffe said. "They believe the ewe's death is not the work of wolves, or a rabid boar, or a human, but the work of their fabled beast."

"The cook, Marielle, mentioned such a creature when she saw the vicar yesterday morning," Ophelia said.

"The peasants here are grievously backward and super-stitious. They have no village priest in Vézère, you know, no church. The villagers—my servants among them—have been whispering among themselves that the beast has been angered."

"By us," Larsen said, pointing to Ophelia, Banks, and then himself.

"Us?" Ophelia said.

"Interlopers," Larsen said. "Enjoy their privacy, I under-stand."

"One of the maidservants has already given her notice, and my groom has threatened to quit as well," Griffe said.

"We must venture out into the wood without delay," Larsen said, back to drumming his fingers. "What the beast needs is a bullet between the eyes."

"We will set out on the hunt directly after breakfast," Griffe said. "Luc tells me that the hounds are fed and watered and eager as eels to go."

"Good morning, everyone," Ivy said, sailing in. She stopped. "Why the long faces? If it's about the slaughtered sheep, the maid Clémence already told me. Hideous, isn't it?" Her eyes sparkled as she sat.

"Child, what is this?" Banks murmured, fingering a rib-bon in Ivy's curls.

"A *silk* ribbon, Papa," Ivy said soothingly. "Only silk."

Ophelia hid her frown in her coffee cup. For a moment, Banks's neck had looked like it might pop.

* * *

On his way down to breakfast, Gabriel encountered Bernadette on the stairs. She was weeping.

"Mademoiselle Gavage. Pray, what is the matter?"

"Lord Harrington." She grabbed the banister. "I did not hear you coming. I am—I am well, *quite* well."

"Might I be of assistance? Is it the item stolen from you?"

Bernadette's breath caught. "Who told you about that?"

"Only Miss Stonewall. She is most concerned for your happiness."

"Oh. Dear girl." Bernadette's face looked hard. "It is true, I am most saddened by the loss of my . . . it was a brooch, you see, a hairwork brooch, a love token given to my father from my mother, and it is—oh, *là*—it meant so very much to me. I have upset myself searching for it again this morning."

Gabriel offered a clean handkerchief, and Bernadette took it. "Perhaps it will turn up."

Bernadette shook her head. "Diamonds, you see, were inlaid around the edge." She blew her nose into the handkerchief.

"Ah." In that case, the brooch would have been attractive to a thief, despite the hairwork, a sentimental touch that Gabriel had always found slightly repulsive. Lovers would snip a lock of their hair, or in a macabre vein, bereaved people would snip locks of hair from the deceased. The hair was looped, knotted, braided, and preserved under glass.

Bernadette said, "Once, some of our silver was stolen by a girl I had enlisted as a scullery maid when my own maids were convalescing after the measles. She was from two villages away, and I did not know her, and, well, she took the silver to a secondhand shop in the central street of Sarlat. To sell it, you see. Everyone is most keen to set out on the hunt this morning, particularly after a beast slaughtered one of the ewes in the village—"

"Good heavens."

"—yet I am torn between going to the shop in Sarlat to see if the stolen things are there and—"

"Say no more," Gabriel said. "Remain with your guests. Go on the hunt—look, the sun is shining. I shall ride into Sarlat and check every secondhand shop. I meant to go to town today anyway, as I must send a telegraph in order to work out what's to be done with young Master Christy."

"Oh, thank you, Lord Harrington. You are ever so kind." Bernadette pressed the handkerchief into his hands. "Please, do not—do not mention this to anyone. I do not like to speak of that brooch."

"Very well."

"Cripes, I do not believe I shall be able to walk five minutes in these things," Henrietta said. She collapsed onto a divan in her bedchamber.

"They're only flat boots," Ophelia said. "Surely you have worn flat boots before."

"Not since early girlhood." Henrietta smushed out her lower lip.

"Pouting is not going to work on *me*, Henrietta. I'm not one of your imbecile gentlemen."

"You could have fooled me in that ridiculous hat. It resembles a top hat for a midget."

"It's for hunting, and anyway *you* told Artemis to lend it to me."

"Did I?" Henrietta duckwalked to the mirrored wardrobe. She squawked. "A spot!"

"I don't see anything," Ophelia sighed. She'd only come to fetch Henrietta because the others were downstairs ready to set off on the hunt. She should've guessed she'd be sucked into a whirlpool of vanity.

"You don't *see* it? It looks like that Italian volcano—what is it called? Mount Vestless?"

"Vesuvius." Mount Vapid, more like.

"It is because of all that rich dessert Mr. Larsen forced me to shovel down after dinner last night. Chocolate mousse, and that berry tart, and more chocolate mousse. He said that he adores ladies with hearty appetites."

"Does Mr. Larsen have anything to do with those flat boots?"

"He said he appreciates ladies who are able to manage themselves in proper hunting boots."

"*Are* you managing, though?"

"Oh, do shut up, Ophelia. I have not had the luxury of wearing men's boots day in and day out, as *you* have. Men's boots don't come in regular ladies' sizes. Perhaps when you and Griffe are wed, you might share shoes with him. Just think of the saved expense."

Ophelia kept her trap shut. Because Henrietta's livelihood had always depended upon the enthrallment of gentlemen, she looked upon every other woman as a potential threat to her next meal. Insulting other ladies was like breathing to her.

"By the by," Henrietta said, "it wasn't very subtle of you, smearing pâté on that veil. There are other ways to delay a wedding, you know. Find yourself a good strong purgative and come down with influenza on the morning of the wedding."

"It wasn't me!"

"If you say so."

Bernadette had assumed that Gabriel's motive for searching for her brooch in Sarlat was gallantry. So he experienced more than one twinge of conscience as he rode down the château drive. In fact, he had wished for an opportunity to pay another call on Madame Genepy. He would go into Sarlat after that.

His thoughts floated to Miss Flax as he rode along the gritty beige road. His feelings for her, last month in Paris, had seemed like a perfect love, emerging from nowhere fully formed. But she had so easily affianced herself to Griffe, and with that *ease*, and with the deception it entailed—and she really meant to marry him!—and Gabriel's perfect love had dissolved away. Miss Flax was an intriguing young lady, he allowed. But she was also a confidence trickster with a proclivity for quandaries. Not to mention a weakness for absurd disguises.

And perfect love? An illusion. A fevered wish.

Gabriel refused to face the withered, dying thing, deep inside of him, that despaired that perfect love did not, *could* not, exist.

Madame Genepy's granddaughter Lucile answered at Gabriel's knock. She hugged a ratty shawl close.

"You again?" she said in French, giving him a sour once-over.

"Good morning, madame. I was passing on my way to town and wondered if Madame Genepy might be well enough to tell me more of her tale."

"She's sleeping. Heart's not well."

"Has she seen a doctor?"

"What business is that of yours?"

"I beg your pardon." Gabriel paused, reluctant to leave, hungering for just one more snippet of the tale. "Tell me, has your grandmother ever read the de Villeneuve version of the *Beauty and the Beast* tale?"

"She does not know how to read. I have read it, though." Lucile curled her upper lip. "De Villeneuve stole the tale."

"Stole it? From whom? Did Madame de Villeneuve perchance travel to this village?"

Lucile shook her head. "My great-great grandmother—Osanne was her name—went to work as a domestic servant in Paris when she was young. Times were difficult those days—or so Grandmother says—with famine that struck the village and the animals of the forest alike." Lucile clutched the shawl tighter at her throat.

Gabriel wondered if she was thinking of the slaughtered ewe.

Lucile went on, "Osanne found work in the household of Madame de Villeneuve. She must have told her mistress the tale—for she was, after all, a storyteller, always eager for a willing ear. Madame de Villeneuve changed the tale, of course, adding things here and there, leaving things out. I once read the tale in an edition in the bookshop in Sarlat. Fanciful trash. It bears little resemblance to Grandmother's tale."

"In what way?"

"Oh." Lucile looked past Gabriel's shoulder to the road, and she stepped back a little. "The house is growing cold, me standing here with the door open."

"Very well." Gabriel turned to go, but then stopped. "Your grandmother's tale made mention of palaces of stone—castles, she said. Is there a particular castle in this vicinity to which she referred? Local sites sometimes correspond to local tales."

At first Lucile's face was blank, but then something sly crept in. "Yes. One of the ruined castles up the valley. I could take you there if you like—you will need someone to show you around. Parts of it have crumbled away, and more are in danger of giving way and collapsing into the river below, but I know which parts are safe. There are certain pictures carved into the stone that might interest you. Pictures of beasts."

Gabriel's fingertips prickled. "I would very much like to go. As will, I am certain, other guests from the château—those who are weary of the hunt by tomorrow, of course."

"Might we leave at ten o'clock in the morning? I could walk up to the château, then, if, of course. . . ."

"Splendid, and yes, I will of course pay you for your time. Good day, madame."

11

Twenty minutes later, Gabriel rode into the center of Sarlat. Its tight streets and carbuncled, teetering buildings were relics of the town's medieval prosperity. This century had left the town behind. Although it was still beautiful, it seemed unable to rouse itself from an enchanted half doze, wedged at the bottom of two intersecting valleys. The railways had bypassed it.

Men hunched at their pipes and morning wine at inn windows. Shopkeepers opened their doors to admit fresh air. Women in cloaks chattered, children frisked towards school, and two dogs snuffled in a slushy alleyway.

After riding up and down the central street twice, Gabriel finally spotted the secondhand shop Bernadette had mentioned. Its sign was faded to a collection of golden paint flecks, and the window was so grimy that he had at first taken it to be untenanted. But then the door swung open, bell jangling, and someone tossed out a hissing cat.

"Shoo!" a man said. The door slammed.

Gabriel found an iron ring to tie his horse to and went inside the shop. Dust tickled his nose, and the floorboards moaned.

"Oui?" the shopkeeper said, popping out from behind a shelf of old books. His gray hair was parted exactly down the middle and plastered with oil.

"Good morning," Gabriel said in French. "I wished to inquire if you have purchased any new items in the past day."

"You wish to *buy* or"—he peered closely at Gabriel—"you have had something stolen?"

"Buy."

"Good. Because I do not, do not, deal in stolen goods. I am always very careful to ask. I can spot a liar a mile off." The shopkeeper tapped his temple. "It is all about the eyes and the way they move. You, for example, I knew instantly that you were lying when you said you did not have anything stolen, by the way you looked into my eyes and away. Only liars do that, you see."

"Fine. I am looking for stolen items. But I will pay for them."

"I see, I see." The shopkeeper bustled behind a counter. "And do you intend to involve the . . . police? Do not lie to me, monsieur."

Gabriel *had* meant to involve the police, if he did indeed find the items stolen from the château. But this shopkeeper was twisting his arm. "I will not involve the police. Now, pray show me what you have acquired in the past day."

The shopkeeper pulled a felt-lined tray from the display counter and set it on top.

"Amethyst bracelet, fine filigree work, solid gold, *old* gold—and this hairwork brooch—see the diamonds?"

"I'll purchase both. Anything else? This may seem peculiar but, perchance did the seller bring a jawbone with these pieces of jewelry?"

"A *jawbone*? Good heavens, no. The, ah, *seller*, brought

only the bracelet and the brooch. Now, a *different* seller brought in a violoncello with only one small crack in the—"

"No, thank you." Gabriel brought out several bank notes and placed them, one by one, on the counter. "Tell me about the person who brought you the jewelry yesterday."

"I simply *couldn't*." The shopkeeper gazed meaningfully at the bank notes.

Gabriel brought out another bank note and placed it with the others.

"The cook from Château Vézère—I know her by sight because her brother cleans the gutters of my house and she sometimes—"

"The cook!"

"Could I interest you in a pair of spectacles?" The shopkeeper pulled out another tray. "Not a single scratch on the lenses."

"No, thank you. Good morning." Gabriel shoved the bracelet and brooch in his greatcoat pocket and left.

Where was the jawbone now? Had the cook kept it? If so, why? It certainly wasn't fit for making soup. Perhaps she had not recognized its significance and had simply thrown it away on a refuse heap.

At the Sarlat telegraph office, Gabriel sent a telegram to D. J. Montgomery, Esq., in London, Sir Percival Christy's solicitor. The message indicated that young Abel was, in effect, stranded in the Périgord as the result of the sudden death of his escort. Gabriel requested that the solicitor advise him on how to proceed. He asked the telegraph office to send the response on to Château Vézère, no matter the extra expense.

Next, Gabriel stopped at the police station, where he was told that Knight's parish in Cricklade, Gloucestershire, had been heard from, and Knight's body was already in transit. It would take three or four days to reach Cricklade.

Gabriel set off for the château.

He found himself eager to tell Miss Flax what he had

learned. He pushed the sentiment to the farthest reaches of his mind, and forced himself to think instead of Miss Ivy Banks's radiant face.

"You appear uneasy, Miss Stonewall," Larsen said to Ophelia. They, along with Bernadette, Griffe, Banks, Ivy, Forthwith, Henrietta, and Madame Dieudonné, were filing through a muddy vineyard. Behind them loomed the château, in front of them a dark, dripping forest.

Ophelia *was* nervous; a few paces ahead, Henrietta wielded a large, loaded shotgun. If no one was accidentally shot today, it would be a miracle.

"Is this your first hunt, Miss Stonewall?" Larsen asked. "Or is it the talk of beasts? Pray do not worry; I have killed hundreds of beasts in my time."

"I confess this is my first time hunting," Ophelia said.

"My sister tells an untruth," Forthwith said. "She's a marvelous shot. Known as the Killer of Cleveland because of all the baby rabbits she's bagged."

"Indeed?" Larsen said.

"Oh. Yes," Ophelia said, jabbing Forthwith with her elbow. "I meant, this is my first time hunting *boar.*"

Ophelia had half hoped to stay behind at the château, because with everyone out hunting, she would've had free rein to search the house high and low for the ring. But she couldn't think of a good excuse—*sick headache* always rang false—so here she was. With everyone together, however, she could observe the gentlemen with Madame Dieudonné to see if anyone showed signs of a prior acquaintance. And while she was at it, she may as well ask everyone what they thought of Knight's death. Everyone was studiously avoiding the topic. It was downright eerie.

As they walked, Griffe and Banks were engaged in subdued conversation. Ivy walked a little aloof, and she appeared to know precisely how to handle her gun. Madame Dieudonné hobbled along in high-heeled boots, wincing.

A footman with an enormous pack strapped to his back brought up the rear. Bernadette had told Ophelia that their luncheon was in the pack.

Larsen said, "I will tell you how it all occurs, Miss Stonewall, to set your mind at ease."

"I do pity the beasts," Bernadette said softly. She opened her mouth to continue, but seeing Larsen's sharp, reprimanding look, she closed it again.

"Does one always pursue wild boars on foot?" Ophelia asked Larsen.

"Yes. Boars keep to the thickets, you see, places horses cannot go. Places even *we* cannot go. That is what the dogs are for. They flush them out, surround them so there is no escape, and then we blast them. Not in the head, of course, for we like to keep those for trophies. In my villa outside of Bergen I have seventy-two beasts' heads mounted on the walls."

"Sounds impressive," Ophelia said.

"Ever had roast boar, my dear?"

"No."

"Ah, then you do not yet understand. Luscious, gamy, dark meat. There is the thrill of the hunt, too, the pursuit—Do you have him? Will he get away?—a contest of wills. Makes a man feel alive. Alive, I say!" Larsen shook his gun towards the sky.

"You know, we really ought to have a roast boar for the wedding feast," Forthwith said, smirking.

"Splendid," Larsen said.

"I shall add it to the list," Bernadette murmured, looking a little ashen.

Ophelia reckoned it was time to bring up the topic of the dead vicar. "A pity Mr. Knight is not alive to hunt with us," she said.

"Knight?" Larsen looked befuddled. "But we did not

know him, and vicars do not hunt—except for heathen souls. No, a man like that must tend to his sermons and such. No sport for them. Besides, he had a weak heart—that is what killed him, *ja*?"

"There *are* belladonna berries in the orangerie," Ophelia said. "There was also Miss Banks's vial of traveling sickness medicine, empty, beside his body."

"Yes, that was most strange," Bernadette said.

Larsen grunted. "Why speak of such things when we are on the hunt? Let us enjoy the day, Miss Stonewall, and let the past alone."

This was like confabulating with a brick wall. "Bernadette, where is Monsieur Tolbert?" Ophelia asked.

"Holed up in his room, at study. I told him even scholars can do with fresh air and exercise, but he insisted that he has no time for the out of doors."

"And where has Professor Penrose gone?"

"The professor? He has"—Bernadette forced a little laugh—"he said he had some business to see to in Sarlat. He will catch up to us later—he insisted that he could track us through the wood by our footprints, although I do not understand how a professor could do such a thing."

Oh, Professor Penrose had all *sorts* of tricks up his sleeve.

They reached the top of the vineyard and plunged into the trees. The wet tree boughs and trunks were black against the snow, which was unmelted in the shade. The bare undergrowth was black, too, and as the hounds bounded and squiggled forward, birds flapped up into the sky.

Ophelia wouldn't have said the forest was creepy, exactly. But it certainly wouldn't be her first choice for a picnic.

The party had rearranged itself upon entering the wood, so Ophelia found herself walking next to Griffe. He showed no sign of yesterday's sinister humor.

"I mean to have much of this forestland cleared someday," he said. "All of it that lies on western or southern slopes, that is. The peasants struggle each year to bring in enough crops to feed themselves because they have been using the same small fields year after year. The soil is exhausted. It must lie fallow. They require more pastureland for their livestock, too. The methods they use now? Archaic, *absolutement*. One shepherd or shepherdess following a tiny herd about. They do not have enough livestock to slaughter for meat, and use them only for milk. I tell them over and again that this valley is rich, fertile, that they could all grow fat and prosperous if they would only clear more land and adopt scientific farming methods."

"They do not wish to do so?" Ophelia asked.

"Stubborn, trapped in their traditional practices. If it is not the way of their forebears, why, they will not do it, either. Badly educated. I attempted to found a village school a few years ago, but after it was built and the schoolmaster was hired, not a single child went. They soon drove the schoolmaster away, claiming he was making their hens stop laying eggs. *Mon Dieu*, they would drive me out, too, if given the opportunity." Something flickered in Griffe's eyes. "They loathe me."

"But this is your land, is it not?"

"But of course it is my land!" Griffe boomed.

Ophelia blinked.

"Forgive me. You have given me an idea, *ma chérie*. I knew you would make a most insightful and practical wife."

Not in a thousand years.

"It *is* my land," Griffe said, "and so I will clear it. With the trees gone, perhaps the peasants will at last be convinced to undertake new farming practices. A brilliant notion, Mademoiselle Stonewall."

"I did not really suggest—"

"No need for modesty." Griffe scooped up her hand and kissed it.

Ophelia tried very hard not to flinch.

"Tsk tsk, sister," Forthwith murmured. "Wait until your wedding night, *please*."

Ophelia accidentally trod on Forthwith's boot.

* * *

They crunched around in the woods for hours, following the lively dogs and never seeing a boar—although Larsen did point out some fresh boar's droppings with glee.

"We are drawing closer to the devil," Larsen said. "I smell its musk."

"Oh dear," Bernadette said, "perhaps we ought to stop for luncheon, then."

"Now?" Larsen bellowed.

Bernadette shrank, but she said in a small voice, "We must revive ourselves for the, ah, showdown with the devilish beasts."

Larsen grunted. "You make a tolerable point."

Bernadette blushed and looked away. She harbored tender sentiments for Larsen, yet Larsen was oblivious. Just like a gentleman.

"*S'il vous plaît*, we must stop," Madame Dieudonné said, speaking for the first time. She creaked to a stump and sat. She looked weary and sallow underneath a thick layer of powder and rouge.

Ophelia went to her. "Madame, are you well?" she asked softly.

"Serves her right, coming along in those silly high-heeled boots," Banks said.

"She ought to be in a convalescent home," Forthwith muttered, throwing stones at blackbirds in a tree. "Or in a coffin."

"I am well, my dear," Madame Dieudonné said to Ophelia. "Beauty requires pain."

"All right," Ophelia said doubtfully. "Where is Meringue?"

"As much as *le petit monsieur* possesses a hunter's spirit, he does not enjoy getting his feet wet, *tant pis.*"

Bernadette said something to the footman in French. The footman removed his pack, and in minutes a small folding table was laid with clean linens, white wine, glasses, china and cutlery, cold meats, cheeses, bread, and fruit. Then the footman, sweating a little, stepped into the shadow of a tree.

The hunting party dug in. The dogs were given water, off to the side, but their wagging tails and lolling tongues suggested they longed to get back on the trail of the boar.

Ophelia sat down beside Banks on a fallen log. After an exchange of pleasantries, she took a deep breath and said, "Poor Mr. Knight. What do you suppose happened to him?"

Banks froze, a chunk of cheese halfway to his mouth. "Happened? What ever do you mean, *happened*? Struck down by a heart ailment, the doctor said."

"But he did seem to crash around ever so much before he died. And there are belladonna plants in the orangerie."

"Belladonna? What does a well-bred young lady know about belladonna?"

"I paid attention during my botany lessons."

"Well, don't go weaving fanciful scenarios. Real life isn't like those novels you young ladies weaken your minds with. My advice to you, Miss Stonewall, is not to trouble with such morbid matters. Mr. Knight is resting in peace now, and you, why, you have a forthcoming wedding. The greatest day of a woman's life." Banks made a hollow dry cough.

"Papa," Ivy called from several paces off.

Banks, still coughing, waved her off.

"He has had a terrible chest cold for a week now," Ivy said to no one in particular.

Once Banks's coughing had subsided, Ophelia said to him, "His death seems to me terribly unfair, though."

"Unfair?" Banks said. "*Unfair?* By God, what has this to do with justice? Struck down by a heart ailment! I'll tell you something, miss. I believe just as much as the next man in eye for an eye, tooth for a tooth—nay, I daresay I believe in it *more*. But whatever sins Mr. Knight may have committed in his life, well, perhaps he got off scot-free, dying early."

Ophelia's skin crawled. No wonder Ivy had her scent

bottles lined up like soldiers on her dressing table; she'd been raised by a tyrant.

While Ophelia spoke with Banks, she watched Henrietta in animated, flirtatious conversation with Larsen. Henrietta perched on a rock, sneaking her flat-booted foot out from beneath her skirts and twisting her ankle about. Larsen juicily approved of the boots. Bernadette watched in dejected silence.

Henrietta, blossoming under Larsen's approval, took up her shotgun and began posing with it, tittering all the while.

Banks said to Ophelia, "She does not appear to know how to use that thing. And just look at Larsen, grinning like a fool. Proves that all the gold in the world cannot buy sense."

Ophelia looked curiously at Banks. His voice was scalding with hate. Why? He and Larsen had claimed to know each other only by reputation. Could that have been a fib? Or did Banks only hate Larsen because Larsen was the richer fellow?

Then, *bang!* Everyone ducked. From a tree, a blackbird plopped down onto the snow, dead as a doornail.

"Did *I* do that?" Henrietta asked.

Larsen was clapping. "You have bagged your first game, Mrs. Brighton. We shall make a fierce huntress of you yet."

Little did Larsen know that Henrietta was already the finest hunter of them all.

12

G abriel had promised to catch up to the hunting party as soon as he returned from Sarlat. But by the time he'd left his horse with the château stable boy—who grumbled that the groom had abruptly quit—he found his mind fixed upon the jawbone. Although a fossil was not the sort of relic he usually concerned himself with, he felt he would like to—no, he *must*—see it for himself. Some deep intuition told him it was meaningful.

If, of course, it existed at all.

If the cook had taken all the stolen items from the vicar's trunk, what had she done with the jawbone? Might she have stashed it in her chamber for some reason?

After some bumbling about, Gabriel found the servants' quarters on the top floor.

He silently cracked a door. Occupied by a gentleman, judging by the trousers slung on the chair, the empty wine jug, and the unemptied chamber pot. Revolting. He closed the door and tried another. A bed and—

"Excusez-moi," a woman behind Gabriel said in a sharp voice.

He sighed and turned. A plump blond maidservant glared up at him. "What are you doing, snooping in my room?" she asked in French. "What do you take me for? Simply because you are a fine, rich gentleman does not mean that you might have *anything* you like."

"I beg your pardon, miss, you are mistaken. I have only lost my way." Gabriel bowed and moved towards the stair.

"I have heard that line before," the maid called after him. "I heard it just this morning!"

Heard it from whom? Gabriel wondered. At any rate, perhaps it would be best if he went to join the hunting party now.

After the picnic luncheon, the footman was left behind in the forest clearing to pack up the mess and carry it back to the château. The hunting party set off once more.

The dogs were fizzling out. Their tails wagged lower, and they walked rather than bounded. But still, the dogs sniffed along a hillside and then steeply down to a small, gushing creek. High above, scrubby oaks jutted from stone cliffs. Ophelia kept to the back of the party, mainly to avoid being in front of Henrietta's shotgun. Bagging that blackbird had dangerously inflated her confidence.

As Ophelia grabbed a tree trunk to step over a tangle of brambles, she saw footprints in the snow, off to the side of the trail.

Footprints? None of the hunting party had strayed so far to the side. No one was paying Ophelia any attention, so she elbowed off the trail and bent to examine the prints.

A man's. Small, and still fresh—no dirt or twigs or melted edges. They led almost straight up the hillside.

Was someone spying on the hunting party? One of the servants or the villagers? This could be important.

Fear made ship knots of Ophelia's innards, but she refused to acknowledge that. Besides, she had a shotgun.

The hunting party was moving away, but she could handily catch up with them; Madame Dieudonné was setting a sluggish pace.

Ophelia hitched up her hem in one hand, tightened her grip on the shotgun with the other, and followed the footprints.

Gabriel found the hunting party's track and hiked swiftly after them through a vineyard, into the wood, alongside a hill, and down into a valley.

This was the same tributary valley in which he'd searched for the caves yesterday.

After a while he heard voices up ahead but, oddly, no hounds baying. He was certain they would have brought out the hounds, which Griffe had said were kept specially for the boar hunt.

Near the stream, Gabriel noticed a man's boot prints and a woman's slightly smaller prints—both fresh—leaving the main track and disappearing up the thicketed slope.

Curious.

Gabriel prided himself on various forms of restraint and self-discipline. However, restraining his curiosity had never been a strong suit. He followed the footprints.

Bare, slick outcroppings of limestone and clinging plants made the going rough. He went up for about fifteen minutes. After hoisting himself up a particularly steep bit, Gabriel couldn't find the footprints. Dash it all. He bent to look for them. He backed up—and bumped into a solid body.

He swung around.

Miss Flax, breathing heavily, eyes glowing, said, "Following me again?" A shotgun was slung over her arm.

Did he only imagine that Miss Flax's eyes glowed to see *him*?

"Not for a moment did I suspect these were *your* prints all the way up here, Miss Flax." The stream was almost directly below.

"He's up there," Miss Flax whispered, gesturing with her shotgun farther up the slope.

"Who?"

"Tolbert. Those are his prints. I saw him. He's been fibbing about being chained to his desk. Come on, before we lose him."

After several more minutes of climbing, they arrived on a shelf of limestone. They heard gentle scrabbling sounds coming from behind a boulder. They crept close to the boulder and peeked over.

Tolbert crouched beside a satchel. He found something inside—a lamp—lit it, and, taking the satchel, ducked into the black mouth of a cave. His lamp illuminated smooth stone walls before he turned a corner and disappeared.

"I'd pay a nickel to see what he was up to in there," Miss Flax whispered.

"He is a zoologist. I have no doubt he is searching for fossils."

"Oh, indeed? Then why is he being so secretive about it, saying he's studying in his chamber when he's really gallivanting?"

"We might chalk it up to a pathologically secretive nature. He is not keen to discuss his research, I have noticed. Come, let us go back down and join the others. It would not do for Tolbert to see us spying on him."

"Oh, fine," Miss Flax said, glancing with longing at the cave's mouth.

They picked their slippery way down.

"Tolbert might notice our footprints," Miss Flax said.

"Yes. Nothing to be done about that. I'll come back later, after he has gone." As soon as the words were out of Gabriel's mouth, he knew he'd live to regret them.

Miss Flax narrowed her eyes. "You cannot possibly mean

to edge me out of this when it was I who first discovered his footprints."

"Of what concern is it to you what Tolbert is doing in there?"

"I'm investigating the murder. And the stolen jewelry."

"Oh yes—I've found that."

"*What?*" Miss Flax spun to face Gabriel so quickly, she lost her footing and slipped. Gabriel caught her arm and steadied her. She was panting. "You found the stolen jewelry?"

"Yes. It seems the cook sold it to a secondhand shop in Sarlat. I surmise that she stole the items from Mr. Knight's trunk. I bought the items back."

"Including a ruby ring?"

"A ruby ring? Why, no. Only Miss Banks's bracelet and a hairwork brooch belonging to Mademoiselle Gavage. You don't mean to say that your engagement ring has gone missing?"

Miss Flax bit her lip and blinked up at the sky. Gabriel would have fancied she was trying not to cry, except he could not picture Miss Flax crying. When she looked at him again, her eyes were dry. "Yes. My engagement ring has gone missing, and if I don't find it soon, then—" She stopped herself.

"Then what?"

"Never mind."

"Perhaps the cook still has it."

"All right, but what if she doesn't? And even if she does, how will I get it back?" Miss Flax started down the hill again. "One thing's clear—I had never thought of the cook as the murderer. She seemed honestly in hysterics when she was standing over the vicar's body. Still, she could've been pretending. I must quiz her. If *she* stole my ring . . ." Miss Flax shook her head.

Was the ring of such sentimental value to Miss Flax? Or perhaps it was only that she did not wish to upset Griffe by having already lost a family heirloom.

Either way, Gabriel remembered his status as Miss Ivy Banks's betrothed and withdrew into silence.

At the bottom, they turned up the stream path. Presently, they rounded a bend.

"Look, there are the others—they have stopped," Miss Flax said. "I wonder if Madame Dieudonné has finally crippled herself with her high-heeled boots." She slanted Gabriel a sidelong glance. "Listen here, professor, don't you *dare* sneak off to that cave without me, do you hear?"

"I wouldn't dream of it."

"I know that bland look on your face. You have no intention of letting me in on your excursion to the cave. Come to think of it, professor, why is it that you're so keen on spying on Tolbert?"

"It is not Tolbert I am interested in. It is his fossilized jawbone."

"The tooth, you mean."

"Not precisely. I'd like to see the entire jawbone from which the tooth fell. If, that is, it even exists. I only glimpsed a sketch of it in Tolbert's notebook."

"Why? That can't possibly have anything to do with a fairy tale, and yet I see that mad glow in your eyes. Wait. It *is* about a fairy tale, isn't it? Are there fossils in fairy tales?"

Gabriel adjusted his spectacles. "Of course the fossil has nothing to do with a fairy tale." That was precisely what he'd been hoping. "The very thought."

"Hmph."

"Why do *you* wish to visit the cave?"

"I wish to see what Tolbert is up to. He's sneaky. The château is chock-full of sneaky folks, and one of them stole that ring."

"Fair enough."

Gabriel had no intention of bringing Miss Flax along on his return to the cave. Creeping about with her in the night-time woods was not a safe proposition. For a variety of reasons.

* * *

Ophelia knew that Professor Penrose had no intention of bringing her along on his excursion to that cave. Well, she'd see about that.

They joined the hunting party. Only Ivy threw them a narrow look; the others were clumped around the pack of dogs, who lay together in the snow.

"What is the matter with the dogs?" Ophelia asked Bernadette.

"They became slower and slower, and now they—well, look at them. All they wish to do is go to sleep. I fear they are ill."

The dogs were curled into tight balls with their backs pressed against one another for warmth.

"Perhaps they are weary from all that running around," Ophelia said.

Forthwith said, "It appears to me that they've been fed some sort of sleeping draught—probably at luncheon."

Sleeping draught? Madame Dieudonné took sleeping draughts. What if she had fed some to the dogs to cut short the hunt? Then she wouldn't have to admit to being too old to keep at it.

"Must call off the hunt, now," Banks said. "Turn around, send for servants to bring the dogs back to their kennel."

"But we are so close to the beast, I feel it," Larsen said.

"Look, the sun is already setting." Forthwith pointed to the orange sun behind bare trees. "We might come back tomorrow. Brr! Chilly out here." He rubbed his arms.

"It isn't so dark," Ivy said. "It feels so fresh and wild at this time of day, with all these wonderful shadows." She stroked her wooden shotgun stock.

Banks watched his daughter closely. It looked to Ophelia as though he would've liked to reprimand Ivy but couldn't think of what for.

They left the dogs and trekked back to the château through the falling dusk.

13

No sooner did Ophelia sit down in her bedchamber to unlace her hunting boots than there was a rap on her door.

Bernadette pushed through. Her eyes and nose were pink. "How could you do it, Mademoiselle Stonewall? You could have simply told me it was not to your liking."

"Do what? You can't mean the *dogs*."

Abel, breathless, appeared beside Bernadette. "There you are, Miss Stonewall. Take your jolly sweet time, don't you? I've made the most marvelous discovery."

"Not now." Ophelia turned back to Bernadette. "What is the matter?" A mad hope rose up that it had something to do with the missing ring. Maybe Bernadette had found it.

"But if *you* did not do it, then who?" Bernadette said.

"Perhaps if you'd explain . . ."

Bernadette swung around. Ophelia followed her to her private boudoir. Abel trotted along behind them, making impatient noises.

Bernadette pointed. The wedding gown, which Ophelia

had last seen that morning pinned for alteration, lay crushed on the carpet. Pins shimmered nearby.

"It was not you who tore out the pins?" Bernadette asked.

"No!"

"Have you got any more of these chocolate drop things?" Abel asked, holding out an empty dish. His cheeks bulged.

Bernadette wept into her hands.

"I am very sorry," Ophelia said gently, touching Bernadette's shoulder.

Bernadette jerked away. "Be gone."

"You don't really suppose that I—"

"Is this all but a great jest to you?"

"It was not I who did this, Bernadette. Please believe me. Come along, Master Christy."

"She thinks you've got cold feet, then?" Abel said cheerfully once he and Ophelia were out in the corridor. "Or maybe it's all a ruse to make you look bad because she thinks you'll usurp her as lady of the manor, banish her to one of those drafty dowager's cottage things with just enough of an allowance for bread crusts and—"

"What is it that you wished to tell me? Did Gerard return?"

"No."

Drat. Ophelia tried to walk faster than Abel, but he simply broke into a jog.

"Golly those were splendid chocs," he said, panting. "Well, I was hot on the trail of a rose beetle today—in the orangerie, you know—and I saw the most peculiar thing. There's this fountain in there, a stone face sort of spouting water into a pool with lily pads and all that?"

"I saw it, yes."

"Well, there's a great fuddle of dead goldfish floating in there."

"That is very sad, but I really must go and prepare myself for dinner."

"I believed you were a clever lady, Miss Stonewall—for an American, I mean."

"I *am*—" Ophelia held her tongue. Had she really been about to defend her intelligence to this spotty, thirteen-year-old rotter? "What am I supposed to make of dead goldfish in the orangerie?"

"You wondered what happened to those traveling sickness tablets—the empty bottle, remember?"

Ophelia stopped in her tracks. "Do you mean—?" She glanced up and down the dim corridor and then lowered her voice. "Are you suggesting that the goldfish were poisoned with the traveling sickness tablets? That the tablets were dumped into their pool?"

"Precisely."

"That the *murderer* dumped them into the pool? To make it look as though the vicar had swallowed the lot?"

Abel nodded. He had a smudge of chocolate on his nose. "This means the vicar most likely died eating belladonna berries—as we have suspected all along."

"But this is *proof.*"

"You ought to speak to the lady to whom those traveling sickness tablets belonged. Perhaps she saw something."

"Ivy?"

"Don't like her much?"

"Why do you say that?"

"You look like you've taken cod liver oil."

It was true; Ophelia hadn't once quizzed Ivy about the vicar's death. Ivy had a prickly sort of atmosphere around her. "I'll ask her tonight."

But first, the cook Marielle. "Will you accompany me to the kitchen, Master Christy?" Ophelia said. "I require a translator."

"You must say please."

"Please."

"All right."

They set off.

"Don't you intend to pick my brains on the matter first?" Abel asked. "Or am I merely a linguistic dray horse?"

"Someone could overhear."

"Well, then *whisper*, for pity's sake."

"It's—"

"I won't translate if you don't tell me."

Ophelia unclenched her teeth. "Oh, fine." She whispered as softly as she could and still hear herself over Abel's wheezing; they were walking briskly. She explained how the professor had discovered that Marielle had sold Ivy's bracelet and Bernadette's brooch, and that Marielle might still have a ring that Ophelia was missing.

"A ring? You never told me you are burdened with ulterior motives." Abel scrunched his mouth.

Ophelia shrugged. "Now, I *had* figured that Mr. Knight or someone else had made the rounds of the château that night, pinching valuable items from various bedchambers, and then stashing them in Knight's trunk. At first when I heard that Marielle had sold some of the missing jewelry, I assumed she'd gotten into Knight's trunk after the police said it was to be left behind. A kind of theft of opportunity, you see."

"Peasant," Abel said.

"However, now it occurs to me, what if Marielle is the murderer?"

"What motive could she have?"

"I don't know. Either way, I must speak to her."

Dinner preparations were under way in the kitchen. Something that looked an awful lot like a ground squirrel was roasting on a spit in the fireplace. Ophelia gulped. Surely they wouldn't serve ground squirrel. This was Château Vézère, not Arkansas.

Marielle stirred a copper vat on the stove, her back to them. The two kitchen maids were at the table, but although vegetables were mounded on one end, they were at work with fabric and scissors at the other end. The maids jumped when they saw Ophelia and Abel enter. One maid squeaked, and Marielle swung around. She waved her wooden spoon, gravy flying, and scolded in French.

"She wishes for us to leave," Abel said to Ophelia, backing up, "so why don't we simply—"

"No." Ophelia gently took Abel's shoulder. "Stay."

Marielle was still yelling, and the maids were bundling up their cloth and scissors and stuffing them into a basket. The cloth was pale gold and rough-looking, like homespun flax. Why did the maids seem so guilty? Was it only because they weren't working on dinner?

"Ask Marielle where she was during the night the vicar died."

"That's rather blunt, don't you think?"

"Go on."

Abel sighed, and said something to Marielle.

Marielle's face flushed and her eyes narrowed. She shouted, gesticulated with her spoon, and turned back to her pot.

"She says we had better leave or there will be no dessert for me," Abel said, panic edging his voice up half an octave. He scampered up the stairs.

Ophelia followed. "She said more than that."

"She said she stayed at her sister's house in the village that night, because her sister has a baby and is desperate for sleep." Abel wrinkled his nose. "I do hope that wasn't a rodent down there on the spit."

That was that. Marielle had an alibi. But she still could've stolen the ring—not to mention Tolbert's jawbone.

In the salon before dinner, Ophelia asked Ivy if she'd seen or heard anything amiss the night the vicar had died.

"Why, no," Ivy said. She was leafing idly through a folio of scenic prints. "Why do you ask, Miss Stonewall?"

"Just . . . curious." How feeble that sounded.

Ivy made a dainty yawn.

At dinner, Griffe said, "The dogs were brought back to their kennel by horse cart, and I am told they are still sleeping soundly now. I instructed my man Luc to keep a close eye on the kennel all night. Locked it tight myself, with a new lock."

"You are the only one in possession of a key?" Professor Penrose asked.

"Of course. My dogs were drugged! Raised them from whelps, I did, each one, and to think some harm might befall them—what if the drug does not wear off? What if—"

"There, there," Bernadette murmured. "I am certain they will awake fresh and healthy in the morning."

"They had better." Griffe gulped from his third or fourth goblet of wine, narrowly studying his guests as he did so. A bread crumb had somehow become lodged in his eyebrow.

"The dogs were drugged during luncheon," Ophelia said, "with the food they were given, correct?"

Silence fell.

Ophelia went on, "So what if the drugs were really meant for *people*, not dogs?"

"*Nei, nei,*" Larsen said, shaking his head. "Someone meant to cut short the hunt. Spoil the sport for the rest of us." He gnawed angrily on a small bone.

"I fancy she's attempting to distract us from the matter of the *wedding gown*," Ivy stage-whispered to Bernadette.

Bernadette stifled a sob in her napkin.

Penrose intervened by telling everyone about the excursion to a ruined castle he'd arranged for ten o'clock the next morning. "I fancy that will keep us all amused while the hunting dogs convalesce."

Everyone but Larsen agreed that a ruined castle sounded amusing. Nothing was going to keep Larsen off the trail of the beast.

After midnight, Gabriel bundled himself in greatcoat, boots, and a fur cap. He stashed a lantern, matches, and a loaded Webley Longspur revolver in various pockets and left the château through the kitchen door. He crunched across hardening slush.

As he passed the stables, he heard the soft nickering of a horse within, and then a form appeared out of nowhere.

Gabriel froze, every nerve in his body zinging. "Who goes there?" he whispered in French. His breath puffed in the air.

The form moved closer. "I don't know what you're saying, Professor, but I reckon your accent is impeccable."

Gabriel smacked a palm to his forehead. "Miss Flax! What in the deuce are you doing out here? Are those trousers you're wearing?"

"Borrowed them from my fake brother. Hiking up to that slope in a hoop skirt once was one time too many. Shall we go?"

"You're not coming. This is madness." Gabriel glanced back at the darkened château. Please God, that motion in a second-story window was only his fancy.

"I *am* going, whether you like it or not." Miss Flax strode— yes, *strode*, for she wore a pair of baggy trousers beneath her great furry cloak—towards the formal gardens.

Gabriel had no choice but to follow. Miss Flax was infuriating. Intractable, stubborn, and by God, she would stop at *nothing* to do exactly what she wished.

Gabriel wondered why the corners of his mouth kept twitching upwards.

They reached the bottom of the formal gardens and traversed a bridge over the ornamental canal, which separated the bottom of the gardens from the vineyard.

"Are you not afraid, Miss Flax?" Gabriel asked as they passed between gnarled rows of grape vines. This was an old vineyard; the branches were so tangled and thick one couldn't even see two rows over.

"Afraid? No. Why would I be?"

"Murderers, thieves, and rampant beasts are not enough to frighten you?"

"I do not have the luxury of wallowing in fear, professor. I've got a task at hand, and I mean to keep it in my sights."

"Collaring the murderer and finding your precious ring." Blast. Why had he said it like that?

"It's not *precious*," she said stiffly. "I mean to say, it's surely quite valuable, but the point is . . . well, I'll be straight with you, professor. I must find the ring in order to give it back to the count."

Everything inside of Gabriel went still. Hope struggled to the surface. "Why?"

"To break things off. I never meant—this ruse has already gone on too long. I've only kept it up on account of Henrietta."

"I did not know you were so obligated to her."

"I'm not. Not exactly. I can't. . . ."

"What is it?"

"You'll think poorly of me."

"I don't believe I'm capable of it."

"You don't understand what it is to be flat broke and completely alone in the world."

"Flat broke, no. But alone? I daresay I do know what that is like." Gabriel concentrated on the rhythm of his feet on the rutted earth. After he'd left Miss Flax in France three weeks earlier, he had never felt more alone.

Miss Flax was silent, and Gabriel waited. At last she blurted, "I lost all the money I'd saved—someone stole it, really—all the money for my passage back to America, and Henrietta said she'd pay me to keep up the engagement for two more weeks, bring her to this hunting party, see, for she'd heard Mr. Larsen would be here, and, well, it's as clear as day what her intentions are with *him*."

"Yes."

She paused. "You don't think poorly of me?"

"No, Miss Flax. I only worry about how Griffe will take it when you break things off."

"I know. I feel awful about it. And I'm running out of time. That's why I had to come along with you tonight, don't you see? I must find some new clue to help me figure out who did in Mr. Knight. I've been up against a brick wall, and Tolbert is just as much of a suspect as the rest."

"I could have reported to you all I saw in the cave."

"Perhaps, but you might not see what *I* see. You're looking for other things. Fairy-tale things."

Gabriel could not argue with that.

They'd reached the wood. They found the path the hunting party had taken earlier.

"Should we light a lantern?" Miss Flax whispered.

Gabriel looked up. The moon was three days from full, and only a few filmy clouds obscured its light. "I think we ought to save the lantern fuel for the cave, if we are able. We do not know how deeply it goes into the earth."

"Do you reckon we'll find the cave again?"

"I am certain of it." In the Crimea, years ago, Gabriel had been a cavalry scout. He had a good head for terrain.

14

They found the entrance to the cave. Ophelia's boots were leaking, and she had to keep pulling up the trousers she'd nicked from Forthwith. Still, trousers beat skirts by a mile.

Penrose lit his lantern, and they ducked inside. The light bounced off shiny-damp limestone walls, about ten feet high. The tunnel took a curve a few paces in. The floor was fine gravel, and it appeared to be well-worn by feet. Hopefully human feet.

The cave narrowed and they were forced to bend forward. Then suddenly, the cave opened out into a spacious cavern. Penrose held the lantern high to take the cavern's measure. It was roughly the size of Château Vézère's dining room, with vaults of limestone marred by scratches and by black and reddish dirt. . . .

Ophelia's breath caught. No, not scratches. Not dirt. "Holy Moses," she breathed. *"Pictures."*

Penrose angled his lantern. Animals seemed to waver

and leap. Exquisite, sweet-faced animals etched into the stone walls and tinted with black and brown-red pigment.

"Look, a herd of buffalo," Ophelia said. "And is that a deer?"

Penrose only nodded, his eyes riveted to the pictures. His profile was almost boyish with wonder, and Ophelia felt a mysterious tug.

They moved slowly alongside the wall. A bear here, with a lovely-shaped head. Then a sort of furry elephant. A lion. A snake. As Penrose tilted his lantern this way and that, the shadows from the stone's natural bumps and divots made the animals almost seem to move.

"Who made these?" Ophelia asked.

"I don't know, but surely people very long ago, for much of the color has been drained away by seeping moisture—see?"

"This is most certainly what Tolbert was visiting this afternoon."

"Yes."

"Why do you suppose he keeps telling everyone he's in his chamber studying, when he's really roaming about the countryside?"

"Tolbert is, shall we say, *jealous* of his work. He doubtless intends to document this carefully, in academic style, before sharing it with anyone. He'll wish to get all the credit for its discovery. I must document this somehow. Photography would never work in here, even with many lanterns. Perhaps paper tracings—"

"What's this?" Ophelia had almost stepped on something at the base of the cave wall.

Penrose crouched and held the lantern over it. "Good God," he muttered. "Is it . . . a *shrine*?"

Small earthenware dishes held what appeared to be chocolate drops, purple berries, and loose pearls. A clay vase held a red-and-white-striped rose.

Churches in New England didn't have shrines. They didn't even have stained-glass windows.

"Pearls," Ophelia said. "Madame Dieudonné was missing a pearl necklace." But—she looked carefully at the shrine— no ruby ring. Still, the pearls connected the shrine, very loosely, to the missing ring. There was hope yet.

"This resembles the offerings people of the Orient assemble for their gods or ancestors," Penrose said.

"Those are belladonna berries, professor." The skin of Ophelia's back felt all itchy and crawly, and she stole a glance to the black gap where the cave continued into the earth. Someone could be back there. Watching.

"Miss Flax," Penrose said slowly. "Look at this." He lifted the lantern, illuminating the picture on the wall above the shrine.

Heavens to Betsy. A carved, black-painted beast, half man, half boar, undulated in the light.

The body of the beast was like a man's, although the feet seemed—Gabriel squinted—yes, they seemed to have hooves. But the head! It was unmistakably that of a furry boar, with large pointed tusks and tiny round ears.

A slight crunching sound made Gabriel and Miss Flax freeze. Their eyes met.

Silence.

Gabriel knew that somewhere in the shadows, someone or something lay in wait.

Miss Flax, wide-eyed, in those awful trousers, seemed at once horribly vulnerable and dear beyond measure. The pistol tucked into Gabriel's waistband felt newly heavy. He picked up the lantern and slowly stood, willing himself not to exude the essence of fear in case whatever was watching was an animal.

"*Come,*" he mouthed to Miss Flax, wrapping his free hand around her wrist. "*Slowly.*"

She stayed very close to him as they walked steadily out of the cave.

They emerged into the cold, damp night. The moon glowed whitely above. The air tasted of soil and rot.

"Shouldn't you extinguish the lamp?" Miss Flax whispered as they started down the rocky, ice-slicked slope. "So they can't see us?" She tugged her wrist free of his hand so she could climb.

"Wild animals are afraid of light." Gabriel longed to grab her wrist again, to enfold her, keep her safe. If something were to befall her—

"It wasn't an animal in there," Miss Flax said. "It was a human being. I could *feel* it. Animals don't make one feel so frightened."

"Not any animals?"

"No. Animals never seem *evil*, and I felt something evil up there in the cave."

Gabriel had felt that sense of evil, too. And he didn't wish to mention it, since they were at least twenty minutes away from the château, but he still felt it *now*.

"Who do you suppose set up that shrine?" Miss Flax whispered.

"Tolbert."

"You sound certain."

"He is not the cold-blooded man of science he pretends to be. A few years ago he stole a great fossil lizard bone from his place of work in Paris."

"To sell it?"

"No, that is the amazing part. I was told he had it arranged in his bedchamber on some sort of cushion."

"That's nutty."

"Indeed. Yet human beings seem to have an impulse for religious worship, and zoologists are not immune."

"Do you suppose he was hiding in the cave tonight?"

"I don't know."

"Well, if Tolbert set up that shrine, he somehow got his hands of Madame Dieudonné's pearls. Maybe he has the ring, too. Maybe *he* murdered Mr. Knight."

"What of a motive?"

"Well, don't forget I found a fossilized tooth in Mr. Knight's trunk."

"How could I?"

No creature, human or beast, emerged from the shadows during their hike. Gabriel's muscles relaxed when Château Vézère could at last be seen, a boxy silhouette beyond the vineyard.

"Never thought I'd be so happy to see that house," Miss Flax said softly. They passed between softly rattling rows of grapevines.

"You did not once wonder what it might be like to call such a house home?" Gabriel kept his voice light. His ancestral home in England was, embarrassingly, perhaps six times larger than Château Vézère.

"Mansions aren't for the likes of me. Give me a trim little house with a shady porch and an apple orchard, and I'll be as happy as a queen."

"And does Queen Ophelia live alone in this house?"

"Yes. Unless friends need to be taken in."

"You never meant to marry?" Bother that tightness in his voice.

"My father abandoned my mother, Professor Penrose. He was a schoolteacher, had gone to college in Boston, even, and I suppose he fancied himself at bottom too good for Mother. So when I was small, he just left. Mother supported my brother Odie and me by becoming a maid of all work on a farmstead—in New Hampshire. Worked like a slave for the lady of the house. Mrs. Beecher. Now *she* was a wicked witch out of a fairy tale. The thing I remember most about Mother was her hands. Red and shiny, her knuckles swollen, and her palms were as rough as a cat's tongue. So gentle she was to Odie and me, though. I don't remember Father, but Odie does. Did." Silence.

"Your brother is—?"

"I don't know. I lost track of him during the war. He signed himself up for a soldier, you see, and one day my letter to him came back from his camp unopened. I wrote to his colonel, but I never got a reply. I reckon that's *one* way to tell a lady that her brother is dead."

"But he could be alive still."

"Don't go trying to make me hope, Professor. He's gone. Mother's dead, my father may as well be dead, and to answer your question, yes, I'd rather live alone in a nice clean house with nobody bothering me—or *leaving*."

Miss Flax's voice was clear and purposeful, but Gabriel heard the pain. For the first time he understood her iron-nailed stubbornness, her resolve to make the best of her life at all costs and—he eyed her baggy gent's trousers—using any means necessary.

"But you," Miss Flax said, breaking the heavy silence, "you will soon be a married fellow, with a wife and children, and a mansion or two?"

"I have an estate in England, yes." Why did Harrington Hall suddenly sound utterly bleak compared to Miss Flax's porch and apple trees? "These days I confine myself mainly to a town house in Oxford. I enjoy simplicity, Miss Flax."

"Does Miss Banks enjoy it, as well?"

He didn't answer, feeling obscurely reprimanded.

They emerged from the vineyard and approached the stone bridge that arched over the ornamental canal and into the formal gardens. Moonlight-bleached statues of angels flanked the bridge.

A figure sprang from behind one of the statues. Something was the matter with it. It was too bulky on top—

Miss Flax screamed and stumbled backwards. The figure brought out some kind of club, swung it high above Miss Flax, and brought it down with a sickening thunk. Miss Flax collapsed.

Gabriel cried out, lurched forward. He had only the briefest, confused impression of a boar's head, glittering dark eyes, pointed white tusks, fur. Something horribly heavy smashed the top of his head. Fireworks sparkled, he was falling, and then all was silent black.

He was submerged in foul-tasting, icy dark water. The canal. He fought to the surface, gasping, the weight of the lantern and the pistol in his pockets dragging him down. He paddled arms and legs, swinging his head, searching.

Where was Miss Flax? "Miss Flax!" he cried.

Nothing.

Why was this canal so blasted *deep*? He swam to the side. Moss slicked the stones. After several tries he finally got a finger hold. He heaved himself up and over the balustrade. Panting and shivering, he clambered to his feet.

A dark lump on the snow. Fur cloak. Boots jutting.

"Miss Flax," he croaked, staggering over. He threw himself beside her and turned her face.

Her eyes fluttered open. "Professor?" she whispered. She lurched upright. "Where is that man who hit me?" She squinted into the darkness. "What a coward, wearing that silly costume."

Gabriel helped her to her feet. "We should not give chase. Allow me to see your head."

She rubbed her crown. "There's a lump. Not bleeding. Who *was* that?"

"Heaven knows. Tolbert? Let us go."

As they traversed the formal gardens, Gabriel peered into the shadows—left and right, left and right. No motion except waving branches and rolling clouds.

They didn't speak until they'd bolted themselves into the dim kitchen.

"Someone's not too happy about us seeing that cave, I'd guess," Miss Flax whispered. She went to a bench along the wall, poured out a glass of water, and drank it down. "Water?"

Gabriel nodded. She poured him a glass, and he gulped it. He still tasted the rank canal water.

"Good night, Professor," Miss Flax said. She hesitated.

Their gazes snagged together and held for too long. Wordless, half-formed things clamored in Gabriel's mind.

"Good night," he finally said.

She left.

Gabriel fell asleep wondering how he would explain the knob on his head to Miss Banks.

Ophelia woke with a pulsating headache and a foggy sense of dread. Then it all came back. The cave. The pictures. Madame Dieudonné's pearls and the belladonna berries in that shrine. That ninny in the boar's costume clobbering her over the head.

She touched her head and winced, feeling a tender lump. Thank goodness for complicated hairstyles.

She got out of bed, put on Artemis's dressing gown, and went down the corridor to use the lavatory and the wash-room. When she returned, Clémence was arranging a tray of coffee things on a table.

"Bonjour," Ophelia said.

Clémence tossed her a scornful look and left without a word.

For the first time, Ophelia looked at the clock. Twenty past nine. She had overslept. The excursion to the ruined castle was at ten o'clock, and she'd be darned if she missed the chance to see most of the folks who might've clobbered her last night all in one place.

On her way to the wardrobe, her eyes fell on Forthwith's trousers. Oh no. Clémence had hung them on the fire screen to dry.

Would Clémence tell Bernadette or Griffe about the trousers? Surely she'd tell the other servants. Folks would know that she, Ophelia, wore trousers in secret. Or, worse, folks would suppose that fellows paid her nighttime visits and forgot their trousers when they left.

Number one, Ophelia would return the trousers to Forthwith's chamber and deny *everything* if anyone asked. Number two, she would find out if the driver Gerard had returned.

The parakeet cheeped.

And number three, she'd find some fresh newspaper to line the bottom of the birdcage.

Ophelia poured a cup of coffee and doused it with cream. She took sips as she got dressed. One thing about the French: Their cows made the nicest cream.

When Ophelia picked up Forthwith's trousers to return them to his chamber, something fell out of a pocket. A hankie—a *soiled* hankie. Blotched with purplish, belladonna berry–colored stains.

Hold it. Could *Forthwith* have killed the vicar? Forthwith was obviously scamming Larsen. If the vicar knew about the scam, if Forthwith thought his scam was threatened, well, that could be a fine motive for murder.

Ophelia stuffed the hankie back into a trouser pocket. She went to Forthwith's chamber and knocked. No answer. She went in, dashed to the trunk from which she'd stolen the trousers last night, stuffed them in, and hotfooted out of there.

Next stop, Gerard's chamber. Ophelia heard rustling inside. *At last.* Unwilling to delay her confrontation even one second longer, she flung open the door.

"There you are," she cried.

A lady squealed, the bedclothes heaved, and Gerard thunked out of bed and onto the floor. Utterly unclothed.

Oh.

Ophelia inched the door shut, whispering, *"Pardonnez-moi."*

Gerard scrabbled to his feet, hiding his front with crossed hands. Ophelia was treated to his soup-chicken hindquarters as he climbed back in bed.

A yellow bouffant head thrust out from beneath the bed-clothes, and Madame Dieudonné uttered what sounded like curses.

Ophelia slammed the door and bolted for the stairs.

No, no, no. How could she ever forget *that* sight?

Abel had said he'd heard a lady with Gerard the night the vicar was killed. That had ruled out Gerard as a suspect. If Madame Dieudonné was Gerard's hide-and-seek partner, that meant *she* had an alibi, too. Which, if nothing else, whittled down the range of murder suspects.

Ophelia found a newspaper in the abandoned breakfast room. It was four days out-of-date and in English—probably for the benefit of the château's English-speaking guests.

Not that the parakeet would be picky.

Ophelia took it upstairs. She removed the soiled news-paper from the bottom of the birdcage and threw it in the fire. She folded a fresh square. As she did so, she noticed a headline: "Empty Train Stalls Travel to Paris."

The brief article described how the train traveling back and forth between Avignon and Lyon was completely sold out for a ten-day stretch but, oddly, no one was *riding* in the train. No one knew who had purchased all those tickets. The railway offices wouldn't say.

Ophelia smoothed the newspaper at the bottom of the bird-cage. "There you go, little one," she said to the parakeet.

The parakeet promptly tried out the new paper.

Ophelia didn't know where in France Avignon and Lyon were. Something niggled at the back of her mind. Then it was gone.

15

"Madame Genepy was awake when we called upon her this morning," Ivy said to Gabriel. Her voice was faintly taunting. "She told me more of *La belle et la bête*."

"Oh?" Tense, Penrose leaned forward on the seat.

The carriage jostled on the road on its way to the ruined castle. Miss Flax sat quietly beside Ivy, looking tall and plain in her brown bonnet beside dainty Ivy. Banks sat next to Gabriel. Lucile, Tolbert, and Madame Dieudonné traveled in a second carriage. Larsen had gone out hunting, Forthwith had taken a carriage into town, and Griffe had stayed behind at the château to meet with the woodcutters he had summoned. Bernadette had stayed home to bake wedding cakes and write invitations. Henrietta was, presumably, still sleeping.

"Would you tell me exactly what Madame Genepy said?" Gabriel tried to squelch the envy in his voice. *He* should have been there, listening to that tale. But Ivy had visited Madame

Genepy that morning, bringing her broth like a ministering angel, while Gabriel was still sleeping.

"Well," Ivy said, "there was a bit about a beautiful maiden who was to be the bride of the beast."

"Ah—as in the de Villeneuve tale? The daughter sacrifices herself to save her father." The maiden sacrifice motif was typical of animal groom tales.

"Actually, Madame Genepy didn't mention a father. The maiden sacrifices herself—what did she say?—for her people, or something of that nature."

"Her people."

"Then the maiden married the beast." Ivy's eyes glowed. "The beast Madame Genepy described sounded precisely like the one that was seen in the village last night."

"What's that?" Banks asked.

"Oh, Papa, don't you ever pay attention? Another sheep was killed in the village last night, and one Madame Haut, awake to nurse her baby in the night, saw a beast going along the edge of the field and into the wood."

"A wolf?" Miss Flax asked. "A boar?"

"The woman claimed that the beast walked upright like a man," Ivy said with a shudder, "and that it had a boar's head."

"What these peasants need is a woolen mill," Banks said. "That river of theirs has got enough vim to run one, I daresay. Keep them employed and keep their heads from rotting with humbug. Men with beasts' heads! Pshaw."

Gabriel kept his hands quite still on his knees, but inside his gloves his fingertips buzzed almost painfully.

Madame Genepy's beast matched the description of whoever had hit Miss Flax and him over the head last night. Madame Genepy's beast *also* matched the description of the beast in the cave picture. Here, then, was absolute proof that her tale was as ancient, if not *more* ancient, than Gabriel had hoped. He must make paper-and-pencil rubbings of those animals in the cave—and that beast—while he still had the opportunity.

What was more, this rendered the hybrid jawbone in Tolbert's sketchbook not simply a scientific anomaly. It made it a fairy-tale relic.

Gabriel must have it. He *would* have it.

The ruined castle clung to a stone outcropping above the Vézère River. The carriage rumbled across a bridge and began a curvaceous ascent through a steep, thick forest. The two carriages stopped halfway up, beside an abandoned inn.

Everyone piled out of the carriages. They started the final ascent to the castle via a derelict stone staircase.

Gabriel fell into step beside Tolbert, at the rear of the group. "I say, it is rather fascinating that this local legend contains a beast that possesses boarlike traits."

"I have no interest in legends. I am a man of science." Tolbert's voice was muffled by his fur collar.

"Oh, I do not doubt it. However, I did see your sketch of the hybrid jawbone—"

"This again? That bone was doubtless an anomaly. A freak of nature. One of its kind, not a proper species."

"You saw it, then?"

"But of course I saw it. I am not in the habit of sketching pictures from my imagination." Tolbert stopped. "What is it you *truly* wish to say to me, Lord Harrington?"

"I will be blunt: I happened to see some wondrous cave paintings. Most were animals that, while no longer found in the Périgord, did not seem far-fetched. A bear, bison, a rhinoceros. However, there was one painting that depicted a boar-man hybrid, a creature that might have had the same sort of jawbone that you sketched in your notebook. But of course, you have seen this painting, this cave."

"No. No, I have not."

Gabriel decided not to mention that he had seen Tolbert enter the cave yesterday afternoon.

"Are you spying upon me, Professor? Ah, yes." Tolbert

made a bitter cackle. "I may not be as privileged as you, Lord Harrington. My father was a shopkeeper, not an earl. But I have dwelled within the hallowed halls of academia long enough to know when another scholar is attempting to encroach upon my research."

"Am I?"

"My God, you disgust me." Tolbert started up the steps.

Gabriel followed, saying, "You have no interest in the cave painting I mention?"

"No. I am a scientist, and as such, I have not the slightest interest in artworks—and at any rate, this picture of yours sounds like a fraud, or the prank of adolescent boys."

Gabriel was thoughtful as he walked the rest of the way up to the ruins in silence. Why was Tolbert lying? Was it really due to academic jealousy? For if Tolbert had indeed discovered a new species, a species that linked humans with boars, well, what a stunning find. He would become famous the world over. Tolbert *must* have seen the cave paintings—it would be difficult to miss—even if he had not arranged that shrine. And Gabriel rather thought that he *had* arranged it.

Everyone clumped together at the top of the steps. Lucile led the way through lichen-laced walls into a courtyard. Towers and battlements teetered up into the blank gray sky.

Inside the castle courtyard, the party dispersed. Banks and Ivy linked arms and spoke cozily, pointing out architectural features of the castle and using terms—portcullis? bailey?— that Ophelia had never heard before. Tolbert scowlingly studied an archway. Penrose and Lucile went off together. Madame Dieudonné looked lost without her poodle, and she kept sending Ophelia fretful looks.

Ophelia did not wish to discuss Madame Dieudonné and Gerard and whatever they had been doing under the bed-clothes earlier. There was no need *at all*. She'd come along to observe the others, to see if whoever had been dressed up in that boar's head last night would give themselves away.

So far, no sign. They all seemed wrapped up in themselves. No one even looked at Ophelia. Maybe the attacker had been someone else, then. A servant. The blacksmith. *Griffe*.

Drawn by the sweeping, wintry vista, Ophelia wandered to the farthest battlement, just beside a crumbling tower. Wind licked up from the valley, stinging her cheeks. She placed her hands on the hip-high wall and leaned over. Far, far below, rubble cascaded from the base of the cliff into the river.

Dizziness rocked through her.

"Mademoiselle Stonewall," someone said.

Ophelia jumped. "Madame Dieudonné." She pressed a hand to her heart, stepping back from the wall. "You startled me."

"I am so pleased to have the chance to speak to you"— Madame Dieudonné's eyes swiveled left and right—"in *privacy*."

"If it is about the, um, the coachman and—"

"No, no."

"Oh." Good.

"Although, my dear, there is no shame in my profession."

"Your profession?"

"I am a courtesan, as was my mother and my grandmother before her."

"Oh." Ophelia knew all about courtesans, having played one in *The Rise and Fall of Love*.

"I have been reduced by circumstances to such as that vile coachman. How he has enough money to pay, I do not know."

Bribe money, maybe? "Madame, have you spoken to Gerard about the broken-down stagecoach?"

"*Non.*" Madame Dieudonné caressed her own cheek. "Courtesans specialize in removing gentlemen from the cares of their everyday lives. We are not wives, nagging and shrewish." She was so close, Ophelia smelled face powder mingling with coffee breath. "You should remember to be more like a courtesan and less like a wife when you are married. You will be happier. The count, he is a man who does not enjoy nagging, eh?"

Ophelia drew back. "You know nothing of the count and me."

"*Non?* Would it surprise you to learn that I knew him before I arrived at Château Vézère? Ah, I see that it does."

Actually, Ophelia had guessed Madame Dieudonné had previously known a man in the château, but she hadn't suspected it was *Griffe*. "Where did you meet him?"

"Ask him."

"All right, I will."

Madame Dieudonné sidled closer. "I know, Mademoiselle Stonewall, that you are investigating the death of Monsieur Knight."

"Well, I—"

"Do not lie. I have no patience. First, I found you snooping in my chamber, and today you intrude without ceremony into the private chamber of Gerard? No, do not attempt to deny it. I know that the vicar's death was not the work of fate, as the police would have us believe. *Oui*, Monsieur Knight was murdered."

"Yes, you told me of your suspicions already, but *who*—"

From the tower above, a bit of loose mortar fell. Madame Dieudonné stiffened. Ophelia squinted up to see a blink of motion, someone drawing back from the wall.

"Not here," Madame Dieudonné whispered. "Someone is listening. Later. Pray come to my chamber, after everyone has gone to bed, and I will tell you everything."

"Why didn't you tell the police what you know?"

"I want nothing to do with the police." Madame Dieudonné flinched, as if remembering something.

Maybe something involving the Monte Carlo police.

"I will tell you what I know," Madame Dieudonné

whispered, "and *you* may take it to the police. *Et*, leave me out of things."

Ophelia felt that cloak-and-dagger shenanigans were best left to Shakespeare. But there was likely one or more persons within earshot right now. "All right," she said softly. "I'll meet you tonight."

She left Madame Dieudonné and circled around the tower, hoping to discover who had been standing over them and, just maybe, eavesdropping. She found herself in a crumbly passage with a staircase that sank down into blackness, and then in what appeared to be a half-ruined chapel. When she at last found stairs leading up, there was no one at the top of the tower.

It could've been anyone listening. Hopefully it had only been the professor.

Ophelia went back down the stairs and looked into a closet-sized chamber jutting from the side of the castle. A stone platform filled the chamber, in which a round hole was carved. Peculiar. She looked through the hole. *Eek*. Nothing but empty air between her and the rubble way, way down at the base of the cliff. The river flowed by.

Her neck prickled, and she spun around. "Oh! Miss Banks." What was the *matter* with these folks, always sneaking up on you? "What in tarnation are you doing there?"

"*Tarnation*, Miss Stonewall? My, what quaint vernacular you Americans employ. I think I read that expression once in a Mark Twain book, but I never would have guessed it would trip off the tongue of a Cleveland heiress." Ivy smiled. Her eyes flicked past Ophelia to the hole. "Having a peek down the latrine?"

"Is that what it is?" Ophelia inched away from the hole. "Imagine having to balance yourself over eternity like that every time you needed to go."

"My, you are coarse, aren't you? *So* sad for the Count de Griffe." Ivy inched closer. "For it *is* the count you wish to marry?"

"Of course."

"I have been meaning to tell you, Miss Stonewall, I finally realized where I have seen your friend Mrs. Brighton before."

"Oh?" Ophelia's pulse sped up.

"Mm. It is so very odd, because I distinctly remember seeing her likeness on a theatrical placard in London a few months ago, advertising some American variety show performing on the Strand. Low, vulgar stuff. Why was Mrs. Brighton, widow of Cleveland's high society, on that placard, Miss Stonewall?"

Ophelia knew precisely why: Even though Henrietta had quit Howard DeLuxe's Varieties a year ago, Howard had never bothered to remove her likeness from the placards. Howard was cheap.

Ophelia backed away from Ivy, but with the latrine hole just behind her, she didn't have much wiggle room. "You are mistaken, Miss Banks. That couldn't have been Mrs. Brighton."

"Oh, it was she. I never forget a face. She is an impostor, and quite clearly she hopes to get her hooks into Mr. Larsen."

"Have you suggested this theory to anyone?"

Ivy smiled. "Not yet. I prefer to keep things up my sleeve until *just* the right moment. I fancy that's something that you and I have in common, Miss Stonewall."

Ophelia slipped past Ivy, through the latrine doorway and away down the corridor. Despite the cold wind whapping through the ruined castle, beneath her corset and chemise she was damp with sweat.

"Stags," Gabriel said to Lucile. "These are the beasts you believed would interest me?" He studied the stags and oak leaves carved in a door lintel. True, de Villeneuve's tale made mention of white stags with golden antlers. But Gabriel wasn't interested in de Villeneuve's tale.

"Well, yes, stags," Lucile said, sounding hurt.

"They are very fine," Gabriel said quickly, "but for some reason I had thought the beast would be . . ."

"The beast from Grandmother's tale." Lucile's voice went hard. "The people of this valley *do* think from time to time of things not concerned with Grandmother's tales."

"Of course. I merely misunderstood."

"If these carvings are not good enough for you—" Lucile shrugged.

"They are fascinating. Are there others in this castle?"

"Boars, down below. Carved on the wall built around the old wellspring. The wellspring is dry now, but in the old days it supplied water for the castle."

Gabriel's heart thumped. "Boars?"

"Go around this corner here." Lucile pointed. "There is an arched doorway halfway along. Go through the doorway and down the steps. You cannot miss the round wellspring wall. I will not go with you. Those steps frighten me."

Biting wind swirled as Gabriel rounded the corner. He leaned his weight into it. Daylight illuminated the first stretch of steps, but then they coiled away into tar blackness. A stagnant odor rose up. The steps were alarmingly tall and steep, too, and although iron rings in the walls indicated that rope handles had once hung there, now a man would have to press tight to the walls all the way to the bottom.

Gabriel peered down. He was sure on his feet; he could easily—

A stiff shove hurtled him into darkness.

He scrabbled to gain a hold on the walls as he tumbled on his hip and then over his shoulder. Fingernails snapped. His thoughts jumbled. His entire skeleton rattled, and then he caught hold of one of the iron rings. He stopped. He clung to the ring, panting. Nothing felt broken or popped open, although heaven knew he'd be bruised. If he had continued down the steps like that, gaining momentum all the way, he would have broken his neck.

Which, doubtless, had been Tolbert's intent.

Gabriel crept up the steps. Pain jolted and throbbed. When he reached the top, he wasn't surprised to find nobody there.

When he entered the courtyard, everyone was assembled. They all looked cold-pinched and eager to leave. Tolbert would not look at Gabriel but buried his tortoise face in his collar. Yet his carbon-black eyes sparkled.

16

When Ophelia went to her chamber to change for luncheon, she found Abel lounging on her sofa, reading. A plate of brown cake sat at his side.

"Oh, hullo," he said without taking his eyes from the page. "How was the castle? Dreary as all get-out?"

"Master Christy. What are you doing in here?"

"Well, I fancied reading my book in peace, and my own prisonlike garret was giving me frostbite. Nice coal fire you've got in here."

"Have you seen Gerard?"

"Don't you think of anything else? As a matter of fact, he's gone for good." Abel forked a hunk of cake into his mouth and kept reading.

"What?"

Abel heaved a sigh and put down his book. "It seems Gerard had been harassing the maidservant Clémence, which greatly angered the Count de Griffe, and he sent Gerard packing while you lot were at the ruined castle. Quite a lot of roaring on the count's side. Rather possessive of his servants, I'd say."

Ophelia slumped into a chair. "But Gerard was probably bribed by the murderer, and now I'll never be able to speak to him."

"If it's any consolation, I rather doubt he would've told you the truth." Abel tipped his head towards the cake. "Would you like some? It's awfully good, nice and buttery and nutty. Mademoiselle Gavage is an excellent baker when she isn't bursting into tears or in a dither, yapping about veils and gowns and things."

"Did Bernadette *give* you this cake?" Abel's wedge was approximately one-quarter of an entire cake, and it hadn't been neatly cut.

"More or less. Go on. Try it. I'm using the fork, of course, but you could break off a bit with your fingers. I won't tell anybody." He forked another bite into his mouth.

It was all so undignified, but Ophelia gave in. The cake smelled too scrumptious, warm and sugary. She broke off a piece.

Abel watched her. "Ripping, isn't it? A local specialty, I understand. *Gâteau aux noix*. By the way, your parakeet looks melancholic. He could probably do with some live grubs. Birds don't only eat seeds, you know."

"Perhaps later." Ophelia chewed more cake. The last thing she required was grubs writhing around in her bedchamber.

Ophelia could scarcely touch her luncheon. Lucky she'd eaten all that cake. Meanwhile, that skunk Ivy chattered gaily with her father and Bernadette about fossils, never looking at Ophelia. Tolbert did not join in this discussion. Silently, he hunched over his plate, toying with his fork. Madame Dieudonné ate with Meringue hidden on her lap. Gobbling sounds could be heard.

Henrietta still hadn't come downstairs, and she'd sent word with the maid that she had a sick headache.

Just as well, since Ivy was onto her.

Professor Penrose had a pink scrape on his cheekbone, and his spectacles frames looked a little mangled. Ophelia hadn't been able to ask him about these on the carriage ride back from the ruined castle. What had happened to him?

Larsen was still hunting, and Griffe was out on his estate making plans for the felling of the forest with the head wood-cutter.

Everyone seemed to be *waiting* for something.

"Is there any news from the blacksmith regarding the repair of the whippletree?" Madame Dieudonné asked Bernadette.

"Why yes, there is—I had nearly forgotten. I have been in such a state over the wedding preparations. A village lad brought word that the ironwood required to replace the cracked whippletree will arrive today, so you will be able to set off for Bordeaux the day after tomorrow."

"Ah, Dieu merci," Madame Dieudonné murmured, feeding a bit of meat to Meringue.

"But my parcel has not yet arrived from Bordeaux," Tolbert said in a whining tone. "I cannot leave the château before my parcel arrives."

"I am certain we will be able to arrange something," Bernadette said firmly. She couldn't hide that she wished Tolbert out of her house.

Ophelia couldn't blame her. And what was in that parcel?

After luncheon, Ophelia decided a snoop through Griffe's study was in order. After all, with him out on the estate with the woodcutters, this could be her only chance. Maybe Madame Dieudonné really did know who had murdered Knight, and the whole thing would be sorted out tonight. But if she was mistaken, well, Ophelia ought not waste any time when she could be searching for clues. Not with a wedding scheduled for the day after tomorrow.

Of course, Ophelia wouldn't go through with the wedding. But she still clung to a hope that she'd find the ring and be able to break it off with Griffe in a dignified way.

Griffe wasn't the softhearted fellow she'd taken him for. What if he had killed Knight? Wait—what if *he* had stolen the ruby ring? If he knew Ophelia planned to break it off with him, taking his ring back would be one way to make things more difficult for her.

The study lay in a remote section of the main floor. Ophelia crept in. Tobacco smoke and stale wine mingled with a musky, confusing scent. Dozens of stuffed animal heads decorated the walls. Stags, a fox, wolves, even a tiger and a rhinoceros and—*oh-ho*—boars. Lots of boars. Although Ophelia had no way of knowing if a boar's head had been stolen from the study, she would wager that that ninny last night had gotten his boar's head mask from here.

A glass-fronted case displayed pistols and shotguns.

How comforting.

Empty wine bottles covered the desk, and the drawers held nothing but boxes of cigars and matches. But there was a promising cabinet behind the desk, filled with little drawers.

Ophelia dug through. Lots of papers, some personal-looking and some with a more businesslike appearance. Unfortunately, they were all in French. She supposed she could pinch some and ask the professor or Abel to translate, but she wouldn't know where to begin. The papers were disorganized, and there were sheaves of them.

One caught her attention, though, because of the way it was crammed at the back of the bottommost drawer. Not as though anyone had wished to hide it; more like it had been stuffed away in a fit of anger.

She pulled it out and smoothed it on the desktop. It looked like a letter.

"Mademoiselle Stonewall. You have unearthed my secret."

Why oh *why* did this continue to happen? Ophelia turned. "Count. I—"

Griffe shut the study door behind him. "No need to explain. What young lady would not rummage into the past of her fiancé?" He came to her side. He smelled of the fresh air, and he still wore a coat, hat, and gloves. He was breathing hard. He poked the letter with a fingertip. "The evidence of my youthful indiscretion."

"I don't understand."

"My father died too young and as a result, I became the Count de Griffe too young, at only twenty-one. I was mad with grief over the loss of both my parents, and I was also drunk with all of my newfound power and wealth. In those days, if I saw something I desired, I took it. When I grew weary of it, I cast it aside. And I could not be sated by any vice."

Ophelia's eyes drifted to the empty wine bottles on the desktop.

Griffe went on, "I became a gambler, and one terrible evening in Paris, I lost a portion of my ancestral estate to a pockmarked, greedy fop from England." He took Ophelia's chin roughly in his hand and made her look up at him. "I have reformed."

Ophelia wrenched her chin free and stepped back. She bumped the desk and a bottle fell over. Wine gurgled out across the desktop.

"I have reformed," Griffe repeated.

"People don't change," Ophelia said. "And if you ever touch me roughly again, Count, I'll tell your sister— *everyone*—about it. Is this why you're so intent on hurrying up the wedding? Because you saw something you desired, and now you're going to take it, no matter what?"

"I sense—I *know*—that you are attempting to get away." Griffe's cheek twitched.

"I'm not some—some rodent in a trap. I'm a *person*."
Ophelia took a deep breath. "Madame Dieudonné told me
something peculiar this afternoon. She told me that she was
acquainted with you before she ever set foot in Château
Vézère—"

"Lies!" Griffe slammed his fist on the desk.

Everything in Ophelia went cold and still. "I will not be
shouted at," she said in a quiet, dignified voice.

"If you mention that old woman's loathsome falsehood
to anyone, you shall *never* be the Comtesse de Griffe."

"You would break off our engagement?"

"Oui."

Tempting. Mighty tempting.

Ophelia returned to her chamber to compose herself. She
wouldn't admit to herself that Griffe had frightened her,
exactly. But she couldn't help wondering what else he could
be hiding, besides a rotten temper, a checkered past, and a
secret acquaintance with Madame Dieudonné. Griffe had
even traveled to England in the past month. Could that
journey have been somehow connected to Knight, or to the
heart complaint tablets with the English label?

Bernadette was waiting in Ophelia's chamber, eyes red,
hair disheveled, hands clasped like a soprano's.

Not this routine again.

"How *could* you, Mademoiselle Stonewall?"

Ophelia stopped in the doorway. "What is it?" Her eyes
fell on the plate of cake crumbs Abel had left. "The cake. I—"

"Do not pretend to innocence. Garon told me that you are
reluctant to marry this week—all the more reason, he quite
wisely said, to bring it about—but for you to stoop as low as
this? At the very least, I had supposed you were a young lady
of dignity and—and *normal* appetites. I baked five *gâteau
aux noix* this morning. Five! Two are utterly gone—now I

see that you have devoured them—and the others were found dumped in the slop buckets destined for the village swine."

"I didn't know that it was—"

"I do not know if you wish to marry Garon or not, Mademoiselle Stonewall"—Bernadette had gone rigid and quiet—"although an ill-bred *bourgeois* like you does not deserve his devotion. However, it has become clear that you do not wish for me to make the preparations for your wedding. You reject Maman's veil, gown, and, *oui*, the cake that was her own receipt. Should I assume you do not desire my presence even at the wedding ceremony?"

"Of *course* I wish for you to be there."

"Then why this—this *sabotage*?"

Ophelia didn't know what to say. Bernadette didn't believe a word she said.

"I see that you have no answer," Bernadette said. "Very well. Your silence is an answer unto itself."

"Which chamber is Monsieur Tolbert's?" Ophelia blurted.

"I beg your pardon?"

"Tolbert. He, ah, loaned me a book and I wish to return it."

Bernadette narrowed her eyes but replied, "His chamber lies in the southwest corner. Good afternoon." She glided stiffly out.

Ophelia looked at the plate of cake crumbs. Abel was certainly capable of eating two entire cakes, little rotter. But he didn't seem mean-spirited enough to dump the others in slop buckets.

So who had? In Ophelia's doggedness about discovering the vicar's murderer, she hadn't spent much time wondering who was sabotaging the wedding preparations. Ivy, perhaps, to make her, Ophelia, look bad, or dour Clémence, or even Bernadette, supposing her tears and indignation were a sham. . . .

Ophelia went to Tolbert's chamber. He was so very

secretive—the sneaking, the lies, and that mysterious parcel—so she knew almost nothing about him.

His chamber was locked.

There were hours to kill before Madame Dieudonné planned to tell Ophelia who she believed the murderer was. The clocks seemed to slow.

Ophelia decided to try to speak to Madame Dieudonné now; why wait? After all, the stagecoach was slated to leave soon. But when she went to Madame Dieudonné's chamber, she heard snoring, and when she peeked in, she saw the old woman snoozing. Her wig sat on the table beside the bed, and Meringue was licking her pink scalp like a lolly. Meringue saw Ophelia and growled a warning.

Ophelia closed the door; she'd have to wait.

She put on her cloak and went for a walk around the formal gardens, circling them four times. That killed only an hour, but she didn't wish to venture into the forest. She didn't even go near the ornamental canal, where that costumed ninny had clobbered her last night.

Heading back to the house, she encountered Professor Penrose in the side court.

"Ah, Miss Flax. Good afternoon. I've just spoken with the old gardener, Luc, about the belladonna berries in the orangerie." He lowered his voice. "In brief, he propagates the berries, along with other medicinal plants, in order to sell them to an apothecary as a way to earn a bit of extra money. He begged me not to mention it to the count, however, since evidently neither he nor Mademoiselle Gavage know of the scheme."

"But surely Griffe and Bernadette know about the belladonna plants," Ophelia said.

"Of course. It is Luc's mercenary scheme that they are unaware of, and I also suspect that Griffe and his sister are not entirely aware of the *number* of belladonna plants in the orangerie. There must be a dozen."

Ophelia decided not to tell Penrose about her plan to meet with Madame Dieudonné. Penrose had a bad habit of poo-pooing such notions. "What has happened to your spectacles, by the way?" Ophelia asked him. "They're bent."

"Ah, yes. I trod upon them by mistake."

Liar.

"Well, I must go," Penrose said, suddenly awkward. "Miss Banks and I are supposed to play chess. Would you care to join us? We could take turns."

"No, thank you." Ophelia didn't know how to play chess, but she wouldn't admit it to the professor. Besides which, the less time spent in Ivy's company, the better.

"Well then, I will see you at dinner."

After that, Ophelia went inside, bathed, and read some more of the de Villeneuve *Beauty and the Beast* that Penrose had given her. She was at the part where the snobbish fairies explained how the beast could *only* marry a lady of royal extraction. Ugh. She flung it aside.

"Perhaps we should all play a game," Ivy said in the salon after dinner. Everyone was assembled except Tolbert, who'd left just after dessert. "Wouldn't this château simply be *splendid* for a game of hide-and-seek? All these funny rooms and passages and hidden staircases? Not to mention the suits of armor."

Banks smiled indulgently. "My little Ivy always did love hide-and-seek. Drove her governesses quite out of their skulls with all her hiding and creeping."

Ophelia wasn't surprised.

"Perhaps a game *would* be nice," Madame Dieudonné said, winking a shriveled eyelid at Ophelia. Did she mean to tell Ophelia who the murderer was during the game? That didn't sound too wise.

"I have a better idea," Forthwith said. "I'll show you the marvelous new trick I've been practicing."

One could practically hear the inward groans. Forthwith's nightly conjuring tricks had grown tiresome.

"A game would be most diverting . . . ," Bernadette said.

Larson grunted. "Bit like hunting, what?" He hadn't killed anything that day, and he was in a simmering temper as a result.

Henrietta said, "Oh, hunting. I *did* so miss hunting while I was abed today," and angled her décolleté in Larsen's direction.

"Perhaps tomorrow, my dear," Larsen said vaguely.

Forthwith was sulky. "The trick won't take long, you know, and I've been practicing my fingers to the *bone* with the thing."

"Allow the young gentleman to show us his trick," Griffe said, "and there will be time enough later for hide-and-seek." He sent Ophelia a look that was both longing and hostile. Did he mean to corner her and demand an explanation for the cakes in the slop buckets?

"Why, *thank* you," Forthwith said in a surly tone. He sprang to his feet and went to a crimson curtain hanging against one of the walls. Ophelia hadn't noticed *that*. A gilt chair stood in front of the curtain.

"Goodness, what is that?" Bernadette asked. "Did the servants help you bring that curtain in?"

"A conjurer never gives away his secrets." Forthwith clasped his hands and spun to face the group. "I require a volunteer from the audience. A beautiful lady—"

"*Moi!*" Madame Dieudonné cried, reeling to her feet.

"Marvelous," Forthwith said with an incredulous white grin.

Madame Dieudonné dumped Meringue in Ophelia's lap and went to Forthwith's side.

Meringue circled twice and curled up in Ophelia's lap. He smelled faintly of sausages and perfume.

Forthwith whipped the crimson curtain open, revealing one of the many mirrored panels that decorated the salon walls. "Ladies and gentlemen, is vanity not the bane of the gentle sex? Is it not vanity that drives even *la plus belle du monde* to the brink of despair to see her face wither and fade?"

Madame Dieudonné's smile was slipping.

Forthwith continued. "Yes, in the end, perhaps vanity causes ladies to simply merge with their reflections and—*poof!*—*disappear.*" He took Madame Dieudonné's hand. "My dear lady, step this way." He whispered a few words in her ear, and she nodded.

Forthwith attempted to hand Madame Dieudonné up onto the chair, but she was not able to lift her foot so high. Forthwith hoisted her by the waist. She kicked arthritically and Forthwith staggered, but at last she was standing upon the chair and facing the mirror.

"Now, ladies and gentlemen," Forthwith said, "I shall cause this lady . . . *to vanish.*"

"He seems ever so *adept* at this," Ivy whispered loudly to her father.

Forthwith whipped the curtains closed. He held up his hands like an orchestra conductor.

The audience held its breath.

Forthwith whisked the curtains open. The mirror shone. No Madame Dieudonné. "Ah, where has she gone? To join, perhaps, the fairyland of self-deception and enchantment that exists inside the mirror? Let us ask her when she returns." He closed the curtains again, flourished his hands, and cried, "She returns!" He whipped open the curtains.

Madame Dieudonné had *not* returned.

17

Forthwith closed the curtains and tried again. Still no Madame Dieudonné.

"Where has she gone?" Bernadette cried.

"Forthwith, this isn't humorous," Henrietta said.

"What are you playing at, young man?" Larsen bellowed.

"She is supposed to—you see—" Forthwith raked fingers through his hair and pushed the curtains aside. He shoved the mirror, and the entire wall panel swung inward.

"Great Scott, what is the meaning of this?" Banks said.

"The château is full of such hidden doors," Griffe said. "The house was built in an era that wished for servants to be invisible."

"Well then, she must be somewhere behind the panel," Larsen said.

Forthwith pushed the panel further inward. Darkness yawned, and Ophelia felt a draft. "Madame Dieudonné?" he called.

Silence.

"Perhaps she meant to begin the game of hide-and-seek," Ivy said.

"Silly old woman," Larsen muttered.

"I *do* agree," Henrietta said.

Ophelia shushed Meringue's whining by patting his head.

"The passage leads to a servants' stair and, beyond, the kitchen," Bernadette said. "Our servants do not use these old passages anymore, and there are no lights, and the dust and cobwebs—"

"We must search for her," Penrose said. He grabbed a lit candelabra and disappeared into the passage.

Everyone waited. No one's eyes met.

A few minutes later, Penrose returned, his face begrimed and a lock of hair loose across his forehead. "No sign of her. We ought to search the château. Come on, then. We cannot allow an elderly lady to be lost."

Everyone armed themselves with candles and gas lamps and dispersed.

Ophelia took a hurricane lamp and carried Meringue. She began with a search of the library, just next door to the salon. She felt queasy. Someone had, maybe, overheard Madame Dieudonné say that she knew who the murderer was. The murderer was, to Ophelia's way of thinking, among them. So what if the murderer had made Madame Dieudonné vanish . . . for good?

But that was silly. This was all because of Forthwith's conjuring trick, and Madame Dieudonné had volunteered for that.

Ophelia found nothing of interest in the library. She searched the music room, and then the artillery gallery. Nobody. Room after room she checked, and she passed the others doing the same. What in Godfrey's green earth had become of Madame Dieudonné?

All the while, Meringue whined and squirmed in Ophelia's arms.

Wait. *There* was a notion: Meringue could sniff out his

mistress. Ophelia plopped him on the floor, and instantly he scampered off. Ophelia followed him.

Meringue trotted past several doors and up and down two short staircases. They were approaching Griffe's study.

A loud crack sounded, somewhere nearby.

Oh no.

Ophelia dashed down a long corridor and around a corner. The study door was wide open. She looked in.

Milky moonlight bathed the chamber. The eyes of the stuffed animal heads glittered. She caught a sweet whiff of burned gunpowder. A shadowy woman—*Henrietta*—stood in the center of the room, holding something shiny. Another woman—yes, it was Ivy—stood nearby, palms clamped across her own mouth. They both stared down at a black lump on the carpet.

Henrietta turned to Ophelia. "I do believe she's dead."

Ivy burst into tears.

Meringue bounded over to the lump. He whined and circled.

"Dead? Madame Dieudonné is *dead*? How can that—?" Ophelia rushed in, dropped to her knees, and turned the lump over. Madame Dieudonné's eyes and mouth gaped, and a hole in her forehead trickled black. Her bouffant wig was halfway off, revealing shiny pink scalp.

Mercy.

A dry sob heaved up from Ophelia's chest. She hunched over and tried to hear a heartbeat, hear a breath. Nothing. Nothing at all. She swung her head up to Henrietta and recognized at last that the shiny thing Henrietta held was . . . a gun.

Meringue began to lick his dead mistress's hand.

"Stop," Ophelia whispered. *"Stop."* She scooped up Meringue and stood.

Ivy sobbed.

Then there were others in the chamber—Forthwith and Larsen, rushing in with lamps. They froze when they saw Henrietta, her gun, and the bleeding corpse on the carpet.

Larsen spoke first. "Good God, Mrs. Brighton, what have you done?"

"Done?" Henrietta said in a small voice. She looked at the gun and dropped it as though it scorched her. "Miss Banks, tell them I haven't done anything. Tell them how you and I came upon the body—together—and then I picked up the gun—"

"I—I am not certain *what* I saw," Ivy said through her tears. "Everything was so very dark, and did I not come upon you already here?"

"No!" Henrietta cried. "We arrived together, stupid girl!"

Larsen put his arm around Ivy. "Now see here, Mrs. Brighton, that is no way to speak to a young lady in shock."

"But I am in shock, too!" Henrietta said.

"No, I daresay you are not," Larsen said coldly. He crouched to pick up the gun with his handkerchief, slipped it in his pocket, and led the weeping Ivy away.

Ophelia, Henrietta, and Forthwith looked down at the body. Then they looked at each other.

"Oh, let us get away from that horrible thing," Henrietta said.

"Wait," Ophelia said. "Look." She pointed to a second door, slightly ajar.

"*I'm* not going over there," Henrietta said.

"Nor I," Forthwith said.

Ophelia rolled her eyes and went to the door. It led into a gaming room, and from there, another door led back out into the corridor.

Ophelia looped around and met Henrietta and Forthwith in the corridor. "That is how someone might've gotten away," she said. "And did you see the uncorked bottle of brandy on the table? Madame Dieudonné must've sneaked in for a tipple. Probably wished to give us all a scare with the conjuring trick, or else she got confused back there in the servants' passage. And that gun must have come from the gun cabinet in the study. It's open. Henrietta, this isn't going to be pretty." She shushed Meringue's whines again. "Miss Banks knows that you're an actress—she told me as much this afternoon."

"Oh, God," Forthwith said.

"What of it?" Henrietta said.

"She knows you're using a false name and that you're only pretending at wealth. That you're an opportunist. All sorts of sinister motives could be wrung out of this."

"You know I didn't kill Madame Dieudonné, don't you?"

Ophelia paused. Truth was, she *didn't* know; she hadn't seen the murder with her own eyes. But she did know Henrietta, had known her for years, and she was sure that Henrietta wouldn't ever murder anyone. Fleece, yes, and double-cross, scam, woo, and betray. But not murder. She nodded. "I believe you."

"How on earth did that Goody Two-shoes discover my identity?" Henrietta asked. "It has been a year since I gave up acting."

"She has some sort of uncanny memory for faces," Ophelia said, "and she saw your likeness on a theater placard in London a few months back. It's only a matter of time before she catches on to me being an actress, too, and you, Forthwith, being a slick theatrical deceiver."

"Conjurer of the stage would suffice."

"But slick theatrical deceiver is so much more accurate. Why in tarnation have you been performing tricks? You're pretending to be a soap heir."

"It's because he's a show-off," Henrietta said. Then to Forthwith, "I *told* you vanity would be your undoing."

"Then that makes the two of us."

"We ought to take off tonight," Henrietta said. "The police won't be here for ages."

"With what conveyance? Where would we go?" Ophelia asked. "Into the forest?"

Henrietta swallowed.

Forthwith held up a hand. "Hold on a moment—we. Why do you refer to *we*, precious Henny? I believe you're the only one who has been caught with the smoking gun—literally. It was so very dramatic: the moonbeam, the—"

"You would cut me loose?" Henrietta asked in a scalding whisper. "You said we were two peas in a pod, Forthy."

"Oh, we are. Which means that I have no intention of scrapping my own plans for you."

"What exactly *are* your plans, Forthwith?" Ophelia said.

"Never you mind."

Sneaky devil. "Henrietta," Ophelia said, "listen. If the three of us are packed off to jail tonight, part and parcel, well, there won't be anyone left to act on your behalf. No one to stand up for you, to insist—or prove—that you're innocent. Mr. Larsen won't, for starters."

"How quickly he leaped to comfort Miss Banks," Henrietta said. "How quickly he assumed I was a killer—and after all I have done."

"What precisely *have* you done?" Forthwith asked.

"As far as I can make out," Ophelia said, "you've been devoting yourself to tricking the poor old man, Henrietta."

"Precisely. *Devoting.* And now look at me! My legs positively ache from those wretched flat boots he suggested I wear, and I've grown fat and spotty from the rich food he forced me to try. I feel like one of those *foie gras* geese."

"I wasn't going to mention it . . . ," Forthwith murmured.

"Oh, shut up, you selfish beast."

Meringue growled. Ophelia stroked his head. "When we are questioned, Forthwith, we must keep up our ruse as brother and sister and distance ourselves from Henrietta, claim we were oblivious to her tricks, claim that although we are all three from Cleveland, we only met Henrietta last week at Artemis Stunt's apartment in Paris."

"Fine," Forthwith said.

Ophelia knew he was agreeing for his own sake, not Henrietta's.

"I *knew* I should have started going to church," Henrietta said. "Or at least confession. Artemis says it's wonderfully refreshing to have your conscience wiped clean regularly, quite like a good clay face mask."

"They wouldn't allow you through the church doors, Henny," Forthwith said, kissing Henrietta's cheek. She slapped him, and he laughed.

Several pairs of footsteps and harassed-sounding voices grew louder.

Ophelia took one last, long gander at Madame Dieudonné's body on the carpet. She cradled Meringue to her chest and squared herself to face the music.

And, quite possibly, the murderer.

The Sarlat police arrived hours later, having been summoned by a servant on horseback. The first thing they did was lock up Henrietta in the dining room. She cursed them roundly, but submitted. What else could she do? And she was already half drunk.

The second thing the police did was announce that they would perform a search of the château. They corralled everyone in the salon and told them to await questioning. A gendarme guarded the door. Ophelia overheard Bernadette saying that the servants had been gathered in a similar fashion down in the kitchen.

Ivy was summoned for questioning first.

18

❧⚬❧

Ophelia sank into a chair in the salon, still holding Meringue, who did not seem to wish to leave her. Poor thing. He was destructive and smelly, but he was an orphan now. Ophelia untied his blue bow, scratched his fuzzy ears, and covertly studied the others.

After all, one of them could be a murderer. Twice over. At first, she reasoned that the murderer must've been at the ruined castle that morning, in order to have overheard Madame Dieudonné. That only left Tolbert, Banks, Ivy, and the village woman Lucile. But then she realized that someone could've overheard what Madame Dieudonné said at the castle, and *passed it on* to one of the folks who'd stayed behind: Larsen, Griffe, and Bernadette. Lucile could've even told one of the château servants.

That there could be a team of murderers working together, well, it was enough to give you goose bumps.

Yet everyone in the salon wore an innocent expression, all wide, worried eyes and churchy voices. Ophelia was pretty certain that no one would miss Madame Dieudonné. No, they were all worried about their *own* necks—with the exception of Professor Penrose. *He* was probably worrying about that crusty old jawbone.

"Miss Stonewall, I see you have a new friend," Penrose said, sitting beside Ophelia. He patted Meringue's head, and Meringue wiggled his tail.

"He likes you," Ophelia said. "Maybe *you* ought to adopt him."

"That wouldn't be very favorable for my studious image, would it?"

Griffe watched them over the brim of his wine goblet.

The police clearly did not wish for their questions and methods to be shared, so after each person was questioned, they did not return to the salon.

Ophelia's turn was brief. In fractured English the police inspector, who resembled a badger in a suit, asked for Ophelia's version of events, starting with Forthwith's mirror trick and ending with Henrietta holding the gun.

"Is Mrs. Brighton guilty?" Ophelia asked.

"But of course." Inspector Pierot chuckled. "Why does no one see to it that young ladies are educated in logic?"

"Is it illogical to think that Mrs. Brighton was telling the truth, and that she did indeed pick up the gun only after the fatal shot had been fired?"

"Why are you so very certain that Mrs. Brighton is innocent?"

"Oh, she is surely guilty," Ophelia said quickly.

"Mademoiselle Banks told me that not only did she come upon Mrs. Brighton just after the shot was fired, but she recognized her as a variety hall actress whom she had once seen on a theater placard in London."

"A variety hall actress? How shocking."

"What is more, my gendarmes performed a search of her chamber and discovered a pair of diamond cuff links belonging to Monsieur Banks. He says they disappeared on the night that Mr. Knight was murdered."

"Oh?" Planted. The murderer must have *planted* those cuff links. Which meant the murderer was trying to frame Henrietta. "She is a thief?"

"Of course. Clearly an opportunistic and grasping huntress, always on the scent of money."

Not too far from the bull's-eye. But Ophelia doubted Henrietta would steal cuff links, even diamond cuff links. Those were chicken feed compared to Henrietta's grandiose matrimonial aims.

"You appear surprised by all of this, Mademoiselle Stonewall, yet you arrived from Paris with this cunning woman."

Fingers crossed that Henrietta and Forthwith would keep the story straight. "Yes, but I only met her a week ago at the Paris home of the authoress Artemis Stunt. Mrs. Stunt tends to keep"—Ophelia cleared her throat—"rather *bohemian* company."

"Why do your parents allow you and your brother to consort with such company?"

"Artemis Stunt is an esteemed authoress, Inspector, and my father, although a soap manufacturer, enjoys reading in his spare time. He believed—correctly, I might add—that Mrs. Stunt would be an amusing hostess for my brother and me during our time in Paris."

Miraculously, Inspector Pierot swallowed it. "Very well," he said. "You may go."

Ophelia took a deep breath. "Inspector, this is going to sound a little funny, but Madame Dieudonné, well, this afternoon she told me she knew who murdered Mr. Knight. She said that she'd tell me who it was, and what proof she had, tonight. Someone must have overheard her saying this—someone in the château, or else the village woman called Lucile—and I reckon this is why she was killed. To keep her quiet."

"Monsieur Knight died of natural causes," Inspector Pierot said absently, shuffling through his notes. "Is that all, mademoiselle?"

"You can't possibly still suppose Mr. Knight died of a heart ailment," Ophelia said.

"Ah, I do. The two deaths are unrelated."

"All right, then, what about this: The whippletree on the stagecoach—the stagecoach that broke down, carrying both people who are now *dead*—was deliberately broken. The blacksmith in the village told me as much."

Inspector Pierot finally lifted his eyes from his notes. "Have you been playing detective?"

"I may speak with whomever I like. I will be the Countess de Griffe in only a few more days, Inspector. I reckon I'll have some clout in this neighborhood. I won't be dismissed like this. I—"

"I have known the count since we were both children, mademoiselle, and I would advise you not to pull too hard at the leash. He has a nasty temper."

Ophelia's breathing went shallow.

"Now then." Inspector Pierot's smile didn't make it to his eyes. "You may go. Do not return to the salon until I have finished questioning the others. In fact, as you have had such a great shock, I advise you to retire for the evening. And please, no more quizzing the village folk. You may . . . regret it. The occupants of Vézère are strange. Secretive."

Was that a warning or a threat?

Ophelia stood. "Will you arrest Mrs. Brighton—or whatever her name is?"

"She has been arrested already. We will take her to the jail in Sarlat tonight."

Oh *no*. "And Madame Dieudonné?"

"We will carry her to the morgue."

"Good. For I would not sleep a wink knowing a murderer or a corpse were still in the château."

* * *

After Ophelia left Inspector Pierot in the library, she went straight to the dining room. She rattled the door handles, but both sets of doors were locked. She supposed the police would've also locked the door that led from the dining room to the servants' passage.

"Who is there?" came Henrietta's muffled voice from inside.

"Ophelia."

"*Do* something, Ophelia. This is all your fault! If it weren't for you and your silly scheme—"

"*Shhh.*" Ophelia glanced up and down the corridor. No one was within earshot. Probably. "*My* scheme?" she whispered through the keyhole.

"You get people into jams with your odd, childish, *theatrical* taste for costumes and deceptions—"

"That isn't true." Was it? Ophelia considered herself to be a wholly practical lady. Yes, from time to time she resorted to drastic measures, but only in a pinch and when much was at stake. Henrietta was making her sound . . . *frivolous.*

"All I desire is to return to Paris." A glugging sound was followed by Henrietta smacking her lips.

"Are you drinking?"

"Nothing else to do in here. Bottles and bottles of wine on the sideboard. Why did I ever leave Paris? That Larsen doesn't care a whit for me. He fancies he longs for a lady, but what he *truly* desires is a lumberjack in a hoop skirt."

"I'm going to figure out who did this," Ophelia said. "Have you any notion?"

"Miss Banks. Little bitch."

"But you said you came upon the body together."

"We did." Another bottle-glug noise. "We were going along the corridor together when we heard the shot. We entered the study together. Madame Dieudonné was dead. I picked up the gun."

"Then why did you say it was Miss Banks?"

"Because . . . I *wish* it was her. She requires being taken down a few pegs." There was a thump, as though Henrietta had collapsed against the other side of the door.

"Henrietta? Henrietta, I'll get you out of this scrape. I promise."

"Ha! Think quite a lot of your lady detective abilities, don't you?"

Not precisely. But Ophelia did have a solid history of iron-gritted determination. "I must go now," she whispered, hearing approaching footsteps.

"If only I could flee," Henrietta said, "simply flirt my way out of those policemen's clutches and hop aboard the next train. Only, this godforsaken place doesn't have a train station for fifty miles around."

It was true; Ophelia recalled all too well the long stage-coach ride from the Limoges train station. Something shifted at the back of her mind. What was it? Something about train stations and railroads and being trapped—

A man cleared his throat just next to Ophelia. She started and, since she was still crouched, she tumbled backwards. Her crinoline and petticoats poofed. "Oh. Professor Penrose." She scrambled to her feet.

"Miss Flax," he said, giving her a hand. He held Meringue awkwardly, like one would hold a stack of books. "Your dog."

"*My* dog?"

"Who's that?" came Henrietta's muffled voice. "Professor Penrose? Professor! You must get me out of here."

"Good night, Henrietta," Ophelia said.

"Drat, the bottle's empty," Henrietta said.

Penrose led Ophelia across the corridor, into the salon. "No one wishes to look after the dog," he said. "I have heard everything from vague claims that he is a nuisance to intricately detailed accusations regarding his mode of, ah, tending to his bodily requirements. Funny things have been found on the Aubusson carpets." Penrose released Meringue onto the floor. Meringue scampered to a sofa and lifted his leg.

"No!" Ophelia cried, swooping him up. She turned to Penrose. "I must take him outside."

"Miss Flax." Penrose's voice was very low, and his eyes glittered behind his spectacles. "May I vehemently suggest that you do *not* attempt to free Henrietta—"

"What? How could you even suggest that? She is innocent."

"Is she?"

"Yes."

"She was caught with a gun in her hand, standing over a dead body. Might I propose that you do not know her as well as you believe you do?"

"Maybe I don't know *you* as well as I believed I did, Professor."

His jaw tightened. "Leave this place, Miss Flax, before it is too late. Poking about in this business at this juncture would be foolhardy. This isn't a stage play."

Why was everyone suggesting that Ophelia was some sort of drama-mad dingbat?

Penrose went on, "Whoever is behind these two murders will stop at nothing to protect themselves. They might attempt to frame you for the crimes—"

"You mean, *Henrietta* might attempt to frame me," Ophelia said in a flat voice.

"Yes. She is desperate."

"She's only drunk. And disappointed that she didn't captivate Mr. Larsen."

"If the murderer is not Henrietta, but someone else who still walks free, you could be in mortal danger. If it is a matter of means, I will purchase your railway ticket to Paris—I'll purchase your steamship passage back to the United States, if you will allow me to. It is only a matter of time before the police learn that you and Forthwith are impostors, too. All they need to do is telegraph whoever it was you said you were staying with in Paris—"

"Artemis Stunt." *Crumbs.* Please oh please, Artemis, be gone at one of your country house parties.

"The police will likely telegraph her tomorrow. Go, tonight, before it is too late."

Why was he so confounded eager to get rid of her, anyway? Ophelia set her chin. "No. No handouts, for starters, and second of all, I couldn't leave even if I wished."

"Oh?"

"The *ring*. Remember?"

"You wouldn't go through with the wedding simply on account of not being able to produce the ring? Surely Griffe would understand."

Oh, Penrose would be surprised. "I don't mean to go ahead with the wedding, but I certainly mean to figure out who stole the ring—and murdered two people—and that means staying put here at the château." Ophelia really shouldn't be talking about such things with another lady's fellow, and it was unconscionable speaking about Griffe like this in his own house. But it was time to tell Penrose the whole truth. "I *never* meant to marry Griffe. I only wished to, well, to nettle you."

"Nettle me?" Penrose knit his eyebrows.

"Yes. It was foolish, and childish, and awfully unfair to Griffe. So now I must simply buckle down, find the ring, collar the murderer, and be on my way."

"You make it sound simple."

"Well, as a matter of fact, Henrietta gave me an idea of where to start. Have you any notion where I might find a railroad map of France?"

"Then you *do* mean to leave."

"Not at all."

"I believe there is a booklet of French railway timetables that must have a map in it in the library. I saw it days ago."

"The library?" Ophelia chewed her lip. "That's where Inspector Pierot has set up camp."

"Not any longer." Penrose went to the salon doors. "Yes, I hear them coming to fetch Henrietta."

Ophelia and Penrose closed the salon doors most of the way and peered through the crack. Inspector Pierot and two gendarmes arrived, with Griffe and Larsen just behind. Griffe produced a ring of keys, and Inspector Pierot unlocked the dining room doors.

Henrietta must've been sitting and leaning on the doors, for when the doors were opened, she rolled out onto the carpet with an empty wine bottle in one hand.

"Disgraceful," Larsen muttered.

"It's your fault, you dried-up, stringy old codger," Henrietta said, not bothering to get up off her back. "*Your fault!* Do you see my face? My feet?" She lifted a leg and swiveled it.

Larsen and Griffe exchanged that special chummy gentlemen's look that said *Hysteria—SO sad.*

Inspector Pierot shook his head. "Madame, please rise. And do put your ankles and petticoats away."

"People pay big money to see my ankles and petticoats!" Henrietta shouted.

"Woman," Griffe said, "—for I will *not* address you as madame or mademoiselle, not only because we know not what you truly are or from whence you came, but because you are a wretched and deceitful creature and it is fitting that you grovel upon the floor, since you are indeed lower than the worm that crawls—"

"Oh, get to the point," Henrietta snapped. Now both her feet were in the air, and she studied them as though pondering a purchase at the shoemaker's.

Griffe flushed. "Very well. I shall. Even if the police, for some deluded reason, set you loose, do not cross my threshold again."

"She will not be set loose," Inspector Pierot said.

The gendarmes bent to grab Henrietta's arms. She kicked

each of them in a tender portion of their anatomy. They both doubled over with an *oof*. Penrose, hidden beside Ophelia, winced. The gendarmes recovered and dragged Henrietta to her feet. They led her, cursing and thrashing, away. Inspector Pierot, Griffe, and Larsen followed.

"Will you show me where to find that railroad timetable?" Ophelia whispered to Penrose. She ignored the sick hollow feeling in her stomach.

"Meet me in the library in a few minutes."

He didn't need to explain to her that they shouldn't be seen sneaking around the château together.

19

$\backsim\!\infty\!\sim$

Ophelia waited a few minutes, and then collected Meringue from his project of de-tasselling a cushion. She took him out into the side court to do his business. He didn't. Not hopeful for the château's parquet. The moon was almost full, a blameless white disk. The wind rushed through tree branches. Far in the distance, something howled, long and lonesome. Meringue growled, hackles rising. Ophelia felt too, too cold.

She went back inside to the library. Penrose arrived moments later, shut the doors, and pulled a booklet from a shelf. "The French railway timetables," he said softly.

"Thank you." Ophelia plopped Meringue on the floor and took the booklet. "Good night."

"Good night? You don't intend to tell me about your marvelous deduction?"

"Not after you told me to go to America immediately and never come back."

He scratched his eyebrow. "That is not *precisely*—"

"It's like this." Ophelia flipped through the booklet and found a map of the entire country of France with, it looked like, every railroad line. "I happened to see a peculiar newspaper article about an empty train running back and forth between—what was it?"—she squinted at the map—"yes, between Avignon and Lyon."

"And?"

"Just give me a moment." Ophelia studied the map. *Holy Moses.* "Look at this, Professor. See, the stagecoach started out in Marseille, bound for Bordeaux. Now, Mr. Knight, Madame Dieudonné, and Abel Christy were all on board, and they all wished to get to Paris. But see? Bordeaux is far, far off the path between Marseille and Paris—Paris is almost a straight shot north from Marseille, but Bordeaux is way over here on the west coast. But *we* are just between Marseille and Bordeaux, here in the Périgord."

"Wait a moment. If Knight, Madame Dieudonné, and Master Christy all wished to go to Paris, why in heaven would they go via Bordeaux? And in a stagecoach, no less?"

"It's because of that train in the newspaper article. See, they couldn't travel from Marseille to Paris by train because one critical leg of the journey, between Avignon and Lyon, was all sold out for many days. So instead of waiting around, they decided to travel by stagecoach to Bordeaux. Mr. Knight and Abel were to take a ship from Bordeaux to England—Abel told me as much—and Madame Dieudonné planned to take a different railway route to Paris, once she arrived in Bordeaux."

"And they collected Tolbert only miles from here, in Sarlat."

"Yes. He always meant to go to Bordeaux, in order to pick up the parcel waiting for him."

"It strikes me as odd that Knight and Madame Dieudonné were not willing to wait in Marseille until the railway route opened up again. After all, even factoring in a week's wait in Marseille, the stagecoach journey would take just as much, if not more time, and stagecoach travel is far more strenuous than train travel."

"Madame Dieudonné seems to have been in a lather to leave the South of France. Something about casino creditors."

"Ah."

"And Mr. Knight was in a hurry to collect a reward from the Christy's family solicitor in London, for the safe delivery of Abel."

"That sounds rather odd."

"Because he was a vicar?"

"Well, yes. Oughtn't he have escorted Master Christy to London out of a sense of duty or charity?"

"Not if he was hard up. Mr. Knight wasn't exactly the smug saint he pretended to be. He had wine stains on his shirt when he died, and Madame Dieudonné and Abel both say he was unpleasant and sneaky. And that scar on his neck—someone tried to murder him once, I'd bet."

Ophelia studied the railroad map again. The Avignon to Lyon line stretched north–south through the belly of France. "Now here's what hit me when Henrietta said she was trapped here in the Périgord, on account of the lack of close-by railroad stations. I'd already suspected that the murderer planned things out in advance by bribing the stagecoach driver, Gerard, to make the coach break down in front of the château gates. Well, what if the planning stretched back even further? What if the murderer bought out all the train tickets on that route, knowing that it would force Mr. Knight and Madame Dieudonné to travel by stagecoach to the Périgord? What if Mr. Knight and Madame Dieudonné were *lured* here, lured all the way from Marseille?"

"A trap."

Ophelia's neck prickled. "It's calculated. Devious."

"*If* your theory is correct."

"It must be. Otherwise, what could we possibly make of the absolute *coincidence* of both murder victims—supposedly strangers to everyone in the château—just showing up here, unannounced and by surprise?"

Penrose said nothing, but his tense jaw told Ophelia that he was taking her theory seriously.

Ophelia went on, "Whoever bought out the tickets on that train route, well, that would be mighty costly. Which means the murderer is very, very rich."

Griffe, Bernadette, Larsen, and Banks were *all* very, very rich, so this didn't narrow down the suspects much.

"How could we learn who bought out the train route between Avignon and Lyon?" Ophelia asked.

"I suppose the railway ticket office in one of those two cities would have the answer."

"Could we—could you—send them both a telegram?" Ophelia's ears went hot. "I could pay you back some other time—I promise I would."

"I'll go to the telegraph office in the morning." Penrose studied her. "And yes, pay me back when you are able."

"I will." Some folks might've thought it petty, a rich lord asking an unemployed actress to pay back such a small sum. But Ophelia breathed a sigh of relief. It was awful, going around begging favors all the time on account of being flat broke. The professor was allowing her to keep her dignity, and she liked him for it.

Not, of course, that Ophelia had *any* prospects for money on the horizon. With Henrietta in jail, there wasn't much hope of ever receiving the sum Henrietta had promised her in exchange for sticking out the engagement for two extra weeks. Although, of course, Ophelia felt mean to even think of that.

"Speaking of telegrams," Penrose said, "I nearly forgot what I wished to tell you earlier. I've heard from Sir Percival

Christy's solicitor in London—a courier boy brought a telegram to the château earlier this evening. Mr. Montgomery
is most distressed to learn that Mr. Knight is dead and that
Sir Christy's son is stranded in the Périgord."

"His *son*?"

"That is what he said."

That was funny. Abel had led Ophelia to believe that Sir
Christy was only his protector and that he was descended
from Nubian blue bloods.

"At any rate, because Montgomery knows me by
reputation—he is on retainer for a certain branch of my
family tree—he has requested that I escort Master Christy
to England as soon as I am able. Although now, with the
police launching a murder investigation, heaven knows when
that will be."

"You must have a good reputation, Professor."

"I make an attempt." He smiled.

"I must go now." Ophelia felt suddenly shy. "Meringue.
Meringue?" Ophelia made a kissy noise that she knew made
poodles come running. No Meringue. She heard snuffling
noises over by the windows and went over. Meringue was
gobbling something off the floor behind the drapes. Ophelia
bent to see. *Cake crumbs.*

Someone had been eating cake—her wedding cake, by
the looks of it—behind the drapes. Someone had heard
everything she and Penrose had said.

Ophelia picked up Meringue, who was smacking his
fuzzy chops. Good thing the eavesdropper had only been
Abel. She'd have a word with him first thing in the morning
regarding keeping his trap shut.

No fire, up in Ophelia's chamber. The parakeet was
puffed up on its perch, eyes shut. Ophelia got the fire going, and in its orange glow she noticed an envelope on her
pillow.

She picked it up.

Mademoiselle Stonewall

was all the envelope said.

Griffe was at it again. She opened the envelope.

Ma Chérie,

I will be occupied all day tomorrow, directing the wood-cutters and tending to other business. Pray meet me in the orangerie before breakfast. I would most enjoy choosing together the flowers with which to decorate our wedding altar. I will await your presence at eight o'clock. Do not be late.

Griffe

The orangerie? How spooky, although not as spooky as the prospect of more time alone with Griffe. But the trouble was, Ophelia couldn't stir the pot. She couldn't risk being banished from the château now, because if that happened, she wouldn't be able to sleuth any longer.

When she crawled into bed, Meringue was already sprawled on her pillow. She lay her head on the lumpy mattress and tumbled into dreamless sleep.

Gabriel could not sleep. His fascination with, desire for, the fossilized jawbone had been eclipsed. He could not stop thinking of what Miss Flax had told him: that she had never intended, not for a moment, to marry Griffe. That she had accepted Griffe's proposal only to nettle him, Gabriel.

He sank into a chair in his bedchamber and lay his forehead on a palm. He had been desperately in love with Miss Flax, in Paris, and now he was realizing something else, something that he'd been suppressing: He was desperately in love with her still.

Yet he'd affianced himself to Miss Ivy Banks.
What had he done?

Ophelia woke at dawn groggy and unrested, yet anxious
to begin the day.

She developed a plan as she dressed in a green woolen
gown.

If her theory about the railroad route was correct, then
the murderer had access to a great deal of money. Larsen
could be eliminated as a suspect because Ophelia had heard
him snoring the night the vicar had been killed.

Which left only Griffe and Banks, unless Bernadette and
Ivy somehow had access to their family fortunes. Ladies
usually did not; she must check on that.

Two suspects. That was manageable, wasn't it?

Ophelia changed the parakeet's seeds and water, noticing two grubs at the bottom of the cage. Ugh. Although the
parakeet *did* have a little more pep this morning. Next, she took
Meringue out to the front of the château. As Meringue sniffed
about, selecting the perfect spot, Ophelia kept thinking.

Regarding motives, well, if Griffe or Banks were the murderer and they'd gone through such trouble and expense to lure
the stagecoach to Château Vézère, then they must have known
Knight or Madame Dieudonné before—and they must have
held a grudge. Madame Dieudonné had claimed she'd known
Griffe before, and Griffe had flown off the handle when Ophelia had asked him about it. On the other hand, Banks could
have known Knight in England. The only connection between
Banks and Knight that Ophelia could work out was that Banks
owned silk and woolen mills, and Knight had had those bobbins of silk thread in his trunk.

Chopping sounds started up in the distance, hollow and
ringing. Ophelia squinted towards the lacy, bare trees. How
many woodcutters had Griffe employed? A dozen?

She made a kissy sound for Meringue, and he came

trotting. It was time to meet Griffe about flowers in the orangerie. She'd deposit Meringue in the salon first. She couldn't very well leave him outside if there were marauding beasts out here. Meringue might have a certain swagger, but he'd look like an hors d'oeuvre to a wolf.

The orangerie was quiet when Ophelia entered, except for the gurgling fountain. No dead fish—or live fish—in the lily pad pool.

"The fish died." That was Griffe. Ophelia turned. "They were found by Luc, floating lifeless, every one. It must have grown too cold, or perhaps the water became unclean." Griffe had not shaved, his eyes were bloodshot and pouched, and although his clothes looked clean, Ophelia caught a whiff of sour wine.

"Good morning, Count. Roses, do you think? I am content with roses—any will do."

"Eh? Brides are customarily more particular about the arrangements of their weddings," Griffe said.

"Oh, well, I've always been practical. 'Efficient Ophelia' is what everyone calls me back home in Cleveland." She strolled through the plants so she wouldn't have to look at Griffe.

He followed her. "Is this, then, why you are upset?"

"Upset? Me?"

"Because your mama and papa, your friends from Cleveland, will not be at our wedding?"

"I believe I already told you as much. I wish to marry later, in the spring—"

"*Non.* The solstice. It is a special time. The magic in the air will sanction our union."

"If you say so."

"Why do you not wear the ring I gave you? I have noted this, day after day."

"Oh, it's—well, it's a bit uncomfortable, honestly. Too tight."

"You should have told me. A goldsmith could make it larger. Bring it to me, and I will have it sent out. I wish to see it on your hand when we say our wedding vows."

"All right. Certainly."

"Why is it, Mademoiselle Stonewall, that I feel as though you no longer care for me? I lay awake last night, drinking glass after glass of wine, wondering, attempting to understand why you do not"—Griffe stopped Ophelia with a hand—"why you do not return my regard. *Pour quoi?*" He tried to rake his other hand through his mane, but it was so tangled that his fingers caught. "Everything seems to unravel. My plans, my hopes—crushed."

Did killing Knight and Madame Dieudonné have anything to do with those plans? Ophelia shrugged Griffe's hand off. They had stopped next to the rack of gardening tools.

"Three more animals had their throats torn out last night," Griffe said, moving closer to Ophelia. "A cow and two sheep, near the village. The woodcutters, are they able to chop fast enough? The wilderness seems to encroach."

Ophelia took a step back. She was just in front of the gardening tool rack now. Her poufy skirts bumped something, and the tools rattled.

"What is more," Griffe said, "Banks has fallen deathly ill."

"He has? What is the matter?"

"I would have guessed his heart—my own father was afflicted with a disease of the heart. I have seen the gasping for breath, the coughing, the ashen skin. He has taken to his bed and I have sent for a doctor. Mademoiselle Banks protested this, for she says this has occurred before, that it is not his heart, that he will recover within days. She cannot admit it to herself, even, that her dear papa might die soon. Ah, so much death in my home." Griffe stepped still closer. Ophelia had no room left between herself and the gardening tools. Griffe brushed her cheek with the back of his hand.

"Count," Ophelia said in a crisp voice, twitching away from his touch, "do the ladies of Château Vézère have, I mean to say, are they allowed to enjoy the family fortune? Does, for instance, your sister Bernadette have a fortune of her own?"

Griffe jerked back as though she'd slapped him. "Money, mademoiselle? *Money?*"

"Well, your sister's money."

"I do not believe it." Griffe emitted a humorless bark. "But of course. These are questions your papa would have asked, no? And I would have in turn inquired what sort of fortune he meant to settle upon you when we married? Ah! Where is the sentiment *romantique*? I thought you desired me for love, but *non*. How could I forget the American spirit, so mercenary, ever *bourgeois*?"

He'd gotten hold of the wrong end of the stick. "Wait just a moment—"

"Not to worry, *ma chérie*." The endearment sounded bitter now. "The women of this family have their own apportionments. You may spend what you wish, once we are married, just as my sister does." Griffe checked his pocket watch. "I must go—*mais*, first . . ." He nudged himself against Ophelia, pushing her back against the gardening implements. His fleshy lips hovered over hers as he murmured, "I believe one kiss from by betrothed is my due."

"Not till our wedding night." Ophelia ducked under his arm. The pitchfork fell and clanged on the floor. She made a beeline for the door.

"I *will* make you love me," he called after her.

She turned. "You cannot force love."

"*Non?* Wait and see."

Ophelia's heart swelled with fury. But she would *not* panic.

She left the orangerie.

20

Bernadette *did* have access to her family's money, then. How could Ophelia discover if she had bought out the Avignon–Lyon train route? Was there a way to, say, pry into her bank account? Did Bernadette *have* a bank account? As much as Ophelia hated to think it, it would probably be cleverest to simply await the train ticket offices' responses to Penrose's telegrams. Had he gone to town yet?

Ophelia loathed thumb-twiddling. Perhaps she ought to speak to Banks. After all, he was still on her list of suspects simply by virtue of being well-to-do.

But when she went to his bedchamber, the door was shut and there was no answer to her soft knock. He must have been sleeping, then. Well, he *was* ill.

What next? There was Abel, who'd been eavesdropping—and dribbling cake crumbs—in the library last night. Ophelia hiked up to his garret. The door was ajar, and she saw his dumpling-shaped form under the bedclothes, facing the wall.

"Still abed?" she said softly.

"Go away." Abel didn't turn.

"Are you sore with me?"

"No. Go away."

"All right. But first"—Ophelia stepped into the chamber and shut the door—"first I would simply like to request that you do not mention anything that you may have overheard in the library last night, between Professor Penrose and me."

"I cannot imagine to what you refer," Abel mumbled into his pillow.

"I found cake crumbs behind the drapes."

"What cake?"

"You aren't fooling me. That *was* you last night."

A pause. "Would you bring me a cup—no, a pot—of tea and some bread and butter and jam?"

"Most certainly not." Ophelia was already out the door.

If Griffe was going out to meet the woodcutters, she might check his chamber for some sort of clue. Such as, oh, a receipt for a mountain of train tickets between Avignon and Lyon.

But in the family wing, Ophelia didn't know which bedchamber was Griffe's, and besides, every door was locked. Clémence came upon her, bed linens heaped in her arms, as Ophelia tried the last doorknob.

"Mademoiselle?" Clémence said.

"Oh." Ophelia released the doorknob like a hot coal. "I was searching for a—another lavatory. The one near my own chamber has been occupied ever so long." She mimed pulling the lavatory flush-cord.

Clémence shrugged and kept going. She did not speak or understand English. Would she tell Bernadette and Griffe that Ophelia had been snooping in the family wing? Without a doubt.

Breakfast, then. And after that, chew her fingernails and wait to hear from the ticket offices.

* * *

Gabriel felt old, older than his thirty-five years. Stiff limbs, quilt batting between the ears. Four cups of strong coffee had done nothing to remedy it. He'd passed a sleepless night, filled with sweating regret, snippets of Miss Flax's words, and visions of Miss Ivy Banks's reproachful pout.

Perhaps getting his hands on that jawbone—the jawbone that was likely the relic of a fairy-tale Beast—would make him feel fresh and spry again. He would make the briefest nip into the cook's chamber to look for the jawbone before he rode into Sarlat to visit the telegraph office.

A window in the servants' stairwell was ajar. Chopping sounds rang in the distance like flat, relentless tribal music.

Creaking on the stairs below made Gabriel pause. He turned. The stairway was empty to the landing. Beyond the landing, a stair tread sighed.

"Show yourself," Gabriel called.

Silence. Then Tolbert edged into sight.

"What are you playing at?" Gabriel asked.

"I followed you, Lord Harrington. Following you always yields the most fascinating findings. Now, some would assume that you were simply seeking out a maidservant for a romp in a featherbed, but I know that set to your shoulders."

"Do you, now."

"The hunched-forward stance of a fanatic intent on his prize. My jawbone, is it not? Ah, I see from your expression that I am correct. Searching for it, where? Here in the servants' quarters? Why?" Tolbert's tongue flicked along his lower lip. "You believe a servant has it? One of the villagers?"

"You are entirely mistaken. I merely seek out someone to remove the soiled laundry from my chamber."

"I am frankly insulted that you would expect me to believe such—what do you highborn English say?—ah, piffle."

"We could stand about all day trading insults—and I

must say it is tempting—but I've more pressing things to do."

"Such as finding the jawbone—*my* jawbone."

"Is it yours? I seem to recall that you denied its very existence."

"You saw my sketch—stole a look at that, too. You are a thief, Lord Harrington. Such a nasty habit."

Gabriel went up the rest of the stairs. Tolbert knew exactly what he, Gabriel, was doing here, so why not perform the search of the cook's chamber while he had the opportunity? He went to the cook's room. Open. Tolbert crowded in behind.

With Tolbert watching, Gabriel searched the chest of drawers. Nothing but garments. He peered under the bed. A colony of dust bunnies. He pawed through the drawer in the nightstand and even looked under the pillow and patted all over the quilts. Nothing.

Tolbert sneered. "How sad—is your day spoiled, Lord Harrington?" He pulled something from his jacket. A revolver. He cocked the hammer and took aim at Gabriel's chest. "Leave the Vézère valley. Leave today, or I will kill you."

Gabriel quickly assessed the tremor of Tolbert's hand. If he hit Gabriel with a bullet, it would be through sheer luck. However, Tolbert was unbalanced. Unbalanced was dangerous. "Leave?" Gabriel asked. "Why?"

"I have made this region my place of study for the past two years, and you fancy you may simply burst in at the last moment and snatch away all that is mine? The miles I have walked, surveying the land in the hopes of sighting a fragment of a fossil or the clue to a cave's entrance." The revolver shook. "The rocks I have cracked open like a diamond slave. All of my study, sweat, and time has gone into this, and you, like the lord you are, hope to steal all of the credit? No."

"I presume, Tolbert, that you do not refer only to the jawbone."

"Ha! Attempting to trick me into revealing everything?"

"There *is* something more, isn't there?" Gabriel said. The burning began again in his heart, the burning that had been eclipsed, for a few brief hours, by thoughts of love and Miss Flax. Gabriel knew the stories of the Yeti, the Loch Ness Monster, the furred man-beast of the American Rockies. Could it be that Tolbert wasn't simply hunting for fossils but for a *living* relic? "What is out here in the hills, Tolbert? What, besides caves filled with paintings and fossils? *What?*"

"Ah, you perspire, Lord Harrington. Human after all, then."

"You enjoy toying with human beings."

"Human beings are of no interest to me." Tolbert's finger stroked the gun's trigger. "They are so frightfully predictable, you see. Science, now, hard facts, *those* are truly alluring."

"Science? Hard facts? You are dabbling in the stuff of fairy tales, man."

"*You* believe this matter concerns fairy tales. I believe— no, I *know*—that I have discovered a missing link in the history of *Mammalia*. That, Lord Harrington, is more magical than any woman's puerile story."

"Why have you set up a shrine in that cave? Is *that* but a scientific experiment?" Gabriel detected nothing in Tolbert's eyes. No honesty, no deceit. Only a wall.

"I saw the shrine of which you speak," Tolbert said. "That was not my doing."

"Then whose was it?"

"God knows. The peasants, perhaps—superstitious, in-bred fools—or that teary mess, Mademoiselle Gavage. *She* is positively worshipful of the forest creatures, you realize."

"What evidence have you?"

"I came upon her in the wood, singing a nursery song to a rabbit."

That didn't sound worshipful. That sounded *batty*. Although, Gabriel had noted that Bernadette did not eat any meat.

Gabriel said, "I was told that you made off with a bone of the great fossil lizard *megalosaurus* that belongs to the natural history museum in Paris. That you kept the bone enshrined upon a pillow in your bedchamber—"

"Lies! I have enemies." Tolbert regripped his pistol handle—his fingers must have been sweaty—and stepped closer. "Who told you that? One of your Oxford, how do you say, *chums*?"

"Never mind." Gabriel pushed past Tolbert, into the corridor.

The young boy, Abel Christy, peeked out a door. "Lord Harrington?" he said, rubbing his eyes.

"Go into your chamber and lock the door," Gabriel said.

Abel shut the door, and the latch clicked.

Gabriel turned to Tolbert. "You will go now, and take your damned gun with you. Go on, then. You would not shoot me."

"I would."

"No. You are a coward."

Tolbert's hooked little face turned purple. He clubbed Gabriel across the cheekbone with the gun's butt.

Gabriel grabbed a fistful of Tolbert's shirt. "Go," he growled, and half threw, half pushed Tolbert towards the stairs.

"You will not have that bone!" Tolbert shrieked up the stairwell as he retreated. "You will not have *any* of my prize! Leave this valley, Lord Harrington, or you will never get out alive!"

Gabriel didn't respond. He pressed fingers to his cheekbone. No broken skin, but it throbbed like the dickens. After a minute, he went downstairs, too.

If Tolbert did not have the jawbone, and the jawbone wasn't in the cook's chamber, then perhaps the cook had taken it elsewhere. Somewhere outside the château.

Gabriel went to the stables and found a freckle-faced stable boy napping in one of the stalls.

Gabriel rapped on a post.

"Oui, monsieur," the stable boy said, struggling upright.

Gabriel tossed a coin, and the boy caught it. "Prepare a horse for me. I must ride to town."

"*Oui, monsieur.*" The boy's eyes slanted to and from Gabriel's bruised cheekbone, and then he went to fetch a horse.

As the boy finished with the saddle, Gabriel said, "Tell me, lad, where does the château cook go on her days off?"

"Marielle? To her sister's house in the village."

"Who is her sister?"

"Marguerite, the midwife—the blacksmith's wife."

"The woman who claims to have sighted the beast two nights ago whilst nursing her child?"

"Yes."

That the cook's sister was also the blacksmith's wife was nothing strange. Such interlacing was common in small villages. Still, unease rolled in Gabriel's belly. He didn't quite know why. "Do you suppose Marielle will be at her sister's home today?"

"Well, that is uncertain. The whole village is preparing for a"—the stable boy ducked his head, rubbing his nose with a knuckle—"for a celebration. The women are all making pinecone garlands at Jeanne's house today."

"For the upcoming wedding?"

"What? No! Oh—do you mean the count's wedding?"

"Of course." Why was the lad so unnerved? "Thank you." Gabriel mounted the horse and set off for Sarlat.

"There you are, Miss Stonewall," Ivy said when Ophelia seated herself at the breakfast table. Only Ivy and Forthwith were there, sitting side by side. "You must miss your friend Mrs. Brighton awfully—is that why you appear so pale? *So* sad she was forced to spend the night in jail—but then, I suppose she must get used to it." Ivy buttered a roll.

"Good morning," Ophelia said. Meringue bounded in from somewhere and hopped onto her lap. "Your father has taken ill, the count tells me."

"Yes." Ivy fluttered her eyelids. "But he takes turns now and then—no one really knows why. I'm certain he'll be well by tomorrow.

Ophelia looked around at the untouched place settings. "Where is everyone?"

"Larsen's already out stalking his beast," Forthwith said, "and God knows where everyone else has gone."

"I fancy everyone's afraid of being murdered," Ivy said, "so they're hiding. Of course, I believe one of the servants did it. The locals here are frightfully devious."

Forthwith checked the clock on the mantel. "I must be going, myself. The count has given me the use of his coachman and carriage to drive into Sarlat this morning."

"Oh? Whatever for?" Ivy asked.

Forthwith paused, and then flashed a smile. "Why, to call upon the wretched Mrs. Brighton in jail."

He was up to something. Ophelia was sure of it.

"That deceitful creature?" Ivy said. "Why would you visit *her*?"

"Mrs. Brighton is indeed a sorry example of womankind," Forthwith said, "but I feel it is my duty as her countryman to see to it that she is being treated in a humane fashion by the police."

Ophelia said, "I'll go with you." She would figure out what Forthwith was doing in Sarlat if it was the last thing she did.

"Sister, that will not be necessary. In fact—"

"You cannot talk me out of it."

Forthwith sighed. "Oh, very well. But I wish to leave in ten minutes. The carriage is supposed to be waiting in the front drive then."

Ophelia cut open a boiled egg and spooned it into Meringue's mouth.

"How revolting," Ivy said with a shudder. "Mr. Stonewall, do you always allow your sister to display such barbaric manners?"

"I would thrash her soundly if we were back in Ohio."

"You'd wind up with a black eye, too," Ophelia said.

Ivy looked shocked.

"I can't very well starve the poor animal," Ophelia said. Meringue licked egg yolk from his muttonchops.

"Why don't you take him to the hunting dogs' kennels for some kibble?" Forthwith asked.

Ophelia shook her head. "And risk him being poisoned?"

"There *is* quite a lot of poison floating about this place, isn't there?" Ivy said. "I first thought that, of course, when Mr. Knight was discovered with all those bottles of medicine lying about in the orangerie, and then I thought it again when Madame Genepy was taking heart tablets when I visited her yesterday."

"Was she?" Ophelia asked.

"Oh, yes. And then I thought of poison *again* when I saw Bernadette putting some little tablets in bits of cheese, and *then*—"

"Wait," Ophelia said. "What was that about Bernadette putting tablets in cheese? When?"

Ivy scrunched her forehead, finger to her cheek. For a young lady who purportedly read Latin and Greek, she certainly excelled at looking like a numbskull. "I suppose it was the morning before we all went out hunting together. The day before yesterday. I wished to ask her about borrowing a pair of gloves for the hunt, and I found her in the pantry, poking tablets into bits of cheese and placing them in a basket. I thought nothing of it, although she did seem startled to see me. She gave the basket to a manservant and led me upstairs."

"That was the day the hunting dogs were poisoned," Ophelia said. Meringue gobbled more egg off the spoon.

"Was it?" Ivy took a pixie's bite of roll and chewed. "I think I will be *ill* if I must continue to watch you feeding that horrid poodle. Mr. Stonewall, can't you do something? Make it all just—*disappear*?"

Forthwith's jaw was tight. But he could not resist showing off—he never could. "Very well, Miss Banks. I will consent to making my sister's egg and spoon disappear but not, alas, the poodle, for fear of a black eye." He whipped out a handkerchief from his pocket. Something thunked on the floor beside him.

Ivy looked down. She gasped.

Ophelia looked under the table. A brown medicine bottle, just like the one she'd seen in Knight's pocket, lay on the carpet.

"Are those . . . heart tablets?" Ivy said, touching her throat. "Is that the bottle that was found in poor Mr. Knight's pocket, Mr. Stonewall?"

"The police kept that bottle," Ophelia said.

"It isn't mine," Forthwith said.

"But it fell from your pocket," Ophelia said.

Forthwith bolted to his feet, knocking his chair to the floor. "Well, it isn't mine!" He stormed away without righting the chair.

"*Well* then," Ivy said, and took a prim sip of coffee.

Ophelia didn't know what to say to Ivy. But she did know that she must ride with Forthwith to Sarlat and find out what he had up his sleeve. She got up. "Would you mind Meringue for a few hours?" she asked, plopping the dog on Ivy's lap.

Ivy stiffened. "Oh. I suppose. Animals simply *adore* me. I've got a King Charles spaniel at home. Little Roddy."

Meringue growled.

"I'll take that as a yes." Ophelia righted Forthwith's chair and went to fetch her cloak and bonnet.

21

The carriage ride to town was awkward. Forthwith kept tossing Ophelia dark looks, and she tried to keep up the sprightly routine.

Why hadn't she thought of Forthwith as a suspect before? Forthwith had a motive for both murders: to keep his true identity concealed. If Knight or Madame Dieudonné had discovered that he was really a conjurer of the stage, not a soap heir from Ohio, well, he might've been inclined to permanently shut them up.

Of course, Forthwith didn't have a penny to his name— supposedly. And if Ophelia's theory about the bought-out train route as a way to lure the murder victims to Château Vézère was correct, then Forthwith couldn't have afforded it, for starters.

But . . . what if Forthwith had an accomplice? An accomplice such as Larsen? Had Larsen snored all through the night the vicar had been killed while Forthwith did the dirty work? Because it sounded as though Larsen had the wherewithal to buy up every train ticket in France for a year. Forthwith might have a motive for murder quite, quite different than simply trying to cover up his confidence artist tracks.

And—oh mercy, of *course*—Forthwith's parlor tricks had been integral in both murders, had they not? That first night, he'd performed the trick with the rosebush, and Knight had died clutching a rose. And then Madame Dieudonné's disappearance through the mirror, well, what if Forthwith had orchestrated that trick only to give himself—or Larsen—a chance to kill?

"That wasn't my bottle of heart tablets, quite obviously," Forthwith said out of the blue, after ten minutes of jostling along the winding road in silence.

"Oh?" Ophelia affected disinterest.

"Someone must have placed it in my pocket. To make me appear . . ." Forthwith scratched his upper lip. "Appear guilty." He twitched a curtain aside and peered out the carriage window. He wore a greatcoat over a jacket, but neither was buttoned, and Ophelia saw an ivory pistol handle. "Miss Banks," he said.

"Miss Banks?"

"I suppose she put that medicine bottle in my pocket. She was sitting just beside me at the breakfast table—she could have done it easily. Do you think it was only a coincidence how she talked of all the poison floating about the château, and then, lo and behold, I discovered a bottle of medicine in my pocket?"

"You didn't believe what she said about Bernadette putting tablets in cheese, do you?"

"It didn't have the ring of truth, no. Miss Banks is a liar."

"Have you proof?"

"I simply *know* it. Call it magician's intuition."

"Why would Miss Banks spread falsehoods about Bernadette? Why would she plant a medicine bottle in your pocket? She was with Henrietta when the shot that killed Madame Dieudonné was fired. Miss Banks isn't the murderer."

"She planted that bottle to stir up trouble. Or to make us nervy. You said Miss Banks might know that we're not who we claim to be, Ophelia, so perhaps she's having a bit of fun with us. There is something not right with that young lady. She's as pretty as picture, oh yes, but her eyes have got this weird glitter. They remind me of animal eyes—you can't quite get through to the other side."

Ophelia agreed. But she was so suspicious of Forthwith, she couldn't help wondering if he was disparaging Ivy only to muddy the waters.

Gabriel watered his horse at an inn and left it there. He walked through the center of Sarlat towards the telegraph office. Cafés spilled out from the crooked medieval buildings facing the square in front of the Hôtel de Ville—the city hall. Men drank coffee and read newspapers, bundled in coats, their faces turned up to the pale sunlight.

Gabriel glanced idly at the men as he passed, but his breath caught when he recognized a face: Gerard, the stagecoach driver who had been expelled from Château Vézère for harassing the maidservant Clémence.

Gerard sat at an outdoor café table with a lady. The lady wore lip paint and dangling earrings, and she laughed like a donkey, head tipped back.

Gabriel approached. "Good morning," he said in French. "Aren't you the stagecoach driver, Gerard?"

"That I am, that I am," Gerard said, "and I recognize you, my lord, from the château. Course, the likes of me aren't good enough for the count and his house. Hell, I am not even good enough for his wenches!"

The painted lady brayed with laughter.

Gerard was drunk, and apparently he was a generous drunk, for he invited Gabriel to join them. The painted lady looked Gabriel up and down as he sat. Having doubtless assured herself of the fine quality of his coat, she smiled.

They made pleasantries. Despite the early hour, Gabriel accepted a glass of wine—it was a solid Bordeaux—and said, "What a fine vintage. Rather costly stuff, I daresay."

"Nothing but the best for sweet Emerald." Gerard stroked the back of the lady's neck.

"Does the stagecoach company pay you so well?" Gabriel asked.

Gerard's eyes narrowed. "What a rude question for a lord. But then, you're drinking with the likes of *me*, so . . ." He grinned, showing tea-colored teeth.

"You destroyed the coach's whippletree, didn't you?"

"Coach broke down all by itself."

"Rubbish. The whippletree rings were cut."

"I think I'll just show myself to the gent's." Gerard stood on swaying legs. "When I get back, I trust you and your toffee nose'll be gone." He staggered off.

"Well?" Emerald said, leaning her bosom over the tabletop.

"I beg your pardon," Gabriel murmured. He stood and followed Gerard into the gloom of the café.

Gabriel found him relieving himself into a stone basin in the murky rear courtyard. Gabriel didn't wait for him to finish; there was something to be said for catching a man at his most vulnerable.

"Who paid you to disable the stagecoach?" Gabriel asked.

Gerard fumbled with his trousers. "No one."

"Don't make me lose my temper."

"A soft-pawed highborn gent like you?"

"My paws are not particularly soft."

Gerard licked his lips. "I didn't choose to get mixed up in this. I just want out of this godforsaken valley. It smells bitter—food's bitter, wine's bitter, the very air smells bitter. Like death."

"Enough of the poetics," Gabriel said. "Tell me who paid you, and I'll be on my way."

"They said they'd kill me if I told anyone about any of it."

Good God. Miss Flax had guessed correctly. The murderer *had* bribed the coachman to destroy the whippletree. "Who?"

"I laughed at the time but now, with two murders up at the chateau, I know they mean it."

"Who?"

"Don't know."

Gabriel withdrew the Webley revolver from his jacket. He didn't mean to use force with this pitiable drunk, but a display of intimidation was, alas, required.

Gerard stepped back, bobbing his Adam's apple. "What I mean to say is, I never knew who it was on account of I got my directions, and the first packet of money, well, anonymously."

"Tell me everything."

"I drive the Marseille-to-Bordeaux route every fortnight, and we always stop at the same inn here in Sarlat to feed and water the horses and change passengers. Well, this last time we stopped in Sarlat—"

"Four days ago."

"Yes—a letter was waiting for me—a woman brought it out from the inn, said it had been left for me, she knew not by whom."

"A letter."

"Well, a letter, and a nice thick packet of money. The letter only said, brief like, to cut the whippletree rings three miles outside of Sarlat, on the Vézère River road."

"Just before the Château Vézère gates, then."

"As it turned out, yes."

"Did you keep the letter?"

"I'm not a fool. Burned it."

"Did it say anything else?"

"It said that if I did the job well and kept my mouth shut, there'd be more money coming. But if I slipped up . . ." Gerard's eyes shifted about, never landing on anything. "If I mucked it up, I would be killed. They've been watching me these days past. I feel it. What a relief, getting out of that château, despite the free wine and vittles. Now, I reckon I'm a dead man, you knowing all this, making me tell. You've killed me, my lord."

Gabriel left Gerard standing there.

After visiting Henrietta, Ophelia and Forthwith paused on the police station's steps. The police station was the same sulphur-yellow stone as every other building in town, and although it lay across the street from a pretty park, it still gave Ophelia's chest an iron-cold feeling. It didn't have enough windows.

Forthwith put on his tall beaver hat. "Well, *that* was revolting. All that clinging, all those tears. The pimples on her nose! I feel as though I need to bathe. I wonder if they'll really chop her head off in the public square."

Ophelia felt sick. Guillotines were supposedly more humane than, say, hanging, but they gave her the all-overs. "I've never seen Henrietta so low," she said. Henrietta's curls had been matted, and last night's face paint circled her eyes.

"Mm, quite a disaster, wasn't she?" Forthwith checked his pocket watch. "Listen, meet me back here at the carriage in half an hour. I have some business to attend to."

Ophelia bet he did. "Allow me to accompany you."

"Heavens no, Ophelia. We aren't *friends*, let alone siblings, and we needn't keep up the ruse in private. Feeling lonely, now that your fiancé has turned into a rude lout and that Penrose fellow has found a prettier, younger lady to woo?" Forthwith trotted down the steps and off down the cobbled street.

Ophelia waited until he'd rounded the corner before following. The street curved, sloping gently down, and funneled out into a web of busier streets. She spied a beaver hat, bobbing in the current of pedestrians, and followed it.

The beaver hat ducked into a café. Ophelia poked her head in.

There—the beaver hat! But wait. That wasn't Forthwith; it was a middle-aged gent with a waxed moustache. She had followed the wrong person.

Drat.

"Mademoiselle?" a waiter said.

"Pardonnez-moi," Ophelia murmured, and went back out onto the street. She looked left and right. No Forthwith.

Ophelia wandered along the street, searching for Forthwith. Old buildings rose up crookedly, and none of the streets went in a straight line. How she missed good old New England, with its right-angled white buildings and fresh fields.

Aha. Here was one of the apothecary's shops. She might ask about the château gardener peddling those belladonna plants in the orangerie.

She pushed into a cramped shop whose walls were built, floor to ceiling, with carved shelves full of bottles and jars.

The shopkeeper, an elderly woman in a black gown and dyed curls, helped the lone customer. Ophelia loitered until the customer bunked off. When Ophelia had the shopkeeper's ear, her pitiful French could not express her question well. She left the shop, cheeks hot, with the distinct impression that the shopkeeper thought *she* wished to purchase a large quantity of belladonna berries.

After more wandering, she found a second apothecary's shop, the dingier, dustier sort.

"Oui, mademoiselle?" the portly man behind the counter said.

Ophelia managed to make her question understood: Did Château Vézère's gardener sell belladonna berries to him?

"Non." The shopkeeper frowned and said in French, "Only the grand lady of château comes here, for her sleeping tablets."

"Mademoiselle Gavage?"

"Oui."

"Merci, monsieur." Ophelia went out.

Sleeping tablets! Maybe Ivy hadn't been fibbing about Bernadette putting tablets in bits of cheese, after all. But then, did that make Bernadette the murderer? If she was, Ophelia realized she ought to be back at the château, not tailing Forthwith in Sarlat.

Actually, it was nearly time to meet Forthwith back at the carriage, anyway. Ophelia went in that direction. Half a block later, she spotted Forthwith up ahead, leaving a shop with a small parcel tucked under his arm. He hadn't seen her, and he walked with a jaunty step in the direction of the carriage.

Grand.

Ophelia waited until he was out of sight before hurrying to the shop from which he'd emerged. IMPRIMEUR, the hanging wooden sign read. She peered into the display window. Stacks of fancy stationery. A printer's shop.

Inside, it smelled of flat ink and sweet, pulpy paper. Printing presses of gleaming wood and brass occupied half the shop, and two men in shirtsleeves bent over their work. A shop counter and shelves with stationery filled the other side.

Had Forthwith simply been purchasing stationery? He wasn't exactly the letter-penning sort. Ophelia approached the young woman at the counter.

"*Pardonnez-moi, l'homme avec le chapeau*, um, beaver," she said, tongue scrambling.

"I speak English," the woman said with a smile. "If you prefer."

Thank Theophilis. "I do prefer. The gentleman who left a few moments ago—wearing a beaver hat—"

"The American gentleman?"

"My brother. He forgot part of his purchase, and asked that I collect it for him."

The woman furrowed her brows. "Why did he not come back himself?"

"Oh. Too hungry. He is going directly to the café."

The woman gave Ophelia a funny look, but turned and

checked one of the cubby holes in the shelf behind her. "He left behind nothing from his order."

"His order of stationery," Ophelia said, trying to sound sure of herself.

"Stationery? Why, no. The American gentleman collected his order of the strange little labels with the beast upon them."

Ophelia's jaw fell. "I beg your pardon—beast?"

The woman's expression closed. "You are his sister, you say?"

One of the men at the printing presses called something to the woman that Ophelia couldn't understand, but she reckoned it was something to the effect of *is there any trouble?*

"Well, I must be going." Ophelia left before anyone could stop her.

22

〜❧〜

Now it was certainly time to meet Forthwith back at the carriage; Ophelia saw a clock tower. What could Forthwith be doing, having labels printed with beasts on them? He was surely at the bottom of this mystery. And Larsen was mixed up in it somehow, too. To top all, Bernadette bought sleeping tablets at the apothecary's shop. Was there no one in the château who *wasn't* a scheming scab? Besides Abel and the professor, of course.

As Ophelia passed through a crowded square, she saw Professor Penrose step out of a storefront. Speak of the devil.

He saw her. There is a moment, Ophelia reckoned, when you could see the truth in people's faces. Most of the time, people were actors, going about performing the person they *hoped* to be. But when someone caught sight of you unexpectedly (or when you saw your own face by accident in a mirror), you saw through the mask.

When Ophelia saw Professor Penrose see *her*, she read surprise on his face, followed by vulnerability, hopefulness, friendship, and . . . *love*? But when he'd said he loved her last month, he hadn't really meant it.

Her heart stuttered and her feet stopped. Walkers flowed around her.

In a flash, Penrose's face arranged itself into the genial, composed expression he customarily wore. He smiled as he walked towards her.

"Miss Flax. Good morning."

"What's happened to your face? Things keep *happening* to it. Oh. And good morning."

Penrose touched the pink welt on his cheekbone. "I'm not certain I ought to tell you."

"Professor."

"Tolbert."

"What!"

"Smacked me with a revolver."

Ophelia's hands went cold. "Why?"

"He is unbalanced, and rather angry that I am—or so he believes—searching for the fossilized jawbone, which he considers his."

"You were searching for it. Where? In his chamber?"

"I'd already checked there."

"You're very busy."

"Then that makes two of us." Penrose's mouth quirked. "I went to look through the cook's chamber, in the hopes that she had hidden the jawbone there—and your ring, actually—after withholding those items from the secondhand shop. Although why a woman of that sort would keep a fossil, I've no notion. I keep worrying that someone has given it to their dog to chew."

"Then you didn't find it?"

"No. I merely succeeded in further agitating Tolbert. I'm firmly convinced now, however, that it was he who set up that shrine in the cave. He may be, vocationally speaking, a man of science, but he has the heart and soul of a fanatic. Oh—I spoke with the stagecoach driver, Gerard. He's here in town, and you were correct. He was bribed by an anonymous person to cause the stagecoach to break down, just before Château Vézère's gates. He received a packet of money for his trouble—and to keep his mouth shut."

"I knew it. He didn't say who?"

"I don't believe he knows, truthfully."

"A packet of money, then? Yes, the murderer is someone rich."

"Speaking of which, I've just come from the telegraph office. I sent messages to both the Avignon and Lyon ticket offices of the Compagnie des chemins de fer de Paris à Lyon et à la Méditerranée."

"What in tarnation is *that*?"

"A railway company with an excessively convoluted name. I'll check back first thing tomorrow for a reply."

"Thank you. And I *mean* to pay you back."

"I know that you will."

"I must go. I've come into town with Forthwith, and I fancy he won't wait more than a minute for me if I'm late. Tolbert isn't the only one brandishing a gun, you know. Forthwith has one."

"Now?"

"Yes."

"Ride with me back to the château—we could hire another horse. Better yet, do not return to the château at all. People are behaving oddly, and whoever the murderer is, well, they'll become desperate—they already *are* desperate, actually— and they must know that you're snooping about in this business."

"Not go back? No! I'm getting closer to the murderer, I feel it. Besides, I can't run off without returning the count's ring, and I certainly can't allow Henrietta to go to the guillotine."

"I do understand. But—"

"And I wish to ride back with Forthwith to—to ask him about something." Ophelia didn't wish to tell Penrose about the printer's shop and what the shopgirl had said about beast labels. Nor did she have any inclination to share her suspicions about Forthwith and Larsen being in cahoots. Penrose's knee-jerk response was to treat her like a demure, delicate lady. Which she wasn't.

"Please don't ride with Forthwith," Penrose said.

"I must."

"There must be a better way. A safer way. Would you take my revolver?"

"*You're* carrying a gun, too?" Ophelia rolled her eyes. "It's like the Oregon Territory hereabouts."

"Take it."

"No. I could never use it, and letting others see that you've got a weapon only makes their blood boil. In the circus, the ringmaster always fired a gun—only a blank—up into the air to mark the beginning of the show, and let me tell you, some of the sauced fellows in the audience got the wrong idea more than a few times, and whipped out their *own* guns. Caused a stampede in the audience, once, and then one of the elephants got into the mix—don't *look* at me like that, Professor. No, I'm going to ride back with Forthwith. I'll see you soon."

Penrose grabbed her arm. "Miss Flax, I beg you not to—"

She shook him off and turned tail. The professor was so confounded bossy.

Forthwith was waiting inside the carriage. His legs were crossed, and he bobbled his foot impatiently. The paper-wrapped parcel sat on the seat beside him. "I haven't got all day, Ophelia. Lord. Where have you been?" He rapped on the ceiling, and the carriage rumbled forward.

Ophelia stuffed down her unease. What of it if she was trapped in a carriage with a possible murderer?

"Where have I been?" she said. "Oh, wandering around. Quaint little town, isn't it? My *Baedeker* says the town center dates to the middle ages." Ophelia inched to the edge of her seat, eyes on Forthwith's parcel. "Funny, isn't it? Back in America, I reckoned the buildings from the colonial days were ancient, but that's nothing, is it?" She snatched up the parcel and tore off the brown paper. Dozens of little paper rectangles cascaded out.

"What in hell are you doing?" Forthwith yelled. He fell to his knees and began frantically to gather up the papers.

Ophelia held one up—they were all the same. There was a beast on the label as the woman in the printer's shop had said, sure. But not the half-man, half-boar variety. No, Forthwith's little papers were printed with the image of an American buffalo. Words curved over and under the buffalo:

Stonewall's Magic Buffalo Soap

"Patented and Pure"

Est. 1867

Forthwith grabbed Ophelia's wrist, hard. She cried out, and he nipped the paper away. "You may be an accomplished trickster, darling, but it is I who specialize in sleight of hand," he snarled.

"What *is* all this?" Ophelia said. "Did you kill Mr. Knight? Did you kill Madame Dieudonné?"

Forthwith gathered up the last fallen papers and stuffed them into the torn wrapping. "Damn it, you dirtied them, Ophelia."

"Tell me!"

Forthwith got back on the seat. "You suppose I killed those two? Why would I?"

Ophelia pointed at the torn parcel. "To protect whatever scheme you've got cooking. The sneaky talks with Mr. Larsen. The gun in your jacket—yes, I saw it."

"Knight and Madame Dieudonné were both strangers to me. I didn't kill them. God, what a waste of tuck *that* would be. Why murder people when you might simply outfox them?"

"Stonewall's Magic Buffalo Soap? What is that? And if

it's so magical, why didn't you launder that belladonna-stained hankie of yours?"

Forthwith slitted his eyes. "How do you know about that?"

"Oh. I may have borrowed your trousers to, um, climb a cliff."

"What?"

"Never mind. The point is, I saw the hankie."

"That wasn't mine. It was planted, just like that bottle of heart tablets this morning."

"By Miss Banks?"

"Maybe. Whoever planted the hankie probably hoped a servant would find it. Don't you see? The murderer is creating distractions. Smoke screens. Magician's bread and butter, you understand. Make everyone look the other way while you do your business."

"All right, then what about Stonewall's Magic Buffalo Soap?"

Forthwith lounged back in his seat and folded his arms. "It's quite simple. I hatched a scheme, during that wretched journey here during which Henrietta did nothing but gush like a girl in pigtails about that cadaver Larsen. He sounded ripe for the picking, and when Henrietta mentioned his fascination with the American West—the plains and tepees and antelopes bounding into the sunset and all that rubbish—well, I had a brilliant notion. Since I'd already been recruited to play your brother, Mr. Stonewall the soap heir, I decided to get Larsen to invest in my soap company."

"What soap company?"

"My false soap company, which employs a secret, patented ingredient derived from the gopher claw bush, one that has been used for eons by the natives of North America."

"It has?"

Forthwith snorted. "Of course not. There is no such thing as a gopher claw bush. But Larsen liked the cut of my jib, and that was the important thing. I spun him a tale of woe, about how I yearned to break away from Father's tyrannical clutches—old man Stonewall, don't you know—and build a company of my own. He utterly sympathizes and, provided I produce a solid business strategy that could convince other investors, he is prepared to invest a small fortune in my company."

"But you haven't *got* a company." Ophelia rubbed her temples. "What do you—you mean to accept a small fortune from Mr. Larsen and then—what?"

Forthwith made a lazy, abracadabra wave. "Vanish."

"You're a thief. A confidence man."

"Well, you would know, Ophelia dear. And if you so much as breathe a word of this, I'll expose *you* as an actress faster than you can say *guillotine*." Forthwith smiled.

Ophelia scowled out the carriage window. Given that Forthwith had the morals of a brick, he could be lying about all of this. He still could be the murderer. Yet for some reason she was inclined to believe him. The soap, the investment—it all rang plausible to her ear. But with Forthwith off the list, who was left? Only Griffe, Bernadette—mustn't forget the sleeping tablets and the cheese—and Banks, who was, if nothing else, very rich.

With Henrietta wilting in jail, and with only a day until Ophelia was supposed to walk down the aisle—only a day left, that is, to find the missing ring—it seemed like an impossibly long list.

Gabriel located the blacksmith's shop from a long way off, by the dirty ribbon of smoke rising from its forge. As he drew closer, walking along the muddy track into the village, he heard the prismatic clang of hammer on iron.

The blacksmith—Gabriel had been told he was called Marcel—was at work, then. But the stable boy had said all the women would be elsewhere, making garlands for some village celebration.

Gabriel slowed, formulating a plan. The shop stood to the side of a cottage. No smoke rose from the cottage chimney. Gnarled fruit trees clumped behind the cottage, and beyond that spread a field dotted with sheep. Cottages stood on either side of the blacksmith's cottage, but at a distance of several yards and screened by more trees.

Gabriel could simply sneak around and enter through the back—provided no one was home. And the clanging of Marcel at his forge would be a constant indication of *his* whereabouts.

If anyone asked Gabriel what he was about, he could say he wished to hear firsthand the woman's account of seeing the beast.

A pause in the clanging made Gabriel stop. But a moment later, the hammering started up again. He picked his way to the rear, crouched behind a fence, and watched the cottage windows. No motion behind the dark, leaded panes. After several minutes, Gabriel crossed the weedy garden.

How odd that a village woman did not tend her garden. Surely her family would benefit from the crop of greens or onions or herbs that this little plot could yield. Perhaps the villagers gardened in a communal plot.

Gabriel knocked gently on the door, and waited. Nothing—and no barking dogs, thank God. Come to think of it, dogs were oddly absent in this village.

He slipped through the door—unbolted—and found himself in a one-room living space half lit by small windows. Low-beamed ceiling. Unlit hearth, ashy and smoking. A pile of frilly, wild-looking mushrooms on the table.

He listened for creaking floorboards, but if anyone was upstairs, they were still. Outside, the clanging went on and on.

Gabriel sprang to action. All he desired was the jawbone, and there weren't many places it could be hidden in this humble place. He checked the mantelpiece and the crude chest beside it. Nothing but a half-made gown of pale gold, homespun flax. He found a small cupboard under the stairs, but that was filled with broom, mop, bucket, and rags.

He turned to the table, covered with food preparation in progress: the mushrooms on the cutting board, a bowl of shelled acorns, a pile of swampy-smelling greens, a wild game hen, dried berries. This explained why the woman of the house did not bother with her back garden: All of this food had been foraged or hunted from the forest.

In the china hutch, stacks of mud-colored stoneware. Gabriel opened the hutch's lower doors. The odor of decaying wood puffed out, and he cringed as his hand plunged through sticky cobwebs. But—there *was* something. Not a jawbone, but . . . a piece of paper.

Gabriel studied it, and his breath frayed.

It was a pencil drawing, black-and-white and scientific, of a skeleton. Tidy little labels—*a. b. c.* and so on. *Tolbert's* hand, Gabriel was convinced. The skeleton was of a creature that appeared to be, in some respects, human—the rib cage, pelvic bones, limbs, and spine were certainly human, if with a rather hunched and sturdy appearance. But the skull and the feet? Like a boar's, tusks and hooves and all.

A door crashed open. Gabriel shot to his feet, keeping hold of the drawing. He spun around to see a man barreling towards him with an upswung hammer.

23

The man with the upswung hammer was presumably the blacksmith Marcel.

"What in hell are you doing in my house?" Marcel bellowed in French. "I will crush your skull!"

"I came to reclaim my drawing," Gabriel said, waving the paper.

Marcel stopped, and the hammer fell to his side. He panted. "What do you mean? That is not yours."

"It is. I suppose you got it from the zoologist, Tolbert?"

A pause. "No. Well, yes. He gave it to my wife. She took a foolish fancy to it. He called upon her yesterday, said he had learned of her sighting of the beast. He wished to ask her if the beast matched the creature in his picture."

"And did it?"

"Why in hell should I tell *you*?" Marcel hefted the hammer.

Gabriel tensed. He still had his Webley tucked in his jacket, but he would not use it on a man in his own home.

"Why tell me? Because, as I said, this drawing is stolen property. Or perhaps I should request the police to assist me."

"I could bash your skull in now and bury you in the woods."

"Oh? The woods are rather bustling at the moment."

"I know places those damned woodcutters do not. Secret places." Marcel lifted the hammer and lunged.

Gabriel dodged to the side, feeling the breeze of the hammer. It hit the hutch, and pottery crashed and splintered. Marcel bellowed.

Gabriel was at the back door, and he picked up a small wooden stool. Marcel was making another Spanish bull's charge with the hammer.

"Oh, go on and keep the damned thing, then," Gabriel said, and allowed the drawing to drift to the floor.

Just as Marcel was upon him, Gabriel swung the stool and whacked him under the chin. Marcel crashed to the floor, and the hammer skidded into a corner. Gabriel snatched it up, now wielding the hammer and the stool. He was the same height as Marcel, but far outbulked.

Marcel crawled to the drawing and grabbed it. Bright blood dripped from his lip and spattered across the paper. "Meddling outsiders," he said. "Everything was fine until you lot arrived."

"So you say, man, but it seems that at least one of us meddling outsiders—Tolbert—has given you something to treasure."

"This?" Marcel wadded up the drawing. "I care nothing for this. Tolbert is a lunatic, a snob, his Paris ways! Bothering my wife. She has a baby to mind and women to help."

"Well then, if the picture means nothing to you, why don't you burn it and be done with it?" Gabriel gestured to the smoldering ashes in the fireplace. "Go on."

Marcel hesitated, but then got stiffly to his feet. He tossed the drawing onto the ashes, and after a few seconds, it blazed up and, blackening, curled upon itself.

If that drawing had been meaningful to him, he did not show it.

Marcel grabbed a pewter pitcher from the mantel and came barging towards Gabriel.

Dash it all.

Gabriel slipped out the back door, tossing aside the hammer and stool as he tore through the garden, around the cottage, and onto the main village track. What had Marcel meant about meddling outsiders? Why had his wife kept—and hidden—the picture of the skeleton? One thing was certain: The tension in this valley was tightening as surely as a hand at the throat.

On the track, he slowed to a brisk walk, and he didn't look back until he reached the château gates.

Gabriel stopped in the château only briefly, to fetch a roll of paper, pencils, a gas lamp, and matches. He stuffed it all into a satchel. It was time to document the animals in the cave, before it was too late. If the villagers hadn't known about the cave before, well, they probably did now, and the woodcutters moved ever closer, too.

Passing through an upper corridor, Gabriel glimpsed, through a cracked door, Banks abed. He paused to look in. Banks's face was like grayish rubber, his eyes sealed shut, his chest rising and falling too quickly beneath the covers. A sick nurse sat in a chair beside the bed. When she saw Gabriel, she tapped a finger to her chest—his lungs, did she mean?—and shook her head.

Twenty minutes later, Gabriel arrived, panting and sweating, at the bottom of the slope below the painted cave. The woodcutters' hacking echoed off the cliffs. He started up through the rocks and wet brambles. Patches of snow remained in the shade. He saw boar's footprints stamped across one patch, and what he fancied were a chillingly large wolf's prints in another.

At the mouth of the cave, Gabriel lit his lamp and ducked inside. Even inside, cool and damp, axe hits scrambled the air, but as he followed the cave deeper into the earth, all sounds thinned out until he was immersed in flat, primeval silence.

When the lamp illuminated the shrine before the boar-man painting, Gabriel's heart faltered and then sped.

A bone leaned against the wall of the cave. *The* bone, the jawbone—or, properly speaking, one half of a jawbone—at once human and tusked. Along with the jawbone, a fresh rose floated in a bowl of water, and new sweets and plump, shiny belladonna berries filled the other dishes. Yet those other things blurred into the darkness; to Gabriel's eyes the jawbone alone seemed to glow with a holy light.

He picked it up carefully, and pain thrilled up his arms. Fossilized. How old was it? Old enough for tooth and bone to have rotted and been remade, bit by bit, in stone.

He turned it over, studying it from every angle. It could not be a hoax; he could see the striations of the natural stone. This was a priceless specimen, precious to science, to human history, to posterity. What had Tolbert been thinking, leaving it in a cave like this? A wild animal could carry it off, and it would be lost forever.

Tolbert was mad. Mad, and dangerous.

Gabriel wrapped the jawbone in a clean handkerchief and slid it into his satchel. Then he unrolled blank paper, took out a pencil, and got to work.

When Ophelia and Forthwith alighted from the carriage in front of Château Vézère's stables, it was to see Bernadette laboriously mounting a horse.

"Hunting? Splendid," Forthwith muttered to himself, pushing open the door. "Hello, there, Mademoiselle Gavage," he called. "Going to the forest to meet Mr. Larsen? Shall I accompany you?"

Ophelia clenched her teeth. Forthwith wished to show Larsen those soap labels immediately, and she felt powerless to stop him. Because if Forthwith tattled on her . . .

"Oh, that is not necessary." Bernadette arranged her riding skirts over her side saddle. The rust-colored velvet flowed over her chestnut horse, making Bernadette and horse appear as one, like one of those satyr critters.

Ophelia stepped down from the carriage. When Bernadette saw her, her expression cooled.

"Blasting a gun at innocent animals will soon set my mood to rights," Forthwith said.

Bernadette's lips made an O. "Excuse me?"

"I meant, you don't intend to ride alone in the woods, Mademoiselle Gavage, with beasts *and* beastly woodcutters both roving about?"

"I wish to bring luncheon to Monsieur Larsen and my brother."

"Are they hunting?" Ophelia asked.

"Monsieur Larsen is hunting, yes, and Garon is overseeing the woodcutting. Join us later, Monsieur and Mademoiselle Stonewall, after you have changed into your hunting costumes—it will not be difficult to find us, I think. Monsieur Larsen and Garon said they would stay on the creek trail until I joined them, so we will wait for you."

"All right, then." Forthwith, hugging his torn parcel, went towards the château.

Ophelia hesitated. Would it be mad to quiz Bernadette about poison tablets and cheese?

Bernadette ignored the way Ophelia was loitering and called, "Georges, *le panier.*"

Le panier? That meant "basket."

Georges, a manservant, came forward with a small wicker basket, and he and Bernadette fussed until it was tied to her saddle horn with a ribbon. "Luncheon for the gentlemen," Bernadette said to Ophelia in a distant tone. "Only a little wine and meat and my brother's favorite cheese, *cabécou.*"

Cheese. Oh. Mercy.

Bernadette continued, "You must remember, since you *will* be his wife and must look after these sorts of things. Goodness knows what you mean to do with sorry old *me*. Garon enjoys his *cabécou* with a little honey, and walnuts."

"*Cabécou.* I'll remember."

Georges started towards the château.

"*Will* you remember?" Bernadette looked down her nose at Ophelia as she nudged her horse into motion. "My brother tells me you have not given him reason to believe you will be a tractable wife." Bernadette swung her horse around, and it clip-clopped across the side court, towards the path to the vineyard and the woods.

Forget about scary Griffe and his even scarier sister—although, how wrong Ophelia had been about *them*. No—Ophelia hitched up her skirts and followed Georges—the more pressing matter, the maybe life-and-death matter—was the cheese in that basket.

Bernadette was out of sight by the time Ophelia caught up to Georges.

"Excuse me," Ophelia said, breathless.

Georges stopped, brow furrowed. "*Je ne parle pas anglais,*" he said. He did not speak English.

Drat.

She must find a translator. The kitchen, maybe. Ophelia beckoned Georges to follow her. He made a snooty, *Crazy American lady* face, but followed as Ophelia led him to the kitchen.

The kitchen stank of sour milk. The fire was out. A mountain of copper pots, dirty china, and decayed vegetables filled the sink.

Where had the servants gone?

But there was Abel, slumped at the table, still in his striped nightshirt, eating honey straight out of the jar.

"Master Christy! Would you help me?" Ophelia said. "I've got to ask this manservant here, Georges, a question. I need a translator."

"I suppose," Abel said with a listless shrug. He licked the dripping honey dipper, staring blankly into space.

"Where have all the kitchen servants gone?" Ophelia asked.

"They've quit. Angry about the woodcutting." Abel dipped for more honey.

"What's the matter with you?" Ophelia asked.

Georges shifted with impatience.

"The matter?" Abel said. "What is the reason for this brief flash that is human life? We are but ants beneath the crushing foot of the divine, we are a flutter of an eyelash amid the vast waste of the cosmos—"

"Never mind, there isn't time—tell me later."

"My, how *feeling* of you." A drop of honey slid down Abel's chin. "You could not even *begin* to comprehend the melancholy that has descended upon me."

"You might be surprised. Now. Would you ask Georges if he recalls Bernadette—Mademoiselle Gavage—doing anything peculiar with bits of cheese two mornings ago, before we all went out hunting?"

Abel asked him.

Georges looked surprised and then wary. He said something.

"Well?" Ophelia said.

"He says Mademoiselle Gavage did pack a basket of cheese and asked him to add it to the hamper, but she said he was not to touch it under any circumstance after that, as it was special cheese for her, only."

"Have the hunting dogs gone out today with the Count de Griffe and Mr. Larsen?"

Abel inquired.

"*Oui,*" Georges said.

Mercy, mercy, mercy. If Bernadette was taking poisoned

cheese out to the woods today, it could be meant for a pack of dogs. But it might also be meant for Griffe or Larsen.

"Come with me, Master Christy—I need you to translate for me some more," Ophelia said. "Let's go to the stables—hurry."

Abel stood—he wore small shiny boots and knee socks under his striped nightshirt. "What is happening?"

"No time to explain."

Georges watched Ophelia and Abel crash out the kitchen door.

They raced around the château to the stables. "Ask the stable boy to saddle me a horse," Ophelia said breathlessly.

Abel translated, and the stable boy nodded and beckoned them to a stall, where two horses were already saddled. "He says he'll just change one of these for a lady's saddle and—"

"For pity's sake, there isn't any *time*." Ophelia yanked open the stall door, coaxed the horse out by its bridle, and mounted astride. The stable boy gawked.

"I shall come, too," Abel said, unlatching the other stall.

"You're in your pajamas—you'll freeze!" Ophelia's horse pranced in place.

"I'll have you know, I'm an excellent rider," Abel said. "Here, I'll just put on this smelly coat." He pulled a work coat from a peg—several sizes too large—and shrugged into it. He led an enormous black stallion out of its stall and struggled to get his foot in the high stirrup. The stable boy lifted Abel by the waist and plopped him into the saddle.

Ophelia nudged her horse's flanks, and they were off.

Ten minutes later, Ophelia and Abel were trotting along the creek trail. Red woodsmen's caps and glinting axe blades flashed. Chopping echoed. A great tree groaned as it gave way and crashed through the underbrush. All the birds had fled. A sense of doomsday twined through the trees.

Bernadette and her basket of cheese had gotten a good

head start. What if someone else died? Ivy had told Ophelia about Bernadette poisoning the cheese hours and hours ago, and Ophelia hadn't acted. In truth, she hadn't quite believed Ivy; Ivy seemed prone to exaggeration.

As a way to distract herself, Ophelia asked Abel, "What is the matter with you, Master Christy, still in your nightshirt and plowing through the honey?"

Abel clung to the saddle horn, sliding from side to side. "It is all your fault."

"Go along!"

"It's all because of you and that pompous professor in the library last night."

"So that *was* you hiding behind the drapes and eating cake."

"That is entirely beside the point."

"What *is* the point?"

"Sir Percival Christy is my father."

"Yes. You hadn't mentioned it—"

"Because I didn't know! He never told me. All these years—all my *life*—he led me to believe he was merely my protector and that my deceased father had been a prince. But now, well . . . Miss Stonewall, I will not blame you if you do not wish to associate with me any longer when I tell you that . . . Sir Christy is not married to my mother. Mother is very grand and beautiful, you know, but she isn't of royal blood."

"I don't care a jot about royal blood. You are still the same person you were yesterday—and so is Sir Christy, and so is your mother. I am sorry that you heard the news in that fashion, and that it came as a shock, but you'll be all right. Now you know who your father is."

"I'll be *all right*?" Abel snorted. "No. Now I'm merely—merely one of your sort. A commoner. I'll never be king. My blood's not blue. It's *red*. I feel as though I've died."

"Buck up, Abel. You'll soon realize that life will go on as before."

24

Ophelia let Abel wallow. The trail had grown rougher and she needed to concentrate on riding.

After another ten minutes or so, Ophelia saw three horses with three people astride, farther up the trail. She recognized Bernadette's rust-colored habit and Griffe's flowing mane of hair, and she heard Larsen's guffaw. Spotted hunting dogs milled around the horses' legs.

Thank goodness; the dogs were alive and kicking, and so were Larsen and Griffe. So far. Ophelia urged her horse faster. Behind her, Abel *oof*ed and panted with exertion.

Bernadette, Larsen, and Griffe looked surprised to see Ophelia and Abel. They were stopped close to the stream, no trees obstructing the view of gray, churning water. This was just below the painted cave, Ophelia realized.

"Mademoiselle Stonewall, I did not realize you would be joining us," Griffe said. He held his rifle across his saddle, and his eyes were guarded. Hurt. As though *he* had a right to look hurt when he'd thrust himself upon her that morning. "And who is this? Young Master Christy?"

"By God, the lad is in his pajamas under that coat!" Larsen bellowed. "This is earnest hunting, not child's play. Return to the château at once!"

"I do not mean to hunt." Abel lifted his brows. "It's a bit, well, barbaric, don't you think? What about capturing the creatures instead of slaying them? Then you might study them from a scientific perspective."

"What is he saying?" Larsen asked no one in particular.

"Cheese, Bernadette," Ophelia said, drawing her horse up. Bernadette balanced her cheese basket against the saddle horn. "*Special* cheese? Not for your brother's luncheon, though. For the dogs."

Bernadette tucked her chin back.

"What is this?" Griffe asked. "Cheese for the dogs?" He turned to Bernadette. "You do not feed cheese to the dogs, do you? They must have meat, only meat."

"What ho," Abel murmured, dismounting. "What have we here?" He toddled off towards the trees.

Bernadette's eyes were locked on Ophelia. "I know not what you mean about cheese, dearest sister-to-be. Do you require a lie-down?"

"Do you mean to say that there's nothing funny about the cheese in that basket?" Ophelia asked.

"French cheese is always a bit funny," Larsen said. "Chunks and lumps of mold—"

"I will have you know," Griffe said, "all of the cheese we eat is made in our château's own creamery, not—"

"Poison," Ophelia said. "I'm talking about poison."

Bernadette was frozen on her saddle.

"Go on, eat the cheese," Ophelia said.

"You have injured my feelings beyond measure," Bernadette said in a small, cold voice. "And the answer is, no, there is nothing at all wrong with the cheese in this basket."

"Prove it, then," Ophelia said. "Eat some."

"I am not hungry."

"Surely you can manage one bite."

Bernadette turned beseechingly to the men.

"Oh, for pity's sake," Larsen said. "Miss Stonewall's *head* has gone as runny as cheese. Give me the cheese, and I shall eat some. I have worked up an appetite." Still on horseback, Larsen reached over, pushed aside the cloth on the basket, and took a lump of cheese. He lifted it to his lips.

"Non!" Bernadette cried, slapping his hand so the cheese flew into the air. One of the dogs opened its chops, caught the cheese, and gulped it.

"It's poisoned," Ophelia said. "I'm sure of it—and that dog will prove it in a little while when he drops dead." She looked at Bernadette. "You didn't quite manage it the first time, did you? The cheese meant for—who, your brother?— ended up in the bellies of the dogs that day. So you meant to take another stab at it today. Why? Is it to do with the family fortune?"

"Look what I've found!" Abel yelled from the edge of the trees. He'd pulled up a mossy fallen log.

"Not now," Ophelia called back.

"What does Mademoiselle Stonewall speak of, sister?" Griffe said, face red. "Answer me!"

"Mademoiselle Gavage?" Larsen said. "What is the meaning of this? Poisoning the hounds? Attempting to poison your brother?"

"Who is that up there?" Griffe shouted up the slope, into the thicket.

A gunshot split the air. Larsen said, *"Oog,"* and crumpled off his horse like a puppet whose strings had been cut.

A gunshot cracked the cushiony silence of the cave. Gabriel froze, his pencil hovering above the rubbing he was making of a carved bear.

Larsen was out hunting, he knew. Had he finally bagged his beast?

On another wall of the cave, the dancing boar-man flickered secretly in the shadows.

Curiosity overcame Gabriel. He rolled up the paper and stuffed it with the pencil in his satchel, next to the handkerchief-wrapped jawbone. Taking up his lantern, he headed towards daylight.

"Thorstein!" Bernadette leaped from her horse in a billow of velvet. She fell at Larsen's side. "Thorstein! Oh, Thorstein!" She looked up blindly at Griffe and Ophelia. "He has been shot! Thorstein, you cannot be shot." She threw herself over his body.

Griffe dismounted and charged up the slope, hacking through the thicket with the butt of his shotgun. "I will find you and hunt you down!" he yelled.

Ophelia checked on Abel. He was on his knees, peering under the fallen log, seemingly oblivious to the events around him. Ophelia dismounted and kneeled beside Larsen. "Where has he been shot?"

Bernadette didn't even lift her head as she swung a fist and punched Ophelia in the arm.

"Ow!" Ophelia cried, clutching her arm. "I've got to see where he's been shot—oh. Wait. Look—it's only his shoulder, see the—"

"Get away, you little viper," Bernadette snarled.

"We must go," Ophelia said. "There is a shooter up there." One of the horses whinnied. A dog barked, and others growled.

Bernadette wept into the crook of Larsen's neck. "Thorstein, you cannot die!" she said in French. She said some more things that Ophelia struggled to understand, although she was pretty sure Bernadette said something like, "It cannot be that I loved you all these years for naught." Ophelia most certainly picked out the words *amour* and *trente ans*.

Ophelia had already guessed that Bernadette harbored sentiments for Larsen, although thirty years really took the cake. Why wasn't Larsen saying anything? That gunshot wound on his shoulder couldn't have killed him. "Come on, get up," Ophelia said. "It isn't safe to stay here."

"Thorstein, *je t'aime!*" Bernadette wailed.

Larsen stirred, and managed to hoist himself on his elbows even with Bernadette burrowing into his neck. *"Précieux Bernadette, est-ce vrai?"*

Ophelia understood that: "Precious Bernadette, is it true?" Larsen touched the hairwork brooch Bernadette always wore. The brooch must have been some sort of love token from *him*.

Larsen and Bernadette kissed.

Ophelia glanced away, embarrassed. Most of the dogs rambled around, snuffling the ground, twitching their tails, and growling . . . except for one. The one who had eaten the cheese. Its ears drooped and it lolled on its haunches, panting.

"Bernadette, you *did* poison that dog," Ophelia said.

"Not to kill him, you twit. Only to slow him down. All I wished was for the hunting to cease, the heartless killing of the wild creatures—why?"

That made a sort of mad sense.

Griffe crashed out of the brush, panting, red scrapes criss-crossing his face. "I could find no one. The shooter has fled and—ah. I see that Larsen and my sister have at long last made amends."

"Only his shoulder was shot," Ophelia said. "We should go."

"They have always loved each other," Griffe said. "A grand love affair in the youth, *oui*? But Bernadette could not bear his hunting—she is so softhearted, you see. Cannot even eat the flesh of a trout. Larsen married another, but she never forgot her mistake. His wife died last year. Hope was born again. *Oui*, he told me in confidence that he came here to win her hand." Griffe's expression closed, as though he'd remembered that he was sore with Ophelia.

Larsen wished to win Bernadette's hand? Then all those things Henrietta had fancied Larsen had been saying—hints about the sort of lady he esteemed—hadn't even been directed at her. They had been compliments aimed at Bernadette. *Bernadette* wore flat boots and enjoyed being out of doors. *Bernadette* ate heartily and never skipped dessert.

And yet . . . if Bernadette and Larsen loved each other, could they not also be accomplices in murder?

"You are correct; we must go," Griffe said gruffly. "The shooter may return. Perhaps it was an honest accident, and the shooter is too ashamed to show his face."

Doubtful.

A man on horseback emerged from the bend in the path; they hadn't heard him coming over the gush of the stream. Forthwith.

"Only my brother," Ophelia said. Yet Forthwith carried a shotgun on his shoulder.

Forthwith's face clouded when he saw Larsen and Bernadette on the ground. "What's this? Has someone taken a tumble?" He brought up his horse beside Ophelia and Griffe. "Good God—is that Larsen? Has something dreadful occurred?"

Forthwith's kindly act was about as convincing as a shark's.

"No need to work yourself into a lather," Ophelia snapped. "He's going to be right as rain, and anyway, you only care about him so far as you can fleece him with your crooked soap business." She gulped. How had *that* slipped out?

Griffe frowned. Forthwith, pale, shifted his eyes between Griffe and Ophelia like a wind-up toy.

"What did she say?" Bernadette asked, turning. "Crooked soap business?"

Larsen, his head in Bernadette's lap, was laughing.

"What in the name of God is this all about?" Griffe said. "Soap business? Fleecing?"

"Nothing," Ophelia and Forthwith said in unison.

"I will tell you what it is about," Larsen said. "This young man here meant to trick me into investing a fortune in his fraudulent soap manufactory. Magic Buffalo Soap, he called it, with some tommyrot ingredient that does not even exist—what is it? Hare's paw bark?"

"Gopher claw bush," Forthwith said coldly. "How did you know?"

"I may be old, but I am not a fool, young man. I was alive to your tricks from the very beginning. You have an oily way about you—not, mind you, that that is an impediment in business."

"Then why did you allow me to attempt to convince you?" Forthwith shouted. "The time I have wasted, all that blathering! And I've invested money, too, in those preposterous soap labels you had me print up! *Damn* you, man."

"Turned the tables on you nicely, did I not?" Larsen said. "Made you understand the value of hard work. All of this effort and money you have invested in attempting to fool me, why, you could have used all of that to start a *real* soap manufactory."

"There is no such thing as gopher claw bush, you stupid little man," Forthwith said.

"It does not matter. It makes a good brand, and that is the important thing with manufactories."

"Damn you!" Forthwith said. He swung on Ophelia. "And damn you, too, Ophelia Flax, for throwing me before the cart."

"Ophelia *Flax*?" Griffe said with a frown.

Ophelia stopped breathing.

Griffe loomed closer. "What does he mean, Ophelia *Flax*?"

"Oh. I—"

"She's an actress," Forthwith said. "A variety hall actress, just like her longtime friend, Henrietta Bright. Actresses are a duplicitous breed, dear count. They never can tell when to stop acting and start behaving like honest women."

Ophelia's hands shook. "That's funny, because I've always found that conjurers of the stage have the same sort of problem—Forthwith *Golden*."

"Conjurer of the stage?" Griffe said slowly. "Variety hall actress? Tell me there is some mistake. You are not siblings from Cleveland?"

"I am very sorry, Count," Ophelia said softly. "Things seemed to take on a life of their own—but I meant to come clean, to break off our engagement, just as soon as I got Henrietta out of jail—"

"You came into my home, my family, under false pretenses?" Griffe sounded dazed, but his eyes were flinty. "Break off the engagement, you say? This, then, is the meaning of your reticence, your aloof ways. No coy bride, you, but a slatternly trickster!"

"I—"

"*Go,*" Griffe said. "Collect your things from my house and be gone."

"I'm sorry," Ophelia said.

"Sorry? Meaningless! And you as well—whoever you are," Griffe yelled at Forthwith, "leave at once!"

"Master Christy," Ophelia called to Abel.

"I wish to stay here," Abel yelled back, digging under the fallen log. "I've made the most spectacular discovery!"

In silence, Ophelia and Forthwith mounted their horses and set off towards the château.

"Report your lodgings to the Sarlat police," Griffe shouted after them, "or I shall do it myself and recommend your arrest!"

"Leave my mother's ruby ring behind!" Bernadette screamed.

Ophelia nodded without turning. All around in the long-shadowed trees, the chopping echoed on and on.

* * *

When Gabriel at last reached the bottom of the slope, it was to find Griffe and Bernadette helping a bleeding Larsen onto his horse.

"A sniper?" Gabriel said once they'd described how Larsen had been shot. "One of the woodsmen?"

"God only knows," Griffe said.

For the first time, Gabriel noticed Abel digging in the dirt. "Master Christy, come along. It isn't safe here."

Abel looked up, dazed. "Where is Miss Stonewall?"

"Miss Stonewall is here?" Gabriel asked.

"*Was* here," Griffe said. "And it seems her name is, in truth, Miss Flax. An actress. That supposed brother of hers is some sort of charlatan conjurer."

Oh no. They'd been discovered.

Griffe went on, "What a fool am I! I might have known with him performing tricks night after night. How blind we all are."

"Where have they gone?" Gabriel asked.

"To hell, I hope."

"Oh, let us hurry," Bernadette cried. "Thorstein is bleeding ever so much."

Bernadette, Griffe, and Larsen rode in the direction of the château.

"Be careful," Gabriel called after them.

A stallion as large as a knight's charger nibbled dead grass at the trail's edge. "Is that your horse?" Gabriel asked Abel.

"What? Oh. Well, in a sense. I rode it here, if that's what you mean."

"It'll carry the both of us. Come on."

"Now?" Abel stared down at his pile of dirt. "But I've found something simply amazing, a *lucanus cervus*, only it's got—"

"There is a sniper in the woods. On the horse *now*."

Abel folded something in a handkerchief and went—inexplicably, in a nightshirt and boots—to the horse. Gabriel helped him up, got onto the saddle behind him, and pressed the horse's flanks.

25

An orange sun was melting into the hills when Ophelia and Forthwith set off down the slushy château drive. On foot.

Cold wind rattled the trees. Ophelia lugged her battered carpetbag in one hand and Meringue in the other, folded under a flap of her cloak. She'd left the trunks of Artemis's finery behind, and she'd packed at breakneck speed. She had no wish to be in the château when the others returned. She had carried the parakeet in its cage up to Abel's garret and left it there with the jar of sunflower seeds and a note: *Don't feed it too many grubs.*

Forthwith walked a pace ahead of Ophelia. He carried only one smallish valise. "Damn it, Ophelia, what were you thinking, mucking everything up like that? I despise you."

"I told you, I'm sorry."

"*Sorry* doesn't help much, does it?"

"We'll go to Sarlat. I haven't any money but—have you?"

"A bit. But Sarlat is three miles away, and it is growing

dark. The days are so blasted short. It's like a nightmare. Walking three miles? We should've stolen some horses."

"And risk arrest? We've no choice but to walk. Beggars can't be choosers, Forthwith."

"My God, you sound like my aunt Gertrude. How I loathed her. She used to lock me in a trunk when I was naughty. Do you know, that's how I became a magician?"

As soon as Gabriel dismounted the stallion outside the château, he went to where he believed Miss Flax's chamber was.

She was already gone. Forthwith was, too. Had they managed to hire a carriage so quickly?

"Why are you peering into this bedchamber?" Ivy asked, making Gabriel jump. When he turned, she was only inches away. Why hadn't he heard her?

Gabriel raked a hand through his hair. "Miss Stonewall, and her brother—"

"Haven't you heard the news, Lord Harrington? They weren't siblings at all. They were impostors, just like that Henrietta creature. They've been turned out." Ivy's eyes were shadowed. She must have been exhausted, with her father ill. . . . "Now it's only *us*. To be perfectly honest, those Americans didn't quite fit in, anyway."

"Where did they go?"

"They left on foot. I saw them from the window."

"On foot! To the village?"

"Why do you wish to know?"

Gabriel let out a breath. He hadn't reasoned it through, but he realized he'd been about to get back on a horse to search for Miss Flax. But here, *this* vision of beauty standing before him, was his future wife. He would stay. He *must* stay. Mustn't he? He could send for word of Miss Flax tomorrow.

"Has the doctor come?" Gabriel asked Ivy.

"Yes. He said there is something the matter with Papa's stomach, and that he must continue to rest. Why don't you go change, and then we could play chess downstairs in the salon." Ivy had not seemed to notice the welt on Gabriel's cheekbone. But of course, she was preoccupied. "It is a pity that Papa is not well enough to watch. He does so enjoy it when I make a checkmate."

At dinner, Griffe floundered in a drunken rage, railing against the deceiving Americans and the trickery of women in general. All the kitchen servants had fled out of anger regarding the tree felling. The meal—cured meat, cheese, stale bread, and wine—was served by Clémence. She stood behind Griffe's chair and refilled his wine goblet each time it grew low, an almost maternal expression on her face.

Larsen and Bernadette were oblivious to Griffe, gazing adoringly into each other's eyes across the table. Larsen's gunshot wound had proved to be superficial, and Bernadette had bandaged it with care.

And Tolbert? Nowhere to be seen. In fact, Gabriel hadn't seen Tolbert since he had struck him with his revolver in the servants' quarters that morning. Perhaps he had finally gone on to Bordeaux to collect his mysterious parcel.

How their numbers had diminished. Yet still, the murderer had not been caught. Gabriel eyed Griffe. *He* was mad enough to kill, at least tonight. No one spoke of the sniper in the wood, but one might've cut the anxiety in the dining room with a butter knife.

Young Master Christy dined with them, since it was not fitting to leave the lad alone in the kitchen without any company. He shoveled food into his mouth steadily, staring, wordless.

Ivy seemed spent. "Lord Harrington," she said after the dessert of stale preserved fig cake, "I think I will go to bed—could we play chess tomorrow, instead?"

"Of course," Gabriel said, suppressing a sigh of relief. He would not be good company tonight. He rather loathed himself at the moment, actually. He had been taught from the cradle to believe that he was a gentleman. Yet what would a gentleman do in this circumstance? Remain loyal to his betrothed or throw it all off and go chasing after a confidence trickster of an actress? Clearly, a gentleman would remain loyal to his betrothed. So why did it feel so bloody *awful*?

Later, when Gabriel was making his way to his own bedchamber after attempting—and failing—to read in the library, he passed Banks's door. It stood half open, so he looked in.

The nurse at Banks's bedside had been sleeping, chin on chest, but she started awake at Gabriel's arrival. "I was only resting my eyes," she stammered in French.

Gabriel replied, "I only wished to see if Mr. Banks has improved." He hadn't; he was still gray, sleeping, his whole body collapsing upon itself. That is what death looked like.

The nurse said, "Perhaps, monsieur, we should send for the doctor again."

"Oh?"

"Monsieur Banks woke this afternoon, only for a moment, and asked for his heart medicine."

"I was told that the doctor said he hadn't a heart ailment, that it was something to do with his stomach."

"I could not understand what the doctor said to the young lady, monsieur, because they spoke in English. Still, Mr. Banks asked me for his heart medicine."

Gabriel wished to ask Ivy about this, but she had retired hours earlier. Should he wake her? It was improper for him to knock on her door at this hour, or, really, at *any* hour.

Still, he went to her chamber. If Banks could be saved simply by taking the proper medicine, well, Gabriel must see to it.

Ivy did not answer his knock. He sought out the maidservant Clémence and asked her to enter Ivy's room, but they soon discovered that the door was locked. Ivy must haven fallen into a profound sleep.

Gabriel resolved to send for the doctor first thing in the morning.

* * *

Gabriel slept with the jawbone and the loaded Webley under his pillow. Neither gave him peace of mind. For although he had in his possession an unspeakably important relic, both scientific and folkloric, Miss Flax had been cast out, and he knew not where she'd gone.

His bedclothes tangled, and he perspired through his nightshirt. He gave up and got out of bed. But a glass of cognac at the fireside only succeeded in further disordering his thoughts.

He should've ridden out after Miss Flax. She was penniless, alone—unless you counted that louse Forthwith— and in danger of arrest. Gabriel hadn't done the right thing by her from the very beginning. She was, if nothing else, his friend, yet he had not valued, not protected, their friendship. He ought to have helped her more instead of chasing his private goals. He never should have allowed her to engage herself to Griffe. He should have *never* proposed marriage to Miss Banks.

Tomorrow he would find Miss Flax and help her out of her predicament. *That* was the gentlemanlike thing to do.

Soothed a little, Gabriel returned to bed and at last fell asleep.

He woke at dawn to frigid wind gusting through an open window. Drawers lolled halfway out. Wardrobe doors splayed. Garments were scattered across the carpet.

Tolbert in search of his prize.

Gabriel reached under the pillow. The jawbone was still there. He must find a better place to hide it until he could carry it back to Oxford.

Clémence waited upon breakfast: more stale bread, cheese, and tepid coffee. Bernadette and Ivy were listless and ashen.

Griffe was unkempt and red-eyed. Larsen was already gone hunting despite his wounded shoulder, and Master Christy was reportedly making a mess with books in the library. Tolbert still had not shown his face.

Gabriel sat beside Ivy and said softly, "Your father—has his condition at all improved?"

"Worse." Ivy stifled a sob with her balled-up napkin. "He grows worse."

"The nurse told me last night that he has been asking for medicine—heart medicine."

"But why?"

"He seems to believe that he had some, that he misplaced it, and that it's all he requires to become well."

Ivy shook her head. "But he's hasn't *got* a heart condition. It is his stomach. It has always been his stomach—and the doctor from Sarlat confirmed as much. . . ." Her voice crumpled.

"I am sorry that I mentioned it. Perhaps he has grown delirious." Gabriel bit into rock-hard bread. He supposed it would only distress Ivy if he were to summon the doctor again.

"I apologize for my poor hospitality," Bernadette said. "We must hire new staff—perhaps from Sarlat, or even Paris. Dear Clémence will be promoted to housekeeper as a reward for her devotion to the family."

Perhaps that was why Clémence, standing just behind Griffe's chair, appeared so radiant this morning.

"Traitors, the lot of them!" Griffe roared. "Paid them better than anyone for fifty miles around, and this is the thanks I get! I cut a few trees—my *own* trees—and they stomp away like petulant children? What is more, my own footmen—*former* footmen—were brawling with the woodsmen last night. Disgraceful. I intend to hire even *more* woodcutters. Finish the job even faster. That will teach those fools."

"Brawling?" Gabriel said. "Was anyone hurt?"

Griffe made a dismissive gesture. "A black eye here and broken tooth there. Nothing the brutes did not deserve. Now I must go into town myself to fetch the telegram the head woodsman told me is waiting for me at the telegraph office—Sarlat is a damnable rumor mill—even though I am occupied with the tree felling and this wretched beast nonsense. The woodsmen, by the by, claim to have seen a beast walking upright through their camp last night—"

"Indeed?" Gabriel said.

"Drunken scoundrels," Bernadette murmured.

"—so that telegram is going to sit and rot because now I have no servant to go and—"

"I will fetch it for you," Gabriel said.

"Eh?" Griffe said. "I would be most obliged."

"You might keep to your overseeing of the tree cutting, and I will have a spot of exercise riding to town."

"I suppose that actress—Miss Flax, was it?—is in Sarlat," Ivy said. "And the stage conjurer, of course."

"Probably," Gabriel said into his coffee cup.

A window burst in a shower of glass. A rock hit the table, bounced, and rolled to a stop beside Ivy's plate. Bernadette screamed, and Ivy dissolved in weeping.

Gabriel and Griffe dashed to the broken window to see a clutch of adolescent boys in peasants' attire scattering into a stand of trees.

A straggler turned and shouted in French, "That is only the beginning!" before disappearing.

Ophelia unglued her eyelids. Where in tarnation was she? She didn't recognize the long crack running down that plaster wall, nor that window with such a deep wooden sill. Her head rested on her lumpy carpetbag, and that licking on her hand, what—?

She struggled upright. Oh. *This* nightmare, still going strong.

She was wrapped in her cloak on the cold floor of a boardinghouse, and Meringue was licking her hand. There was Forthwith, curled up like a lima bean in the chamber's only bed. What a gent.

Yesterday evening, they had walked almost halfway to Sarlat before a man driving a cart loaded with quarry stones had offered them a ride. Once in Sarlat, they'd slogged around until they found a boardinghouse with a vacant room. And here they were. The stinky shared lavatory was down the hall, and breakfast wasn't included.

Ophelia got up and prodded Forthwith. "Wake up. We've got to report our lodgings to the police station before Griffe tells them tales."

"Go away, you traitor," Forthwith said.

"If we don't, we'll look like fugitives."

"Mnngh." Forthwith rolled over.

"We've got to *do* something. They're pinning it all on Henrietta and they'll try to pin it on *us*, too."

"Surely they'll see the light."

"No." Ophelia set her chin. "*Allow* those bunglers to take charge of our fates? Let me show you something." She went to her carpetbag and dug out her box, the one in which she used to keep her money and the ring. She tossed it on the bed. "Open it."

Forthwith looked at the box groggily and sat up. "Henrietta's birthday gift to you. I helped her select it in the shop, you know. You carried this with you all the way from Paris?"

"Open it."

Forthwith opened it and pulled out the slip of paper. "*I make my circumstance.*" He snorted. "I took you for a reasonable young lady, Ophelia, so why on earth are you toting about gibberishy little notes?"

"It's not gibberish. Those words mean . . ." Ophelia swallowed the knob in her throat. "It means that one must not succumb to fate but take the reins. In this case, it means not allowing nincompoops and lazy police officers to decide—what are you doing?"

Forthwith had been poking at the bottom of the box. Something clicked. He smiled. "Just like a lady in a crinolette, this box has a false bottom."

26

Ophelia blinked.

"It's a magic box," Forthwith said.

"Henrietta gave me a conjurer's box? Why?"

Forthwith pulled out a roll of banknotes. "To fool you. God, if I'd known you had all this boodle, I would've allowed you to foot the bill for a proper hotel."

"That's my money!" Ophelia snatched the banknotes, unrolled them, and counted. It was almost all there—every German and French banknote, although the coins of little value were missing. Henrietta had probably removed them because of their telltale jingling. "Why didn't you *tell* me it was all there? I would *never* have come on this horrible journey to the Périgord! I'd be in New York by now!"

"You just answered your own question." Forthwith stretched back and lit a cigarette. "Henrietta was so keen to get to this godforsaken moist underarm of a provincial hell—"

"In order to meet Mr. Larsen."

"Yes—that she hid your money to force your hand. She

didn't wish to actually *steal* your money, because as she explained to me, *that* sort of fraudulence was entirely beneath her. I often wonder how she would've turned out if she had ever gone to Sunday School as a wee one."

Ophelia's hands shook. Magenta splotched her vision. "I ought to leave her in that jail and let her fend for herself."

"Come now, Ophelia, that doesn't sound like you. You're the long-suffering older sister we all wish we had. You know, I could have told you from the start that that pompous walking liver spot, Larsen, wasn't the *slightest* bit smitten with her. He had ulterior motives for being at the hunting party himself."

"Yes, I know. He wished to woo Mademoiselle Gavage."

"Not that. Something else. You see, Larsen knew Mr. Banks already, had known him to my way of seeing things, *long* before they had arrived at Château Vézère."

"But they claimed to know each other only by reputation."

"Lies. They had secret little snarling spats every opportunity they got. I know because Larsen made me trail after him like a motherless whelp."

"He didn't *make* you do that."

"Didn't he?" Forthwith gusted cigarette smoke. "Have you considered Larsen as a murder suspect?"

The thought had crossed Ophelia's mind only yesterday, when she'd learned that Bernadette and Larsen were in love. Larsen had snored through the night of the vicar's murder, but Bernadette could've been his accomplice. "Well, I *have* noticed that people in love sometimes forget all about their moral obligations to the rest of mankind."

"Here's something: If Larsen knew Banks before, and if there is bad blood between the two of them, well, Banks is ill now. Deathly ill. What if that is Larsen's doing?"

"You suggest that Larsen is *poisoning* Banks? Why not do him in quickly, instead of making him merely ill?"

"To make him suffer, of course."

Ophelia paced. How could she get back into Château

Vézère to continue her sleuthing? Could she go in disguise? Pose as, say, some sort of gypsy lady in search of a glass of water?

Forthwith went on, "At any rate, you oughtn't be angry with *me*, because if you hadn't come to the Périgord, you wouldn't have found Professor Penrose again."

"What does he have to do with it?"

"Oh, come off it, Ophelia. You're in love with him, and he's in love with you."

"He is engaged to marry Miss Banks, or has that escaped your notice?"

"She's not for him. He can't take his eyes off you. Why are you allowing him to get away? He's staggeringly rich, Henrietta says—"

"His wealth means nothing to me."

"No? You're a morally righteous young lady who's just so happened to put on a costume and pretend to be a rich heiress from Ohio?"

"I *had* to do it."

Forthwith snickered. "Not everyone would have resorted to such a bizarre theatrical ruse. No, I think you sleep soundly at night by distancing yourself from people like Henrietta and me. But the truth is, you're just like us. A survivor, at all costs."

"I *am* a survivor. And trust you me, I don't like tricking people, not one little bit. Folks can only use the abilities they have. I never finished school past the age of fifteen. I can't read fancy books, I don't know any important people, and I'll never have enough money to sway anyone. But I'm resourceful, I'm good at disguises, like it or not, and I try hard."

Forthwith flicked ash on the floorboards. "And you've somehow managed to conquer the heart of an English earl who's got slathers of money."

"I told you, money means nothing to me."

"Money means nothing to you? Look at the lengths to which you've gone—going along with Henrietta's dirty little scheme—just to cobble together enough for steamship passage back to America. Money would change everything for you."

"I don't need his money," Ophelia said quietly.

But she suddenly knew with her entire mind, body, and soul, something else: She needed Professor Penrose. Raw impossibility yawned before her.

She went down the hall to the lavatory and splashed cold water on her face.

She wiped the water from her eyes and looked into the tarnished mirror above the sink. In that silly *Beauty and the Beast* tale, Belle had met her reckoning when she'd seen, through her magical looking glass, the Beast dying in his garden. Bunkum indeed, except that, well, for a moment Ophelia fancied she saw the professor's face in the mirror, and while he wasn't dying, she saw the death of hope for a future with him.

She could not leave France without telling him that she loved him, too. She would solve these murders, come clean to the professor, and be gone.

Ophelia went back to the chamber and put on her cloak and bonnet. Forthwith was already asleep again. Ophelia collected Meringue and her roll of banknotes, made a leash for Meringue out of a long corset lace, and left.

She took Meringue to do his business in a park. Then she went to the police station and reported to a clerk where she and Forthwith were staying. After that, she bought hot rolls and a hunk of cheese. She started back towards the boardinghouse.

She would eat, and then she'd arrange to rent her own chamber, because sharing with Forthwith was as unbearable as it was unseemly, even though they had told the proprietress that they were siblings. After that, she would find some sort of conveyance to carry her back to Château Vézère, where she would burst in and demand that Larsen explain how he'd known Banks previously. Or something along those lines.

At a public pump, Meringue stopped to lap at a trough. As Ophelia waited, she munched a roll. She had the tingly feeling she was being watched. . . . *Yes.* That stringy-looking fellow in brown farmer's togs, crouched on the steps of a church. She'd never seen him before, yet his eyes were stuck on her.

"Come on, Meringue," Ophelia whispered. They hurried the few blocks to the boardinghouse. As she stepped across the threshold, she glanced left and right—

My sainted aunt. The stringy man in brown was down at the corner, hands in pockets, staring right at her again. Ophelia pushed inside.

In the chamber, Forthwith lolled in bed smoking, and another man stood at the window. His back was turned to Ophelia, but she recognized Professor Penrose in an instant. He held an envelope.

"You brought food?" Forthwith said. "Splendid."

Penrose turned. His face lit in that peculiar way when he saw Ophelia, but in a flash it was gone. "Miss Flax."

"Professor."

"I'm hungry," Forthwith said. "Oh—and an officer of the police called while you were out. Something about a stolen ruby ring and how the count and his sister will demand your arrest if you don't return it promptly."

So it had finally come to that. Ophelia set down Meringue and tossed the parcels of food at Forthwith. "What brings you here, Professor Penrose?"

"To be honest, three things." Penrose crouched so Meringue could sniff his glove. "I am ostensibly in town to fetch a telegram for Griffe." He waved the envelope in his hand.

"Oh. How is Mr. Banks?"

"He has not improved."

"What of Abel?"

Penrose smiled a little. "Making a tornado of the naturalia

books in the château library. He has a caged parakeet on the table beside him at all times, for some reason. He's as happy as a clam. There is something else I wished to speak of, Miss Flax. Perhaps outside—"

"No," Ophelia said, too quickly.

"What is it?"

"Nothing. Well, *something.* There was a fellow out there, skinny as a rake in drab brown sort of farmer's clothing— I've never seen him before, but I fancied he was . . . following me. He's down in the street."

Penrose tensed. "Are you certain he was a stranger—not one of the château servants, perhaps?"

"He could've been one I've never seen before, I suppose."

Penrose told her how village boys had thrown rocks through the château windows that morning. "Something evil is brewing. Tolbert is missing, too, but he left all his things behind at the château. I have reason to believe he hasn't gone far—perhaps he is staying in the village, or on a nearby farm."

Forthwith munched bread. "I am certain the man you saw was of no account, Ophelia. You can't have slept well on the floor."

"The floor?" Penrose's eyes softened. "Miss Flax, I chiefly wished to come here in order to ask if there is anything at all I might do for you."

She *could* ask him to help her get to the bottom of how and why Larsen and Banks had known each other before. . . .

Penrose went on, "There is something else, too, of a more, ah, private nature." He lifted an eyebrow at Forthwith.

"You wish for me to scram," Forthwith said through a mouthful. "Fine. Off to the lavatory with me, because there is *nothing* more pleasant than eating one's breakfast in a lavatory of a three-hundred-year-old building shared with two dozen drunks. So long." He stumped off.

An awkward silence descended.

"You . . . you are also occupying this chamber?" Penrose said, looking at Ophelia's carpetbag.

Her ears burned. "It isn't—"

"Miss Flax, I know you to be a lady of the most ironclad principles, and you need not explain anything to me."

"Thank you." She looked at the envelope in his hand. "Who is Griffe's telegram from?"

"I know not, but it is from Cricklade, Gloucestershire."

"From Mr. Knight's parish!"

"I daresay they wish us to know that they've received the body."

"What if it's a clue?"

"Why would someone from a parish in England be in possession of a clue?"

"That lawyer in London possessed a clue about Abel Christy's father, didn't he? Aren't you curious?"

"I am not in the habit of reading other people's letters."

"Oh, I've seen you do it."

Penrose straightened his spectacles. Nettled again.

"I'm certain you didn't come here to quibble with me, Professor."

"I came to ask for your assistance, Miss Flax, something I could not ask of anyone else."

Ophelia almost said, *What about Miss Banks?* but kept her lips buttoned.

"I trust you, Miss Flax."

"What is it?"

"The fossilized jawbone." He patted his jacket. "I must keep it somewhere away from the château."

Of course. Penrose wasn't truly here to check on her; he was here on account of his moldy old fairy tale obsession. "You mean *hide* the jawbone. Where did you find it?"

"In the cave. Tolbert had added it to his mad little shrine. I did not wish to leave it there for fear that it would be destroyed by the elements or carried off by an animal."

"Doesn't it belong to Tolbert?"

"I have grappled with this, and I have concluded that no, it does not belong to him. It belongs to all of mankind, to science or, at the very least, the French nation. I could not risk it being lost or destroyed."

Ophelia searched Penrose's eyes but detected only a smidgen of maniacal glow. "Fine. I'll keep it safe for you, but only under one condition."

"You always drive a hard bargain, Miss Flax."

"I believe in bartering. It's ever so efficient. I'll guard your fossil if you allow me to read that telegram."

Penrose laughed. "Good heavens, no."

"Then I won't hide your jawbone."

"My chamber was ransacked last night. Tolbert is mad with desire."

Ophelia folded her arms.

Penrose paused. He handed over the telegram. "Only be gentle with the seal. I'd like to stick it again."

Ophelia already had it open. "It is from someone called Mr. Appleberry—oh, he says he is the curate in the Cricklade parish."

"You see? We ought not to have—"

"Mercy." Ophelia reread the brief message. "Professor, that body they sent to Cricklade—it wasn't Mr. Knight."

27

❧

" The wrong body? How can that be?" Gabriel took the telegram and scanned it. It was true; Appleberry regretted to inform the Count de Griffe that the body delivered to the vicarage was not Cecil Knight but a total stranger. "Then where, by God, is Mr. Knight?"

Miss Flax cupped her elbows in her hands and began to pace. Brow furrowed, dark eyes flashing, she resembled a librarian on the warpath. "I should've guessed this ages ago," she said. "That very first evening, Mr. Knight—or, I ought to say, his impostor—refused wine from the count. Yet he had a wine stain down the front of his shirt when I saw his body in the orangerie. He had that terrible scar on his neck, too, which at first made me think he'd tussled with criminals, although he blamed it on the heathens. Then Master Christy told that Mr. Knight—or, the person he *believed* to be Mr. Knight—was a stranger to him, that he met him only for the first time on the dock in Marseille. *That* means that the impostor knew of Mr. Knight's plans to meet Master Christy."

"The impostor could have known this firsthand from Knight," Gabriel said, "or he could have stolen a letter from Sir Christy regarding the boy's ship, or he could have come across the letter by happenstance and seized the opportunity."

"Any way you bake it, Professor, one thing's clear: In order for the impostor to have met Master Christy at his ship without any impediments, he must have *done* something to the real Mr. Knight to keep him out of the way."

"Mr. Knight could be far away, and safe."

"Maybe. But I've got a sickly feeling about this. If the murderer—the count or Mr. Larsen or Bernadette, most likely—lured their victim all the way here by buying up those train tickets and bribing the stagecoach driver, he . . . or she . . . is a spider. A webmaker, see. If they planned all that out, well, they must've planned all the rest out, too." A nauseous notion hit Ophelia. "What if the murderer killed the real vicar? I mean to say, what if the murderer paid someone *else* a great deal of money to kill him, in the same way they paid a great deal of money to clog up the railroad route and have the stagecoach break down? We've got to contact someone in Marseille—the police, I reckon—and learn if a man who could've been Mr. Knight was murdered in the days before Master Christy's ship landed in Marseille."

"What of the police here in Sarlat?"

"Those thugs?" Miss Flax tilted her chin. "If I walked into their gendarmerie, they'd probably take the opportunity to throw me in a cell. Remember, Mademoiselle Gavage and the count demanded the ruby ring back, but I don't have it. Would you show me where the telegraph office is?"

"As you wish." Gabriel battled with an inappropriate frisson of glee that Miss Flax and he were, once again, back on the scent. Together.

They left the poodle chewing Forthwith's boot and walked the few blocks to the telegraph office. Along the way, there was no sign of the brown-clad man Miss Flax hàd worried had been following her, although the streets were clogged for the market.

At the telegraph office, they sent a message to the Marseille police station, asking if a gentlemanlike Englishman had been killed on or around December tenth. They decided it would be expedient to indicate that the telegram was from Lord Harrington, but Miss Flax insisted upon paying the fee, and she repaid Gabriel the money she'd promised for the telegrams to the train ticket offices, too. They meant to check back for a reply in an hour's time. The telegrams transmitted over the wires within seconds, but they wished to give the police time to look into the matter.

"It is only a remote possibility that the murderer killed the real Knight, but it is certainly worth asking," Gabriel told Miss Flax as they stepped out onto the crowded street. He touched his coat, felt the shape of the jawbone beneath. Still there.

"Hmph," Miss Flax said. "You can't argue with a hunch."

"Forgive me if this is indelicate," Gabriel said, "but I happened to notice your rather healthy roll of banknotes."

"My savings. I found it last night—it wasn't stolen after all. Oh—before I forget, for it is really very trivial and unimportant—earlier you said you came into town for three reasons."

Gabriel's heart squeezed. "Yes. Yes, I did say that."

"Yet you only told me *two* reasons you had come—to ask if I'd hide the jawbone and to ask if there was anything you could do to help. What was the third reason?" They were caught in a tide of pedestrians oozing through the street towards the marketplace.

"The third reason?" The third reason—which was really the *first* reason, the first thought in the foremost portion of Gabriel's mind, was that he was in love with Miss Flax and must tell her so again, for he now knew that he could marry no other, that he did not wish to converse with another at any breakfast table in his future, or look upon any other in his bed. He opened his mouth.

"Give it over," someone with a gravelly voice said in French into Gabriel's ear. A gun barrel dug into his back. "The bone. We know you have it."

"Run, Miss Flax," Gabriel said, not moving his head.

"Run?"

"Run."

"Not without you," she whispered, eyes on whoever was behind Gabriel.

"I'll join you shortly. I promise."

She blinked. She dodged sideways through the crowd and ran down a side street. Gabriel didn't make another move until she was safely out of sight. Then, in a fluid motion, he spun around and socked his assailant in the jaw. The gun went flying. Bystanders screamed. The assailant crashed to the paving stones, bellowing.

Well, well. If it wasn't Vézère's village blacksmith, Marcel, with his ship-rope sinews and bulging bull's eyes. Charming.

Someone else was upon Gabriel, a reedy man in brown, leaping for Gabriel's neck with a knife. Gabriel kicked the man's belly, and he folded.

Gabriel shouldered through the jabbering throng and ran the way Miss Flax had gone.

"We will have the bone!" Marcel yelled behind him in French. A gunshot cracked, and then another. Glass shattered, and a woman wailed.

Gabriel dashed around the corner around which Miss Flax had disappeared. He froze. More twisty, tight medieval streets jutted off from where he stood like spokes. Which street had she chosen?

"Over here!" he heard her call.

There she was, hiding in a gloomy doorway. Gabriel dashed over, took her hand, and they were running again, towards the only street above which they could see the sky.

Footsteps and gunshots banged out behind them. Thank God Marcel was a poor shot. He would need to reload soon.

"We could run to the police station," Miss Flax said, panting.

"That may be our safest option. Here's the marketplace." They burst into the bustling square.

"You cannot hide!" Marcel bellowed behind them.

"We really ought to hide," Miss Flax said.

Hand in hand, Gabriel and Miss Flax waded into the crowded center aisle between the market stalls, edging and ducking around chattering women and baskets, laughing men and slinking cats.

"Here," Gabriel said, tugging Miss Flax into a space between two awning-covered carts. They crouched. Soggy cabbage leaves, bread crusts, and fish scales littered the paving stones.

Marcel passed; he hadn't seen them.

"What about the other one?" Miss Flax whispered. "The—*oof!*" The brown-clad man had come up behind them and clamped a hand over Miss Flax's mouth. He dragged her back, kicking and flailing. Her bonnet tumbled off.

Gabriel sprang upon the man and ripped his hands from Miss Flax's shoulders. As soon as she was free, Miss Flax bolted.

They had an audience now, gawking market-goers in the mood for entertainment.

Well, one must give the people what they wished for.

Gabriel punched the brown-clad man's nose. A sickening crunch. The man staggered into a barrel of red apples and sent them rolling. Hoots and cheers. Gabriel sprinted through an opening in the circle of onlookers. Where had Miss Flax gone? Where was Marcel?

Gabriel swung his head, but the marketplace was a confusion of color and motion—wait. There she was, on the church steps, swinging open the enormous doors.

By the time Gabriel was on the church steps, someone was just behind him. Marcel. They crashed against the doors at the same moment. They staggered together into cool, incense-scented dimness.

Miss Flax was nowhere to be seen.

"I will have the jawbone." Marcel's heavy shoulders rose and fell. His gun dangled at his side.

"No, I don't believe that you will. Why do you desire it?"

"It belongs to the land here. Outsiders coming and stealing away things that have been here since time began? That is sin. The bone belongs in Vézère."

"Ah. Well, at any rate, I haven't got it."

"I know you have. I saw you take it from the cave yesterday."

"It was you who searched my bedchamber last night?"

"But of course."

Gabriel's mind felt like a deck of cards fluttering in the wind. He'd been so intent on Tolbert. If it had been *Marcel* all the time . . . Could Tolbert be dead?

"Give it to me," Marcel said, advancing. "I know you have it inside your jacket. I have been watching you all day, have seen you touching your jacket to make certain it is safe."

Blast.

"Now." Marcel's split lip, where Gabriel had hit him with the stool yesterday, was scabbed. Marcel lay the tip of his gun barrel on Gabriel's forehead. "Give. It. To. Me." He pulled the hammer.

"You would murder a man in a church?"

"I care nothing for these churches."

"Why not?" Gabriel hoped to distract Marcel, and it worked: Marcel's eyes slid to the glimmering gold altar. "It is a *young* religion. Young things are always stupid."

Gabriel snatched Marcel's gun by the barrel and twisted so hard he sent Marcel crashing to his knees. The gun skittered across the stone floor and under the pews.

"Professor!" Miss Flax's muffled voice cried from the stairwell behind Marcel.

Gabriel and Marcel locked eyes.

"No," Gabriel said.

"Why did I not think of it before?" Marcel was on his feet and barreling towards the staircase. "The *girl.*"

"Miss Flax!" Gabriel shouted.

She had nowhere to go but up.

Fear zinged through Ophelia when she heard the panic in the professor's voice and the stomping footsteps.

Marcel. He was coming.

She went up. She hadn't meant to dodge into some endless staircase. She'd hoped the door led to a closet or a passageway. Up she went, stumbling again and again. The steps were more shallow than she thought they ought to be, with slippery dips from centuries of feet. A stitch in her side made her gasp for breath, but she went still harder. Her hair came loose from its knot and tumbled down her back. Below her, the footsteps came, steady and heavy.

There *must* be another way down, once she made it to the top. True, the wooden church spire in Littleton, New Hampshire—the only other church tower she'd been in— had one ladder, to reach the bell. Nothing else up there but a steep tumble of roof—

Here. Here was more light pouring down the stairs and— yes!—she was at the top. A bell, massive and metal, hung from crisscrossed fat beams. Doves flapped away. Ophelia looked around wildly.

There was no other way down.

Only open, arched windows on all four sides, dizzy flashes of rooftops, chimneys, hills, sky.

Ophelia dashed to the side farthest from the stairwell. Marcel erupted from the stairs, black hair wild, sweat pouring.

Their eyes met across the bell's well. One second. Two.

Marcel rushed one way, and Ophelia ran the other. They had completed one full circle when she stumbled next to one of the open windows. Rooftops and sky came rushing forward, but she broke her fall, fingernails digging into the stone sill.

Marcel had her by the hair. Deep, tight, panicky pain. She yelped. More clattering footsteps were coming up the stairs.

"Get *off*, you big oaf!" Ophelia yelled, jabbing her elbows.

Penrose appeared in the corner of her eye. His face registered horror. He advanced, and in soothing French he spoke to Marcel. Ophelia caught the gist of his meaning: "Do not do anything rash, Marcel. You would not have an innocent young woman's blood on your hands."

"What do I care of her blood?" Marcel sneered. "She is nothing to me, a stranger, and an American, no less."

Penrose pulled something from his jacket. Ophelia expected a revolver, but no: It was . . . a jawbone.

Marcel loosened his grip on her hair.

"You desire this, no?" Penrose said.

"You damn well know that I do."

"You may have it. But first release Miss Flax."

"Why should I trust you?"

"You needn't." Penrose shrugged and moved to replace the bone back in his jacket.

"No," Marcel said, almost growling.

"I shall come closer," Penrose said, "and place it in your hand as soon as you release Miss Flax."

"At the same time," Marcel said.

"Very well. At the same time." Penrose came closer and held out the bone. Marcel released Ophelia's hair, snatched the bone, and strode towards the stairs.

"Miss Flax," Penrose murmured, gathering her to his chest.

Ophelia felt rag-doll limp and wet-eyed, so even though the professor was another lady's betrothed and she, Ophelia

Flax, was *not* one to wilt into a fellow's arms like a popped dirigible, well, it somehow happened anyway. She pressed her face into his shoulder, eyes squeezed shut. His solid arms wrapped around her. His breath warmed her ear, her cheek.

They stood like that, wrapped together in silence, for such a long moment that a few doves fluttered back to the rafters.

Penrose pulled away a little to see her. "Miss Flax, when I saw—when I thought he might . . . I have been prideful and stubborn and blind. The third thing I meant to tell you today . . ." He took a deep breath. His arms didn't loosen. "I wished to tell you that I am your friend, and I will help you no matter what occurs. I wished to tell you that you are not alone. Do you understand? You are not alone, and you won't ever be alone. No matter what happens next, or where we find ourselves on our separate paths through life."

Ophelia's belly twisted itself into knots, and she clung fast to his arms—Ophelia Flax, *clinging.*

Penrose went on. "What I mean to say is . . . last month, at the château in the Loire, I offered you a love speech, but I did not offer you what is more important still: a speech of friendship. Although, as you well know, I do love you."

"How can you make love speeches to me when you are otherwise engaged? Miss Banks—"

"I was numb when I returned to England last month. I felt as though a part of me had perished. No sooner had I expressed—or, perhaps, merely attempted to express—my sentiments to you, Miss Flax, than you became engaged to Griffe. Miss Banks . . . well, I have done her a grievous disservice to propose marriage to her. I am ashamed of that. I must apologize to her, and I must . . ." Penrose smoothed a breeze-blown strand of hair from Ophelia's eyes. "I must break it off with her. Immediately. Then, perhaps, I will be able to ask you an important question with a clear conscience."

An important question? The professor meant to ask her to be his wife? Ophelia's thoughts clamored. She couldn't have her own dairy farm in Vermont or New Hampshire if she married an English earl, could she? Fear twisted up inside her, too: Her father had abandoned Mother. And, shouldn't a fellow ask a lady if it was all right to ask her to marry him? Or. No. Was that right?

She pulled away, smoothed her cuffs, tidied her hair.

"I do apologize," Penrose said. "This is too much. You have had a great shock. Let us leave this place."

By the time Ophelia and Penrose were in the market square again, she had patched up her composure and knotted her hair. If the professor meant to propose marriage—and she still wasn't *entirely* sure that's what he'd meant—well, she had her answer ready. Right now, she had other fish to fry.

"Marcel could be the murderer," she said, scanning the crowd.

"Because of the jawbone?"

"He seemed ready enough to kill *me* for it."

"God, do not remind me of that."

"Maybe Marcel killed Mr. Knight's impostor over the jawbone. The impostor *did* have it in his trunk—remember the tooth?"

"All right, then: Marcel killed Mr. Knight's impostor for the jawbone. But what about Madame Dieudonné?"

"Why do murderers kill for the second time? Isn't it because it turns out that someone knows too much?"

"But how could Marcel have known of Madame Dieudonné's plans to divulge the murderer's identity to you? He wasn't at the ruined castle that day."

"No, but the village woman Lucile was."

"Good Lord. I hadn't thought of her. It was her idea to take us all up to that castle in the first place, you know. I wonder if *she* pushed me down the stairs."

"She pushed you down the *stairs*?"

"I survived. I've been so fixated upon Tolbert." Penrose

paused. "But then, what of your theory about the wealthy murderer luring their victim to Château Vézère at great expense?"

"I don't know. Could we return to the telegraph office and see if the Marseille police have responded?"

"All right."

The Marseille police had not responded, but still, a telegram was waiting for them.

The telegram read,

LORD HARRINGTON: MY NAME IS MR. CECIL KNIGHT. HAVE JUST BEEN RELEASED MOMENTS AGO FROM MARSEILLE JAIL, WHERE I WAS HELD FOR FALSE CHARGES RELATED TO PUBLIC BRAWL ON TENTH DECEMBER. THE MAN WHO CONVINCED POLICE TO ARREST ME BECAME KNOWN TO ME DURING PAST DAYS THROUGH SPEAKING WITH OTHER PRISONERS. JACK POTTER. ENGLISH SHIPPING AGENT WITH LOW REPUTATION FOR SWINDLES. READ IN NEWSPAPER OF DEATH OF POTTER POSING AS ME IN PÉRIGORD. ASSUME HE STOLE MY TRUNK FROM LODGINGS IN MARSEILLE AND MET MASTER CHRISTY'S SHIP ON ELEVEN DECEMBER. WILL TRAVEL TO SARLAT AS SOON AS FRAGILE HEALTH ALLOWS. PLEASE ADVISE REGARDING SAFETY OF MASTER CHRISTY.

"A shipping agent," Ophelia said. "Maybe that's why he had those bobbins of silk thread in his trunk. They must have been commercial samples."

"Indeed. And who at Château Vézère is rich as Midas and works in shipping?"

"Mr. Larsen, of course. Oh gracious—what about Mr. Banks, ill abed? Mr. Larsen and Mr. Banks might have known each other before—Forthwith told me as much earlier today, and it slipped my mind. Suppose Mr. Banks turning up there fuddled Mr. Larsen's plan—

"What plan, exactly?"

"Why, to lure Mr. Knight—Jack Potter—to the château and murder him. I'm frightened for Master Christy. He might speak like a college lecturer, but he's only a little boy, and now he's got no one looking after him, and if Mr. Larsen is a killer—"

"Are you suggesting that this is all some mad plot that will end in Master Christy being harmed?"

"I don't know."

"It strikes me as odd that the murderer in the château seems to have pulled strings to lure this impostor, Jack Potter, yet this telegram indicates that Jack Potter *himself* had a hand in things."

"In getting the real vicar jailed, you mean."

"Yes. And what of Marcel and his jawbone?"

Ophelia held up one palm. "There is the matter of the vicar and the trains and Marseille and the whippletree—that is one thing." She held up her other palm. "But there is also the matter of Marcel and the jawbone and that cave. And the beast. Are the two matters connected? Maybe. Maybe not. But I can't help thinking that they *are*. Let's telegraph the vicar and tell him Master Christy is safe—so far—and then we ought to go straight to the château."

"We'll hire a carriage, and I'll leave the horse I rode here at the inn."

28

⁓❦⁓

Château Vézère had a deserted air when their hired carriage rolled to a stop in the front drive.

"Look!" Miss Flax pointed. "Every last window on the first story is shattered."

"The village boys returned, then." Gabriel jumped down from the carriage and handed Miss Flax out. He instructed the driver to wait, and they went inside.

The foyer's marble floor sparkled with shattered glass. Cold wind swayed the chandeliers.

"I've got a bad feeling about this, Professor."

"Let us check the salon."

They walked so close their shoulders touched, and Gabriel had the oddest sense of walking towards his fate. Or his doom. Somehow, though, walking to his fate or his doom alongside Miss Flax felt, well, it felt *right*.

They found Bernadette and Griffe speaking in low tones before a meager fire in the salon. Both looked up, wide-eyed, haggard.

Griffe stood, flushed. "What is *she* doing here," he asked, eyes locked on Miss Flax.

Miss Flax lifted her chin. "Where is Mr. Larsen?"

"Larsen?" Griffe scoffed. "What do you want of him? Another of your filthy little scams, eh?"

"He is hunting," Bernadette said, glancing to the windows.

"He must be found," Gabriel said. "I'll ride out and find him myself."

"Why? He has done nothing!" Bernadette cried.

What a peculiar thing to say.

"Get that wench out of here," Griffe said to Gabriel.

"Watch your tongue, man. Miss Flax will stay by my side until all of this mess blows over. You were wrong to send her away, Griffe. Have you no heart? A young lady, defenseless and penniless, cast out with nothing but a charlatan conjurer for company? For shame."

"I will not be reprimanded in my own home!" Griffe shouted. "I will not have my wishes ignored!"

"Garon," Bernadette murmured. She tossed Miss Flax a curdling look.

How wrong Gabriel had been about Bernadette. He had taken her for a meek domestic creature. Yet now she really did seem capable of murder.

"Where is Master Christy?" Miss Flax asked.

"What do you care of the child?" Bernadette said.

"He's a young boy without a protector."

Gabriel strode to Griffe and passed him the curate Appleberry's telegram. "Your telegram, Count, and here is another of mine, from a gentleman by the name of Mr. Cecil Knight."

Griffe stared at the envelopes. "They have both been opened already. What is the meaning of this?"

"Go on, read them."

Gabriel saw Miss Flax slip away. She'd be searching for the boy.

When Griffe at last looked up from the telegrams, he

said hoarsely, "That man in the orangerie was an impostor? *Mon Dieu*." He tossed the telegrams to the carpet. "I have been deceived again and again. There is no dignity, no *vérité*, left in the world." He sagged back in his chair. For the first time, Gabriel noted the wine bottle beside Griffe, the empty glass. Griffe shaded his eyes with a hand. "Leave me. For God's sake, *everyone leave!*"

Bernadette, aflutter, began to gather up her embroidery.

"Where is Miss Banks?" Gabriel asked. He'd check on Miss Banks and then ride out to the woods in search of Larsen.

"At her father's side," Bernadette whispered.

But Ivy was not at her father's bedside; the weary sick nurse was reading her Bible in the chair beside Banks, who did not move beneath the coverlet. His eyes were closed, his breathing thick, his face like mud.

"Has he improved?" Gabriel asked the nurse in French.

She made the sign of the cross. "No, monsieur. He has worsened. He has not taken food or water for near twelve hours now. He does not move or speak. We must summon a priest."

"And you, madame? Have you had food or water or sleep these twelve hours past?"

"Water and food. No sleep."

"I should send for someone to relieve you, a village woman perhaps—"

"Sacredieu!" The nurse made another sign of the cross. "From the village Vézère? I would rather keep my eyes open for a month than leave this poor man to one of those heathens."

Gabriel's eyes fell on the vase of fresh roses beside the bed. "Who has brought those roses?"

"The beautiful daughter. She is in despair. She comes to him again and again, new roses every six hours. As though roses could make him live."

Gabriel went to the hired carriage waiting in the drive. He

instructed the driver to go to Sarlat and return with the finest doctor in town. What a fool he'd been not to do it earlier.

"Tell the doctor to bring medicines of all kinds. For the lungs, in particular, and the stomach. And the heart. Oh, and also . . . summon the police."

The driver nodded, already flicking his horses with his whip.

Gabriel started for the orangerie.

Penrose had said something about Abel making a mess of the library books, so Ophelia checked there first. No Abel, although an avalanche of open books threatened to spill off one table.

The kitchen. Of course. Ophelia hurried for the kitchen stairs, refusing to allow her thoughts to flit to the bad things that might've befallen Abel.

She turned a corner and crashed head-on into someone. Clémence, arms piled high with some glossy white garment, fear in her eyes. Without a peep, Clémence hugged the garment to her bosom and continued on her way.

Ophelia stared after her. Had that been the countess's wedding dress? She continued to the kitchen.

"Abel! Oh, thank goodness you're all right!" she cried when she saw him at the table. The parakeet sat in its cage on the table next to him.

"Well, of *course* I'm all right." Abel didn't look up.

Ophelia went closer. Abel wasn't looking at a hunk of cake or a pot of jam; he was looking at an enormous insect. Ugh. He was sketching a picture of it with pencil and paper. "What *is* that, Abel? Is it . . . alive?"

"Heavens, no. It went to the killing jar as soon as I'd transported it from under that fallen log in the forest to the château. Don't look at me like that—it was dying, anyway. Goodness knows how it survived so long into the winter. Beetles like this usually die off in the autumn. Beautiful, isn't it?"

Ophelia looked at the cream-colored beetle, the size of a field mouse, with crablike pincers and iridescent golden antennae, and lied, "Splendiferous." Her skin crawled.

"It is an unknown species, I am certain of it. I checked every book I could find in the library. I've discovered a new species!"

"Excellent. Listen, I wish you would come with me to Sarlat. It isn't safe for you here."

"Why ever not? If you refer to those village lads, well, they won't do anything to *me*. It's the count they despise."

Ophelia took a big breath and began the tale of the telegrams, the wrong body, and the true, still-living Reverend Cecil Knight.

Ivy bent over a rose plant in the orangerie, snipping with hooked brass clippers. Her cheeks were flushed, her hair becomingly arranged. Never had she appeared so lovely.

"Lord Harrington," she said. "I did not hear you come in. Is everything all right—is Papa—?"

"I have just been to see your father. He is . . . he is alive." Gabriel's voice cracked. Was he truly going to jilt a lady who was about to lose her father? "I have sent for a doctor. We'll soon set things to right." He mustered a lukewarm smile. "Miss Banks, there is something I must tell you."

"Oh?" Ivy's brow was a placid lake, yet she beheaded a perfect rose. It dropped silently to the floor.

"I must put an end to our engagement to be married. I am terribly sorry."

"Is it that coarse little American actress?" Ivy asked with a brittle smile and unblinking eyes. *Snip* went another perfect bloom onto the floor.

"If you refer to Miss Flax, then yes."

"Where is she? Eavesdropping again? She's a *terrible* eavesdropper. You'll never be able to keep on help with a creature like that under your roof. And your mother—have you thought of your mother? She shall drop dead when you bring a variety hall actress home." *Snip*—another headless stem.

"I cannot allow you to speak of Miss Flax in that way."

"My, my. You have a heart after all, Lord Harrington. I did not think it possible. What a coup for Miss Flax. Isn't it every actress's dream to snare a wealthy aristocrat? I daresay I've read at least ten rubbishy novels to that effect." *Snip, snip, snip.*

Gabriel placed a gentle hand on Ivy's shoulder. She went on snipping, now at spiny bare stalks. "Ivy—"

"Miss Banks." She flashed pearly teeth. "Now that our understanding has been terminated, you must refer to me as *Miss Banks*, and you mustn't touch me—although I believe, Lord Harrington, this is the first time you have *ever* touched me, is it not?"

He removed his hand.

Ivy hacked at the tough central stalk of the butchered rose bush. She grabbed the stalk with one hand to steady it. "Oh!" She held out her hand. They both stared at the blood seeping through her cotton glove. "Papa would be so very angry if he saw me wearing these gloves."

"Please, Miss Banks, put the clippers away."

"Very well!" She dropped the clippers and they clanged on the stone floor. She ground one of the roses beneath her heel—was it an accident?—before swishing silently past Gabriel.

"Where are you going?" he called after her. His guts churned with guilt.

"For a ride, I think. Perhaps along the river. It will be sublime under the full moon tonight."

"A ride? That would be madness, Miss Banks, riding in the dark—and it *will* be dark before too long. There are hunters abroad, rough woodsmen, the villagers—"

"And the beast?" Ivy stopped, hand on doorknob. "What an imagination you have, Lord Harrington. No, I do not believe I could have lived with that. I am a lady who keeps to the facts but you, well, I was *most* disappointed to discover that you still believe in fairy stories." She slipped out.

Gabriel dashed outside but could not see where she'd gone; the side court was empty. How had she disappeared so quickly? Did she really mean to ride out into the falling dusk?

From the front of the château came jeering voices, shattering glass, and the hollow boom of something heavy colliding with a door.

Gabriel ran to the front corner of the château and peered around it. A clump of men—a dozen or more—flowed up the front steps. Torches blazed. Dirty sap smoke puffed into the ever-deepening sky. One man wielded a pitchfork, another some sort of crude bludgeon, and others, hunting rifles. They all hooted as two burly forms battered their shoulders again and again against the front door. The door bowed and splintered; it would not hold for long.

Gabriel dashed back the way he'd come and tried a side door. Locked. He stripped off his coat, wrapped it around his fist, and smashed a window, again and again until all the shards had been cleared. He shook out his coat, shrugged it back on, and climbed through.

He found himself in the artillery gallery. He raced through dim corridors to the grand salon.

Griffe sprawled, snoring, in the armchair where Gabriel had left him. He cradled a wine bottle.

"Wake up!" Gabriel said, shaking him. "They've come for you. The villagers have come for you. Come along, we must hide."

Miss Flax burst into the room, Abel at her side. Abel carried a brass birdcage. "Who's that battering at the door?" Miss Flax asked.

"I daresay the villagers had their fill of Griffe's tree felling. Come, help me with him. He's senseless. We might hide in the secret servants' passageway."

The three of them—Abel insisted upon helping with a serious air—dragged the snoring Griffe to the door hidden in the wall panel, the same door through which Madame Dieudonné had disappeared during that fateful conjuring trick. Inside, it smelled of dust and mildew, and it was pitch-black. They stretched Griffe out on the floor. Miss Flax and Abel stuffed themselves inside.

"Why the birdcage, boy?" Gabriel asked Abel.

"It's my parakeet," Abel said, as though that explained everything.

"Just a moment." Gabriel dashed back out into the salon just as a huge splintering crack sounded at the front of the house. The marauders had breached the door.

"Hurry," Miss Flax cried. "What are you doing?"

Gabriel snatched up a candelabra stuck with tapers and a box of matches. He ducked back through the hidden door and shut it. Stifling blackness. Their own quick breathing. Then, men's voices, closer and closer. They heard the salon doors being booted open, muttering voices, crashing glass. Then the men were gone.

29

$$\text{\textit{e}}\!\!\sim\!\!\times\!\!\sim\!\!\text{\textit{o}}$$

Ophelia dared not speak for an aching eternity. Abel pressed beside her, hot and sweaty, hugging his birdcage. The parakeet didn't make a sound. The professor crouched on Ophelia's other side, his shoulder against hers. That was reassuring. Griffe went on snoring, and his wine breath soon fumed up the passage.

"Where is Miss Banks?" Ophelia whispered. "What of Mr. Banks and his nurse? Bernadette—oh!—and the maidservant, Clémence, is still here."

"We must hope that they are safe. Those men are half mad with blood lust and, probably, drink. It is the count they wish for. Once they fail to find him, they will leave."

They waited for another long stretch. They heard boots stomping, doors slamming, distant guffaws, curses, whoops. After fifteen or twenty minutes, silence at last fell.

"They're gone," Ophelia whispered.

"Yes," Penrose said.

"Allow me out of this hen coop," Abel said, struggling to

his feet by bracing his entire weight upon Ophelia's shoulders. He fumbled around, stepping on everyone, until he found the door and spilled out into the salon with his birdcage.

Ophelia blinked, even though the salon was lit only by thin blue moonlight. Penrose helped her up—her feet had fallen asleep and they felt like two wooden mallets. They dragged Griffe back out onto a carpet and Ophelia fetched a pillow for his head. Penrose lit a few gas lamps.

When Ophelia kneeled and lifted Griffe's head to slide the pillow under, his eyes opened.

She froze.

"You," Griffe said thickly. He moistened the roof of his mouth with his tongue.

"I will just be going," Ophelia said crisply, "but first I thought I'd prop up your head, for you've had far too much to drink, and I would not wish for anything bad to happen to you if, for instance, you were to be sick."

Griffe struggled upright. "Mademoiselle—was it Flax?"

"Yes," she said, drawing away. She felt Penrose's eyes on them.

Griffe said, "Mademoiselle Flax, I have been most ungracious, most unkind to you. I am sorry. In Paris, I fell in love, not with you, I see, but ah! with the mysterious creature you pretended to be. You tricked and betrayed me, and for that I am most angry, but as I drank wine—my father's vintage, there is but one bottle left, now—I gazed into my own heart and saw that there is no actress so fine that she could pretend your sweetness or your good heart." Griffe fumbled for Ophelia's hand, and she allowed him to take it. "You possess a good heart, Mademoiselle Flax. You made strange, *oui*, foolish choices, yet I cannot but forgive you."

Ophelia's mouth opened, but she couldn't think of what to say.

"I beg your pardon," Penrose said, "but I must go check on Mr. Banks and the nurse. Master Christy, would you stay here with Miss Flax?"

"Fine." Abel was arranging the parakeet's cage on a table. "But I still haven't gotten to show you my beetle."

Penrose ruffled Abel's hair. "Soon, lad. Soon." He left. Abel slumped moodily on a chair and slid a little specimen case from his pocket.

"What is more," Griffe said to Ophelia, "I was unkind to you, unforgivably rude, when you asked me about what Madame Dieudonné had told you. It is true, we knew each other, Madame Dieudonné and I, long ago, in my youth. My cousin Roland, older than I and worldly, brought me to her, a famed Parisian courtesan, to initiate me into the ways of love."

"Oh. Um." Ophelia tugged her hand away from Griffe's. "No need to spell things out too—"

"She fell in love with me, I but a hapless and selfish young man, she more than twice my age though still a great beauty. I spurned her without a thought. When she returned to the château after all of these years, I did not at first recognize her. She had altered her name and time had not been kind. She felt slighted over again for that. When at last I realized it was she, I was too mortified to admit knowing her to anyone, least of all to you, my betrothed."

"But you had nothing to do with her death?"

"*Non!* I would never . . . I have been angry, I have behaved poorly, but Mademoiselle Flax, you must know that I would never kill another human being."

Ophelia waited for her gut. Finally she said, "I believe you."

Griffe smiled fuzzily, like a baby newly awoken. "We both had secrets, *oui*?"

Ophelia nodded. *"Oui."*

"Oh, *monsieur le comte!*" a woman screamed. Ophelia and Griffe looked up to see Clémence bouncing in. She threw herself upon Griffe and kissed him all over his face, hands, and neck, and Griffe seemed helpless to stop her. In fact, he almost seemed to be enjoying himself.

Ophelia frowned. Of *course*. Clémence was in love with Griffe. The devotion, the jealous behavior towards Ophelia.

Ophelia suddenly knew that Clémence had been behind all the sabotaged wedding preparations.

Griffe managed to push Clémence away. Clémence was dewy-eyed, her blond hair tumbling. Griffe said something in French about noblemen and servants, and fat tears rolled down Clémence's cheeks.

Ophelia cleared her throat. "I beg your pardon, Count— and I do realize this is really none of my concern—but I would like to point out that you engaged yourself to one Miss Stonewall of Cleveland, Ohio, who was *not* a noble-woman."

Griffe shook his head. "But a *servant*—"

"Fiddlesticks! Just look at Clémence! All she needs is a new gown." Ophelia reckoned Clémence had just the one. "Can't you see that she loves you, Count? That's a finer thing than money and titles. You love her, too—I can tell. Admit it to yourself and you'll be ever so much happier. And listen, if you were able to convince yourself that you were in love with me, an actress—and did you know I once worked in the circus?"

Griffe's jaw wedged open.

"Well then, surely you might return the love of this beau-tiful lady." Ophelia got to her feet. More pins and needles. Ouch. She limped over to the fireplace to get a blaze going again, leaving Griffe and Clémence to work things out be-tween themselves.

Gabriel bounded up the stairs two at a time and hurried along the upper corridors. Paintings had been ripped from the walls, vases smashed. He smelled urine. In Banks's chamber, the sick nurse huddled in prayer beside the bed. Banks lay as before, breathing throatily, eyes shut.

"The men!" the nurse whispered in French. "The heathen men!"

"Did they harm you, madame?"

"No. They said they wished for the lady."

"The lady?" Gabriel's heart turned to ice. *Ivy.* Young, beautiful—they could only wish for Ivy. How could he have been so *blind*?

He ran downstairs and out onto the twilit front drive. He looked left and right. Nothing but rattling bare trees and the low-slung moon.

He ran to the stables. Perhaps Ivy had gotten away on horseback before the village men had come.

The stables rustled with the sounds of upset horses. No Ivy and, of course, no groom or stable boy. He pushed out of the stables again. He stopped, and tipped his head. Yes. There. Hoof beats, thudding closer. Ivy returning. She would have realized the folly of going for a ride at such an hour.

Gabriel went out to the front drive, and the hoof beats thumped louder and louder. A horse galloped up the drive, mane and tail streaming.

The horse did not have a rider.

"Something has befallen Miss Banks," Professor Penrose cried, bursting into the salon. His usually composed face was in motion, as though it couldn't settle upon a sentiment. He scarcely noticed Griffe and Clémence on the carpet, murmuring and embracing.

"What has happened to Miss Banks?" Ophelia asked. "The men—?"

"I do not know." Penrose raked a hand through his hair. "God, I do not know. Her horse has just returned without her. I broke things off with her—that was more than an hour past, now—and she said she would go for a ride along the river road."

"But that is madness!"

"Well, she *is* mad," Abel muttered, still sulking with his beetle box.

"She insisted," Penrose said, "and before I could stop her, well, the village men arrived—oh God."

"You suppose she went off, brokenhearted and distraught?" Ophelia asked.

"Well, naturally." Penrose paced back and forth.

Ophelia could picture Ivy *pretending* heartbreak, to make Penrose feel guilty and such. But it wouldn't be at all like Ivy to go off like a poetic damsel and, say, drown herself in a mill pond.

"I must go search for her," Penrose said. "Miss Flax, please stay here at the château and look after"—he looked at Griffe and Clémence—"well, perhaps the count no longer requires looking after, but Mr. Banks does, and so does Master Christy."

"I do not require looking after," Abel said. "I am not the village idiot."

"You're a youth," Penrose said, stopping before Abel. He sucked in a breath. "What . . . is that?" He pointed to Abel's specimen box.

"I have discovered a new species of beetle."

"May I?"

Ophelia sighed. Sidetracked by a bug at a time like this?

The three of them peered into Abel's specimen box.

"It is a stag beetle," Abel said. "Stag beetles are named for their prominent antennae, which resemble stag's antlers."

"But it is *white*," Penrose said. "White and gold."

"I've never seen anything like it," Abel said. "Isn't it lovely?"

Penrose slowly shook his head. "I have been utterly blind. The villagers having no church, the sick nurse and her talk of heathens. Madame Genepy's tale. De Villeneuve's tale as well, in fact. . . ."

Ophelia and Abel exchanged glances: *Had the professor gone off his rocker?*

"Would you mind explaining things a little more clearly, Professor?" Ophelia asked.

"De Villeneuve's and Madame Genepy's tales both made mention of white stags with golden horns. I believe they refer to the beetle or, at least, the original tale *meant* a beetle and de Villeneuve misunderstood and changed it to an actual stag. I misunderstood. I misunderstood *everything*, hearing only what I wished to hear, or hearing what I assumed I would hear in advance, rather than keeping my mind receptive to something new. Madame Genepy's tale *is* something new—or, rather, something very, very old, older than any tale I have encountered. Don't you see? Hers is not a medieval tale; it is a tale rooted in the very beginnings of human history. When she began her tale saying *In this land before time*, why, that is precisely what she meant. When she spoke of the Mother of the Seasons, she did not mean the Virgin Mary—she referred to some primeval goddess. And the animals—oh my God, the animals! She spoke of how this valley has been slumbering; when she spoke of the loss of all the creatures, she meant all those creatures on the walls of the painted cave—the bison and bears, the rhinoceroses and mammoths and snakes."

Ophelia struggled to follow. "So you're saying that it's a really old tale that Madame Genepy tells, and that her tale is rooted in the ancient animals that used to live in this valley?"

"Yes. Her tale is the tale of this valley, and of the loss of the ancient creatures that once roamed here. And now Miss Banks . . . they have taken her, I know it!"

"Who has taken her?" Abel asked.

"The villagers."

"But why?"

"My heart is sick. These tales, the animal groom tales of which the *Beauty and the Beast* tale is one . . . they are believed by scholars to have their origins in primeval rites of sacrifice."

"Sacrifice?" Ophelia said.

"Virgins sacrificed to appease beast-like deities."

"You mean to say that the villagers worship a beast-like deity?" Ophelia asked, amazed that such a sentence came from her lips.

"To influence the weather, or save livestock—"

Ophelia thought of the slaughtered livestock.

"—or in an attempt to control forces beyond their scope of influence."

"Such as Griffe chopping down their forest?"

"Yes. And the shrine, Miss Flax! How could I have thought for a moment that that shrine was Tolbert's doing? It was the villagers, the servants, the gardener—all of them."

Outside the windows, the clear full moon was floating higher.

"It is the winter solstice," Ophelia whispered. "Longest night of the year, and a full moon to boot. Nice time for a heathen ritual, wouldn't you say? Professor, what time do you reckon the moon will reach its zenith tonight?"

"Six o'clock."

"Then we haven't much time. Miss Banks said she intended to ride up the river road—we ought to retrace her path."

Penrose took Abel by the shoulders. "Stay here. The doctor from Sarlat should arrive sometime soon, but if you hear anyone besides the doctor coming—*anyone*—you are to shut yourself into the servants' secret passage and stay there until we return. Do you understand?"

Abel nodded, wide-eyed. "You may depend upon me, Professor."

30

In silence, Ophelia and Penrose saddled two horses in the stables. Ophelia chose a gent's saddle; she'd never gotten the hang of those prudish side saddles that made her feel like she was always about to go flying into a ditch.

They rode down the dark château drive. Their horses' hooves made thumps and crunches aplenty, but Ophelia's heart kicked when she heard another, more distant *snap*.

She swiveled in her saddle. She gasped. A form half hunched in the trees—or—she blinked. No, it was only a thicker clump of bushes.

"Is something the matter, Miss Flax?" Penrose asked.

"Right as rain."

They continued on. At the château gates, they stopped.

"Miss Banks said she would ride up the river road," Penrose said, "but surely she didn't mean to ride through the village. She seemed frightened of the folk."

Frightened wasn't the word Ophelia would've chosen. Ivy had been contemptuous of the villagers. Still, she surely wouldn't wish to ride through the village and risk contact with them.

They turned right. They rode in silence for fifteen minutes without seeing a soul. They stopped. Cold wind slapped off the river. Their horses' manes blew.

"Surely we would've encountered her by now, if this is the way she had gone," Penrose said. "She is on foot now. If those brutish villagers carried her . . ."

Ophelia had never seen Penrose seem so lost. Her heart ached to see how his shoulders hitched, as though he were in pain. "Don't hold yourself responsible," she said softly. "Miss Banks is a woman grown. She makes her own choices. Come on, let's ride along the river road the other way."

They turned and broke into a trot. "I should have seen all of this sooner," Penrose said. "Not *after* the villagers stormed the château and kidnapped an innocent young woman."

"I should have seen it, too."

"If they harm her, it is on my head."

Ophelia thought hard. "Professor, you said something about animal groom tales. What did you mean by that?"

"God, it seems silly." He made a hollow chuckle. "These are tales in which a beautiful woman—a human woman—marries a beast. As in *La belle et la bête*, for instance."

"How do these tales usually pan out? I mean to say, what's the happily ever after?"

"Why, that the beast is redeemed and transforms back into a man."

"Because the lady kisses him, is that it? Like that frog prince yarn?"

"Well, no. Usually in animal groom tales, some other mechanism breaks the spell. Water is a common motif." He glanced into the moon-pale gush of the river.

"Water?"

"Enchanted wells, springs, and the like. In the de Villeneuve tale, Belle brings the dying beast water from a fountain, and it is really the combination of the fountain water and Beauty's declaration of love that transfigures the beast back into a man."

Ophelia's nerves prickled. "Professor," she said slowly, "that morning when the cook discovered Mr. Knight's— well, the impostor's—body in the orangerie and she was so frightened about what she took to be beast-goring marks on his belly, well, she said something about a spring."

"She did?"

Ophelia nodded. "She said the Beast is transformed by water from an enchanted spring."

"An enchanted spring." Penrose spurred his horse on. "The ruined castle is built over a spring."

They passed the château gates and kept going along the river road in the other direction.

"Eerie, isn't it?" Ophelia said as their horses trotted through the village Vézère. Not a light shone in a window, although it was suppertime now. "It's almost as though everyone has simply . . . left."

In the blacksmith's hut, embers glowed red in the furnace. A crow cackled on the roof. The last building in the village was a pitch-dark stable. A horse whinnied softly as they passed, and Ophelia fancied she saw the white flash of its eye.

Presently they rounded a bend in the road, and there was the ruined castle: jagged and flat-looking, like a cut paper silhouette. The moon drifted to its left, and Ophelia had the spooky feeling that once the moon was right up over the castle, something might . . . *happen.*

They rode up the steep-pitched castle road and left their horses hitched to trees at the abandoned inn. They went up the stairs on foot.

At first Ophelia thought it was the wind. Moaning. Wailing. But each step up the stairs brought the sounds into sharper focus. It *wasn't* the wind; it was chanting. Dozens of voices chanting, underlaid by the hollow plodding heartbeat of a drum.

Her skin went clammy. Penrose quickened his step, and she knew he'd heard the chanting, too. At the top of the stairs, they stayed close to the castle's outer wall and peered through the archway. The courtyard was empty. The chanting coiled down from somewhere above, where battlements and towers cut the sky like jack-o'-lantern teeth.

Gabriel and Miss Flax crept to one of the towers. Up. They needed to go up, to where the chanting was. Around and around they climbed until they emerged outside, atop a tower with low crenelated walls.

Gabriel gasped, and Miss Flax whispered, *"Mercy."*

On *another* tower, several yards off and below them several feet, a crowd of people stood. Light from the moon, almost directly above, washed down like pale water. Their chanting droned on and on to the accompaniment of the drum.

Gabriel and Miss Flax went to the wall, crouched, and peered over. They were close enough to make out faces. There was Lucile with her grandmother, Madame Genepy. There were the village adolescent boys, for once still and grave. There was the cook, Marielle, swaying, eyes closed and hands raised as she chanted, and beside her the château gardener, Luc. The stringy brown-clad man was there, and Gabriel caught the white flash of his nose plaster. He'd broken it, then. The entire village, it seemed, man, woman, and child, was ringed around an empty center.

The crowd parted. A huge figure in pale flowing robes emerged from somewhere, a wreath in his hands.

"That's Marcel," Miss Flax whispered. "The blacksmith! What's he holding—it looks like that wreath is made of—"

"Belladonna berries."

"What is he, some sort of *priest*? And look what he's got around his neck. It's the jawbone, strung like some kind of amulet."

Marcel lifted the belladonna wreath to the moon, as in offering.

The chanting crescendoed.

Gabriel could scarcely breathe. This was madness. Utter madness. This was the year 1867, for pity's sake. Who in Europe—at least, in the western nations of Europe—partook in pagan rites? And where was Miss Banks? Gabriel scanned the crowd, but he did not see her. There was Tolbert, though, moving in and out of sight at the back of the crowd.

Marcel lowered the wreath and turned, robes swirling. He held out a commanding hand. Again, the crowd parted.

A woman, head drooped and hands behind her back, was led forward by two men. She wore a gown of pale gold.

"Bernadette!" Miss Flax said with a gasp. "That's—they mean to sacrifice Bernadette? *That's* who they stormed the château to find, and we did not even notice she was missing!"

"God Lord, I am a fool. These tales—the de Villeneuve, all of them—the human bride must be of noble blood. Miss Banks isn't of noble blood; *Bernadette Gavage* is. I must go—"

"Look!" Miss Flax whispered. "Here comes . . . Merciful heavens."

A man led forth a huge furry boar by a rope around its neck.

Gabriel bolted to his feet. "They're mad. I must intervene."

"You'll be outnumbered, professor! Please, stay."

Gabriel patted his jacket. His revolver was still there, and loaded.

Miss Flax pointed to a pile of crumbled stones. "We could throw rocks if need be, keeping ourselves hidden behind the battlement. Isn't that what the knights did in the olden days?"

"God only knows what the villagers have planned."

"That boar won't hurt Bernadette. Look at it. It's as docile as a lamb."

"A six-foot-long lamb with bristles and tusks."

"Please don't leave."

Gabriel's heart tugged. Miss Flax was frightened. Had he ever seen her so?

He crouched beside her again.

The boar was led to a stop beside Bernadette. Marcel placed the belladonna wreath on Bernadette's loose, messy hair. Bernadette jerked her arms, which appeared to be tied at the wrist. Marcel cried, "In this land before time began, the Mother of the Seasons made this land lush with animals."

"What did he say?" Miss Flax whispered.

Gabriel translated, adding, "That is how Madame Genepy's tale begins."

Marcel continued, and Gabriel translated softly for Miss Flax. "'But a deep enchantment put the land to sleep. All of the animals turned to stone. Men and women froze into mineral columns.'" Comprehension unfolded in Gabriel's mind. Animals turned to stone? *The animals in the painted cave.* Men and women petrified into mineral columns? Not the marble statues of de Villeneuve's prettified tale; *stalactites and stalagmites.* "'The land will continue to sleep unless Beast and Human are reunited in marriage.'"

"He means to marry Bernadette to a *boar*?" Miss Flax whispered.

"It would seem so. I hope this means she is not in danger." Gabriel translated what Marcel said next: "'That was a magical time, a time of dreams, with no divides between humans and animals, between humans and the world. Today we dwell in a disenchanted world. We have lost the language of the animals. We see only oblivion staring out of their dark eyes. But we may mend this rift, yea, *we may mend it!*'"

This, then, explained the villagers' seemingly backward hostility towards Griffe's scientific improvements. Those improvements included deforestation and more aggressive, large-scale animal agriculture. But the folk of Vézère practiced simple animal husbandry and relied upon hunted meat and foraged wild plants.

Marcel shouted up at the moon, "Mother of the Seasons! Grant us absolution! We are sorry we fell from your grace. Mother, help us!" The crowd moaned, dozens of arms upstretched to the moon. The drum thumped louder, faster. "Mother, take this virgin of noble blood! Make her the bride of this sweet-hearted beast. Through their union gather your people once more to the long-lost bosom of the earth!"

Marcel said something to one of the nearby men, and the man stepped forward to remove the ropes at Bernadette's wrists. Marcel grabbed Bernadette's arm and placed it around the boar's furred neck.

Bernadette screamed.

Gabriel got to his feet. "I cannot stand by any longer. I am sorry, Miss Flax. I shall return." He kissed the top of her head and ran for the stairs.

Ophelia considered following Professor Penrose, but then thought better of it. If things got down to the nitty-gritty, she could do more from up here with her pile of rubble than she could if she rushed empty-handed into a crowd of crazed heathen villagers.

Still, she fought to keep her breathing steady. For if something were to happen to the professor . . . No, it didn't bear thinking of.

She couldn't understand what Marcel was saying without Penrose translating. Marcel was still droning on, arms raised. The crowd kept crying out and moaning, and the drum thumped on.

Bernadette quaked, her arm around the boar. Her face was a mask of fear and disgust. The boar snuffled at something by its hooves.

What would the villagers do when they saw the professor?

Ophelia's skin began to crawl. At first she figured it was on account of the ghoulish spectacle. Then she reckoned it was the chilly wind. But . . . something made her turn.

Gabriel crept through the ruined castle, which was here washed by moonlight, there sunk in shadow. The villagers were appealing to the Mother of the Seasons—their goddess, evidently—to stop the marauding beasts as well as Griffe's deforestation. They were desperate; they felt under attack, and they seemed to think that marrying a wild boar to a lady of noble blood would do the trick.

He followed the throbbing drum and the villagers' moans up a coiled staircase and out onto the top of the tower. He emerged at the back of the crowd; no one saw him.

Where had Tolbert gone?

Gabriel hid behind a heap of stones and watched, ready to spring forward if need be.

Marcel held up a wooden chalice, and through the din of the crowd, Gabriel pieced together that the chalice held water—enchanted water, if Marcel was to be believed—from the castle wellspring. Marcel offered the chalice to the boar, and the boar took a few messy laps. Marcel offered the chalice to Bernadette. Bernadette reared away in disgust.

"Drink!" Marcel yelled in French.

Shaking, Bernadette took a sip. She gagged.

The crowd keened and shouted.

Another woman stepped into the inner circle. The cook, Marielle. She held something up, and it flashed red. A ruby ring.

Marcel spoke in an undertone, now, as priests sometimes did when administering vows. He addressed the boar first. The boar shifted, eyes rolling. Marcel addressed Bernadette, and Bernadette shook her head. Marcel grabbed her hand

and pushed the ruby ring onto her finger. The drum's tempo lunged forward, and the crowd began to dance.

Ophelia's mouth fell open. A dark form stood at the top of the tower steps. Human legs, trunk, arms. But a big, furry boar's head with tusks that gleamed white.

There was a peculiar hissing sound, and Ophelia realized it came from her own lungs. She dove, still on her knees, for the pile of rubble and grabbed the first stone that she could. She scrabbled to her feet, never taking her eyes from the beast in the shadows.

"Come on, then," Ophelia said. "Take off your mask. You might've had everyone else fooled, but I never believed for a second you were real. Who are you under there? Mr. Tolbert? Mr. Larsen? Gerard?"

Silence. The beast's shoulders rose and fell.

Ophelia got a firmer grip on the stone and took a few steps forward. "Come on, then, take that moth-eaten mask off. You made it from one of the mounted heads in the château study, didn't you? How can you breathe in there? Did you poke yourself some nice breathing holes?"

Still, silence.

Who was it under there? It was the murderer, Ophelia was certain, and that ought to have made her turn tail. But by gum, she'd cornered the beast *and* the murderer. Wild horses couldn't pull her away now.

She closed the distance between herself and the beast in one second flat. She chucked her stone aside and took the bottom edge of the beast's furry head in each hand.

The beast grunted and reared back. Weakling. Ophelia tugged harder and downward, so the beast-impostor was bent at the waist and its head was sideways. One last tug and the beast plopped on its rump. The mask was free.

"You little *bitch*," Ivy Banks snarled, splay-legged in gent's trousers.

"What in—what in tarnation are you doing dressed up as a beast, Miss Banks? We came out here, rushed out, *searching* for you. Professor Penrose fancied you had been kidnapped after you'd headed out into the evening with a broken heart."

Ivy tittered. "Just like a gentleman, is it not, to suppose a lady's every action is on account of him?"

"It was you every time, wasn't it? Every time someone spied a beast it was *you* in this nasty old boar's head." Ophelia looked down at the boar's head in her hands. It reeked of rancid animal grease. She dropped it. "You whacked Professor Penrose and me over the head that night—you pushed your own fiancé into a canal."

"Serves him right, cavorting in the night with another woman. It wasn't me *every* time, you know." Ivy got to her feet. "I didn't kill the livestock."

"Then who did?"

"How would I know?"

"You meant to scare the villagers," Ophelia said. "Spook them into thinking their beast legend had come to life."

"Why not? They believe all that rubbish anyway, or did you not notice their little ritual going on just now? They ought to thank me for making their pitiful backwater theology a reality. I got the idea from that hysterical cook the morning Mr. Knight's body was discovered in the orangerie."

Mr. Knight, she'd said. Didn't Ivy know that really had been Jack Potter?

"It seemed a brilliant way to . . ." Ivy pressed her lips together.

"To what?" Ophelia said. "To distract everyone from the fact that *you* murdered a man?"

"Do *I* look as though I could kill a man?" Ivy bent and picked up the stone Ophelia had dropped.

"Yes. You do."

"It wasn't me. Father raised me to be a *lady*. The very *thought* of me cornering Mr. Knight and poisoning him with belladonna in his wine!"

"Then that is how you did it?"

"I told you, it wasn't me."

"But you went through all the trouble of dressing up in a beast costume every night and traipsing about the countryside—"

"It was really quite fun. So very liberating. But you already know the joys of gentlemen's trousers, don't you?"

"You're attempting to convince me that you went to all the trouble of dressing up every night as a moth-eaten boar, even though you didn't . . ." Ophelia's voice trailed off. Who would Ivy go through all that trouble to protect besides herself? "Your *father* is the murderer," Ophelia said. "Why?"

"I don't know. He won't speak to me now, and I did *everything* for him. To save him."

A daughter sacrificing herself to save her father. Now why did that sound so familiar?

"That night," Ivy said, "I saw it all through the orangerie windows. I couldn't sleep, and I'd seen Papa creep into the orangerie from my bedchamber window. I put on my wrap and followed. I was worried."

Worried, Ophelia's foot. Ivy was mad for management and power.

"I saw Papa toast Mr. Knight with a glass of wine. They drank. Soon, Mr. Knight convulsed and Father . . . he did nothing. Only watched a bit, and once Mr. Knight was bleeding horribly from that pitchfork wound—that was an accident—Papa left. But dear Papa had taken no measures at all to conceal his crime. He required my help. I fetched Father's heart tablets from his chamber—"

"*His* heart tablets? Then it *is* a heart ailment!"

"Quite obviously. I went quickly, you see, before Papa returned to his bedchamber. I ran so hard, I had a stitch in my side. I fetched my own traveling sickness medicine, too, because that's got belladonna in it, and I fancied *that* would create confusion as well."

It most certainly had. "You dumped the traveling sickness tablets in the goldfish pool."

"I needed to be rid of the tablets, and the fish pool seemed as good a place as any. Then I recalled how everyone had gone on about the roses, so I placed one in the vicar's hands."

"To muddle things even more."

"Yes, and after all *that*, I fancied Papa would be safe from suspicion."

"Did he know you'd done all that?"

"Oh, no. It was all going just swimmingly until *you* began snooping about, Miss Flax—is that a stage name? Then, I assumed the guise of the beast each evening to further create suspicion."

"And you kept going on about the villagers, how scary and suspicious they were, in an effort to draw attention away from yourself. Why did you kill Madame Dieudonné?"

"I didn't! Papa did. We both overheard her, right here at the castle, telling you that she knew who the murderer was. I saw the look of dread on Papa's face. I knew he would kill her when he could. When we were all searching for her after that silly conjuring trick with the mirror, Papa shot her."

"You allowed Henrietta to take the blame."

"She's a criminal."

"But not a murderess."

"Does it matter? Women like that ought to be locked up. Women like *you*."

"What about tonight?" Ophelia asked. "Why did you come here? Why did you costume yourself as the beast?"

"I hoped Lord Harrington would come here, looking for *me*, of course, but finding the villagers instead."

"So he would suppose the villagers committed the murders?"

"Something like that. And the costume, well, my *goodness*, I could not be recognized, could I? Oh dear. Me and my tripping little tongue!—now you know *far* too much." Ivy smiled and took a step towards Ophelia, stone in hands.

"I cannot have Papa arrested for two murders, can I? Out here in the hills and the trees, your body will simply vanish into the river or over a cliff, or perhaps a wild beast will devour it before anyone notices you are missing." Ivy hefted the stone overhead and lunged.

Ophelia dodged around Ivy and stumbled down the tower steps.

31

The drum boomed, and the villagers rioted and twirled in circles around Bernadette and the boar. Bernadette appeared green. The boar was becoming skittish. Marcel stood a few paces off and watched.

Tolbert slid around the pile of rubble and crouched by Gabriel.

"Tolbert," Gabriel said.

"We meet again, Lord Harrington. You are not a man who gives in easily."

"Nor you, I daresay." Tolbert's chin tufted whiskers, his hair was lank, and he stank of sour feet. "Have you been roughing it, Tolbert?"

"I am accustomed to sleeping out of doors when necessary."

"Guarding your cave from the woodcutters?"

"Yes. And I am so pleased to hear you at last acknowledge that it is *mine*."

"What about the shrine?" Gabriel asked, just to be certain.

"Pah! You continue to believe that was *my* work, even as these insane peasants carouse in a circle around a boar?"

Good point.

"I am here for my jawbone," Tolbert said. His shiny black eyes were fixed, unblinking, on the bone hung about Marcel's neck.

"It was always about the jawbone and the cave," Gabriel said. "Never about the legendary beast?"

"The beast is extinct. But it *once* lived. I have the fossil evidence—or, I shall, once I wrest it from that fool blacksmith's neck."

"You didn't murder anyone?"

"I have neither the time nor the inclination. My interests are scientific."

Perhaps. Yet Gabriel knew that scientific obsession was not very different from other sorts. "What about your mysterious parcel in Bordeaux?"

"It is not mysterious, Lord Harrington. What ever gave you that idea? It is a handmade rock pick from Scotland. My previous one broke. I do hope it has not been injured in transit from England."

The crowd was growing more raucous, and the boar was tugging at its ropes.

"Have you learned anything about this—well, this cult?" Gabriel asked Tolbert.

"It is of a somewhat recent date. Perhaps twenty years old. Begun by Marcel after he nearly died ingesting belladonna berries. He claims to have stepped through the door into the divine realm and spoken, face-to-face, with the goddess. She sent him back to the land of the living to begin his cult. Rubbish, of course. Poisoning oneself is not divine, but stupid. I suspect the cult is a way for Marcel to lord control over others in the village. He is a brute, and secretive. He is a true provincial, too. Resentful and suspicious of anyone who is not from his native valley."

Lucile must've pushed Gabriel down the castle steps that

day. Gabriel had intruded too deeply into the village lore. Likewise, Larsen must have been shot by a villager who was resentful of him hunting on their forestland. Lucile had been lying about Madame Genepy losing her memory, too. That had been a smoke screen. The tale was the same as it had always been.

Crunching footfalls made both Gabriel and Tolbert turn. Four gendarmes clustered at the top of the tower steps, faces slack at the sights and sounds of the villagers dancing.

Tolbert licked his lips. It could be his last chance to get his hands on the jawbone before the police, perhaps, confiscated it as evidence. He rushed forward, elbowing and stumbling through the crowd. Screams and curses. The drumbeat stopped. The boar had broken free of its ropes, and its two handlers struggled to placate it. Tolbert took a flying leap, felled Marcel, ripped the jawbone free, and held it up to the moon, giggling shrilly.

Gabriel dashed through the throng and wrapped his arm around Bernadette. "Come with me, Mademoiselle Gavage," he murmured.

"Lord Harrington," she sobbed.

Marcel swatted the jawbone from Tolbert's hands. It arced through the air and landed at the boar's hooves. The boar sniffed it. There was a long, breathless pause, everyone watching. The boar ate the jawbone.

Ivy was just behind Ophelia. Her footfalls were ladylike, almost silent, and she panted through her teeth.

At the bottom of the steps, Ophelia swung her head left and right. She went left and along a vaguely familiar passageway lit by moonlight through archer's slits. Ivy's lilac scent rose up behind her.

Here was a doorway. *Please let it be the way out.* Ophelia slipped through. No. *No.* A close dark space, walls on three sides—why was it so familiar? She swung around.

Ivy's silhouette blocked the only way out. "The latrine, Miss Flax? Mm. Fitting that you do keep coming here, since you are nothing but a coarse little bit of dung." Ivy grabbed Ophelia's sleeve and twisted. Fabric bit into flesh. Ophelia yelped and tried to jerk herself free. Ivy held fast. She was doubling Ophelia over and pushing her head towards the latrine hole. Death-cold wind gusted up through the opening. Rocks, whitewashed by moonlight, glowed far, far below on their slide into the river.

"Get off!" Ophelia cried, bucking her head and jabbing her elbows like chicken wings.

"Miss Flax!" Penrose's voice cried nearby.

"Mon Dieu!" screamed a woman—Bernadette.

Ophelia twisted hard and sent Ivy crashing against the latrine seat. Masonry crumbled. Rocks showered.

"Help!" Ivy screamed. She was sprawled across a huge chunk of masonry that had cracked free of the wall. She slid headfirst towards the abyss.

Ophelia snatched for Ivy's ankle, but she was too late. A long, sickening wail. Rumbling stones. The professor was yanking Ophelia back onto his chest, and then the entire latrine structure fell, along with Ivy, into space.

A carriage stood in Château Vézère's drive. Lights flickered in the windows.

"That must be Dr. Duclos's carriage," Penrose said to Ophelia.

Ophelia, sore and rattled, dismounted. Ivy's final scream wouldn't stop playing in her mind. "Would you take my horse to the stables, Professor Penrose? I wish to speak with Mr. Banks before the police arrive." The gendarmes and Inspector Pierot had broken up the villagers' festivities at the castle and arrested a bundle of men, including Marcel, for ransacking the château and kidnapping Bernadette.

"Allow me to join you," Penrose said. His shoulders were

set, and beneath a dark wash of stubble, he looked pale. "If Banks makes a confession, it will be useful to have a witness."

"All right."

They left their horses in the dark stables and went to Banks's bedchamber. He was shrunken beneath the blankets, but his eyes were open. The sick nurse was sound asleep in her chair.

"Damned doctor finally brought the right medicine," Banks said in a raspy voice.

"Medicine for your heart?" Ophelia asked. She and Penrose went to the bedside.

"Yes."

Ophelia took a big breath. She told Banks that his daughter was dead, and under what strange circumstances. Then she accused Banks of murdering Knight's impostor, Jack Potter, and Madame Dieudonné.

At first, Banks was immobile with shock, but disgust gradually settled over his spent features. "She meant to kill me? My own little Ivy?"

"You arrived at Château Vézère with two bottles of heart medicine," Ophelia said. "Ivy disposed of one when she planted it upon Mr. Knight's person in the orangerie, in order to muddle things up for the police. The second bottle of heart medicine, she took from you a few days later."

"My own daughter." Banks breathed in and out through cracked lips. "My own daughter wished to *kill* me. She was everything to me, *everything*. Even if she were alive still, I would think of her now as dead to me. Deceitful, wicked child."

"But *you're* the murderer, Mr. Banks," Ophelia said. "And I don't reckon Miss Banks wished to kill you at all. In a roundabout fashion, she was trying to *save* you."

"By taking away the medicine upon which I depend?"

"I think she meant to keep you ill, see, and thus free from suspicion, while she busied herself with directing everyone's attention to the villagers. I found the medicine in your bedchamber, you see—she must have kept it after planting it in Forthwith's pocket in order to confuse the police, when they announced they would search the château after you shot Madame Dieudonné. That's when she placed your diamond cuff links in Henrietta's chamber, too, I reckon. She stole your cuff links, not Jack Potter. She must've meant to give the medicine back to you before you grew irretrievably ill."

In a mad way, Ivy *had* done it all to save her darling papa. Even bringing him to the brink of death. "Mr. Banks, did you know the man you poisoned with belladonna-tainted wine was not really Mr. Cecil Knight?"

"What a brazen little miss you are, trying to extract a confession." Banks's lip curled.

"Did you know?" Ophelia repeated.

"Bah! What does it matter, now? Ivy's gone. My life, my fortune—I built it all for her. Aren't you going to mourn her, Lord Harrington?"

"I will," Penrose said softly.

"What about the man you poisoned in the orangerie?" Ophelia said, afraid that Banks's talkative mood would pass. "Did you know he was called Jack Potter?"

"Well of course! Do you take me for damned fool?" Banks's belligerent words didn't match his feeble voice. "Jack Potter. Low, despicable, vile. Do you know what he *took* from me?"

"Something to do with cotton, wasn't it?" Ophelia said.

"How'd you know *that*? Yes, cotton. Five years ago, during the American War Between the States, there was a British embargo on United States cotton—cut off funds to the rebels and all that. As a result, Egypt finally got a leg up in the cotton trade. I stood to get rich importing Egyptian cotton to my mills in England. I'd never had business dealings in America, but I had plenty of contacts in Egypt already, since I already imported their silk. I hired Jack Potter to arrange shipping routes for all that Egyptian cotton to get to my mills in

England. He double-crossed me. Arranged for *another* mill owner to pay him for all my hard-won contacts. The other mill owner—Kennington's his name—stole all the business out from under my nose. God, I lost out on a fortune!"

"But aren't you still wealthy?" Ophelia asked.

"Doesn't matter! Think what I could have amassed! Had to watch Kennington build a damned palace with money that ought to have been *mine*. Giraffes in his garden! Dishes of gold, they say!"

Banks had been so sour and angry towards Larsen, Ophelia realized, because he was envious of *any* man richer than he. They hadn't known each other, as Forthwith had suggested, but to Banks, it didn't matter. Banks craved to be the biggest—the *richest*—fish in the sea.

Banks said, "I vowed to avenge myself on Jack Potter. To bide my time, to do it well, and to beat him at his own greedy games. I knew he was living in Marseille—knew it for a year. By chance my solicitor in London—"

"Mr. Montgomery?" Ophelia asked.

"Yes. Montgomery mentioned that another client, Sir Percival Christy, was having his charge met at a ship in Marseille and escorted back to England for school. Saw my chance. Sent a letter, supposedly from Montgomery, to Jack Potter—but I addressed it to Mr. Knight. Made it look like the wrong address. I knew Jack Potter couldn't resist the reward I mentioned. Set a deadline, too—got all my ducks in a row. Said I'd come on this hunting trip. All I needed to do was bring Potter to me so I would never be discovered."

"You bought up all the train tickets between Avignon and Lyon, and so blocked travel to Paris for days," Ophelia said.

"I thought that was a brilliant move."

"And, because of the way you phrased that fake letter from the solicitor in London, Potter believed time was running out to collect the reward in London."

"I knew he would choose to take the stagecoach route rather than wait indefinitely for the train. After all, he believed that money would not wait in London forever, and if there is anything Potter cared about in his shriveled little soul, it was money."

"Then you bribed the driver to cut the whippletree rings in front of the château gates."

"Potter drew closer, ever closer. Do you understand how difficult it was for me to suppress my excitement that evening?"

Did Banks truly reckon Ophelia would feel *sorry* for him? What a nut.

"If that—that *daughter* of mine had not gone and muddled it all up, then you would not have gone nosing about. I would not have been forced to kill Madame Dieudonné."

"You killed her because she knew what you'd done."

"That fool of a stagecoach driver must've told her about the bribe, and she must have pieced something together. In bed together, they were."

Penrose cleared his throat.

Ophelia said, "Then you made a fuss over those rare roses in the orangerie, because you knew Potter couldn't resist going and stealing a few to sell the seeds in London."

"Yes."

"Potter also stole jewelry from others," Ophelia said. "As well as Tolbert's jawbone fossil."

"Greedy, I told you," Banks said. "Once I had Potter in the orangerie, well, I had him in the palm of my hand. He remembered me well, of course, although he'd kept it hidden, since, after all, he was disguised as a vicar. Potter a vicar? Ha! Better to dress up a ditch rat like the queen. In the orangerie, I proposed future business dealings. We toasted with wine. Then I stood aside to enjoy the reward for all my careful planning." Banks closed his eyes.

The police would take him to the police station later, when he was strong enough to walk. For now, living with the death of his daughter was punishment enough. That was that. Ophelia felt adrift.

Ophelia and Penrose went downstairs. When they reached the entry foyer, they heard men's shouts outside. Penrose wrapped his arm around Ophelia's shoulders as they went outside together.

A parade of about a dozen woodsmen marched up the drive, carrying torches. Larsen led a large, sinewy gray wolf by a rope. The wolf hung its head, and its ears were slicked back. Its bony shoulders rocked.

"That is the biggest wolf I've ever seen," Ophelia said.

"You've seen wolves before, Miss Flax?"

"Once or twice. In the circus."

"Of course." Penrose's weary voice lilted with mirth.

"Bagged the scoundrel!" Larsen shouted. "This is the beast that has savaged the livestock these few nights past! I will take it to the zoological gardens in Paris!"

The wolf panted.

"Poor thing," Ophelia murmured.

"Do not even begin to think of adopting a savage wolf, Miss Flax."

The thought *had* crossed her mind. "Don't *you* begin to think, Professor, that this wolf cannot account for that jawbone."

"Well, it cannot. The livestock that were killed had their throats torn, as wolves do to their prey. But the livestock had *also* been gored by tusks. The world still holds magic, Miss Flax. There are still things at the edges of our vision that science and reason cannot account for."

"Suit yourself, Professor," Ophelia said. But then, here she was, Ophelia Flax of Littleton, New Hampshire, standing on the steps of a grand château in the middle of French nowhere, with an English earl's arm around her shoulders. Reason could not account for *this*.

32

Two weeks later

Henrietta, despite having somehow gained several pounds in the Sarlat jail, not to mention having her complexion and her spirits ruined, made good on her promise to pay Ophelia. So not only did Ophelia find herself back in Artemis Stunt's stuffy Paris apartment with her original nest egg; she had tripled it.

Of course, she was now the reluctant owner of a petulant poodle, too. But Meringue had shown himself to be mighty trainable if the treats were worth the trouble. He looked much more winsome with his new, close-cropped haircut, too.

Professor Penrose had left Château Vézère for England in a hurry, the day after Ophelia had solved the murders, to escort Abel and the parakeet to the Warbridge School. But he'd promised to return to Paris in two weeks' time, look Ophelia up in Artemis Stunt's apartment, and, well, he'd simply asked if he might go for a walk with Ophelia. She'd said yes. Their parting had been awkward, with lots of darting eyes and unsure words. That was the trouble with sleuthing with someone: Once all the excitement died down, you were left with nothing safe to confabulate about.

Ophelia wagered that Penrose meant to ask her to marry him. She'd had her answer ready all along, ever since he'd hinted at it in the bell tower in Sarlat. And now that she'd had that amazing little snippet of news about her brother Odie—Odie, who she had believed died in the war!—well . . .

Still, when Ophelia found Professor Penrose's calling card beside her plate one morning at breakfast, her belly swooped like swallows.

"Ah, your earl," Artemis said with a knowing smile. "Come to collect his prize?"

"I'm not a *prize*." Ophelia's ears burned.

"Oh, I don't know. When you have gotten plenty of sleep and you aren't in one of your stubborn humors, you can be—"

"No, I mean that I am a person. Not a prize."

Artemis refilled her coffee cup. "I don't understand."

Ophelia didn't bother explaining. Artemis, Henrietta, just about every factory girl, lady circus performer, and actress she'd ever known—they'd all wished to be a prize, a glorified thing that some fellow would marry and whisk away and put up on a bric-a-brac shelf for safekeeping. That wasn't living. That wasn't love.

Penrose called at ten o'clock. The weather was gloomy as he and Ophelia walked into the small park near Artemis's building. Penrose seemed aloof and unable to meet Ophelia's eyes. They spoke of the events at Château Vézère. That was safe terrain.

"Abel is well?" Ophelia asked.

"Yes. Situated at school—which he was glum about, but he did indeed discover a heretofore unknown species of stag beetle, and evidently he will name it."

"Recovered from the shock of learning his father is Sir Percival Christy?"

"Oh, yes. He's moved on to boasting about that." Penrose smiled. "Says he's going to found an explorer's society at his school, lead the other boys out on tramps through the countryside."

They stopped before a fountain filled with dead leaves. Penrose took a deep breath. "Miss Flax, I suppose you know why I've come."

"I reckon that I do, and if you don't mind, I'd like to say something first. It might—well, it might change things."

"Go on."

"I've had news of my brother, Odie."

"That is wonderful!"

"I know." Ophelia's gloved hands shook as she dug out the newspaper clipping from her reticule. She unfolded it, smoothed it out. "It's only a bit of a news story, but his name is in there, clear as day—see?"

"He hasn't—he hasn't gotten into any trouble, has he?"

"No. Go on. Read it."

Penrose read it.

Ophelia knew the tiny column by heart now: One American gentleman by the name of Odysseus Flax was awarded a medal of honor from the mayor of a tiny town somewhere in Switzerland, for catching a thief.

"What is he doing in Switzerland?"

"I don't know. I am setting out for there tomorrow. I must find Odie. He's the only family I've got."

Penrose's eyes look bruised.

Ophelia rushed on. "You and I are friends, and we'll always be friends, Professor, and I do . . ." She gulped down the painful lump in her throat. "I do care for you. Very much. But can't you see? Money and love, they don't mix. We'd never be on equal footing, you and I. You and your title and estate and the university—and, well, me. There isn't anything *to* me."

"I don't agree—but first, *love*. You said love."

"Well, yes." Ophelia met his eyes. "I . . . yes. But true life isn't like a fairy tale. Things between us, the imbalance between us, won't suddenly change—*we* won't suddenly change—simply because we make a promise or two. Don't you understand? I can't be like all those other actresses and chorus dancers, Professor. I can't be like Henrietta. I've got my pride. I can't be *kept*."

"Marriage needn't be like that, Miss Flax. I regard you as my equal—indeed, in many ways you are my superior, as in your resolve, your fortitude, your quick thinking"—Penrose smiled a little—"and your deft hand at disguises. My title, my estate, the university—those have nothing to do with you and me."

"But people don't live only in a house, Professor. They live in a world—a world with other people, customs, expectations. . . . I would never fit into your world, and you wouldn't ever fit into mine."

"Allow me to change your mind."

Ophelia shook her head. "I can't live in your world, surrounded by people who would always think less of me because of where I've come from."

"I will protect you from them."

"You can't. I'm not a china doll." She looked away, the hurt in Penrose's eyes too much to bear.

He didn't speak or move for a good long while. Finally he said gently, "You will travel to Switzerland now, to search for your brother?"

"Yes."

"Have you—"

"Money? Yes, I have enough. You see? *Money*. You've got lots, and I haven't."

"We would share."

"That's not how things are arranged. At any rate, I've got a job that will take me to Switzerland."

"A job? As an actress?"

"Something to that effect. We leave tomorrow."

Another long silence. Penrose pushed his hands into his greatcoat pockets and tipped his head to study the sky. "Miss

Flax, I will not do you the dishonor of attempting to convince you further on the point of matrimony. But I will ask that I might write to you—and, perhaps, ask you to, from time to time, send me a note. If only that I might know that you are well, and safe. And happy."

"All right. I'll write to you, but I won't have a proper address for a while yet, until I've tracked down Odie and, well, I reckon I'll return to America after that."

Penrose scribbled his address with a pencil on the back of a calling card. He gave it to her. "Do not forget me. Please. Good-bye, Miss Flax." He turned and walked away.

He was always just *leaving*. How it made Ophelia's chest ache. Yet, wasn't it true that she was always sending him away?

She spent the rest of the day walking restlessly through the Paris streets, dimly hoping she'd see the professor again. That he'd make her change her mind, somehow, and this cracking feeling in her chest would abate. She did not see him, though, and the cracking feeling kept on.

At any rate, she was right to let him go, because he had only talked of what it would be like if she married him and went to live in England. He hadn't even considered joining her in *her* world.

The next day, Ophelia packed her shabby carpetbag, bade farewell to Henrietta and Artemis, scooped up Meringue, and left the apartment. She had visited her friend Prue in the convent the day before in order to say good-bye. On the street, Ophelia boarded an omnibus bound for the Bois de Boulogne, an enormous Parisian park.

In the Bois de Boulogne, Ophelia tromped across a vast, muddy patch of grass that had been flattened by circus tents. The tents were folded up now and loaded onto the wagons. Circus folk milled about, smoking cigarettes, laughing. There was the tattooed lady, and there was the strong man. An elephant trumpeted and an accordion squalled.

Ophelia had encountered this circus troupe two days ago, the same day she'd found Odie's name in the newspaper. In weak—but improving—French, she'd spoken to some of the performers, really for old time's sake, and learned that they were heading towards Switzerland next and that one of their acts had quit. Ophelia had already been training Meringue to jump over pencils and walk on his hind legs, simply for amusement. Ophelia figured that Meringue could surely advance to leaping through flaming hoops, and that she herself could still ride trick ponies as she'd done years ago. She'd begged the ringmaster for the job, and she'd gotten it.

She had a way to get to Switzerland and a way to keep herself until she found Odie. Who needed an earl with a fortune, anyway?

Ophelia hitched up her skirts to step over a mound of fresh lion dung. "Are you ready, Meringue?" she said softly.

Meringue, still slung over her arm, yawned.

Ophelia climbed up the rickety ladder into a colorfully painted circus wagon. She shut the door.

Keep reading for a preview of
Maia Chance's next Fairy Tale Fatal Mystery . . .

Snow White Red-Handed

Available now from Berkley Prime Crime!

1

Miss Ophelia Flax was neither a professional confidence trickster nor a lady's maid, but she'd played both on the stage. In desperate circumstances like these, that would have to do.

"Who told you that our maid Marie gave notice?" Mrs. Coop said. Her diamond earrings wobbled.

Miss Amaryllis, sitting beside Mrs. Coop on the sofa, sniffed and added, "Uppity French tart."

If ever there were two wicked stepsisters, here they were, taking tea in the SS *Leviathan*'s stuffy first-class stateroom number eighteen: thick-waisted, brassy-haired Mrs. Coop, clutching at her fading bloom in a deshabille gown of pink ribbons and Brussels lace, and her much younger sister, Miss Amaryllis, a bony damsel of twenty or so with complexion spots, slumped shoulders, and a green silk gown that resembled a lampshade. They looked up at Ophelia, expectant and hostile.

Ophelia stood before them, tall and plain in the gray woolen traveling dress, black gloves, and prim buttoned boots she'd borrowed—*stolen* was such a rotten word—from the costume trunks of Howard DeLuxe's Varieties in the ship's hold.

"Your maid's abandonment of her post," Ophelia said, "came to my attention during my midday promenade on the first-class deck."

She needn't mention that her own cramped berth was in the bowels of third class, where it stank of sour cabbage and you felt the ship's engines vibrating in your teeth.

"Embarrassing scene." Mrs. Coop pitched herself forward to reach for a cream puff. "The way Marie threw her apron at me! She always did behave as though she were my—my *superior*."

"It wasn't your fault, ma'am," Ophelia said. "French maids are notoriously fickle. They're not the best for service, I'm afraid."

"But everyone in New York's got one. They're simply mad for them."

"It is my understanding, ma'am, that while a certain . . . class of society cling to the outdated notion that a French lady's maid is the height of elegance, the Van Der Snoots and De Schmeers and"—Ophelia scanned the stateroom's luxurious furnishings—"St. Armoire ladies have of late discovered that a Yankee lady's maid is best."

"Yankee?" Mrs. Coop's bitten cream puff hovered in midair. Yellowish filling oozed from the sides.

"Yes, ma'am. Yankee girls are honest, hardworking, modest, and loyal."

Miss Amaryllis slitted her eyes. "I suppose you're a Yankee girl?"

"Indeed I am. Born and bred on a farmstead in New Hampshire, miss."

That was true. She'd leave out the bits about the textile mill and the traveling circus. They didn't have the same wholesome ring.

"I'll find a new maid when we reach Germany," Mrs. Coop said. "I've made up my mind. Why, if I had known Marie would quit in the midst of my honeymoon voyage, I'd have left her on the dock in Manhattan!"

"Another virtue of Yankee girls," Ophelia said, "is their ability to arrange coiffures, make cosmetic preparations, and, if needed—although I'm certain ma'am has no need—apply powders and tints with a hand as subtle as nature herself."

A lie, of course. But Ophelia was an actress—or she had been up until four hours ago, when Howard DeLuxe had given Prue the boot and Ophelia had been obliged to quit— and putting on greasepaint was one thing she knew how to do well.

"Yankee girls use face paint?" Mrs. Coop said. "Why, you said it yourself. They're as plain as potatoes."

"But they learned from their grandmothers, ma'am, the arts of medicinal plants. My own gran taught me to whip up an elderflower tincture that returns the skin to snowy youth—"

Another fib. But Mrs. Coop's eyes glimmered with interest.

"—and a *Pomade Victoria* of beeswax and almond oil that makes the hair shine like gold, a salve of *Balsam Peru* that makes complexion spots vanish." Ophelia leaned forward. "I could not help noticing Miss Amaryllis's unfortunate condition."

"Why, the cheek!" Mrs. Coop's bosom heaved.

Miss Amaryllis glared up at Ophelia and bit into a biscuit with a snap.

"And," Ophelia said, "a pleasant-tasting tonic of vinegar that slims a lady's waist without effort."

Mrs. Coop's half-eaten cream puff plopped onto her plate.

Ophelia had hooked her halibut.

"Here," Ophelia said, drawing two sealed envelopes from her pocket, "are my letters of reference. I, and my young acquaintance, Miss Prudence Bright, were traveling to England to work in the employ of Lady Cheshingham at Greyson Hall in Shropshire."

Lady Cheshingham was, in truth, the lead character in the risqué comedy *Lady Cheshingham's Charge*, which Howard DeLuxe's Varieties had performed in May. The letters were forgeries Ophelia had penned an hour earlier.

Mrs. Coop fingered the envelopes. "Ah, yes, yes, Lady Cheshingham."

"While already shipboard, I belatedly read a missive I'd received from Lord Cheshingham on the eve of our voyage, which informed me that the lady had passed away."

"Good heavens."

"Yes. A tragedy. She was so young."

"I had heard so many wonderful things about her."

"Miss Bright and I, then, are in want of employment."

Want of employment didn't really pin down the gravity of their circumstances. With the steamship barreling towards Southampton, Ophelia and Prue, with no jobs, only a few dollars, and no acquaintances in England, were well and truly up a stump.

"There are two of you?" Mrs. Coop sounded uncertain. "I—I must ask my husband. We are staying at our castle only until the winter."

Castle? Hm. Surely a figure of speech.

"Of course," Ophelia said, and made a show of tearing at the cambric handkerchief she'd plucked from her sleeve.

But she oughtn't get too carried away in her role. Mr. DeLuxe had always complained that she, having once beguiled her audience, tended to careen towards the melodramatic.

She put the hankie away. "Have you, ma'am, tried Russian face powder?"

Mrs. Coop touched her thickly powdered cheek. "I've always used French."

"Russian is the best, used first by the czarina Catherine. It's got crushed pearls in it—pearls from the North Sea, which restore the complexion to a state of infancy. But don't tell anyone. It'll be our little secret."

"Pearls for Mrs. Pearl Coop," Miss Amaryllis said into her teacup. "How poetic."

"It is easier, Amaryllis," Mrs. Coop said through clenched teeth, "to catch flies with honey than with vinegar."

"Whatever would I want with flies?"

"A figure of speech, dear. Perhaps it would be best if you married your *own* fly, rather than straggling along with Homer and me."

"Homer a fly?" Miss Amaryllis smirked. "More of a frog, don't you think?"

"If I may be so bold," Ophelia interrupted, "it would be a privilege to attend to such lovely, refined ladies."

Mrs. Coop blinked, and Miss Amaryllis leaned against the sofa arm and propped her chin sulkily on her hand.

Mrs. Coop sighed and picked up her cream puff. "It seems we've no choice in the matter. When can you start?"

Ophelia held in an exhalation of relief. "Immediately, ma'am," she said.

"Well?" Prue flung herself face-up on her narrow berth. Her cheeks were blotchy and wet with tears.

Ophelia shut the cabin door. "We have jobs."

"That's splendiferous!"

"I am to be a lady's maid—"

Prue's face fell.

"—and you are to be a scullery maid."

"Scullery maid?" Prue struggled to a seated position. Golden ringlets tumbled around her flushed face and her eyes of enamel blue. She was the closest thing to a china doll that a nineteen-year-old American girl could be. Until, that is, she opened her mouth to speak. "I ain't cut out for a scullery maid, Ophelia. I'm clumsy, for starters, but more than that, I ain't got the *concentration* to peel carrots all day."

Ophelia wholeheartedly agreed. "You'll manage," she said. She stripped off the stolen gloves. "It's only a bit of washing pots and scrubbing vegetables."

"Why can't I be a lady's maid, too?"

"Mrs. Coop and Miss Amaryllis desired but one lady's maid between them. We are lucky they agreed to take you on at all. Don't look so weepy. It's only for a few months, until we save up enough to buy passage back to America. Besides, we don't have another plan."

The plan *had* been to perform with Howard DeLuxe's Varieties in its limited engagement at the Pegasus Theater on the Strand. "Limited engagement" meant for however long gin-soaked London gents would pack the seats to watch the troupe's bawdy skits and musical numbers. "The Lusty Whalers of Nantucket" had top billing, alongside a bit about cowgirls and Indians, a romantic scene in which Ophelia played Pocahontas, and "Paul Revere's Bride," featuring a horse that galloped offstage with a scantily clad Puritan wench.

"We could go find my Ma," Prue said. "Nat—you know, the feller who paints the scenery—told me this afternoon he heard she was in Europe."

"We haven't any notion where." Ophelia sank onto the edge of her own berth. "Europe is enormous, not to mention expensive. And she could just as easily be in New York."

"A scullery maid." Prue's tears were spouting again. "What'll become of me? I ain't got anyone. Ma never wanted me—"

"Now you know that isn't true." Ophelia handed over a hankie.

"If she'd hornswoggled a millionaire into marrying her when I was a baby, she would've left me then."

"Nonsense."

Prue noisily blew her nose.

Her mother, Miss Henrietta Bright, had been the star actress in Howard DeLuxe's Varieties, and like so many actresses, she had supplemented her income with—to mince words—additional business endeavors. Last year, she'd run off with one of her admirers. Some said he was a Wall Street tycoon, others that he was a European blue blood. Either way, Prue's mother had abandoned a flighty girl who possessed all the common sense of a tadpole. Ophelia had no living family of her own—a missing brother and a father she'd never met hardly counted—so she'd taken Prue under her wing.

Ophelia bent to unbutton the stolen boots; they were too small, and her toes felt numb. "You know I have a little money saved up, in the bank in New York—"

"For your farm! You've been scrimping for ages."

"I have." A vision of misty green fields, a white barn, and sweet-eyed dairy cows rose up in Ophelia's mind's eye. It was a vision that often lulled her to sleep, that got her through slushy November afternoons and exhausting double matinee performances. "When I buy my farm someday, well, you can come and live with me there."

Prue wrinkled her nose. "Will I have to milk the cows?"

"Certainly not."

"Snatch it, you're just being nice. You're always being too nice. Just because Mr. DeLuxe sent me packing don't mean *you* should've quit."

Ophelia said nothing as she yanked off the boots. But she knew exactly what became of pretty, silly, penniless girls who didn't have a protector, and the idea of Prue alone on the streets of London didn't bear thinking about.

"You could've been a lead actress someday, Ophelia. And now you're just a maid."

"Fiddlesticks. Acting has merely been a way to pay for my daily bread."

"When you filled in as Cleopatra when Flossie broke her arm, you got a standing ovation and enough roses to fill three bathtubs. You were a stunner."

"In a wig and greasepaint," Ophelia said. "Gospel truth, it doesn't concern me in the least that without Cleopatra kohl-lined eyes or Marie Antoinette rouged cheeks, I blend nicely into the backdrop. I'm five and twenty years of age, plenty old enough to have made peace with myself. I'm not saying I'm some mousy thing who gets stepped on—"

"Course not. You're a beanstalk."

"Not as tall as that, perhaps." In truth, Ophelia *was* tall, and she had large feet, and no corset could mold her straight figure into a fashion plate's hourglass. But her oval face, molasses-colored eyes, and light brown hair were presentable enough. "Anyway, since I'm an actress, a knack for blending in is an asset." She wiggled her blissfully freed toes. "Now. If we're ever to get back home in one piece, we ought to prepare ourselves for our new roles as maids."

"Where in tarnation are they taking us?" Prue said three days later. She scrubbed at the grimy coach window with her fist. Their coach creaked and jostled up the mountainous road like a rheumatic mule. "Everything was all right until we got off at that bad railway station—"

"Baden-Baden," Ophelia corrected from the opposite seat. "*Baden* means baths—it's a thermal resort town."

"That in your book?" Ophelia had had her nose stuck in some book she'd borrowed from Miss Amaryllis for the whole of their railway and boat journey between Southampton and Germany. It was called a *Baedeker*, Ophelia had told Prue. Whatever that meant. Prue hadn't bothered to thumb through it. She considered herself a *doing* kind of person. Book learning gave her the jitters.

Besides, Ma had always cautioned that reading gave a lady a scrunched-up forehead and a panoramic derriere.

Baden-Baden, a German town nestled in plush hills, was called the Paris of the summer months. Leastways, that's what the *Baedeker* said. All the cream of Europe's crop, from Polish princes and British nobles to Italian opera stars and Russian novelists, gathered there to socialize, dance, take the waters, and gamble at the races or in the opulent gaming rooms.

But their coach had left Baden-Baden miles behind, and they were headed up into the mountains.

"I reckoned," Prue said, "when we took that boat to Brussels, we were headed to civilization. But this!" She scowled out the window. Mountains reared up into the chambray-colored sky. "This looks worse than Maine."

"We're in the Black Forest, Prue. Haven't you heard of it?"

"Never."

"Your mother didn't read you those fairy stories by the Grimm Brothers?"

"Read me stories?" Prue bit into one of the strawberry jelly sweets she'd spent her last penny on, back at the railway station. "Not her. But I sure know how to tell real diamonds from paste, and if a gentleman's got a walloping bank account or is just trying to dupe a lady." She chewed hard. The topic of Ma made her feel sore somewhere under her ribs. "Looks like the first-class carriage is getting away from us."

"We are servants now," Ophelia said. Her voice was gentle. "We can't expect to ride with the family."

"Can't expect a decent coach, neither."

"I allow, this coach isn't the most comfortable—"

"It's a rickety old rattletrap." Prue eyed the black wood fittings around the window: carved thorny vines. "Or maybe a hearse."

"We are fortunate to have found employment."

"Well, don't that beat all!" Prue exclaimed. "Look at that castle."

"Where?"

"Up there."

Ophelia followed Prue's pointed finger. "That," she murmured, "beats all indeed."

High on a jutting stone outcrop, framed by pine trees, was a castle. It was built of pale stone, with turrets of various sizes, battlements, walls, parapets, and balconies. It glowed like an enchanted wedding cake in the afternoon sun, and hazy mountains stretched endlessly behind it like a painted theater backdrop.

"Ain't got *those* in Maine." Prue popped another strawberry jelly in her mouth.

"I think," Ophelia said, "that's where we're going to live."